WHITE STONE DAY

By the same author

The Fiend in Human

WHITE STONE DAY

JOHN MACLACHLAN GRAY

 St. Martin's Minotaur ⚇ New York

www.minotaurbooks.com

Library of Congress Cataloging-in-Publication Data

Gray, John, 1946–
    White stone day / John MacLachlan Gray.—1st U.S. ed.
      p. cm.
   ISBN 0-312-28293-1
   EAN 978-0-312-28293-6
   1. Journalists—Fiction. 2. Eccentrics and eccentricities—Fiction. 3. Psychics—Crimes against—Fiction. 4. Oxford (England)—Fiction. 5. Pornographers—Fiction. 6. Clergy—Fiction. I. Title.

PR9199.3.G753W48 2005
813'.54—dc22   2005044413

First published in the United Kingdom by Century

First U.S. Edition: November 2005

10 9 8 7 6 5 4 3 2 1

For Beverlee

I have a fairy by my side
   Which says I must not sleep,
When once in pain I loudly cried
   It said 'You must not weep.'

If, full of mirth, I smile and grin,
   It says 'You must not laugh';
When once I wished to drink some gin,
   It said 'You must not quaff.'

'What may I do?' at length I cried,
   Tired of the painful task.
The fairy quietly replied,
   And said 'You must not ask.'

– Lewis Carroll, Aged 13

Contents

Acknowledgements

I could not have completed this book without the advice and support of Anne Collins, Hope Dellon, Helen Heller and Oliver Johnson. Many thanks to Dr John Hughes, whose discourse abounds with historical oddities.

I am, above all, beholden to Charles Dodgson (Lewis Carroll), whose life and work inspired this entirely fictional account.

Crouch Manor, Chester Wolds, Oxfordshire

Ye golden hours of Life's young spring,
Of innocence, of love and truth!
Bright, beyond all imagining,
Thou fairy-dream of youth!

'Very well, ladies, shall we begin?'

'Please, let's do,' says the smaller girl, pushing strands of wayward hair from her eyes with two small hands.

'Very well,' says her sister, who is slightly older and slightly more ladylike.

The Reverend William Leffington Boltbyn straightens his waistcoat, inhales with feigned gravity, and begins. Before him, the two members of his audience lean forward as though drawn by a string, four lovely eyes limpid with anticipation.

'As you might recall (especially Miss Emma, as our protagonist *du jour*), it was late afternoon, an hour not unlike the present, when the light grows long and the verdant lawns here at Crouch Manor take on a peculiar luminosity . . .' He withdraws his watch from his vest pocket and inspects the instrument carefully. 'About five-twenty-two, I should think,' he says, placing the watch face-up upon his knee.

Whispers Lydia to Emma: 'If he continues describing things I shall lose interest.'

'Be patient,' replies Emma. 'Mr Boltbyn needs to set the scene.'

The vicar resumes. 'Having undertaken a seemingly endless game of croquet, which followed a seemingly endless hour of moral instruction, Emma was beginning to get sulky and bored . . .'

'That cannot be,' objects the older girl. 'I am quite fond of croquet.'

'Very well, let us say that Emma was bored with the moral instruction, though not with the game. In the case of her governess, however, it was the reverse – while she disliked croquet, Miss Pouch never tired of moral instruction.'

'Miss Pouch does not address the ball in the proper manner,' says Emma. 'One cannot strike it properly without parting one's legs.'

'Oh, Emma,' sighs Lydia. 'You are always causing a person to lose the thread.'

Emma turns to her sister and out darts a small pink tongue.

The vicar continues: 'After a characteristically feeble attempt to strike the ball, and becoming overcome as a consequence by heat-exhaustion, Miss Pouch collapsed in a swoon upon the blanket. Now it was Emma's turn – and wouldn't you know, she roqued her governess's ball!'

'Oh yes, Mr Boltbyn, that would be splendid!' cries Lydia.

With a wink to the little girl, the vicar carries on. 'Emma's blue croquet ball now rested in contiguity with the red, presenting Miss Pouch's spirited opponent with an opportunity to avenge any number of slights.'

'A roque is a perfectly legitimate play, you know,' says Emma.

'Quite so. Reassured that a roque is a legal manœuvre, casting an apologetic glance in the direction of her sleeping governess, whose jaw had slackened something like a trout's . . .'

Ha, ha! Both girls laugh aloud. Lydia widens her eyes and moves her lips in the manner of a fish.

'Emma placed her tiny left foot atop her ball, lifted her mallet in a wide arc, and swung just as hard as ever she could, thereby to dispatch Miss Pouch's ball to a distant location, out of play – *Crack!*'

'Crack!' echoes Lydia.

'But wait! Imagine Emma's astonishment as the red ball sped away as though shot from a cannon – tearing across the lawn, ripping through a bed of sweet william and bouncing down the hill, only to disappear in the shadows of Adderleigh Forest!'

'Oh, Emma,' says the younger girl. 'You hit it too hard.'

'Indeed, it is not the first time your sister has underestimated her strength, with awkward results. To make things worse, when she crossed the lawn to retrieve the red ball – it was nowhere to be seen! And what do you say to that, Miss Emma?'

'I suppose I should say that it is very singular.'

'*How very singular*, said Emma to the mallet in her hand as she ran down the hill to the forest, lifted her skirts, dropped to her knees and bent sideways to peer under a wall of vegetation – only to be met by the indifferent gaze of two centipedes and a worm.

'*Oh, dear!* said Emma to her mallet. *I had meant to put Miss Pouch out of play, not lose her entirely!*'

'What did the mallet say?' Three years younger than Emma, Lydia retains a fondness for talking objects.

'On this subject, the mallet had nothing to say.'

'Oh, bother.'

'When her eyes had finally adjusted to the dark of the forest, Emma managed to catch a glimpse of Miss Pouch's ball, whose red stripe stood out in the gloom of the forest – and it was still rolling!'

'"How peculiar," is what I should say then,' says Emma, anticipating his request.

'*How very peculiar*, Emma said, and without further hesitation strode briskly into the forest – reasoning that, since the ball was not rolling very fast, it should be a simple matter to fetch it.

'Yet the ball appeared to have a will of its own. When she reached for it, the ball hurried beyond her grasp like a playful kitten – only to come to rest a few yards further on. This it repeated until she had lost her way. And what did she say to that?'

'Fiddlesticks, I suppose.'

'*Oh, fiddlesticks!* Emma said to the croquet ball. *What a pickle you have got us in!* And the ball finally allowed her to pick it up.

'As you know, Adderleigh Forest is uncommonly dismal and damp. Enormous trunks towered above the girl like the legs of giants. Sharp brambles reached out for her, and slimy creatures squirmed underfoot, which have never felt the sun – not since a time when monsters wallowed in the fens and witches stirred boiling cauldrons of baby soup!'

Lydia squeals in delighted horror.

'A procession of fancied terrors raced through Emma's sensible mind as she stood in what seemed like a darkened room, surrounded by rough, dark columns and a warren of unlit hallways. *So many ways to go – and all equally unpleasant-looking!* she said to her mallet, which had also grown rather tense.

'Perched on a branch high above her head, silhouetted against a narrow slice of sky, two cormorants hovered, their long beaks curved downward. *That will be a dainty mouthful,* said one, *come nightfall!*'

Boltbyn executes a sudden, shrill imitation of a bird, causing even Miss Emma to flinch in alarm.

'*Oh dear!* she cried to her mallet, which had grown quite rigid with fear. *Whatever shall we do?*'

'Surely the mallet must have *some* reply,' protests Lydia.

'Not a word, I'm afraid. Then, to Emma's astonishment, there came a low, gruff sort of a voice from the shadow of a dead tree: *If you keep making such a hullabaloo, you will bring all kinds of beasts, mallet or no mallet.*

'Emma was so startled she forgot to cry out – peering into the shadow of a dead hawthorn tree she glimpsed a small figure in a long tweed overcoat, tiny eyes gleaming just beneath the brim of a hunting cap and, in between, the pointed, upturned snout of a hedgehog.

'*You needn't frighten a person so*, she said, trying not to appear as frightened as she really was.

'To which the hedgehog replied: *You, young lady, were in a state from which the capacity to be frightened issued by itself.*

'*That is because I am lost. Please, can you show me the way back home?*

'The hedgehog replied: Back *is the one way you don't want to go. Unless you have eyes in the back of your head you will run into a tree.*

'*Very well then*, replied Emma, endeavouring to remain calm. *Can you suggest which way I should go?*

'*If I were you, the way I should go would be . . . up. But you needn't listen to me, being a rummager and not a climber.*

'And on that note he turned tail, shuffled into the deeper dark of the forest, and disappeared.

'*Come back!* cried Emma, but received no answer other than a soft shuffling sound. Alone in the gathering gloom, the poor little thing dropped her mallet and Miss Pouch's ball upon the ground, buried her face in her hands, and began to weep.

'At that moment, from immediately behind her issued a most peculiar sound . . .'

Boltbyn abruptly suspends the narrative, to the ardent pleas of the younger member of his audience, at least. (The vicar hasn't an inkling what the 'peculiar sound' is or who is making it, and will require time to come up with something.)

He glances at the open watch on his lap, then at Miss Pouch, still asleep by the fire, her mouth open as though waiting to be fed. Soon Lizzy, the maid-of-all-work, will place the nursery china upon the oilcloth table top; and most significantly, soon the head of the house will arrive for supper. Boltbyn is not partial to the Reverend Lambert, precentor of the Church of St Swithan, whom he considers a vain, pompous ass, shamefully neglectful of his daughters and his young, ailing wife.

'Mr Boltbyn,' pleads Lydia, 'if you don't tell us what made the peculiar sound, I shall be too afraid to sleep!'

'And she will keep me awake with her tossing and turning,' Emma adds.

4

'I don't see why I should,' Boltbyn demurs. 'I have been doing all the imagining while you young ladies loll about as indolent as frogs in the noonday sun.'

Taking her sister's part lest Lydia start to cry, Emma removes the vicar's watch from his lap, climbs upon his knee, frames his face with both her hands and fixes him with an imploring stare. How silly he looks, with his pink cheeks; his silly hair as though parted by his governess! 'Please, Mr Boltbyn? Won't you please tell us just a *little* bit more? Just this once?'

'I sh-shall continue,' he replies, meeting her clear, intelligent eyes. 'But only briefly and on one condition – that each of you must give me two kisses, one on each cheek. And if each kiss is a very sweet kiss, then we might once again find our way into Adderleigh Forest, and follow Emma's wondrous adventures just a bit further.'

The sisters do just that.

Boltbyn takes a moment to think upon what might possibly happen in the next scene. He regrets having invented the hedgehog. A badger would be better, or perhaps a rabbit. Meanwhile, his eyes roam about the nursery – his favourite room, the only place in the house where he feels comfortable.

To judge by the barred windows, the grated fireplace, the bare walls whitewashed against infection, the room has always been a nursery. His gaze falls upon the reproduction of William Nixon Crede's *Bathing Beauty*, in which a young girl has fallen asleep in the bath: a sentimental favourite in nurseries throughout England, and the main source of Crede's renown. The vicar wonders whether the artist's reputation would diminish if they knew that the original painting is *itself* a reproduction – a painted copy of a photograph taken by Boltbyn himself?

Probably not, he thinks. Originality does not count for much these days, if it ever did.

Gazing upon his two friends, the imprint of their kisses still burning his cheeks, the vicar resolves to mark this date in his diary with a white stone, and to accompany it with a rhyme the day has inspired:

> *Elf locks tangled in the storm,*
> *Red lips for kisses pouted warm.*

Long ago, when Boltbyn was a child, playing with his sisters, inventing ways of passing the afternoon, he began his lifelong habit of marking significant days by pasting a small, smooth white stone (gathered from the beach on holidays) in his diary, as a sign of special happiness.

How the white stones accumulated during those charmed, carefree early years! And how dismally they petered out after the death of his mother, the demands of school, and the repetitive burden of daily life.

Until Emma.

It was during a croquet tournament in the quadrangle of Christ Church: the wind blew his hat from his head onto the ground – and impudent Emma spiked it with her umbrella! Her governess was mortified when it emerged that the owner of the punctured hat was none other than Wallace Beverley – Beverley being the pseudonym under which Boltbyn creates his light verse and children's books. How utterly needless were her apologies! For Wallace Beverley had found his muse and William Boltbyn his happiness at once – and all for the price of a hat!

> *With huge umbrella, lank and brown,*
> *Unerringly she pinned it down,*
> *Right through the centre of the crown.*

Emma was barely ten, and on an outing to Oxford with her family. Over the nearly three years of their acquaintance, Boltbyn's diary has been strewn with white stones, whole weeks smiling like rows of little teeth, while his shelves and drawers bulge with photographs of his favourite subject in all sorts of guises, from beggar-girls to wood-nymphs.

The vicar looks upon Emma, photographing her in his mind, fixing in his memory the look in her hazel eyes, still filled with the mystery and wonder of childhood. At the end of this day he can safely affix another white stone to his diary – but for how many more? Soon Emma's eyes will acquire another kind of knowledge – and then the golden light of childhood will die, and he will be alone, an orphan and a widower, at once.

2

Whitechapel, 1858

In the shadow of London Hospital, a solitary pedestrian slouches along Raven Row, wearing corduroy breeches and a muffin hat. It is early evening, the temporary silence before the lamplighter arrives, that in-between hour when the day-creatures have gone to ground and the night-creatures have yet to emerge in their tattered finery.

Buildings of stone and brick loom like the blackened hulks of abandoned ships as he turns up Sneer Lane, looking neither to right nor left. In East London, the unguarded pedestrian does his best to remain invisible.

Passing by the shadowed entry-way of a vacant tobacco shop, through the corner of an eye, he discerns a curious tableau within – something like a Madonna-and-Child. But he does not take a closer look; in this part of the city, curiosity has killed more than cats.

In the entry-way, perched upon a square wicker laundry hamper in front of the boarded-up door of the shop, the figure in question waits for the footsteps to recede, then returns his attention to the child. There is indeed something tender, even maternal, in the way he cradles the slender girl in his arms. His faded, threadbare, once scarlet sleeve is that of a corporal in the Indian Army; the hand that cradles her slim neck is missing its thumb, which appears to have been torn out by the root.

Hovering above him like Joseph at the Manger is a man in a similar uniform, except his stripes and markings have been torn off, leaving a trail of needle-tracks in the shape of the rank of lieutenant-colonel. He seems narrow-shouldered for an officer, with a large head of matted hair that is all but white; standing at attention, he resembles an inverted mop or broom. At present, however, he is bent over his companion, and his outstretched hand presses a cloth over the mouth and nose of the silent girl.

The pleasant sweetness of chloroform disperses quickly, trumped by the immanent reek of the Thames.

'Be careful,' whispers the seated man. 'Mustn't overdo it or she is gone from us and we is gone to the devil.'

'She is not ready,' replies the lieutenant-colonel in the clipped tones of command. 'She has ceased to struggle, yet I feel her breast move more quickly than it should.'

'That is a relief, Mr Robin, at least there is breath left.'

'Of course there is breath, Mr Weeks, I am not an idiot. The point is, we must make certain. Mr Lush warned as how the clever ones will pretend to be asleep. Imagine if she awoke in transit!'

'Granted, Mr Robin, yet I do not like the use of chemicals for this purpose. It is a low business for men who have seen the epic of the race.'

'Focus on the larger picture, Mr Weeks. England is teeming with cashiered troops washed up on her shores, seeking positions. Shall we join them in the workhouse?'

Robin avoids mentioning that he is the more likely of the two to wind up in that dreary institution, owing to the condition of his face. Sunburnt to charcoal during the siege of Lucknow, it is an unsightly film of scar tissue, and his eyes are agony in sunlight without the protection of dark glasses.

'True for you, sir,' says Weeks. 'Especially us last remaining of the 2nd Infantry what has been dealt so poor a hand. We are not in the running for respectable work. Yet it is not healthy for the mind, an English girl being taken.'

'You have seen and done worse, Mr Weeks.'

'It is not the same, is it? Not after the 'orrors o' Bibi-Gar . . .' The smaller man's eyes become distant; his voice starts as a whisper but rapidly gains volume. '*English woman and children in pieces . . . a ghastly puzzle of flesh the well full of it, white women and children, hang the sepoy swine . . .*'

'Fall to for heaven's sake, keep your voice down and your mind on the business at hand!' Robin swiftly produces a flask from an inside pocket. '*Hazar*, corporal, there's a tot for you.'

Weeks drinks deep. 'Thank you, sir. *Hazar* yourself, sir.'

'What you need is a bit of the chemical before lights-out. One sniff and you sleep like a *baba*. It is *pukka* for the bowels as well.'

'That is not the trouble, sir. It is to crush the slavers only to become slavers oursel' – and of an English girl. I know not how to properly confess it at church.'

'It is not a sin, corporal. As in Bombay, it is an industry.'

'*When in Rome*, I suppose, sir.'

'Precisely. Being foreign-born, not England-born, we must adapt to the terrain, learn to think with the mind of one's fellow Britons. And no more of this confession business, please.'

Weeks glances down at the delicate, inert form in his lap, heaves a sigh, and takes another swig from the flask. 'You 'ave a tactical mind, Mr Robin. It is no wonder you reached the elite ranks and not I.'

Thus, the two surviving members of the 2nd Infantry Division, 3rd Infantry Brigade, rekindle their *esprit de corps*.

As India-born Englishmen, Robin and Weeks arrived in London as destitute, unarmed and disoriented as Punjabis. For weeks, they wandered the Embankment as in a wilderness, near starvation, with no more understanding of the ways of London and how to survive here than if they had landed in Timbuktu – less, for in Africa they would at least have known how to deal with the inhabitants, to forage, to plunder, to butcher and bolt.

Eventually they found themselves in the cadaver business – stealing, digging up and, in a slow period, creating corpses for private medical schools unconnected with the Royal College, for dissection by apprentice apothecary-surgeons. Week after week, they loitered on the Embankment, amid the army of unemployed men who gather in front of the warehouses of the East India Company, available for hire by aggrieved men-about-town as man-bashers for a few shillings.

Then, as chance would have it, along came Mr Lush, acting on behalf of a member of the quality, who offered them an opportunity to expand their custom by furnishing a young female subject for 'artistic purposes'. The remuneration was more than encouraging.

The requirement was of a highly specific nature. The creature to be obtained was described in minute detail – gender, features, colouring, stature – as though for a part in the theatre. After several days, the search took them to a gambling establishment in Houndsditch, where they located the perfect specimen, and for a breathtaking stipend.

Robin removes the handkerchief from the girl's mouth and nose. His damaged features soften as he regards her face – the smooth English brow, the pert, pointed English chin. For a moment the two soldiers grow sad together: on the passage from Calcutta they imagined London as a garden, blooming with lovely faces such as this.

'She is ready, corporal, and will easily last the trip.'

Being the more muscular and better-sighted, Weeks lifts the small, limp form in his arms so that Robin may open the lid of the wicker hamper. 'Put her in the basket, Mr Weeks. She has a half-hour to catch the Oxford train.'

3

The Alhambra Baths, Endell Street

Nobody is more squeamish about mortality than the man who courts it in his daily habits.

Edmund Whitty, correspondent for *The Falcon,* crosses Gutter Lane with a scented scarf over his mouth and nose – for London is in the throes of the public ordeal that will become known as the Great Stink, when so many citizens have resorted to covering their faces with their handkerchiefs, the city might be populated by highwaymen.

Looking on the bright side, the Great Stink has trumped the lesser stink emanating from Whitty himself. He has spent another night in a doss-house on Golden Square, where anyone so foolish as to put on a night-shirt awakens in the morning with nothing to wear, his day-clothes having been sold twice over by dawn.

Like any professional on his uppers, Whitty torments himself with past success. Even the putrid air carries memories of a time when the city rang with the Amateur Clubman's eloquent, if somewhat artificial, indignation:

> *It is an historical fact that in ancient times, the Thames functioned as a repository of the dead not unlike the Ganges – a holy conveyance into which one's mortal remains were consigned for their journey to Heaven. Now the Thames is not a river of the dead but a dead river – a boneless, swelling corpse at the heart of Empire, a malign tumour in the heart of the greatest city in the world . . .*

The Ganges reference was pure speculation, and 'ancient times' an unprovable fiction, yet the piece howled with populist outrage, putting *The Falcon* in the forefront of municipal reform. More important, the piece increased circulation by 10 per cent, providing a bonus of £15 for the outraged scribe.

Happy days. Happier than now, at any rate.

Weighted with nostalgia (and the suspicion that he has become that much-to-be-pitied figure among Oxford men, the 'burnt-out case'), Whitty slouches down Tavistock Street past buildings like monstrous blocks of cured meat.

He was on top of the Thames scandal from the beginning. If England were a meritocracy by this point he would now be serving as an adviser to Parliament, spreading insight among the highest circles, at favourable rates.

Following the cholera epidemic of 1847, the Commission of Sewers decreed that all sewage be discharged directly into the drains. Henceforth, the daily excretions of over three million people fell into the pipes below, wound through a succession of infested tunnels, then reconvened in the Thames, from which Londoners drank, washed and fished.

A decade later, the Thames is a boneless, rotting corpse and so is his career, having failed to generate one saleable narrative in over two months – not through lack of industry, but because each piece has been usurped by Alasdair Fraser's most detested rival, the correspondent for *Dodd's*.

To be scooped, spoiled, ruined by Fraser? *The deuce!*

A trickle of sunlight seeps through the iron skeleton of what will become the rebuilt Theatre Royal, which could be named the Royal Tinderbox for its proclivity to go up in flames. Whitty estimates the hour to be seven – he no longer has a watch. Still, his habit of early rising endures, unaffected by a pathetic lack of stimulants. Though he appears as stylishly ravaged as ever, Whitty is a mere husk of his normal self, having retained the form of decadence but not the content.

Yet it could be worse. It is late summer, and he has not yet slept on a swarming straw mattress with a half-dozen naked, diseased strangers. Mind, the doss-house on Golden Square was a frightful place. Bodily sounds that would make a celibate of anyone. And vermin? Before retiring, he managed to scrape a small handful of crab-lice from the bedclothes, and crushed beneath the candlestick like peppercorns.

Surely this degraded state of affairs cannot owe itself to the skill of Fraser of *Dodd's*! When a pugilist suffers defeat at the hands of an opponent, the fault lies in his own art. Whitty is losing confidence, like a man with a terrible blemish on his face, yet, lacking a mirror, and at a loss to see it for himself.

He remembers once having seen a street performer on the Strand, a survivor of brain surgery able to detach his skull at the crown like the lid of a jam-jar, exposing the sphere of gelatinous flesh within. For a penny, he invited pedestrians to press upon one or another part of his brain with a forefinger, causing him to cry out, to laugh, or to flap an arm up and down. Whitty had recoiled from the spectacle; yet should he not envy a man with access to the inner workings of his own mind?

While awaiting the insight that will restore his prospects, one imperative exists: to avoid emitting the odour of failure. For a journalist, failure is like gangrene. As with vomit and shit, failure can be detected in minute quantities. Once a journalist exudes failure, the stench is with him for life.

Until recently, the Turkish bath has occupied an unsavoury niche in the city, a virtual secret to all but a scattering of patrons: officers returned from Turkey and northern Africa, sufferers of joint pains, neuralgia and delirium tremens, as well as a certain set of Mayfair clubmen who use the baths as a meeting-place, with less than salubrious objectives in mind.

For his part, Whitty has come to rely upon the Alhambra as his cocoon – his place of transformation from worm to butterfly, without which he might as well burrow a hole in the ground and die.

Entering the establishment through an inconspicuous door marked 'Employees and Trade', he steps into a tiny vestibule suitable for the shedding of unwanted identities.

First go the gloves – once fawn, now black, tattered and melancholy beyond expression. Next the wool overcoat – once green, now the colour and texture of tree bark. Layers of filthy linen follow, and a pair of boots for which the term 'down at the heel' is no longer sufficient, there being no heel left to speak of. Lastly, his woollen underpants, now a leaden grey as though painted by the London fog.

Having traded his mortifying attire for an equally mortifying exposure of his most private parts, Whitty scurries quickly through the entry-way and down a hall to a booth, whose indifferent occupant hands him a pair of checked towels, the larger of which he fastens about his loins like a kilt.

At last he can face the world, unashamed.

Padding barefoot across the damp ceramic tiles, he passes through a wide archway into a marble sitting room, where five or six foppish gentlemen lean against the sweating porcelain walls, smoking cigarettes. He is shocked but not surprised to recognise Walker of the Treasury, whose checked towel trails across the tiles as though inviting someone to snatch it. Walker and Whitty exchange perfunctory nods and avert their gaze, while the former reddens like a tomato from head to toe.

Hurrying through a second door into the baths, he passes by a tall, angular gentleman with a T-shaped moustache and goatee. American without a doubt: the colonial tourist is an increasing phenomenon in town, buying up ancient furniture and cluttering the landmarks of the city.

In this torpid atmosphere he perches on a marble armchair to await the cleansing process; around him other gentlemen lie face-down on stone couches shaped like crypts. Silent eastern boys slide like ice-skaters across the tiles, appearing and disappearing as though materialised from steam, ministering to the wattles, bristles and appendages like attendants to a herd of walrus.

'Salaam, Mr Whitty, you honour our house with your presence.' The voice is a modulated oriental murmur, with no hint of the street in Cheapside where Ahmed, son of the proprietor, was actually born.

'And to you, Ahmed. Is your father well?' asks Whitty, stretching out naked on the bench so that the two might perform their respective functions – the mortician and the cadaver.

'In the pink, praise God.'

After soaking him with tepid water, Ahmed scrubs each square inch of skin clean by means of a soap-infused sponge on the end of a stick, much as he might wash the windows of a house. Then he gently scrapes Whitty down, from his neck (chafed) to his heels (blistered), using an instrument resembling a small garden hoe. As he planes off the dross, an extraordinary pile of debris accumulates, though it has been less than a week since his last visit. Last, Ahmed's glistening, hairless colleague appears in a loincloth to crack every bone in Whitty's skeleton, knead his muscles, and pinch his toes.

Having completed what is known as 'the sudation', the two attendants silently withdraw, leaving the corpse in a state of languid reflection.

Whitty refuses to put his current misfortune to some sort of curse – though it is true that much of his life has been a matter of fleeing an accelerating train, with varying distances between his rump and the cow-catcher. Even at the height of his success there remained his fearsome debt to the Captain, the result of a wager in the sport of ratting, with compound interest growing like a tumour and default a mathematical certainty.

What troubles him most is the role of Fraser of *Dodd's* in this latest decline – story after story ruined by the Scotsman, often one day in advance of publication.

As he dozes off, faces appear: Fraser, with his knowing squint and sharp little teeth; Algernon Sala, his editor and former schoolmate – in effect, a monocle nestled in a beard; followed by the more welcome yet equally painful sight of dear, dear Mrs Plant, his publican, her skin as white as the moon, her touch as welcome as sunlight. Winding up the procession, his colleagues at Plant's Inn appear as a group, encircling him in the way of tribesmen, waving pens in the air, whooping like savages . . .

'Pardon me, good sir,' whispers the gentleman in the neighbouring chair, causing Whitty to cry out in alarm. 'You have been whimpering in your sleep, or I should not have disturbed you.'

The flattened, courtly accent is undoubtedly American – Virginia, possibly. Whitty opens his eyes to behold the angular gentleman with the T-shaped moustache and goatee. Uneasily, he wonders what he has been saying in his sleep.

The gentleman greets him with a camaraderie Whitty finds instantly annoying. 'As a foreigner in your country, sir, I hope I have not transgressed any rule by speaking to a stranger.'

'By no means,' Whitty lies.

'Might I say that there can be nothing as absurd as two men seated together for an hour without venturing to open their mouths. Are not all men equal, sir? What difference does it make if a man has his breeches on or not?'

'Quite,' replies Whitty, for whom the difference is considerable. 'And yet, men do seem to require a pair of trousers in order to fully enjoy a social occasion.'

'In any event, say I, better that naked men reveal themselves, than suffer the illusion that much is not already revealed.'

Again Whitty wonders what he has been muttering in his sleep.

'For example,' continues the American, 'in your case, even in your nakedness I can see that you live by the craft of writing.'

'And by what evidence have you reached that determination?'

'Are you familiar with the existence of psychic phenomena?'

'Indeed. And I am aware of the goblins in Hampstead Heath, and of Spring-Heel Jack, who jumps over houses and frightens the horses.'

'A sceptical mind. I salute you for it. The suspicious intelligence of the common man is at the heart of democracy.'

'Democratic or not, sir, I do not follow you.' Whitty sighs inwardly, for his moment of repose has been ruined by a crank.

With a wink, the American reaches to the floor beside his chair and retrieves two cigars. 'Will you partake of a cheroot, sir?'

Whitty accepts the offer readily, having had to settle for moist stumps, retrieved from the ashtrays of his club.

14

'Julius Comfort of Richmond, Virginia, sir. I am a visitor to this fair city, on official business.'

'Edmund Whitty, sir, and I am not.'

Introductions complete, they rise to their feet and cross the chamber to draw from a gaslight provided for that purpose. Puffing energetically, they reseat themselves, folding their towels across their laps

Whitty would prefer to smoke his cheroot in peace and let the conversation wither, but the American, having purchased an audience, has other plans. 'Are you familiar with this publication, sir?'

The newspaper is none other than *Dodd's*, and the writer is the man he loves least in London. Having no escape, Whitty reads the article, thinking that it is a high price to pay for a smoke.

THE PSYCHIC PROWESS OF DR GILBERT WILLIAMS
An Eye-witness Account
by
Alasdair Fraser
Senior Correspondent
Dodd's

There exists a natural and estimable tendency shared by the discerning, to dismiss as absurd any testimony as to the experiencing of highly unusual phenomena. This is all to the good, for, lacking a sceptical frame of mind, one rapidly falls victim to one's own imagination, as do savages in foreign lands.

Yet in the modern age it must be admitted that wonders exist (the telegraph, the camera, the indoor privy) which likewise seem to defy nature, and would have been greeted by equal incredulity only a decade ago.

How timely, therefore, is the establishment of the Foundation for Psychic Research, by the noted American authority, Dr Gilbert Williams, endowed by no lesser a figure than the Duke of Danbury, whose mission is to place the field on a firm footing by subjecting such phenomena to the rigours of scientific scrutiny.

For such experiments, Dr Gilbert Williams has served as a willing and qualified specimen.

In 1852, a dozen professional persons observed Dr Williams to levitate his body from the floor and to place his hands upon the ceiling. As well, he has been known to contact entities in the spirit realm before hundreds of eminent persons, including the Emperor Napoleon III.

In this connection, with the ready agnition of Dr Williams and the full co-operation of Mr Albin Lush, Estate Manager for the Duke of

Danbury, your correspondent proceeded to investigate these claims.

The most stringent pains were taken to exclude fraud as a possible factor. The seance room was meticulously examined beforehand, as were surrounding rooms. Walls were gauged for thickness and tapped for hidden compartments or openings. The Medium was stripped naked and all orifices examined by the physician Dr Crockett . . .

Whitty puts the article down, feeling the need of a rest. 'Really, Mr Comfort, did they think the medium to be hiding spooks up his bottom?'

'A necessary procedure, sir, however unpleasant. All must be verified by empirical science.'

'If you don't mind I shall skip to the bottom of the page, for my stomach is not constant.'

. . . Almost immediately, Dr Williams became cataleptic, or something like it. His fingers bent themselves unnaturally backward, his arms and neck twisted around, and his entire body became rigid. For about five minutes he did not appear to breathe. Then he spoke, in a strange, high voice, the following sentence:

Purity when freed from the mortal is strongest, as truth overcomes error!

At this precise moment, the accordion on the piano began to play Auld Lang Syne *all by itself, as though invisible fingers pressed the keys.*

The rendition complete, the Medium began, in the same strange, high voice, to comment on issues of our day, stressing the paucity of knowledge most scientific men possess – for example, that not long ago the spots of the sun were thought to be mountains, whereas today we know them to be great chasms.

But what they do not know is that the sun is covered with beautiful vegetation, and full of organic life.

Is the sun not hot, we asked?

No, the sun is cold. The heat is produced and transmitted to the earth by rays of light passing through various atmospheres . . .

Whitty throws the newspaper forcefully to the floor. 'Surely it is obvious that the writer has entered into partnership with a fraud, acting as his paid shill.'

'A harsh conclusion, sir.'

'I am well acquainted with the writer. Any spirits Fraser might encounter reside in a whisky bottle.'

'Am I to understand that you do not credit the piece?'

'I assure you, sir, that the writer would not know ectoplasm if he were swimming in it.'

'Precisely the reply I had hoped for,' replies the American, giving Whitty's knee a wet slap. 'I have come to the right party for the initiative I propose!'

Blast. It is now obvious to Whitty that the scoundrel plotted their meeting from the first: stalked him to the bath, drew him into conversation, and now intends to harness him in some vanity project – trace his royal ancestry, perhaps.

At the same time, there is always the possibility of remuneration.

Riding this train of thought, Whitty's momentary opportunism trumps his instinct for idiocy. For the correspondent is nothing if not paradoxical: a hypochondriac with a contempt for his own health; a confirmed rationalist who is an avid consumer of every medicament on the chemist's shelf; an elitist who favours the poor; a moralist with a weakness for fallen women.

Nonetheless, he remains coy, if only for purposes of negotiation.

'Sir, in my professional experience it is in the nature of hobby-horses that they are best ridden alone. I advise you to pack up your fascinating experience, your astonishing insight, your personal crusade, escort it to the British Museum, and write your memoirs. There is no virtue in pressing honest journalists in Turkish baths to do your work for you.'

'I have offended you and am sorry for it. I have come not to harm you, but to offer you a substantial profit. I salute your integrity, sir. I admire any man who will turn down good money out of personal principle. Say the word and I shall vacate the premises immediately with sincere apologies, and trouble you no more in this life.'

Turn down good money out of principle?

'I assure you, sir, I intend no such thing.'

'Then lend an ear to what I have to tell you, and what you have to gain.'

'I am a private investigator with the Pinkerton Group, employed by a prominent American family, whose daughter succumbed to a complete cad on the advice of Dr Gilbert Williams – also known as Professor Herbert Zollner of Prague, and as Herr Schrenk-Notting of Konnersreuth, Bavaria; who is in reality Bill Williams of Frankfort, Kentucky, a vicious swindler who, for a substantial bribe, simulated the blessing of a deceased aunt.

'The cad has been dealt with. Yet I have since trailed the villain over two continents, to no avail.

'Mr Whitty, Americans were impressed by the Chokee Bill matter –

how you flushed out the Fiend in Human Form, brought an end to his reign of terror and saved the lives of Heaven knows how many women. Your exploits are the stuff of penny dreadfuls, whose authors have profited more than you have, sir.'

'I am not in the novel business. I merely report events as they occur.'

'You did not report the news in this case, sir. You *created* the news. You *were* the news.'

'Perhaps,' replies Whitty, growing wistful. *So I did, then. So I was, then.*

'The man of whom I speak, Dr Gilbert Williams, is in his own way a monster in human form,' says the American, while rummaging in a briefcase, from which he produces a square envelope of fine-quality vellum.

'I have in my hand an invitation, under the name of Henry Willows, to a seance scheduled on Friday next. I obtained it through old Lord Donlevy, who fears that his nephew, the Duke of Danbury, has become enraptured – mesmerised if you will – by an unwholesome cult. In fact, the seance is to occur at the family town-house on Buckingham Gate.'

Leaning forward, the American speaks with fresh intensity: 'Attend the event, sir, and expose this fraud to the public – for I have no doubt that the charade will be obvious to your trained, sceptical eye.'

'If I may ask,' Whitty interrupts, 'why do you present this opportunity to me? Having uncovered the golden egg, why not eat the omelette yourself?'

'My pursuit has taken me too long. He has me royally pegged and will vanish to some distant corner of Europe the moment he senses my presence. I leave it to you, Mr Whitty, to accomplish what I never can. Expose the scoundrel, and collect your fee.'

A lovely word, fee.

'How much?'

'£10 in advance, and £20 upon delivery of your article.'

Whitty considers the ethics involved, of writing an article and collecting a fee from the party who is to benefit. Such an arrangement carries more than a whiff of corruption.

'£20 in advance and £30 upon delivery,' says the correspondent.

The American produces another cheroot, smiling in a way Whitty does not altogether like.

'I have a confession to make, sir. I have been on your trail for three days. Imagine, the sharpest pen in London living like a stinking beggar!

I assure you that a man of your accomplishment would not suffer such a fate in the land of the free!'

Comfort has him cold. At the same time, he has gone to considerable trouble to make this offer, therefore he must judge it worth his while.

'£15 in advance, £25 upon publication, and not a farthing less.'

'Done.'

Comfort transfers the envelope, then grasps Whitty's hand in a hot, wet palm. 'Your invitation, sir. And your advance. On that note, allow me to bid you a very fine day.'

Whitty opens the envelope to find two banknotes, a tenner and a fiver, as negotiated. For the American at least, everything has gone according to plan.

Mahumud el Khali bin Sai-ud, proprietor of the Alhambra, in a black frock coat and fez, reclines upon a faded pillow, puffs upon a *hookah* and watches Whitty dress, while Ahmed performs the service of valet. Excellent training for his son, to become conversant with details of the English gentleman's way of life.

The bin Sai-ud line is the oldest house in south-western Sudan, having fought many battles with honour before times changed. Now there is no longer a place there for honourable men, Khartoum being overrun by dirty fellows with foreskins, unbelievers, and descendants of slaves who hold a grudge against their former owners. Therefore bin Sai-ud removed his family and relations to London, where the caliphs reign by means of lawsuits and not torture, and where ordinary men may conduct their affairs in peace.

His regard for the English press owes much to Edmund Whitty of *The Falcon*, who came to his rescue during one of London's episodic outbreaks of moral indignation, when Parliament, spurred by the League for Moral Hygiene, resolved to combat vice. Obediently, the Metropolitan Police selected the Alhambra for a symbolic raid, in which the pot-hatted Crusaders would save Christendom from godless Arabs and their harems, and rid the world of sodomy into the bargain. Clearly, the Mussulman stood as designated scapegoat *du jour*.

It is not Whitty's normal practice to ride to the rescue of maltreated foreigners; there are too many of them, and their names too difficult to spell. Moreover, it is generally wise for a London correspondent to keep his head down when Miss Grundy stalks the streets. Yet the hypocrisy was too much to resist – not to mention the opportunity to settle some professional scores.

Shortly thereafter, an issue of *The Falcon* featured a social note by the Amateur Clubman, the pseudonym he employs when baiting the reigning establishment.

> *Having suffered an onset of neuralgia, the Amateur Clubman recently had occasion to elicit the services of the Alhambra Baths, where he encountered several well-connected gentlemen with similar complaints, including Mr Coxwell and Mr Glaisher of the Whigs, as well as Mr Angerstein, MP, the Conservative Party Whip . . .*

A framed copy of the piece now hangs above the proprietor's head like a diploma – another example of Whitty's former style and dash, another memory to torment him in his time of trouble.

Following this piece of reportage, members of the League for Moral Hygiene became curiously mute. A week later, an article appeared in the *Daily Telegraph* on the benefits of the Turkish bath as an economical safeguard against the pollution that bedevils this overpopulated city. Thanks to *The Falcon*, the Alhambra transformed from Sodom to health spa overnight, and Whitty acquired a welcome line of credit.

A dusty stream of sunlight filters through the lattice shutters, casting a dappled pattern onto his precious city clothes, which hang neatly over a chair-back.

Whitty fastens his necktie (stiffened, to put the chin properly at attention) and with painful awkwardness seats himself upon a brocade pillow on the Turkey carpet (bin Sai-ud marvels at the stiffness of the English leg), to help himself to a wad of the proprietor's morning *qat*. Through an archway he can see sons Seven, Three and Six, as well as trusty Ahmed, crouched upon their haunches around a neatly drawn circle of sand on the floor, tracing letters and words in Arabic with their fingers and chanting verses from the Koran. Beyond that room is the kitchen in which, to judge by the sounds heard from time to time, the bin Sai-uds butcher their own goats.

'Esteemed Khali, I spoke at length with an American gentleman this morning and wonder if he might be known to you.'

'He has honoured our establishment only once before, Mr Whitty.' The proprietor raises his voice in order to be heard over the prayers: 'Ahmed, come please, and reveal to Mr Whitty your estimation of the American gentleman.'

Obediently, young Ahmed ceases chanting in Arabic, enters the room and replies in a startling cockney: 'Bloke have the wide-eye of a gamesman. Dunnage be of a macer or a nobbler, could be. Takes arsenic powder for snuff. Wears an 'at wif a finny in the band an' a chif in 'is gally. 'Is clock 'as the colour of an arsenic-eater . . .'

So, thinks the correspondent: A fiver in his hat-band and a knife in his shoe – suitable equipment for an agent with the Pinkertons, and for a dangerous tout. The picture of Julius Comfort remains ambiguous; Whitty allows the £15 in his pocket to cast the deciding vote, and resolves to remain on his guard.

Rising to his feet, he takes his plum-coloured coat (well regarded on Bond Street) from the back of the chair, smooths his waistcoat, and extends one leg to inspect the fit of his peg-top trousers.

Khali extends the tube from his *hookah* to Whitty, who accepts a lungful of spiced tobacco smoke. 'May I enquire as to any change in the prospects of the esteemed journalist?'

'You are a patient man, Khali, and I am in your debt. It is a burden and a sorrow to me and my house – which, at present, we must bear together.'

'Do not disturb yourself, my friend. Should I die, it shall be counted as part of the poor-rate, for which Allah's blessing awaits: a soft couch of petals and a choice of young virgins served with breakfast.'

'Whereas, should I die before payment in full, I shall receive a couch made of nettles, and a choice of toothless hags.'

4

Crouch Manor, Chester Wolds, Oxfordshire

He thought he saw an Elephant,
That practised on a fife;
He looked again, and found it was
A letter from his wife.
'At length I realise,' he said,
'The bitterness of life!'

The Reverend Charles Grantham Lambert seats himself in his comfortless chair, in his comfortless drawing room, where his collected offspring silently awaits the daily reckoning; silently, for it is a rule of the house that nobody shall address Father until first addressed by him. Emma knows this to be common practice in the more respectable households, yet it makes her feel somewhat like a ghost, for it is said that they too must be spoken to before they can speak.

Miss Pouch hovers over her charges, reading her employer's every twitch; with Mrs Lambert so frequently confined to her chamber, the governess must assume full responsibility for the girls' behaviour and deportment.

From the day of his birth to the moment he received his calling at the age of twelve, it was a given that the Reverend Lambert was not only destined for the cloth (the family abounds with clerics) but that his handsome head would surely be measured for a bishop's mitre one day. Now approaching forty-five, he still has the form and bearing, the luminous certitude of one who is firmly anchored to the rock that cannot move.

'Emma's French is pretty well, Miss Pouch, but her Italian is still a worry. Her music may be adequate – I'm no judge – but her drawing could be better . . .' As always, he speaks of his daughter in the third person, so that morsels of praise do not nourish the sin of pride.

'Mr Boltbyn arrived for his visit a bit earlier than usual,' answers Miss Pouch. 'It necessitated a curtailment of her drawing-time.'

'Surely Mr Boltbyn knows better. I wish to speak to him at once.'

'He has left for the day, sir. I shall convey your wishes to him.'

In fact, Lambert is glad that the vicar has gone for the day; the prestige afforded by the author's interest in the girls is offset by the fact that, in Lambert's opinion, Boltbyn is a theological dabbler, woefully lacking in seriousness.

'See that it does not happen again. Mr Boltbyn's amusements are no substitute for an education.'

'I shall indeed, sir.'

'I shall speak to Mrs Lambert about this matter. She should keep a closer watch over what goes on in the nursery.'

'Mrs Lambert was unwell today, I am afraid, and retired for the afternoon.'

'How unfortunate.' Lambert expects she will miss supper – which is also just as well, for in her present state she would cast a pall over the entire meal.

Emma watches her father pore over her notebook as though it were a legal text, knowing that he does so as an alternative to dealing with her mind directly. She has been aware for some time that her thoughts make him uneasy, and suspects that her very existence bothers him in the way of his toothache – as a worrisome daily burden, endured with the patience of Job.

Lambert gives special attention to Lydia's grasp of the Commandments, for her confirmation is only a few months away, and her performance of the catechism before the bishop will surely reflect upon her father. Indeed, he doesn't entirely mind the exercise, for Lydia has proved much easier to control than her elder sister.

Soon enough, Lizzy will bring his tea, then his supper, and he will take respite from his toothache and his various disappointments. For now he listens patiently to Lydia's catechism, which she has mastered quite admirably.

Thou shalt not make unto thee any graven image . . .

Blessed with a baritone suited to preaching and hymn-singing, upon graduation from All Souls College the young Reverend Lambert received an immediate posting at St Alban the Martyr, in the parish of Upper Clodding. The congregation at St Alban were well pleased with their new spiritual leader, who showed an especial interest in the young people. With his manners and breeding, to his parishioners it seemed inevitable that he would receive wider notice as a future leading light in the diocese – an expectation held no less by Lambert himself.

This happy prospect came to nothing. Months and years ground by with no invitation to chair a committee at a synod, no guest sermon at another parish. At times he felt as though he had been beached upon some obscure island to minister to the natives in perpetuity.

(In fact, his ostracism stemmed from a decades-old incident in which a great-uncle accused a fellow clergyman of simony, occasioning a general animosity in the church hierarchy to anyone who bore the name Lambert.)

Unaware that his fate was sealed, Rev. Lambert did his duty. For ten of this earth's revolutions about the sun (still a subject of dispute in Upper Clodding), he conducted holy services, sipped weak tea with the elders, delivered his sermons and read his Bible, while tormented by dreams of missed trains and lost objects. Over time, disappointment surely took a toll upon his disposition; yet his sermons continued to deliver more honey than brimstone, his house-calls provided a wellspring of solace and hope; in sum, their bachelor reverend seemed settled and content.

Thus, it came as no small shock to the congregation when the fixture in the pulpit announced his engagement to one Euphemia Root – familiarly known as 'Birdie', a comely girl of fifteen whose family owned a dry-goods shop in the village.

Less than a month after this startling broadcast, the pair were married by the vicar from Hereford. Nine months later, or possibly less (fingers counted the weeks, the human hand became an abacus), Birdie gave birth to a daughter, who was named Emma. Three years later, Lydia appeared.

It is true that the Church of England does not adhere to the tradition of a celibate priesthood; notwithstanding, among Anglican parishioners the prospect of sexual activity by the clergy is an unsavoury one, even when practised within the bond of holy matrimony.

At service, the presence of his young wife and girls stimulated unwanted fancies among the faithful, and if there is a time and place in which such thoughts should remain absent, surely that place and time is in church of a Sunday morning. To some, the marriage of their vicar came to symbolise the Fall of Man, with the Lamberts as the first couple and a serpent coiled beneath the pulpit. The rift grew wider when Emma blossomed into a miniature version of her well-favoured mother, with an unsettling gaze and an aspect of premature knowing.

Despite the whispers at every tea-table, Lambert continued his duties with stoic determination. Less sanguine was his young wife, for whom the disapproving stares were like needles in the flesh. As the stares and the whispers grew sharper, it became her practice to cover her face with a white veil – not out of modesty, but from a desire not to see the faces of her former acquaintances.

It was at this point of increasing turmoil that Lambert's teeth began to bother him. First one tooth throbbed, then its neighbour, until the entire set took turns. As the affliction worsened, he began to suspect, however irrationally, that a connection existed between his constant pain and his stunted ambitions.

Eventually, word of a chill in the relations between the shepherd of Upper Clodding and his flock (as well as a drop in collection revenue) caught the attention of the bishop, whereupon the Reverend C. G. Lambert at last received a new appointment, as precentor at the Church of St Swithan, Chester Wolds, Oxfordshire, where his fine baritone was to lead the singing – an inferior designation, but in a superior church.

Like a divine intervention a window had opened to admit the warm sunlight of Hope. Surely it will not be long before the Oxford congregation becomes his – for it is well known that the current vicar, Reverend Spoole, suffers from declining health.

Like Job, C. G. Lambert is about to receive his reward.

Thou shalt not bow down thyself to them, nor serve them: for I the Lord thy God am a jealous God, visiting the iniquity of the fathers upon the children unto the third and fourth generation of them that hate me; and shewing mercy unto thousands of them that love me, and keep my commandments.

Emma listens while her sister recites the commandments, thinking that it does not present a flattering picture of the Creator that He punishes children for the sins of the father. And yet, do not the children of drunkards and brutes suffer for the sins of the father? Emma thinks she might understand her father better had she met *his* father; but then her grandfather might have simply pointed to his own ancestors, on and on, back to Adam.

As for Emma's mother, it was hoped that the new position at St Swithan would likewise herald a new beginning, that she might walk freely without her veil. Instead, she chose not to go out at all. Transplantation seemed to have a withering effect, so that now she spends most mornings in bed, her afternoons under medication for nervous hysteria, and her evenings in books.

Thou shalt not covet thy neighbour's house, thou shalt not covet thy neighbour's wife, nor his manservant, nor his maidservant, nor his ox, nor his ass, nor any thing that is thy neighbour's . . .

'You are progressing well, Lydia,' her father interrupts, feeling no need to hear the entire ten. 'Say a prayer that you remain steadfast. Miss Pouch, as I mentioned, Emma's drawing and her languages are a worry. The family cannot afford a finishing governess for her, and you must make the most of the resources God has chosen to provide.'

'Is that clear, Emma?' asks Miss Pouch.

'Yes, miss. *J'attends ce que vous dites. Cela a l'air d'être de la frime.*'

'Quite,' says the Reverend. 'Very good. Off with you, then.'

With the parley at an end, Miss Pouch ushers her two charges out of the room for a half-hour of moral instruction before supper.

The Rev. Lambert warms his hands by the fire, opening his mouth wide in order to admit the soothing warmth into his gums and teeth. Hearing the door open and close, he closes his mouth, leans back in his chair, and assumes an aspect of calm forbearance.

Due to the chronic indisposition of his wife at this critical period in his career, he has come to depend more and more upon Lizzy, the maid-of-all work, a distant cousin taken in out of charity, who has grown to become a presentable, compliant, womanly presence during his wife's indisposition.

'Your tea, Mr Lambert,' she murmurs, setting the tray upon the table in the centre of the room. Heavily laced with laudanum, the beverage will provide hours of comfort, perhaps even sleep.

Reflected in the looking-glass, Emma watches her mother, behind the gauze curtain that surrounds her bed. Coloured glass bottles grace the side-table beside her Bible, among them the sleeping-draught she takes in the early evening. Lydia has been put to bed early with a chill (a window was inadvertently left open during supper), while Father is dozing in the drawing room, having taken something for his toothache.

Sometimes it seems to Emma that, but for the servants and cousin Lizzy, she is the only conscious person in the house.

She has taken her mother's rouge from the drawer – without asking permission, but surely Mother will not mind, for she has no use for it. Her face on the pillow is as white and smooth as if it has been covered with powder of arsenic – something *The Ladies' Home Companion* warns against in the issue spread out on the dressing-table, which

Emma has opened to a feature on 'making-up' by one of the great ladies of the stage.

It should be put on in straight lines under the eyes, for a layer of carmine heightens their brilliancy . . .

Emma longs for clarification of this phrase, for her eyes do not appear any more brilliant, in fact she looks rather like a harlequin.

Three other layers should be gently placed exactly between the nose and ears, never reaching below the mouth. This slight touch of rouge will not altogether vulgarise the face . . .

Twice already, she has had to scrub her cheeks clean, having rendered them, if not exactly vulgar, not exactly ladylike either. Intently she searches her reflection for signs of the glamorous woman of the future. 'Oh, bother,' she says to herself. 'You look like a little girl with make-up on. You don't look like me at all.'

Behind the curtain, her mother opens her eyes to behold a vague form through a silvery mist. 'Who is there?' Birdie calls out, in a small, frightened voice, thinking it might be a ghost.

'It is Emma, mother. Don't you recognise me?' Emma climbs through the curtains, and puts her arms around her mother's neck.

'I didn't at first, my dear,' Birdie replies, holding her daughter close. 'For a moment, I thought it was me.'

5

Fleet Street, west of Ludgate

Holding a scented handkerchief about his mouth and nose, Whitty proceeds south on Bow Street, pausing opposite the half-completed London Opera House to scan the area for suspicious parties, but identifies only the customary array of bottom-feeders, carrying on commerce of the most basic kind:

   – a standing patterer, chaunting his litany of outrages

   – a seller of trotters, eel pie and plum duff

   – the Indian street-sweeper, a fixture for many years

   – a begging street-seller, pretending to offer three pairs of boot-laces, representing his entire inventory

   – Old Sarah, the blind hurdy-gurdy player, grinding out 'Patrick's Day In The Morning' – her only selection – on her defective instrument, accompanied on the cymbal by her companion and guide, an emaciated crone named Liza. The duo compete in cacophony with the farmyard player across the street, also blind, who imitates animals on the violin.

All vie for the attention of a procession of frock-coated gentlemen, handkerchiefs held over their faces with suede fingers, bent forward as though resisting a gale.

Unjustly perhaps, Whitty holds the street-people in the highest esteem while resenting the gentlemen, indistinguishably. Inspired by Khali's prospect of a harem of virgins, he slips Old Sarah a shilling he can scarcely afford, before proceeding along a series of streets that wind down to the Embankment like drains. At last he reaches Ingester Square – the rotting church, the imploding graveyard, the tiny patch of shade under a near-dead tree – and enters the queer brown lump of a building that houses *The Falcon*.

At the editor's office he pauses at the green baize-covered door to review his tiny arsenal of ideas – consisting of Julius Comfort's invitation to Mr Henry Willows, Esq., and the week-old copy of *Dodd's* containing Fraser's pseudoscientific twaddle: could life offer a more soothing unguent for his abraded soul than to make an ass of the brute who has spoiled his career – and to be paid handsomely for the pleasure?

Uttering a silent prayer to nothing in particular, he pushes through the heavy door and into the editor's cheerless office – choked with cigar smoke, splattered with ink, and in a state of perpetual vibration, thanks to the presses and other machinery in the bowels of the building. Never pleasant, the office is made more hideous thanks to gaslight, which has replaced the evil-smelling moon-glow of tallow. Now every splash of dried ink on the Turkey carpet, every layer of dust, every greasy finger-spot, every chip and crack in the plaster bust of some worthy from a previous administration, stands out in macabre relief. The complexions of the occupants (even those who have drunk deep at luncheon) glow with a corpse-like pallor. Hunched over their desks beneath the monstrous, clattering clock, Algernon Sala and his sycophantic chorus of sub-editors and sub-sub-editors appear as in a ghastly intaglio print, an allegorical representation of some death-dealing bureaucracy, charged with administering the mortal procedure of disease and decay.

Which, in a way, is not far from the fact.

Sala sits in the geographical centre of the room like the yolk of an egg, half-visible behind a bruised oaken desk piled high with the business of the day: competing publications to be slandered, novels to be butchered, characters to be assassinated, requests for employment to be ignored.

Presiding over this terminus of shattered hopes, the editor rests his bulk in a creaking, cane-bottomed armchair as he shuffles myopically through packets of telegraphs, newspaper clippings, hand-written reports, scribbled rumours and lies.

In a slow news period, it falls upon the editor to construct issues virtually out of whole cloth, to apply sensational lard to bare bones of facts. In this quest, Sala operates as both master and bird-dog, scanning his desk for meat, then barking a header, to be chewed into copy by his pack of hounds.

Whitty looks down upon his old friend with a mixture of fascination and disquiet. In particular, he wonders at the capacity of the editor to talk, even to think, in the form of newspaper headlines. This facility has enabled Sala to survive a remarkable ten years in this snake-pit of intrigue, despite the unconcealed, patronising scorn of his Proprietor, for whom it is axiomatic that one understands newspapers by reading them, and controls the news by owning it.

To Whitty, it is their shared impotence against powers beyond their control which accounts for their tacit alliance through feast and famine: hence, when on an upswing, Whitty refrains from snapping at competing offers, and when in defeat, Sala does not throw him down the drain. It is the nearest thing to security Whitty has ever known.

At the same time, *The Falcon* has taken a heavy toll on both men.

While at Oxford, Algernon Sala excelled in debate, wrote voluminously, even published an edition of presentable verse. Today, he is like a missionary who has spent too many years speaking pidgin:

'Fellow of King's College dies from anuris of the aorta during visit with prostitute! Header – *His Last Seminar!* Subhead, *Dead in the Arms of a Fallen Woman!*'

'Couple convicted of starving servant-girl, weight 59 pounds, teeming with vermin! Header – *Atrocious Abuse of Servant-Girl!* Subhead, *Beastly and Outrageous Treatment!*'

Observing from the opposite side of the desk, as yet unnoticed, Whitty sees that his friend's eyes have become inflamed, as though by the language he is reduced to working with.

'Good-day to you, Algy. I say old chap, your hyperbole is worthy of the Gothics – absolutely top-drawer.'

'Edmund, dear fellow! Take a seat! I say, you look fecking hale and healthy – *Weighty Matters Cast Aside,* sort of thing?' The editor's monocle glints at the correspondent like the spotlight of a distant search-party.

'Positively of the first water, Algy. Flush with the bloom of cash and collateral.'

'I wish *The Falcon* could say the same, Edmund. Crimea over and done with, cholera gone from the rookeries, royals relatively continent – we are scraping the bloody dregs for shocking outrages, old man. It's a disaster, haven't been out of my clothes since Wednesday.' Returning his attention to the raw meat splayed on his desk, Sala continues:

'Kansas Abolitionist Hacks 5 to Death! Header – *Barbarity Reigns in America*! No, better – *Severed Heads on the Kansas Plain!*'

'Student murders mistress, saws up body! Header – *Student Dismembers Mistress! Bishop Cites Lack of Religious Instruction . . .*'

'Stop, Algy, stop! Give us a moment, will you?'

At the sound of Whitty's voice, Sala's attention returns to the here-and-now. 'Sorry, old chap. There is something obsessive about the writing of fiction.'

'This will be the death of you, Algy,' says Whitty. 'There is more to life than journalism, as surely you know.'

'I do not. But you, seemingly, do. Damn me, you've supplied not a scrap of copy in a fortnight!'

'Not my fault, old boy. *The Falcon* hasn't seen fit to publish.'

'Your last item had already appeared in *Dodd's*. And the one before that.'

'The point stands. You did not see fit to publish.'

'How could I? To do otherwise would violate the Proprietor's fundamental policy – *First in All, Second to None.*'

'What the devil is that supposed to mean?'

'That timing is everything – When to strike, when to draw back . . .'

'And when to play another game entirely.' Whitty says, staring inscrutably into space.

A pause, while the monocle examines him for clues.

As happens often in these conversations, Whitty has no idea what he meant by that last retort. That is one of the difficulties in playing it by ear, in brassing it out: one can talk oneself into performing a face-plant upon the editor's Turkey carpet.

The monocle glitters in the narrow space that separates Sala's beard and brow. 'You seem remarkably sanguine amid the prevailing drought, old man.'

'Sanguine indeed.' This last remark came from Mr Cream, the subeditor, seated behind Sala and to the side, a vole-shaped man with a spidery moustache and a squint. 'Mr Whitty is surprisingly sanguine amid the current infecundity.' Receiving no reply other than a withering look from both men, Cream returns to the copy of *Lloyd's* on his desk.

'Other activities have sparked my interest,' Whitty says.

'Well come out with it, old chap. Inheritance from a distant aunt? *Cash Pours from Unlikely Source*, sort of thing?' Sala removes his monocle and cleans it with his handkerchief, an indicator of concern.

'Other irons in the fire, Algy. *Hunches Bear Fruit. Investments Accrue.*'

Sala's exposed eye narrows before the monocle returns to its position. 'Congratulations, old boy, I must say. But surely you didn't undertake the journey to our office just to declare your disinterest in the profession.'

'Quite so,' contributes Cream, attempting a conspiratorial wink in the direction of his superior. 'A paradoxical peregrination, surely.'

While Cream dislikes correspondents as a general rule, his loathing for Whitty is closer to the bone. It is not just the envy of an homely man for a handsome one, nor the disdain of the prig for the *bon vivant*. It takes all of these and more to create a dislike as intense as this.

Listening to the banter between editor and correspondent, it is obvious to Cream that the normal relation between those who command and those who serve is nothing but a sort of game. Witness these two, who schooled at Rugby (before Whitty's family difficulties), rowed on the same eight at Oxford (before Whitty's expulsion), who stand united by the Old School Tie. This is what enables a dissipated correspondent to speak to an editor by his Christian name (in diminutive form!), and it is what will enable a Whitty, not a Cream, to one day take the editor's chair.

Cream watches with distaste as Whitty, perched upon a corner of Sala's desk, helps himself to one of the editor's cigars and awaits a light, calm as you please – which the editor supplies! In dismay, Cream conceals his face behind *Lloyd's*, listening carefully.

'Got something for us, old man?' asks Sala in an undertone. 'Could do with anything really.'

The two associates eye one another, each searching for clues as to what, if anything, remains between them in this time of adversity.

Whitty observes his oldest friend, a mound of tension and distension, not to mention luncheon. Sala, for his part, eyes a bone-rack in fine tailoring.

'Come now, Edmund. One hates to think the sharpest pen at *The Falcon* has lost its edge.'

Cream lowers his copy of *Lloyd's*. 'Well put, Mr Sala. And a worthy obituary for Mr Whitty: *Arrow has lost its Edge, leaving Correspondent aquiver.*'

'Ah, Mr Cream,' says Whitty. 'Good to see that your snout is, as always, fully embedded in Mr Sala's bottom.'

Three clerks, while on their knees praying to their filing-drawers, titter: *Oh, I say! Fine cut!*

Cream blanches at the obscenity. 'Mr Sala, I protest this foul language. The proprietor would never countenance it.'

'Mr Whitty, please express yourself in more civilised terms,' cautions Sala, a stern expression beneath his beard.

'Very well, I suggest that Mr Cream has set a new standard for obsequious proctology, commonly described as a nose for ooze.'

'Much more mellifluous – don't you agree, Mr Cream?'

The sub-editor ventures no reply while thinking, *I will be revenged on the pack of you.*

Thinks the editor: Another instance of his need for Whitty, for the office is alive with poisonous toadies. 'By thunder, Edmund, you're not thinking of leaving us? Many years' association and all that.'

'It is only an option,' Whitty replies, affecting a pensive, Keatsian air.

'Blast, Edmund!' Sala's descending fist causes tiny globes of black liquid to spatter from his inkwell onto the desk. 'Give over to the fecking Scotsman? Can't have it, old man!'

'Get used to Mr Fraser, Algy. The Proprietor might well tender him an offer.'

'True, the fecking Scotsman seems to have taken the field at present. Uncanny, the way the rascal has developed an instinct in recent months.'

Cream interjects: 'Uncanny is precisely the word for Mr Fraser's intuitive manifestation.'

'Quite,' Whitty says. 'How timely that Mr Fraser should enter the discussion now, for several new and interesting facts have surfaced concerning that Celtic gentleman.'

'Interesting in what way?' Sala and Cream speak in unison.

'Following a persistent investigation I have obtained the confidence of an impeccable source, who leaves no doubt that Dr Gilbert Williams, the subject of Fraser's latest series on psychic phenomena, is in truth a proven humbug with a litter of innocent victims in his wake.'

'Continue, Edmund, old boy. You warm the cockles of my heart with your little tale.'

'A plethora of aliases have come to light: Professor Herbert Zollner of Prague, Herr Schrenk-Notting of Konnersreuth, Bavaria . . .'

'Capital! Foreign names!'

'Only last year he was observed cheating in Biarritz – in the presence of Louis Napoleon himself!' says the correspondent, for added effect.

'A royalty angle!'

'By various means, I have acquired an invitation to our man's little spook show under the name of *Willows* – that is, should I decide to undertake the story.'

Sala's monocle drops to his lap. (The sacks beneath his eyes are a shade of yellow that suggests liver trouble.) 'Dear heaven, Edmund! Can there be any question, with such crisp copy at hand? Naturally, *The Falcon* will provide a substantial advance.'

33

Behind his newspaper the sub-editor takes notes in a round, careful script. At this rate, it should only be a matter of weeks before the proprietor orders the dismissal of Mr Whitty – and, God willing, Mr Sala as well – with a bright possibility of promotion for the meritorious Mr Cream.

6

Bissett Grange, Oxfordshire

I dreamt I dwelt in marble halls,
And each damp thing that creeps and crawls
Went wobble-wobble on the walls.

Strange pictures decked the arras drear,
Strange characters of woe and fear,
The humbugs of the social sphere.

Not far from the town of Chipping Norton, the brougham containing Reverend William Boltbyn and his photographic equipment pauses beside a one-storeyed porter's lodge, nestled in deep ivy, before a set of heavy wooden lodge-gates designed to convey the opposite of welcome.

Nobody in ten years has passed through these gates without a signed invitation from the Duke of Danbury. Artists who ask permission to sketch the house are refused without exception. A photographer who managed to capture the manor by stealth had his negatives smashed, so that the otherwise inclusive *Homes of the British Aristocracy in the Camera: Being Reminiscences of a Peripatetic Photographer* contains no chapter on Bissett Grange. This absence was of less consequence to the photographer than the near-loss of a leg by blood-poisoning, having stepped into a poacher's snare.

An exception to this forbidding directive are members of the Oxford Photographic Society, which the duke has taken under his protection since its founding a dozen years ago, and who roam the estate at will.

As the carriage clatters up the elm-avenue to the house, Boltbyn admires the broad expanse of park; two grazing deer raise their heads at the sound of carriage-wheels and hurry, at their peculiar sling trot, into the shelter of a shadowed copse.

Boltbyn does not look forward to the afternoon. He had thought the society to have progressed well past Sleeping Innocence pictures; moreover, he does not welcome the opportunity to contribute further to the *œuvre* of Mr Nixon Crede.

The entrance to the manor is made of brick, and shaped like a medieval portcullis; above him, Elizabethan gables top a series of fieldstone façades, while before him stands an enormous flower-bed, whose exotic blooms and greenery culminate at the precise centre of the carriage-sweep.

In short, Bissett Grange is a queer, squarish ramble, which has undergone so many renovations as to have lost all trace of its original architecture.

Standing beside the carriage, Boltbyn watches anxiously while two uniformed footmen shoulder his precious camera, lenses, and portable cabinet of developing materials, out of the carriage, up the steps and through the front door. Before entering, he pauses to admire the ancient quadrangle with its stables and coach-houses, so picturesque with the late afternoon sun illuminating the clock-turret and pointed roof.

As always, the reception room contains a magnificent array of hothouse plants, arranged in bowers along the central hallway and in every recess of the gallery – the duke's floral requirements are enormous; like the house, the conservatory is under constant expansion. As always, beneath the bouquet lurks the disconcerting scent of rising damp – a faint, sweetish, rotten emission, a result of inadequate ventilation in one of the renovations. (Within a half-hour Boltbyn will have become insensible to the odour; he doubts that the duke and his servants have smelled it in years.)

The central hallway is a rococo celebration of both European history in general and the Industrial Age in particular, featuring mass-produced figures worth the eyesight of a dozen tradesmen a half-century ago: plaster angels, fish, flowers, tassels, trumpet-blowing cupids against a painted sky, mirrors – alongside genuine marble and bronze sculpture – creating a riot to rival baroque Italy.

At the end of the central hallway – lined with intermittent shrines to former generations of Danburys – Boltbyn can glimpse Danbury's library, in which a collection of pistols takes the place of books; a queer, octagonal, room looking upon an immense lawn, undulating upward as far as the estate's picturesque highlight: the Roland Stones, a public landmark with a prehistoric legacy that might as well have been created for the amusement of Bissett Grange.

Boltbyn follows the footmen up the staircase and down a narrow hall (rendered tubular by Paladin arches, installed on a whim), until they reach a rope, beyond which none may pass. Boltbyn does not find this declaration of privacy especially odd: the Duke of Prescott is said to have built a miniature railway underneath his house, open to none but himself; the Earl of Bridgewater dines alone with his dogs.

Turning left, he enters a room whose windows are permanently sealed to banish exterior light, illuminated by tallow candles in sconces. Towering above him, a series of tall iron lamps of magnesium wire stand ready to flood the area with momentary brilliance. Around the perimeter, a black curtain masks the walls, which were painted years ago by one of the minor Orientalists and may not be erased, having attained the status of art.

Three men apply finishing touches to the setting: chiefly the aforementioned William Nixon Crede – languid and pale, whose paintings are achieved by first photographing the subject, then transferring the image to canvas by means of a *camera obscura*. (His trade secret is safe with the Oxford Photographic Society.)

Even in this dim light Boltbyn can appreciate the classical perspective of trees, stripped of leaves, branches silhouetted like the fingers of crones, receding down a picturesque path, past the multiple jaws of Cerberus the three-headed dog, all the way to Charon the ferryman, and the River Styx.

The foreground is dominated by an enormous dome made of plaster, upon which Psyche will recline. (It was built by Thomas Angley, the architect behind some of the more atrocious renovations at Bissett Grange.) In the meanwhile, Bracebridge Hemyng, the author and critic, pores over a picture-book written by himself, entitled *Great Scenes From Antiquity*, a favourite of householders who wish to celebrate the classics without actually reading them.

A footman gently sets down the camera (two mahogany boxes, connected by a detachable bellows for portability), lens and tripod, another opens the cabinet containing chemicals, solutions, dishes, and glass; and a third footman erects a small velvet tent in a corner of the room.

The photograph will be achieved by the Archer process, an enormous improvement over the collotype process, whose sharpness of detail rivals even the daguerreotype. Properly executed, it is like viewing a scene with a magnifying glass. (Hence its value to Mr Crede and his *camera obscura*.) The disadvantage is the method itself – complicated, messy and accident-prone.

First, the glass plate must be polished to perfect cleanliness, for a speck of dust will appear as a blot. Balancing the plate delicately on thumb and fingers, the photographer must pour the solution so evenly that the liquid evaporates into a smooth film. One slip, the slightest misstep or miscalculation and the photograph is ruined . . .

The door is swung open by an Irish servant and, after a short pause, the Duke of Danbury enters. He wears an immaculate black coat and a violet waistcoat; his wispy fringe of reddish hair has been expertly combed and dressed. In his arms he carries the sleeping, seemingly weightless subject, in a flowing white gown.

Now for the first time, Boltbyn wonders: Why does Danbury insist that they be asleep? For while it may be true that, in the early days of the society, confined to the old collotype process, a photographer would be hard-pressed to achieve any degree of focus using a young, sentient model; but with the introduction of the Archer process, such a precaution became no longer necessary. Still, the Duke continues the practice of giving the subject a mild sedative, in the interests of 'realism'. As guests at Bissett Grange, the members of the society do not argue with their patron. It is not the thing to do.

Danbury arranges the subject upon the rock, in a picturesque attitude. Wonders have been accomplished with make-up, for the face is magnificent, a most perfect, intelligent face, like painted enamel, and . . .

O heavens!

It is astoundingly obvious to Boltbyn why the duke has chosen the subject, and whom she represents . . .

Emma.

The likeness is sufficient to cause him to tremble; were he to speak, all meaning would be lost in a spasm of stuttering.

The Duke of Danbury holds Boltbyn's gaze for a long moment, in which the two men engage in a silent dialogue:

Whatever can this possibly mean?

I think you know.

What is it you expect from this?

I think you know.

With a private nod to Boltbyn, Danbury faces the company as though addressing a class of classics students. 'Gentlemen, for our Sleeping Beauty on this occasion I give you Psyche – dispatched to Proserpine with a bejewelled box so that the goddess might fill it with her beauty.

'Upon her return with the box of secrets, Psyche is overcome with desire to open it, to take a share of beauty for herself. But when she opens the box, she receives not beauty but an infernal sleep, which renders her as still as a corpse. Thus, a young girl discovers the secret of womanhood, and the death of innocence. O what a jealous goddess is time, gentlemen – from whose sharp needle none can wriggle out of reach!'

The duke directs another knowing glance in Boltbyn's direction, though the vicar is at a complete loss as to what it might signify.

'And yet Psyche will be reborn, to be reunited with her Cupid, and they will beget a child whose name will be Pleasure.

'Psyche is the Greek word for the soul, and the butterfly.'

A ripple of appreciative applause erupts, led by Crede and Hemyng.

Crede takes his place next to the magnesium lamp, lucifer poised, while Hemyng prepares an additional plate, infusing the room with ether as though it were a hospital. Boltbyn's heart pounds upon his sternum as he inserts a plate into the camera and bends down to peer through the lens. Thus magnified, he is able to distinguish between the face before him and the face of his soon-to-be-lost friend; still, the likeness is sufficiently unsettling that his hand shakes as he wipes his brow.

Why has Danbury done this? When one gentleman asserts such a confident acquaintance with the private life of another, the question becomes: *What does he know?* Or, *What does he* think *he knows?*

The duke pauses at the door for a final word: 'Gentlemen, urgent business awaits me in London. I remind you that, as with our previous subjects, the model must not be touched by anyone other than Mr O'Day, for the shock of a premature awakening might cause grave injury to the child.

'Good luck to you, Mr Boltbyn. I pray that your work will be a fitting tribute to its subject – and to your own unique sensibility.'

As he leaves, Danbury pauses to whisper to his Irish servant: 'She has an hour under the lights before she begins to smell.'

7

Plant's Inn

For Whitty, as for most London clubmen, a visit to one's drinking-place is the nearest thing to going home.

Straightening the collar of his plum coat, smoothing his new canary waistcoat (retrieved from his tailor after settling the account), he enters a wooden, airless space not unlike the interior of a cigar humidor – worn, scuffed and beaten by generations of elbows, buttocks and foreheads, and as familiar as his walking-stick.

Whitty pauses by the door. A silence descends upon the room, but with no greetings to follow. Curious.

Superficially, all is precisely as it was a few weeks ago. There is Crocker of *The Spectator*, opposite Meggs of the *People's Friend* – the former with a small bandage covering the open sore on his cheek; and there is Cobb, who writes social notes for *Lloyd's* – presumably by clairvoyance, for he never goes anywhere.

None, however, acknowledges his presence. As he crosses to the bar Whitty can sense eyes watching him sideways like egrets, necks swivelling this way and that.

Above the counter floats a thick cloud of cigar and pipe smoke, through which the face of the barkeeper emerges like the genie of the lamp.

'A good day to you, sir,' Humphrey says. His face does not brighten into a mesh of wrinkles, nor does he automatically fetch Whitty's customary drink.

'Puzzled at present, Humphrey. My usual, if you please.'

'Which would be what, sir?'

'What, has your memory failed you? Softening of the brain?'

'Circumstances has changed since you was here last.'

Whitty leans over the gleaming mahogany bar, which remains disconcertingly empty of drink. 'Speak plainly if you please, Humphrey. Am I out of order?'

'Indeed, sir, that were the thrust of Mrs Plant's last indication.'

'I am prepared to settle my account in full, if that is the cause for complaint.'

'That would be welcome, sir, yet there remain issues outstanding.'

'What the devil is my offence this time, Humphrey?'

'Word reached certain ears as to the reason for your absence, which did not enhance madam's regard. Quite the opposite, sir, I regret to say.'

'A curious phenomenon, the modern woman, Humphrey. A terrier in the struggle for emancipation, yet a bloodhound for keeping track of a fellow.'

'Afraid I must remain mum in that regard, sir, for I have never owned a dog.' The barkeeper's eyes dart sideways as though Mrs Plant might spring at him from behind a bottle of Charleson's.

Whitty casts his gaze upon the empty space behind the frosted glass from which Mrs Plant orchestrates the establishment. 'Where is the lady? I wish to pay my respects.'

'Presently at confession, sir.' The barkeeper stares at Whitty's canary waistcoat and will not meet his gaze.

Whitty flicks a bit of cigar ash from his waistcoat, pulls the silver flask of brandy from his pocket and avails himself of a healthy swig: no doubt his chilly reception is based upon the misapprehension that he had gone over to a competing publican.

That can soon be put right, he thinks, and with a pinch of chemist's snuff up the nostril for good measure, he focuses upon the door to the rear snug, a room shaped like a tricorner hat, containing a long table, around which the upper caste of public oracles gnaw one another's entrails for nourishment. He can discern the Scotsman's odious brogue, dominating the discussion as usual.

The barkeeper watches Whitty's well-tailored back as it heads for the rear snug: *A canary waistcoat. Wouldn't you know.*

It never occurred to Humphrey that Plant's might harbour a freak of nature. How is it that he served the party for years and was none the wiser? It required an intellect on Mr Fraser's level to fit the clues together: Mr Whitty's fancy style of dress, his affected Oxford accent; and a frequenter of Turkish baths, where the unnatural swine do their beastly business.

Shaking his head in a gesture of helplessness common to simple men who have seen too much, Humphrey fetches a dish-rag and executes a thorough wipe of the mahogany bar, giving a good scrub to the section upon which Mr Whitty was leaning.

Were he a Roman Catholic, he would cross himself.

Whitty steps into the rear snug where Fraser captains his ship of fools. Lacking an original thought, the man from *Dodd's* endures by means of an affected posture of cantankerous populism and a Celtic willingness, lacking any other weapon, to bite the throat out of an enemy.

'Och Whitty, just my man, absent far too long, guid show!' Clearly, Fraser has not progressed in his effort to form civilised vowels, but he has not lacked for meat: he has gained a stone since they last met; as well, he sports the complexion that goes with good drink and mutton – a deep, ventricular shade of red, a sign of prosperity and good health.

'Mr Fraser. Delightful, to see you flush with the good things in life.'

'Fruits of the work ethic, Mr Whitty. A life spent seeking truth, and forgoing the sport of *backgammon*.'

Unaccountably, Fraser's reference to a common gambling-game elicits a merry response from the three other gentlemen at table: Gosse of the *Yokel's Preceptor* (a guide to London for immigrants from the country), Horne of *Bentley's Journal*, and Ambrose of the *Morning Chronicle*.

'A guid cut, would you not say, gentlemen?' Fraser says to the company. Horne and Ambrose scratch merrily upon their notebooks in reply, plagiarism being the truest form of flattery.

'I am at a loss as to the connection between your capacity for drudgery and the playing of a board game.'

'I should think it would be clear to you, sir. Think of it as a case of East meets West.'

Another round of snickering.

'By a remarkable coincidence,' Fraser continues, 'we were just a moment ago reprehending the outbreak of immorality in public places – in particular, the proliferation of unnatural acts, occasioned by the Canning affair. D'ye recall it, Edmund?'

'Ah yes, Canning, poor fellow. Surprised with his breeches unbuttoned, with a soldier – named, appropriately, Flower – whose dress was in similar disarray.'

'Your empathy is most Christian, Edmund.'

'Did you read about the infant skeletons that lined the walls when Maxwell's on Betty Street was pulled down? The consensual antics of two adults seem trivial in comparison.'

'Trivial, Edmund? May I remind you that a generation ago, uranism – unnatural conversation between men – was punishable by death.'

'And so it remains in your country, a tradition which has provided a charter for blackmailers.' Whitty bites his tongue, unwilling to join further in the argument and thereby contribute to Fraser's newspaper, *gratis*.

'Gentlemen, this is not London, it is Sodom!' pronounces Ambrose. 'I am told that the public houses now must post signs – *Beware of Sods* – while at the Hundred Guineas, the odious creatures are so flagrant as to take on the names of women!'

'The Hundred Guineas, do you say?' asks Gosse, writing as quickly as he can.

'Where are the stocks when we require them?' asks Horne. 'Why has the pillory been abolished? Why are these perverse creatures not in irons?'

'Because it would occasion a surprising emigration from Eton to Newgate,' replies Whitty.

'A guid cut, sir, a guid cut – and from one who should know!'

Whitty hears the scratching of pencils on notebooks, like little teeth gnawing the table-legs. Why does Fraser's flaccid cliché merit recording and not his own, far superior, cut? And why the reference to 'backgammon' – used among ruffians to describe certain sexual acts?

'I should think,' says Fraser, 'that in cleansing the city of this outrageous conduct, the first measure would be to abolish the Turkish baths – which are little more than dens of uranism, as I am sure Edmund will agree.'

Another round of chuckling.

Whitty has had enough. 'I say, gentlemen, there seems to be an amusement going of which I am ignorant.'

'Not at all,' Fraser replies, turning to the barkeeper hovering in the doorway. 'Humphrey, fetch ye a hot gin for Mr Whitty, who has advanced such a spirited defence of sexual inversion. And a guid argument for bestiality as well.' Then he rises from his seat and exits the room winking at the barman as if to say, *What did I tell you?*

8

5 Buckingham Gate

Bill Williams, alias Dr Gilbert Williams, alias Herr Schrenk-Notting, occupies the gloomy back parlour of the decomposing London town-house, in the company of a bottle of the out-and-out and a china teacup. Uncorking his pint, he fills the cup to the brim and downs it as though it were water. These days, in preparing himself for a performance, gin is the spirit he consults.

His hand quivers as he refills the cup, causing it to rattle upon its saucer, and an amount of liquid to spill upon the table top. Williams scoops the gin from the surface, rubs his palms together, and massages the liquid into the skin of his balding pate; for it is proven that applications of alcohol can restore a scalp to fertility.

Williams is a stocky man with a huge head, a wide trunk, and a pair of tiny, woman's feet. Seated he appears dwarfish and standing he appears stout, when in fact he is neither. Thatches of thick black bristle sprout from every region of his body except the top of his head, the one spot he wishes it to cover. Poorly served by nature, the medium has no faith in the Creator as a benevolent force; his intercourse with the hereafter has provided him a living, but no peace, nor comfort.

Equipped with a wealth of experience in the smoke-and-mirrors profession, Williams has grown physically attuned to the natural rhythm of a dodge or fiddle – when a particular location is about to turn rotten – and his senses are telling him that London has reached that point, and more. When he rises in the morning, the hairs at the back of his neck prickle; when he ventures from the house, the hairs on his knuckles stand on end. Such signs must not be ignored, yet to vacate the field with profits at their peak is no way to conduct a business.

It is one of the Creator's little jokes that a location becomes unwholesome precisely at its moment of highest return. Tonight's performance alone stands to net the society over £80 – 400 American dollars – even after splitting the proceeds with his sponsor, the duke. (Williams makes a mental note to set aside 10 guineas for Mr Fraser of *Dodd*'s.) But is the profit worth the risk?

Even more unsettling is the other matter – a development he neither expected nor wished for. On the contrary, it has rendered him a nervous wreck.

As a boy of fourteen, Bill Williams awakened in the pre-dawn November chill of a Kentucky lodging-house, to behold the shade of Daniel Boone, Kentucky's national hero, at the foot of his cot. *Sharpe will be sharped!* came a soundless voice within, and Daniel Boone evaporated like a puff of steam.

Bill slept no more that night, and the next morning feverishly related the encounter to his father, an ex-pickpocket performing magic tricks throughout the state as the Fakir of Ava. His father then approached the *Shelbyville Sentinel-News*, proposing a paid interview, and was promptly ushered out of the building. Two days afterward, however, Solomon P. Sharpe, Attorney-General for Kentucky, was stabbed to death on the steps of the House of Representatives by a disgruntled constituent. *Sharpe will be sharped.*

Reporters flocked like pigeons at their door, leaving the Williams family in clover and the state of Kentucky quivering with excitement at the thought of a psychic in their midst. Accordingly, the elder Williams re-christened his son as William The Spirit Boy, whose stage performances enjoyed moderate success until he began to grow bald in an unboyish manner; at which point he became Dr Gilbert Williams, a respected professor with a degree in Occult Phenomena from the University of Heidelberg.

With a mail-order course of study in mesmerism, a staff of assistants and an array of stage devices common to every magician in America, Dr Gilbert Williams set out to provide spiritual insight and advice from the grave, to anyone willing pay for it.

Never again was Bill Williams to actually experience such a phenomenon as the nocturnal visitation of Boone (thank Heaven, for the event did permanent damage to his nerves); in fact, he has come to regard his work as a form of theatre or music hall, with himself as the actor-manager. He had managed to put the Sharpe episode entirely from his mind – until now.

Bill Williams refills his cup. More gin spills onto the table, with which he fertilises his barren scalp.

Of late, he has come to dread these seances, which remind him more and more of the Boone incident. Images come inadvertently to mind which seem unnaturally vivid. Words emanate from his mouth which are not part of the script, in a voice which is not part of his normal repertoire. Either the medium is losing his sanity, or the spirits with which he pretends to converse have become – with increasing frequency and in the absence of a better description – real.

Is he haunted, or is he insane? And which is worse?

A short distance from Birdcage Walk and practically in the shadow of the palace, the Danbury town-house at 5 Buckingham Gate is a relic of an era when a duke or an earl might be called out of bed in the dead of night to protect the royal family from harm, or scandal, or to perform some service for the Regent on a confidential basis. Hence, the air of shadow and secrecy about the courtyard – the legacy of past conspiracies, embedded in the layers of soot and pigeon droppings, overseen by some granite ancestor who distinguished himself in battle, having apparently suffered the loss of his nose.

The house recalls a time when the Danbury line occupied places of the highest influence. That is why the present Duke of Danbury cannot sell the property, for to do so would be to admit to all of London that the family's station is a thing of the past.

Precious though he holds the Danbury legacy, the duke would not spend a night here, it being singularly gloomy and inconvenient and insanitary.

From past issues of *The Falcon*, Whitty has discovered that the duke habitually lets the residence to whatever fashionable cult happens to have caught the public fancy, from an Indian avatar to a troupe of dervishes from Turkey; at present, 5 Buckingham Gate plays host to the current enthusiasm for 'psychic research'.

Whitty raps the head of his stick upon the windowless front door, made of brass-studded oak and blackened with soot, which immediately opens to reveal a strapping footman in purple livery. Though the initial effect is fine, Whitty notes that his stockings have been mended.

'A very good evening to you, sir. How may we be of assistance?'

Whitty produces the square envelope containing Mr Willows's invitation, while mentally pegging the footman's accent as Irish – Dublin, if he is not mistaken; a foreign quack who seeks to defraud Londoners will find no better henchman than a Dubliner.

'Willows is my name. I trust I am expected.'

Whitty hands over the invitation, noting the calloused knuckles of a tough customer through holes in his gloves as the footman pretends to read it, then executes a reluctant approximation of a bow.

'Be so good as to step inside, Mr Willows, sir, and follow me.'

Taking his hat, gloves and walking-stick, the footman conducts Whitty down an ill-lit hallway into an ill-ventilated reception room, where he is met by the unnerving sight of several persons already on their feet to greet him, with that peculiar dazed expression common among reformed Christians, political radicals, and believers in unorthodox cures.

Whitty remains confident, having purchased from his chemist a bottle of Acker's Chlorodane (a useful tincture of opium, cocaine and marijuana in alcohol) as a bracer. One by one he shakes the hand of a succession of fellow seekers: Miss Lang-Cormack, a wraith of a woman with sallow wattles and fingers like cold macaroni; the Master of Lindsay, whose Christian name he does not catch, a ruddy gentleman with extraordinary tufts of hair growing from his nostrils; the Contessa de Medina de Pomar, who sports a palpable moustache above tight, invisible lips; pale, young Mr Jencken, a barrister from the Temple with the reddened eyes of bereavement; Sir Robert Dorrington-Booth, a jovial, elderly soul who announces that he regards seances as a primer for the hereafter; and Mr Albin Lush, a plump gentleman whose thatch of wiry hair stands on end as though in a state of perpetual alarm, and whose colourless eyes flit from one guest to the other in the way of a schoolmaster taking attendance.

Whitty presents himself as Mr Willows from Leeds in search of a dead aunt; hearing this, his new acquaintances murmur their profound understanding. Having established their unanimity of purpose, all seat themselves on couches and chairs which have been covered with grey dust-covers, as though the house were to be vacated momentarily.

Following a silence not unlike the hush in a surgeon's waiting-room, the door to the back parlour swings open to reveal a moon-faced young woman in a dress that matches the footman's garb, both in colour and disrepair. Shutting the door as carefully as though it were a bank vault, she speaks in a plummy accent, with the underlying musicality of County Cork.

'Good evening, Ladies and Gentlemen. My name is Miss Grendell. On behalf of the Society for Psychic Research, I bid you welcome.' Her solemn aspect conveys no warmth, nor any other emotion; as she speaks, her eyes meet those of each guest in turn before moving on.

'On this occasion I have the honour of introducing to you to our benefactor, who has chosen to attend the evening's proceedings, owing to business in the city. Ladies and Gentlemen I give you his Grace, the Duke of Danbury.'

With a primly theatrical gesture, the moon-faced woman swings open the door to the back parlour and steps aside to reveal a silhouette framed by the doorway. From the company issues a collective sigh, while the contessa's fingers flutter in silent applause.

The figure in the doorway turns, steps forward and speaks in tones so muted that one must restrict one's breathing in order to hear. Even Whitty feels a credulous impulse come over him, an ancient, inherited response to one who occupies a position nearer than one's own to the throne of God.

'Ladies and gentlemen,' states the duke. 'I bid you God speed on your journey of self-discovery. As men of science we ask not for belief, only that you accord your honest attention to what transpires this evening. Miss Grendell, pray continue.'

Danbury surveys the party with the eyes of utter indifference, until he meets the gaze of Mr Lush. Whitty makes note of this.

At a gesture from the duke, followed by a barely perceptible nod from Mr Lush, Miss Grendell continues. 'We ask that you refrain from looking directly at the medium, who may already be making preparations for the spirit world. And be forewarned,' she adds with a barely discernible frown. 'When attention is focused too critically, it detracts from the seance as a whole.'

And might catch a swindle, thinks Whitty.

At another signal he follows his fellow seekers into the back parlour, an oppressive mausoleum of medieval masculinity. The furniture consists of a round mahogany table supported by a central pedestal, several ungainly chairs, and a square piano in the corner. The sole window is shrouded beneath layers of fabric, light being provided by the fire, as well as a chalice on the piano containing a number of wax candles, which flicker spasmodically as though breathed upon. The Duke of Danbury takes his chair – larger than the others, with a cushion and arm-rests – as a signal that the company may do likewise.

No longer back-lit, Danbury presents himself as a smooth, elegant gentleman of medium height, with a balding pate surrounded by a fringe of reddish-blond hair, enhanced by a set of fashionably long, wispy sideburns. The bridge of his nose is decidedly handsome and appears to pull up the centre of his top lip slightly, a well-known sign of breeding. What impresses Whitty most is the duke's poise, the absolute assurance of a man who may do what he likes, when he likes, to whom he likes, and it will be correct because it is he who does it.

A formidable piece of work, Whitty thinks. In researching the subject at hand, he accorded little significance to the name of the gentleman who patronises this faddish enterprise. Seen in person, however, the face seems familiar, as though he encountered it many years ago, in some forgotten context.

Once all are seated, a servant's door concealed in the wainscoting swings open to admit a gentleman shaped like a child's top. Whitty takes in the American trousers and well-cut lounging jacket, but also the trapped haplessness in the man's face, as though he must follow the orders of a feared superior, with no escape at hand.

Dr Williams crosses the room, eyes seemingly directed at a spot straight ahead and above him – employing the steady, unblinking gaze actors use when portraying characters who are seers, or blind, or both. Being so top-heavy, thinks Whitty, it is a wonder he does not simply pitch forward onto his face.

Williams seats himself, then stretches his arms limply to the sides like a choir director, then closes his eyes in the manner of an oriental Buddha.

'You will now join hands,' prompts Miss Grendell. Whitty's left hand reluctantly grips the Master of Lindsay's soft paw, while his right takes possession of Miss Lang-Cormack's cadaverous member. Now that everyone has linked up as though for a game of Ring-Around-the-Rosy, Miss Grendell directs the company to carry on with light conversation, as though it were perfectly normal for a Briton to maintain physical contact with strangers for a period longer than a handshake.

'Be not afraid, and on no account leave your places,' she cautions, moving to a spot beside the piano – situated, Whitty notes, so that it is impossible for anyone at the table to keep watch on herself, the medium and the duke, or to note what might pass between them.

Ten minutes of excruciating silence follow while Whitty endures this unwelcome contact – in one hand a slug, in the other a skeleton; his mind turns to Canadian wolves which, when trapped, will gnaw off a foot and hobble away to freedom.

Suddenly a rapping is heard on the walls – seemingly struck from within the room but no doubt undertaken from outside by assistants. Next come raps upon the mahogany table, at which point that item of furniture begins to tilt upward until it hangs at an angle of about thirty degrees, sloping in the direction of the medium. Looking at the slanted surface, Whitty wonders about the possibility of an unseen pulley or lift; immediately, the table drops to the floor with a loud thump, and the rapping ceases.

'Someone has broken the psychic chain!' Miss Grendell's tone is that of a disappointed schoolteacher. Mr Willows receives a disapproving glare.

Following another momentous pause, Dr Williams rises: arms outstretched in the way of a crucifix, eyes closed, he steps behind the contessa and begins to chop the woman rapidly and urgently about her ears and her back with the sides of his hands. She makes no objection, though the procedure must be none too comfortable. While chopping the contessa, the medium's trance seems to deepen until, groaning aloud, he begins to pace about the room feverishly with one hand to his forehead.

Coming to a halt, the medium declares, in a stentorian basso, *He is very strong and tall!*, at which point he appears to grow several inches, to a height of about six feet, while a gap of some four inches appears between the bottom of his waistcoat and the waist-band of his trousers.

Moving to the window, Miss Grendell gestures silently in the direction of the medium's feet, pointing out that they are now hovering six inches above the floor.

Whitty remains unimpressed, having seen that sort of thing achieved with mirrors. As though in response to his impertinent scepticism, the psychic drops to the floor and, with an embarrassed expression, returns to his seat.

After another unbearable pause, in the voice of a young woman, Dr Williams asks for writing materials. These are delivered into his hand; his fingers have become so rigid that only with difficulty can the moon-faced woman insert the pencil between them. Now his entire arm, seemingly possessed on its own, begins to write a message in French, in a small, feminine script.

'Chantal!' gasps the bereaved young lawyer upon viewing the handwriting, and begins to weep with deep, heaving sobs. In wiping away tears he loses his grip upon his neighbour, breaks the chain, and the writing stops in mid-sentence – whereupon the medium leaps to his feet in a kind of quivering fit, as though the tendons in his neck were about to break through the skin.

David has come back! David's feet are on the ground! he shrieks, in the voice of the old woman.

David? Odd, that that name should come up here and now, Whitty thinks.

Who is the witty man? cries the old woman, seemingly from deep within that bulbous head.

The medium swivels his rigid body forward to confront Mr Willows directly. *Who is the witty man?*

'I am afraid, sir and/or madam, that I do not understand you,' Whitty replies.

'Sir, it concerns David, and the circumstances surrounding his death, and his wish to proclaim the fate of the witty man!' says Miss Grendell, acting as interpreter.

'I fear I know nothing of what you say,' insists Whitty, while the others, the duke in particular, observe him with new interest.

David has come to speak to you. Do you object to his doing so?

'Certainly not, though he has mistaken me for somebody else.'

Then he will now sit down beside you.

A chair next the window moves on its own from the wall, waddles across the carpet and lodges itself between Whitty and Miss Lang-Cormack, who makes room for the animate object as naturally as though it were a child come to say good-night.

David is now seated beside you, and has placed his hand upon your shoulder.

Curiously, he can indeed feel something press his left shoulder with the force of a highly focused wind. Mesmerism, thinks Whitty. That is the explanation.

David wishes the witty man to know that he did not do what he is said to have done, and he did not die as he is said to have died.

'All of this means nothing to me whatsoever, sir,' Whitty insists. He is perspiring despite the chill, and his vision has begun to tunnel.

David wishes you to know that God's justice is very different from man's. That God's justice will see him right. He says that it is the nature of the game we are playing on earth.

'Does David despair of human justice taking its course?' asks Whitty, endeavouring to remain alert, despite the dizziness which has come over him.

Oh dear no, human justice is necessary for the well-being of society. But David cannot interfere, and . . . ah. Something is weighing upon his mind. He wants to know if you sense how hot his tears are.

Seated opposite the seemingly empty chair, Miss Lang-Cormack taps Whitty upon the arm and points to his sleeve, her bloodless mouth in the shape of a smile.

Drops of moisture have appeared upon the material.

Continues the voice of the old woman: *David says, 'Oh Edmund, there are things I wish to tell you that I cannot! That I did not live as you think I lived! That I did not die as you think I died!'*

Edmund?

Whitty hears himself address the medium in a strange, tight whisper: 'Though I am not the person he seeks, I must nonetheless ask, what it is David wishes me to know?'

Abruptly the chair beside the correspondent falls backward with a crash and the medium springs to his feet, palms flat on the table, eyes wide open, exclaiming in a voice which is no longer that of an old woman but that of Dr Gilbert Williams himself – or rather, a terrified Bill Williams, who does not wish to take any further part in the communication.

'I will not permit it! It is too horrible! Oh, it is horrible! It is dreadful! My God, it is so horrible that if he does not stop I shall – Wait! Stop! Somebody has broken the chain!'

Whitty has done just that, having collapsed upon the carpet in a swoon beside the fallen chair.

The Duke of Danbury and Mr Lush exchange a long, significant glance, as if to say, *And what is to be done about this?*

9

Plant's Inn

The enormous old clock above the entrance chimes, or rather clanks, three times – the loneliest time of night, the hour of the wolf.

Notwithstanding an entire bottle of chlordine and a pint of hot spiced gin, Whitty's mental state has not improved. Draped over the empty bar, he lifts a finger to the barkeeper, who does his duty stoically and wearily: Mrs Plant has given him leave to serve the correspondent, and it is a tradition that the establishment will never close while a single patron remains conscious and thirsty.

But where is Mrs Plant? Humphrey insists she is again at confession, but Whitty does not believe this. In his experience, Mrs Plant is not the sort of woman to need dispensation from a male, celibate or otherwise; he thinks it far more likely that she has seen through his carefully contrived exterior, has glimpsed the burnt-out case within, and has no further desire for his company.

Looking on the bright side, he is no longer banned outright, although Humphrey keeps his distance as if Whitty had the pox.

David. His brother. *The* brother – for it is the first-born who carries the family name and estate, who represents the aspirations of his ancestors for a better world. From an early age, David's world was undeniably a better one, in which one young man could excel in every pursuit he undertook – physical, mental, spiritual – with an aplomb simultaneously Roman, Greek – and British. No man was as incandescently British as David.

Six years his junior, Whitty has spent the better part of his life in David's shadow. In the Whitty home on Machpelah Street, the two boys came to occupy more and more distant spheres as they grew up, until by the time David left for Oxford they might as well have been raised on separate continents. Notwithstanding, the spectre of David – student, athlete, distinguished Fellow at St Ambrose College – remained to haunt the lesser boy – especially after the latter was sent down in disgrace.

Following David's sudden death in 1852 at the age of thirty-four, (Whitty's age at this moment), it became apparent that there was no further reason for the family to carry on – the second-born son being an unsatisfactory replacement. And so the house and estate of Richard Whitty, Esq., already in decline, underwent its final disintegration, in the way of an insolvent firm.

At the same time, other versions of David's demise began to surface: that his death only appeared to be a boating accident, that he had 'made a hole in the water' over some scandal or other. Whitty has always regarded these stories as the forgeries of scandalmongers like himself, whose only effect is to highlight David's elevated existence compared to his brother, rummaging in the gutter for nuggets of dirt.

Not quite good enough, old boy. You may impress from time to time, but we both know how inferior you are, how distant from what you should be. How unfortunate that you continue to slouch about London while I have ceased to exist . . .

But what is Whitty to make of the voice he heard this evening at 5 Buckingham Gate? Could it be that the rumours were true? *That I did not live as you think I lived! That I did not die as you think I died!*

The voice of the barkeeper interrupts his gloomy reverie: 'Sir, I beg you to finish drinking, for I am a family man with two children. Surely, Mr Whitty, sir, even a man of your stripe once possessed a family.'

What the devil does he mean by that?

'Reunite with your family, Humphrey,' he mutters through lips which have grown numb. 'Blessings upon you. Yet I seek an audience with Mrs Plant. To that end I shall return tomorrow, and the morrow after that. Unless she sells the place or burns it down, Mrs Plant must eventually show her face.'

Whitty rises, finds his feet and totters out of the building, with the stiff dignity of the truly and consciously impaired.

HOISTED UPON HIS OWN PETARD
A Gadfly Meets His Match
by
Alastair Fraser
Special Correspondent
Dodd's

It gives this correspondent no pleasure to kick a colleague when he is down.

However, when a man plays a leading role in his own misfortune, learns nothing from it, then compounds it with repeated misbehaviour, it falls upon the conscientious among us to be cruel in order to be kind: to take up the scalpel of truth, cut through the skin and lay bare the muscles;

to probe and to penetrate until all is revealed, even to the grinning skull!

We refer, sadly, to Mr Edmund Whitty, who, from time to time, scribbles upon the pages of a tottering weekly, notorious as the most corrupt, irresponsible publication that was ever visited upon any population. Having no equal in disgrace, Mr Whitty seeks to elevate his reputation by undermining another – in this case, by mocking a scientific investigation in the public interest. Of course that is our man's habitual posture: to play the devil's advocate, to muddy the waters of fact, and to float a livelihood upon a sediment of confusion.

Thus it transpires that the correspondent for The Falcon, *under an assumed name, fraudulently presented himself before Dr Gilbert Williams, the eminent psychic, as well as the Duke of Danbury, who accepted Mr Whitty into his home in good faith. Having thus gained entry, this shameless party set about sabotaging the experiment, thereby to dismiss the entire endeavour with the smug cynicism of the professional spoiler.*

What follows should serve as a warning to those who would enter the psychic world with supercilious intent.

In the interest of truth, we must now disclose a painful fact which bears upon the events to follow: that our friend was preceded at Oxford (from which he was later sent down in disgrace) by an older brother, name of David, who died by drowning.

All this is in the public record. Less well-known are the rumours – namely, that the elder Whitty died by his own hand.

When the medium initiated the seance, having attained a trance-like state, what was the first word to issue from his mouth?

David.

And the second?

Whitty.

Overcome no doubt by shame, our man fled the house in what can only be described as a state of dementia.

We pray for Mr Whitty's speedy recovery, and we hope that he has finally received an education.

> *A scandalous writer named Whitty*
> *Who sought to make hay in the city*
> *Himself did expose*
> *And bloodied his nose*
> *And drowned in a sump of self-pity.*

Eastcheap

The black gentleman's brougham, an emblem of upper-class anonymity, drifts with the prevailing current down Gracechurch Street and past the British Bank of West Africa, the driver having been instructed to trace a circular pattern between London Bridge and Tower Bridge. This is not an unusual directive: of the crush of vehicles moving lugubriously through the streets, easily a third serve as temporary offices, meeting-rooms, drinking-rooms, and – with closed window curtains – bedrooms. Contrary to public perception, London does not have a traffic problem unless one is actually attempting to go somewhere.

Directing his horse with slight, automatic movements of the wrist, the half-asleep driver threads his vehicle past the Guardian Assurance and the London and Eastern Trade, then past the Corn Exchange. Meanwhile below him, within the darkened, leather-tufted interior, three men confer:

'Gentlemen, it is my painful duty to inform you that, due to your negligence, the subject died in transit. My employer is greatly distressed.'

Though the speaker is dressed in black, his appearance is strangely comic, in the way of an aged child or dwarf. One gloved hand removes his pot-hat and places it in his lap, uncovering a head of wiry, colourless hair, like the antennae on a specimen of undersea plant life. Thick whiskers of a similar texture frame a pair of cheeks the colour of claret and a punctilious button nose. His eyes, however, are devoid of humour as they await a response from his two companions, with the trepidation of a physical coward in the presence of danger.

'Dear Jesus, Mr Robin, sir, did I not caution you on the chemical?' Weeks says to his superior, while obsessively scratching his arm with the thumbless hand. 'Cursed we be now, sir, damned souls in hell! *Women and children . . .*'

'At ease, Mr Weeks,' replies Robin. His eyes are concealed by dark glasses; a narrow shaft of daylight from between the velvet curtain illuminates his sleeve of faded serge, with its tracings of pips and stripes.

Weeks continues to scratch his arm as though he would like to tear it off, the four fingers clenching and unclenching. '*Women and children . . .*'

'Mr Weeks! Chaffer up, and that is an order!' Robin maintains an impassive countenance – the result of temperament, training, and scar-tissue. 'Tot, corporal.'

Weeks drinks deeply from the pewter flask, while Robin undertakes a formal response to the charge of negligence.

'Unaccustomed as we were to the chemistry, sir, we performed the act as instructed. With respect, we carried out our orders. If trouble followed, it is because we were not properly briefed for the mission.'

'Point taken,' concedes Lush. 'However, I assure you that the courts, and the hangman, would see it otherwise.'

'We of the 2nd Infantry Brigade have faced death before,' replies Weeks. 'Yet before we succumb to the enemy there will be casualties, sir. *Civilian* casualties, if you get my meaning, Mr Lush, sir.'

The estate manager can feel the eyes glare at him from behind the dark glasses; the inside of his mouth grows dry at the thought of what those eyes have seen.

Lush has none of their nerve, their ruthlessness, just as he lacks the duke's sangfroid. With Lush, killing is a miserable business. He is heartsick for weeks afterward; if he is not of the quality, neither is he a brute. His gaze falls upon the mutilated hand of the corporal, like a red claw – a symbol of the unspeakable acts it has committed – and he cautions himself not to push these men too far.

'I assure you there is no need for such dire speculation, gentlemen. As long as you remain under his Grace's protection, your position is secure. As a gesture of his good faith, he has instructed me to remit to you the sum of £10.'

Lush removes an envelope from the side-pocket of his coat, where it has rested next to the most recent issue of *Dodd's*, and places it in the hand of the superior officer.

Robin separates the notes, rubs them between his fingers, and passes them to the corporal for visual inspection. 'Is it really £10, Mr Weeks? And is the currency genuine?'

'It is, Mr Robin. And it is.' The corporal has never before possessed such a sum at one time, on either side of the ocean.

'Most generous of him, sir,' continues Robin, maintaining a neutral aspect. 'One wonders what his Grace might be retaining for such a sum?'

'Only your services, gentlemen – when and as required.' Which will be soon enough, thinks the estate manager.

'Auxiliary troops, sort of thing,' says Robin. 'Such forces might be required to do many things.'

'My employer wishes it known that he is touched by your plight. Soldiers of the realm who have given their all for queen and country, and have been repaid with a handful of dust. A beastly disgrace, was the term he used.'

'Prettily said and most appreciated,' replies Robin, evenly. 'I take it that his Lordship knows a thing or two about disgrace.'

A canny devil, Lush thinks. 'Of course, you are at liberty to refuse his protection. His Grace will intrude on no man's liberty. As Englishmen you may take any course you prefer, however destructive it may prove to your own interests.'

Weeks's hand has ceased to scratch the arm; its mate is no longer clenched in a fist like a knot of wood – nor have his eyes strayed from the cash it contains.

'Give me the money, Mr Weeks,' says Robin. With a curt nod to Lush, he carefully folds the notes into precise rectangles and places them in an inside pocket.

The estate manager permits himself a small smile. Capital. It is done. The photographs are taken; the negatives are sufficiently clear and sharp. They will secure an income for some time, in an industry where distribution is all. And in addition he has secured these brutes, who will see to the other matter.

The air in the carriage having grown insupportable due to the odour of foul bodies and rotten teeth, Lush gives the ceiling three quick raps with the head of his stick in order to bring the carriage to a halt, and the parley to a speedy close.

A chill mist covers them as Weeks steps from the carriage, then assists Robin (virtually sightless before dusk), whose boot he sets upon the brass step-cap, whose arm he steadies for the drop to the cobbles.

'Where are we, Mr Weeks? Damn this city, where the daylight is dim and glaring at the same time! Position, corporal!'

'Eastcheap, I'll warrant, sir,' replies Weeks, gloomily, for the dead girl still weighs upon him. *Eliza*, she called herself when they snatched her off the street. Eliza, who worked at a public house. A good girl she called herself, though of course they all say that. 'Even with this windfall, sir,' he says, 'I'd rather we was back in India.'

'Not an option, Mr Weeks. We must forward ho, or fall on our bayonets.'

'What do you make of it all, sir?'

'That there is more to London than we ever imagined.'

'True,' agrees the corporal without enthusiasm – then glances back over his shoulder, just as the brougham pulls into traffic, unveiling a sight which causes the Indian-born Englishman to gasp aloud.

'Jesus, Mary and Joseph, sir.'

'What is it, Mr Weeks?'

'It is the Tower of London. By my honour, sir, the very thing. Seen it in pictures, sir.'

'Good heavens. Are you sure?'

'I see the White Tower for certain.'

'Do you see the gun, Mr Weeks? The big gun?'

'I do, sir, yes, I believe that is what it is.'

'That gun was cast by Solyman the Magnificent.'

'Go on with you, sir. I did not know that.'

'Studied the Tower in school. Mr Shakespeare mentions it often. By the deuce, I should like to see the spot where they drowned the child princes in malmsey wine.'

The death of children causes the corporal again to sink into a brown study. 'She were an English girl, sir. *English women and children . . .*'

'Stop it, Mr Weeks. We serve the quality now. It is not our place to question our orders any more than if they came from the queen.'

'The queen, sir. God save her!'

'Hear, hear, Mr Weeks.' Robin reaches inside his coat and extracts the folded envelope from his chest pocket. 'Position secured, corporal?'

'Secured, sir!'

'Calls for a spot of leave, I should say.'

'A roust in town, sir? A go at the *bints*?'

'High time, Mr Weeks.'

'Aye, sir!'

'Notify the company at once.'

No harm in a bit of fun, thinks Weeks to himself as the brougham disappears up Crutched Friars. *For we is damned souls already.*

The Falcon

Sala throws his copy of *Dodd's* onto the floor, pulls out his shirt-tail and proceeds to clean his monocle. 'Most distressing, Edmund. How can Fraser have turned you into such a tragic buffoon?'

Lowering his copy of the *Telegraph*, Mr Cream nods agreement, with an expression indicating that he does not find Whitty's humiliation distressing in the least.

'Not so great a mystery as all that,' Whitty snaps. 'When an enemy is supplied with damaging information, anyone can appear ridiculous.'

Sala notes how fatigue and anxiety mar the symmetry of his friend's dyspeptically handsome features.

'Having written a paid advertisement for the institute,' continues the correspondent, 'it is hardly surprising that Fraser has been handed a full account of the event. The mystery in my mind is – who supplied them with the name of Willows?'

'Clearly your original source betrayed you,' offers Mr Cream, a bit too smoothly.

'I find it highly unlikely that the American would engineer such a baroque attack on a strange Englishman,' replies Whitty, thinking, *And pay him £15 for the pleasure*. 'Obviously a third source exists, who knew everything.'

'So many sources,' says Sala, shaking his beard. 'So much tattling. Does nobody keep anything to himself?'

The source of the name Willows is in this office, thinks Whitty. Someone who has been at it for some time. Someone within earshot.

'I don't suppose you might consider that the psychic is genuine,' wonders Cream. 'That is beyond your conceptual purview, seemingly.'

Whitty resists the urge to lunge horizontally and plunge a quill straight into his plump neck.

'Indeed, Mr Cream, it is possible. Just as it is possible that my streak of ill-fortune occurred because I failed to spit and make the sign of the cross upon seeing a black cat.'

'Did you really, Edmund?' Sala enquires.

'Don't talk rot, Algy.'

'In any case, Mr Cream does have a point. We must not forget the possibility that the dead speak from the beyond.'

'People are credulous baboons,' replies Whitty. And yet, he thinks, what is one to make of this? *I did not live as you think I lived. I did not die as you think I died.* Those two sentences burn in his mind like drops of vitriol.

Cream cannot resist prodding the wound. 'Given Mr Whitty's record of late, we should not be surprised that the project is a fiasco.'

'Be quiet, Mr Cream,' retorts the editor. 'I am sick and tired of you.'

The discussion is abruptly ended by the clamorous arrival of a pimpled lout in a tattered wool uniform, with a canvas bag slung over his shoulder.

'What the devil do you want, Sammy?' growls the editor. 'Is it too much to expect a subordinate to knock before entering?'

'Begging your pardon, governor, a message for Mr Whitty.' Sammy approaches the correspondent with an envelope, tripping over a stool.

'Might as well have a horse in the office,' the editor grumbles.

Using Sala's brass letter-opener, Whitty slits the envelope and comes up with a second envelope, of thick Manila paper, addressed as follows:

SOLELY FOR THE EYES OF EDMUND WHITTY, ESQ.

'This might prove interesting,' he says, as he draws out a photograph from the second envelope . . .

'I say, Edmund, what is it? You look as though you have seen – I did not say ghost, out of respect for your sceptical frame of mind.' Sala reaches for the photograph; Whitty snatches it from his grasp, turns, and leaves the room without uttering a word.

With the mechanical gait of a sleep-walker Whitty steps out of the building onto Ingester Square, where he pauses in the inadequate shelter of the only tree in the vicinity – nearly dead, yet not quite ready for the fire. He pauses with no destination in mind, and for no reason in particular he examines the bark of this enduring plant . . .

He sits on the bench, insensible to the moisture soaking the seat of his trousers. He holds the square envelope out in front of him as though it were about to explode.

Blackmail, for certain – but to what end? To extort money from a journalist on his uppers? Or to bar further enquiries into the circumstances of David's life and death?

In either case, the sender has made his point.

The photograph is of the type which has been imported from France and sold on Holywell Street since the invention of the daguerreotype. Such photographs commonly depict a naked woman of a certain type, in a tawdry attempt at a luxurious setting. The most expensive feature a gentleman in a similar state.

This picture is infinitely worse.

It is impossible that it could be an impostor. What actor could counterfeit the small, crescent-shaped birthmark on David's thigh, or the scar from a fractured collarbone after falling from a horse, or the crow's-feet at the corner of his eyes from rowing in the summer sun? Or the lazy smile which Edmund had seen spread slowly over David's face whenever he contemplated his own handsome reflection in a glass?

The female in the picture cannot have attained her twelfth year.

Monstrous.

The oriental wallpaper in the background tells him nothing, for it is a favourite with the fast set in both Paris and London. He slips the photograph back into the envelope and into his coat pocket. Why does he not simply destroy the thing, rip it to shreds, throw it in the putrid Thames where it belongs? Because, even were this the only photograph taken, there might be hundreds of duplicates, ready to be sold beneath the counters of bookshops all over the city. What might he be compelled to do, in order to prevent this from happening?

Watched by the gargoyles across the square, slouched atop the Church of England, Whitty rises abruptly to his feet – too abruptly, for he has to extend one hand to steady himself on the bench, only to cut it on an exposed nail. A bitter oath escapes his throat, directed at various kinds of pain, and he exits Ingester Square at a run, howling aloud, mouth agape, unable to contain himself in the most miserable hour of his life.

The Pith and Paradox

He needs a drink desperately, yet Plant's is out of the question. He decides to calm his nerves in an appalling den near the Embankment, called the Pith and Paradox. It is filled with hoodlums for hire. Whitty is acquainted with its proprietor, a woman of fifty who takes the name Madame Geneva, whose celebrated breasts spill over the counter like tipped bowls of tapioca. When not serving acrid glasses of doctored gin at tuppence a glass, or paying tuppence for a stolen coat worth a guinea, the good woman performs Tarot readings for local judies, bludgers and gonolphs, as though their futures were not sufficiently obvious already.

The moment Whitty enters the Pith and Paradox, it is clear that a change of radical proportions has taken place: an unfamiliar cleanliness and orderliness, a dearth of vomit. The floorboards are no longer carpeted with sawdust, sodden with expectoration, but instead have been swept clean. Nor does the diseased hag-bag at the end of the bar cackle over her gin at the top of her voice, but maintains an almost decorous state of inebriation.

'Mr Whitty,' comes a familiar, welcome, yet unexpected voice. 'I have not seen you in some time.'

Here in Madame Geneva's establishment, in front of the bottles stands Miss Phoebe Owler, in a dress of green velvet, as sharp and as pretty and as *verboten* as ever. Phoebe Owler – who, as a girl of fifteen, sorely tested the limits of his discretion. Indeed, continues to do so to a maddening degree, for she appears not a day older to him six years later; in truth, his vision of her will remain when she is a crone of forty. A wave of feeling breaks over him, that combination of sadness and desire which attends an unconsummated relation with a young woman; in which the better part of one's nature prevailed in return for years of yearning and regret.

'A pleasure to see you as always, Miss Owler. Though I had hoped to see you at the Comedy by now, taking a fifth curtain-call before a delirious audience.'

'You would not have seen it anyway. You were not at the Albert Saloon where I played several parts. Nor were you at the Theatre Royal when I played three matinees as Miss Clayton's understudy.'

'Alas, I was on assignment in Prussia.' Whitty has never been to Prussia; fact is, he lacked the price of a theatre ticket. 'Given your success, to what do we owe your presence at the Pith and Paradox?'

'To my employer. Mr Banks acquired the establishment and has entrusted its management to me.'

'And has this advancement cured you of your stage-sickness?'

'Of course not. Yet I am sufficiently experienced to know that, in the long run, it is impossible to make a living in the theatre.'

'And what of the short run?'

'In the short run, one might as well enter prostitution directly.'

Her eyes flash in that way he likes, indeed, he pursued the topic purely in the hope of seeing her defy him. For a moment she has caused him to forget his current catastrophe – but now it pours back, all of it, and he is in disarray. Fortunately, his drinking habits remain consistent.

'An extremely large spiced gin, if you please, Miss Phoebe, with hot water and plenty of sugar to bring out the flavour.'

'In a spot of trouble are you, Mr Whitty? When you are in trouble you generally pile on the sugar.'

'Nothing that won't be over in a week, at which time I hope to be dead.' Whitty drains the glass in a single swallow.

'Would you care for another?'

'Yes, please.'

'Is there anything I can do?'

For a moment their eyes remain locked together. Phoebe has a knack for this sort of teasing. He can barely constrain himself from leaping over the bar, dropping to his knees and proposing marriage, followed by emigration to Canada. 'No, Miss Phoebe, I am afraid this is a beast I must wrestle on my own.'

With another gin down the neck and a pinch of medicinal snuff up the nose, he totters out of the Pith and Paradox, only to freeze at the door, in a mild panic.

He is about to venture into enemy territory. He is about to be blackmailed – possibly by the one he intends to visit. What if he were held hostage – or murdered by the blasted Irish, with the envelope and its obscene contents in his coat pocket?

With that in mind, he returns to the bar. 'Pardon me, Miss Owler, might I be so bold as to tender a small request?'

'Your requests are always welcome, Mr Whitty. You know that.'

'Here is an envelope I wish to put in your safe-keeping. It contains a letter from my mother, from her death-bed, a document of great sentimental value. If I do not return within a fortnight, feel free to burn it. Should I return for it, I shall pay you 5 shillings.'

'Ten shillings.'

'Six shillings.'

'Seven shillings,' replies Phoebe. Having done her duty by the establishment, she accepts the envelope, leans over the bar, and kisses him softly upon the cheek. Whitty wishes she wouldn't do that.

The arthritic carriage lurches unevenly up Titchfield Street onto Piccadilly, only to become entrapped by the omnibuses, whose sheer multiplicity approximates a series of moving walls. Naturally, their teams of horses emit what amounts to a steady deluge of turd, transforming a street named for the skirt of a woman into a stable. Meanwhile the stone façades of the surrounding buildings create a veritable cauldron of steaming excrement, while intensifying the harsh clatter of horseshoes, the crack of whips, and the oaths of drivers.

Without the dreadful envelope, Whitty feels as though he is rid of a canker. He rests his head upon the rotting pillow, slick from the pomade of a thousand heads, and reviews his position.

The significance of David's death six and a half years ago would be lost on a Londoner today. Thanks to Crimea, the death of an eldest has now become common; parlours all over England feature portraits of dead young men in medieval armour, attended by allegorical women. Photographers have accrued fortunes taking portraits of corpses, framed by locks of their hair.

That was not so when David died. At that time, only rarely did a young man of good family achieve an untimely death: by fever, a fall from a horse – or, in the case of his brother, by drowning while boating on the Thames. Accidental death (to say nothing of suicide) was not tragic or heroic, it was unpleasant and embarrassing, to be discussed in whispers.

Hence, lacking a public forum in which to express their grief, the father, mother and brother responded according to individual temperament: Father chose the path of financial ruin; Mother chose the path of sickliness; and Edmund chose the path of dissolution and trouble. Today, Sir Richard Whitty resides in California, Mrs Whitty resides in Marylebone Cemetery, David Whitty lies beside his mother, and brother Edmund sits in a stinking carriage, on his way to the house of a blackmailer who threatens to pulverise the remaining shreds of the Whitty reputation.

He rests his gloved hands upon his walking-stick and his chin upon his hands, and peers through the curtain, at the sudden greenery of St Charles Square; wisps of fog (ghosts of the Stuarts perhaps) catch onto the branches of plane trees, like swathes of cotton, or bearded heads – severed, then dissolved into mist.

Whitty pounds upon the door with his stick until his arm aches, to no avail, then tries the handle which might as well be welded to the door. Clearly, visitors are not expected at 5 Buckingham Gate.

Returning to the courtyard, he proceeds to a corner of the house and descends a set of crumbling steps to the trade entrance, whose wooden door has gone to rot. Two kicks with his boot and he is inside. He stoops to enter, not to crack his head on the ancient stone lintel.

As a precaution against a meat cleaver welcome, he hollers a hearty and nonsensical *Halloo! Is anyone there?* into the darkness, as though it were the customary thing for a visitor to kick the tradesman's door down, on a visit.

Reassured by a lack of response, he proceeds down a short hallway into the kitchen – deserted, slippery underfoot, heavy with the odour of sheep fat and the eerie silence of disuse. The cast-iron range, set within its predecessor – an ancient open hearth with hooks dangling above – is barely warm to the touch; in front of the stove sits the coal-hod, three-quarters filled, suggesting that the stove was lit this morning.

The meat-table, invisible beneath a cloak of insects the colour of syrup, contains what seems to be the remains of a joint of boiled mutton. In a corner of the room, a rat awaits its turn at the spoils; when Whitty threatens the animal with his stick, it backs away but does not flee.

Clearly, the pantry has been vacated abruptly and unexpectedly. One shelf is piled high with dried soups, pots of beans, grains, as well as the iron black-stone with which Irishmen prepare their dry, tasteless oat-cakes. The next shelf is empty, save for a single bottle with the label of Charleson's; the drawer below gapes open like a toothless jaw.

Whitty concludes that the Irish have left the house, along with every drop to drink in the pantry and every piece of silver in the drawer – only to be expected.

Even so, the back of Whitty's neck suggests a continuing presence – perhaps the rats, perhaps not. Keeping his back to the wall, he sidles down the narrow, oppressive hallway; it must surely lead, eventually, to the back parlour in which the seance occurred. And sure enough, at the end he steps through a low servant's door – which he soon recognises as the hidden door in the wainscoting, through which the medium first entered.

The room, however, has changed somewhat.

The chair from which the duke presided now lies on its side, with one leg missing. The table has been overturned, and the candles scattered about the floor. The drapes have been torn from their fixtures, exposing a thick iron curtain-rod – from which Dr Gilbert Williams now performs his last levitation.

This feat has been accomplished by a rope around the medium's throat, from which he dangles, his tiny feet pointed like a ballerina's, a few inches above the carpet.

The trick was not performed willingly. The broken window-panes behind the psychic, and the rope-burns that scar his neck and palms, suggest that Dr Williams did not cross serenely into the hereafter. Small pools of blood spatter the floor; a trail of blood leads across the Turkey carpet and out of the room. Given that the exit was not effected by the gentleman hanging from the window, the blood belonged to his assailant. Below the corpse lies a chair-leg, stained with blood – the weapon with which the medium fought for his life.

Tied properly, a noose is not easily loosened, and will only tighten further in a struggle. And the final tableau is always the same, struggle or no – a face bloated with blood, a tongue swollen and visible, a pair of eyes protruding as though comically surprised, and the unmistakable smell of a human being who has evacuated all organs at once. Whitty has witnessed the spectacle many times, never without a shudder.

A moment of gloomy reflection comes over him, interrupted by the clip-clop of copper-studded boots, tramping through the kitchen.

'In here, officers!' Whitty calls. 'Get out your handkerchiefs!'

'Good-day to you, Mr Whitty, sir.' Inspector Salmon bends double to enter the door in the wainscoting, one hand with a handkerchief over his mouth, the other clutching his stick.

Highly adroit with a stick, is Inspector Salmon, thinks the correspondent, having felt that stick on more than one occasion. And in return, the inspector has felt the sting of his prose. It is no secret that the inspector's fondest wish is to see him done serious harm.

Salmon inspects the figure before the window, as though it were a side of bacon on special at the butcher-shop. Nodding with an expression of inexplicable satisfaction, he turns to Whitty, while producing a piece of paper from his coat. Now he reads the text, in the way that a preacher reads the Beatitudes.

'Sir, would you be Mr Edmund Whitty, also known by the name of Willows?'

'Whitty was my name when last we met, policeman.'

'As an officer of the Metropolitan Police it is my duty to inform you that a magistrate of the Queen has issued me with a warrant for your arrest.'

'With what am I charged?' Whitty asks this in all innocence, though the presence of a murdered corpse gives him some idea. 'Have you come with anything specific, or shall we improvise as we go along?'

'Do not toy with me, sir, I do not like it.'

Salmon's stick trembles ominously – but does not strike, for three more policemen appear in the open door, one of whom is Constable Stubb, a casual acquaintance and occasional source.

'A good day to you, gentlemen. Good to see you again, Mr Stubb.'

'And you, Mr Whitty, sor.'

'Be quiet, Stubb,' snaps Salmon. 'Can you not tell when you are being mocked?'

Again the trembling of the hardwood stick, and it occurs to Whitty that the inspector himself resembles a stick; with his tall hat, his long great-coat and chin whiskers, he could serve as a giant tooth-brush.

'Sir, I charge you with the murder of one Bill Williams, alias Dr Gilbert Williams, alias Professor Herbert Zollner, alias Herr Schrenk-Notting.'

'And who might that be, Inspector?'

'I shall make note of your impudence, sir. Following a guilty verdict, it will signify a lack of remorse.'

'Your assumption that I am responsible does credit to my physical condition, given that the victim appears to weigh twelve stones.'

'It is known that a man in a frenzy – let us say, over an insult to his family's reputation – can exhibit inordinate strength. It is also known that scandal and disgrace can unhinge a man. But your guilt is for the courts to decide.'

For the first time in their acquaintance, the corners of Mr Salmon's mouth edge upward. 'Send for a carriage, Mr Stubb,' he says, producing a neatly folded sheet of vellum, 'while I document the charge.'

As the constable fits him with handcuffs and leg-irons, Whitty weighs two possible explanations for this unhappy turn of events. It is possible, in theory, that a pedestrian spied the cadaver in the window, notified the constabulary, and that Inspector Salmon arrived on the scene at virtually the same instant as himself. It is more likely, however, that the party who sent the dreadful picture of David, anticipating Whitty's immediate response, notified Inspector Salmon, who awaited him in the way of a duck-hunter or a fisherman. If so, then it follows that it was this person, or his agents, who topped the medium.

While Stubb fumbles with the cold, greasy chain, Whitty probes for information. 'You must have become tired waiting for me, sir.'

'It was not long,' replies the constable. 'We had a good estimate of your time of arrival.'

Right, then.

'By whom, might I ask?'

'I do not know, sir. The information came anonymously, is my understanding of it. There were something about a photograph as well. Do you have that photograph, sir?'

'I know of no photograph, Mr Stubb.'

'That is as may be. If it is on you or in you, it will be found.'

Indeed it will, thinks Whitty, the customary search at Newgate is a thorough, intimate business.

Whitty waddles to the front door, clanking like Marley's ghost, aware that he has acquired a new enemy – one who out-classes Fraser and Cream and, for that matter, even Inspector Salmon. An enemy capable of cold-blooded murder.

Jolted to and fro in a claustrophobic prisoner's carriage redolent with the bodily fluids of its previous passengers, Whitty contemplates what life might have in store. Undoubtedly he is headed for Newgate Gaol – where, without the intervention of Sala, he may await a hearing for upwards of a year – if he does not die of jail fever, in which case the fact of his innocence becomes moot. (Such is the backlog in the courts that a resourceful policeman such as Inspector Salmon can usher a suspect from capture to effective execution without the trouble and expense of a trial.)

As it is, he is in for a miserable week, before word reaches *The Falcon*; before Sala can ascertain whom to bribe.

Whitty peers out the tiny, screened window of the carriage, meaning to take a last, wistful look at grass and trees, as the van rumbles past St Charles's Park, and is surprised to note that the vehicle seems to be heading south on Vauxhall Road. As they turn a corner, he recognises a sign for a mesmeric salon, as well as an advertisement for Down's Hats – landmarks indicating that the vehicle is on Bessborough Road on its way to Vauxhall Gardens. So they are not going to Newgate after all.

The van comes to a stop, and the door is unbolted. The driver appears and hands the prisoner down the step with a great clattering and clanking of chains. They are beneath the ironwork of Vauxhall Bridge, at the top of the Hungerford stairs which lead down to the Thames. Along the shore are the creaking hulks of moored barges, black with coal, and the timber yard, piled with stacks of yellow deal. He remembers a time when periwinkles were caught here.

As Whitty turns to the stone stairway and looks across the river, a terrible premonition occurs.

A boat and oarsman are tied off at the bottom, while on the landing stands a man of middle height – whose arms hang out from his side in the way of a gorilla in a uniform, with a hat bearing the mysterious inscription, *W.S.B.C.* On the landing beside this officer stands Constable Stubb, who hands him a sheet of paper, then returns up the steps.

Brass it out. No time to show weakness.

'Spot of boating, Mr Stubb?' asks Whitty.

'Duck 'im in the river,' says the officer below while reading the charges beneath a torch. 'That'll shaht 'is mouth.'

The torch-bearing oarsman looks up at the prisoner; he would like to see that.

Shoved from behind, Whitty lurches clumsily across the ramp to the steps; the irons are damnably heavy and chafe like the devil. Pausing for breath, he turns to Constable Stubb, who regards him with a curiously apologetic expression. Whitty feels a sudden, inexplicable pang of sadness, as though he were waving farewell to an old and dear friend.

He turns back to the steps leading to the river, which at this hour of the afternoon seems to contain ink and not water; on the other side are the potteries of Lambeth, Cubitt's Yard and St George's Square. To the right he sees a shapeless mass of yellow brick, whose towers, seemingly Egyptian, are silhouetted at uneven intervals against the darkening sky. It is the unmistakable silhouette of the largest and ugliest building in England.

Panic wells up in his sternum; an almost irresistible urge, first to vomit and then to flee, though the only escape is to the bottom of the river.

'Damn you, Stubb, that is Millbank!' he cries, as descriptions of the place flash through his mind – many of which he wrote himself.

'That were not my decision, Mr Whitty, sor. I only takes my orders.'

The Ugliest Edifice in England
by
Edmund Whitty
Senior Correspondent
The Falcon

Always with an eye to the worst of everything, your Amateur Clubman and his associates wish to announce a winner in the field of architecture – Millbank Prison.

Millbank is easily the ugliest edifice in England – perhaps the world, indeed the eighteen acres of Lambeth would be greatly improved were it to contain a Tibetan yurt.

The construction, as far as one can tell, consists of five pentagons within an octagon, perched upon a series of triangles. Its yellow brick façade and multitude of tiny windows evoke something vaguely Oriental. Such a configuration might seem to issue from a Masonic nightmare, yet we are assured that it is all wonderfully scientific. For example, it is said that a great impediment to escape is that the prisoner is too disoriented to find his way out.

Yet the mystery of Millbank does not end with its construction. Admittance is restricted to prisoners and officials, and any interested parties must obtain permission from the Home Secretary of State, who seldom replies, and never complies.

Designed on the so-called Panopticon system, the Millbank keeps the prisoner under surveillance every waking hour of his life, thanks to a complicated system of mirrors. When not under observation, the inmate participates in a regimen of constant cleaning. Yet at Millbank, cleanliness has little to do with health, it being built on swamp land, suffused with vapours that will sicken a man as easily as typhus.

From what we are told of this modern establishment and its innovative governor, those fortunate enough who survive can be found barking mad with the lunatics in Bedlam.

The officer hands his prisoner out of the boat and they cross what was once a moat (now a field of swamp-grass), through the front gate and into a triangular courtyard covered with crushed gravel, swarming with cleaners and trimmers and rakers, all dressed in identical grey uniforms, with a red stripe down the seam of the trousers. They are overseen by a warder in a blue uniform similar to Whitty's escort, but with a different sequence of letters on the hat, and armed with a carbine, whose brass barrel flashes as he moves it to and fro. One prisoner, wearing a kind of yoke, rolls a heavy metal cylinder, which emits a loud, metallic crushing noise. This contraption is followed by at least a dozen men, drawing brooms behind them, marching back and forth side by side, making the gravel and earth appear like the combed hair of a choirboy.

Past the inner gate he smells ammonia, which resembles the smell of piss, the difference being a matter of nuance: while the latter is putrid, the former is oppressively sanitary. The yellow brick mass looming above them is a wide, round turret, with a conical slate roof and a number of vertical slits for windows, like an enormous Martello tower.

He turns to his escort. 'You might at least explain things as we go along.'

'Shaht up,' comes the reply. The small, hooded eyes refuse to meet his – indeed, as they reach the front door it occurs to Whitty that not one of the inmates has cast so much as a glance in his direction; now it comes to him that Millbank adheres to the separate system, a Puritan atrocity in which each prisoner serves his sentence silent and alone, with only his sins for company.

The floors and walls inside the main building likewise teem with inmates, scrubbing with the frantic intensity of squirrels, yet not a sound comes from their mouths. The effect is damnably eerie: in their grey uniforms and prison pallor, they resemble a squad of hygienic ghosts.

Whitty looks about with interest, reasonably confident of his release, as soon as *The Falcon* gets wind of these specious charges. What worries him is that word might not reach Sala for weeks, due to the secrecy of the place. This is clearly what Salmon had in mind.

Situated on the second floor, the governor's room is at the precise centre of the prison – a monastically spare apartment, containing a large writing-table, a small barred window, and with a thick rope stretched across the room, where Whitty is directed to stand.

Through the window he can glimpse the Gothic points of the Houses of Parliament, and a bit of St John's Church; further down the Thames, a lone hansom cab crosses Westminster Bridge. With that glimpse of simple, mundane, free movement he experiences a wave of hollow, aching despair, transformed into a terrified child of seven, snatched from his mother and his governess and the female servants who cared for him, and thrown into a brutal, sterile world of fists and whips . . .

Unlike the boy at Eton, Whitty does not dissolve into bitter tears; yet it is a very near thing.

'Stand up straight and shaht up,' says the warder. 'Here is Governor Whidden.'

Whidden is a compact, cautious-seeming individual dressed in black, with a vicar's wig of a type that hasn't been worn since 1830. By the absence of hair about his ears, Whitty deduces the governor is bald and that the appliance serves double duty, serving his position and his vanity at the same time. Without according the prisoner so much as a glance, Whidden snatches the sheet of charges from the warder, places it on the writing-table, and studies it silently for some time.

He speaks without looking up: 'You have been brought to us on charges of the most serious kind. However, it is not for me to judge your innocence or guilt. You will be treated in the same manner as any other prisoner. Innocent or guilty, you will receive the full benefit of the programme.'

Brass it out.

'This is a disgrace, sir, and the charges against me are preposterous. I demand to see my solicitor at once.'

'I shall overlook that outburst because you have just arrived. Another like it, however, and you shall receive an admonition, and from there a rising scale of punishment for each subsequent offence. Mr Clive here will read you the rules of the institution in due course, along with an explanation of the refractory system.'

The refractory system, from what Whitty has heard, follows an almost mystical principle having to do with the propensity of both plants and people to require light as a source of energy. Therefore, so it goes, if one wishes to reform a man, one must remove the energy that nourishes his misbehaviour. With good behaviour, light is gradually restored to the prisoner, giving life to virtue. Heaven knows what the refractory system will produce when combined with the silent system – a population of lighthouse-keepers, perhaps.

'You will be taken to the surgeon for a thorough examination. Having been judged fit, your hair will be cut, you will be dressed, and you will be placed in a cell in the receiving ward. There you will remain, separate and in silence, for a period of six months. Your progress rests with you as you contemplate your sins and pray for God's mercy, on your journey to the light. Be aware that you are being watched, sir, by the eyes of your superiors and by Almighty God, and that you will answer for every move you make, both here and in the hereafter.'

The governor turns to the officer: 'Mr Clive, you will see to the prisoner's admittance, and that he maintains strict silence.

'And a good-day to you, Mr Willows.'

Upon hearing himself addressed by that name, Whitty's hopes for rescue evaporate. Salmon has buried him in an unmarked grave. He will never be found.

Bissett Grange, Oxfordshire

How cheerfully he seems to grin,
How neatly spreads his claws,
And welcomes little fishes in
With gently smiling jaws!

Nestled in the petals of a red silk dressing-gown, the Duke of Danbury warms himself at the fire before contemplating the duties and pleasures of the day; diminished, alas, since olden times, when a Danbury owned a third of the county's available land, when two-thirds of the population were serfs, and England stood united by ties of blood and service.

In its sober, antiquated elegance, the room maintains a well-bred, co-operative silence. A liver-coloured Maltese named Fetch sits lightly upon the duke's lap, its forepaws crossed, inquisitive face turned upward, intent upon the slightest motion of its master's face.

'Turn out the brute, will you?' says Danbury, lifting neither his voice or his gaze. As with Fetch, the estate manager awaits Danbury's word with the unflagging constancy expected of his position.

Betraying no sign of resentment, Lush rises from his stool, takes hold of Fetch, carries her to the hall in such a way that he will not get hairs on his coat, and hands her to a footman. Returning to the library, he places his stool at an angle from which he can see the duke's face. 'Your Grace is to meet with the solicitors today. Do you wish to ride or drive?'

'Neither. I shall not speak to the solicitors at all.'

'Your Grace did not speak to them yesterday,' Lush says, then switches his mode of expression to the familiar Oxford style, to remind the Duke that they are fellow-alumni, that he is something more than just a servant. 'Sailing close to the wind, Harry. Cash-flow is much improved, but prices cannot remain this high – you continue to run up debts, eh what, old chap?'

'I will not be bullied by clerks. Surely they are not unaware that Uncle will soon join the choir invisible.'

'At present, Lord Donlevy remains sufficiently alive to make troubling statements about your Grace in public.'

'Donlevy is superfluous. Nobody listens to him.'

It is true, thinks Lush, that life at Bissett Grange will become very much easier when Lord Donlevy expires. The duke is the logical inheritor of the Ryelands estate, worth £12,000 a year – sufficient to put behind the regrettable business to which they have had to stoop, periodically, for over half a decade.

Making things doubly difficult, financially speaking, the duke has taken a keen, nay fanatical, interest in resurrecting the atavistic glory of the Danburys at Bissett Grange. The duke's staff are now entirely male as tradition demands. The footmen are Irishmen of Cro-Magnon proportions, while the gardeners, plucked from isolated islands, speak an archaic dialect incomprehensible to the modern ear. Unless addressed by the duke, butlers and footmen face the wall when in his presence.

There are many who suspect Danbury to have a slate loose; yet the same is said of many aristocrats in the countryside, with no loss of status.

'Harry, surely it is the thing to court your creditors, don't you know. Remember that the heirship is not *absolutely* certain.'

'It is too early in the morning for this discussion. Servicing debt is a beastly business.'

True, Lush thinks – beastly in more than one sense.

The estate manager has his complaints, Heaven knows; yet for the most part, he is content. His accounts have made steady progress, with retirement in the offing, which will bring this grovelling to an end, and he will be free and clear.

Taking a heaping spoonful of snuff in each nostril, Danbury says, without sneezing, 'I wish to discuss the family at Crouch Manor and our overtures to them.'

Lush utters a suppressed sigh. 'I sent cards and preliminary pleasantries, as requested. I continue to strongly advise your Grace against it.'

'And if you think I give a tinker's damn what you think, you are catastrophically mistaken.'

The estate manager draws out a notebook and moistens his pencil. His colourless eyes glance at the far wall, containing an arrangement of military pistols. He could make good use of one, right now.

'Shut the door, will you?' Danbury says, while selecting a cigar from the box on the side-table. 'I shan't speak into the corridor.'

Lush obliges. 'Your Grace is set on having them to dinner, then? With the usual crowd?'

'Yes. The photography set is rather a ragged lot, yet Boltbyn must be included. Without the others as well, it would appear odd.'

'It requires very little for Mr Boltbyn to appear odd.'

'I want him under my protection – with the family, of course.'

'London is the largest city in the world. Isn't it the height of folly to pursue subjects so close to home?'

'London is a source of unlimited trouble – as recent events indicate. I want the business to be entirely under my purview.'

Danbury has two voices, thinks Lush. One voice is a superficial drawl, dripping with ennui; the other is a melodious murmur with humorous accents, and a peremptory undertone; a silken sensibility masking a will, or a whim, of iron.

'Are there any other guests your Grace wishes to invite?'

Danbury takes two long, luxurious puffs of his cigar before replying. 'Just be certain that the daughters come. Later we will invite them to tea, together with Mr Boltbyn – and the mother, of course.'

'Harry, I really cannot think what is wrong with the current system.'

'That is because you do not think at all. Now is the time to increase production, to take advantage of the current market. London abounds with policemen and journalists, sniffing about for scandal. There will be none of that sort of thing at Bissett Grange.'

The duke grows greedy, thinks Lush, and overestimates his sphere of influence. The estate manager is worried. A spot on his head has sprouted an itchy rash, like the bloom of a discouraging thought.

He has known the duke for a very long time. As a student of mathematics at St Ambrose College, Albin Lush attached himself to a set of gentlemen-commoners by supplying certain substances and services that were off limits. Eventually, his noble associates deemed his presence worthwhile, and invited them to their gatherings. Then came an opportunity to assist Danbury after the death of the parents. In this position Lush curried favour with his charge by any means necessary, so that when the duke reached his majority there was no question who should manage the estate.

In the years since, however, familiarity has bred contempt on both sides. Lush is well aware that Danbury finds their old-school past an irritant, and he views his superior as an effete squanderer. He knows he will be kicked out of the manor as soon as the duke has the wherewithal to do his own kicking, and looks forward to his emancipation – provided that he has skimmed sufficient cash to fund it. In the meantime, he treads carefully for it is in precisely this mood that Danbury will announce his dismissal.

'Leave me alone, will you?' says Danbury, at which Lush heads for the door, only to be stopped midway by that contemptuous drawl. 'On second thoughts, you will oblige me by bringing pen and paper, and wait for this letter.'

Lush must now stand by while the duke scrawls a brief note in his impossibly elegant, baroque script. 'Tell O'Day to deliver this at once, will you?' he says, passing the letter to Lush without looking at him, as if he were as much an implement as the pen and paper. 'By the way, is the London matter resolved?'

'Not quite, your Grace. The journalist should be rotting in Newgate, but from the newspapers it seems he has mysteriously disappeared. Our brutes will require another £50 to undertake a pursuit.' Lush intends to keep £45 for himself; he will forward the brutes at least a fiver for their trouble.

'Confound their prices, whoever they are. They are bleeding me white over this.'

'I have no belief in psychic phenomena,' replies Lush, 'but we cannot have old issues, for whatever reason. Pre-emptive action was required.'

'In future, stock Buckingham Gate with some sort of religious cult. I've had my fill of psychics.' With a grimace, the duke tosses his cigar into the fire, and partakes of another pinch of snuff.

Spared the presence of his estate manager, Danbury settles into the armchair that once embraced his father and grandfather. Before him the lawn undulates upward as far as Dragon Hill, where the Roland Stones stand like hunchbacked sentries against the horizon – the remains of a neolithic temple and, fittingly, a monument to the ruling class of its era.

As always, one stone dominates – the Knight Stone, its features rotted as though by leprosy. In the Middle Ages, barren women pressed their breasts to it in hopes of a child; in Tudor times witches conducted pagan rituals at its feet. Even today, something about the place evokes vague, disturbing energies, a coalescence of time, light, electricity, and an intensified gravity of spirit.

On the far side of Dragon Hill sits a small cave known as the Wayland Smithy, named for a legend that the shoes of St George's steed were forged within. According to tradition, if a man leaves his horse beside the Smithy with a penny in payment, the horse will be shod upon his return. Men who swear to have witnessed the miracle have worked this soil for so many generations, they might as well be made of it; men whose loyalty Danbury trusts for the same reason one trusts a dray horse – because he knows nothing else.

The Duke of Danbury likewise draws no real distinction between himself, his estate, his legacy and his position, and would no more seek to separate fact from legend than he would take apart his own eye to see how it functions.

And yet, momentous changes have befallen the great families of England. Noblemen have to consider how to afford the maintenance of the grounds, how to finance a hunting party, how to pay for a new roof for the stables. Rather than face this crushing burden, many have let their estates to industrialists and bankers, and retired to France as exiles, driven by penury from the country they once led.

That will not happen at Bissett Grange.

Filling his glass with aqua vitae from the crystal carafe on the side-table, Danbury rises, takes a tiny silver spoon, and scoops a portion of medicinal powder from the little ebony box on the mantel. Waiting for the powder to take effect, he pulls open a drawer in the side-table, removes a stack of photographs and examines them one by one, using a magnifying-glass in order to appreciate Boltbyn's uncanny crispness of focus.

Each depicts the elder daughter of the new precentor at the Church of St Swithan, as an actor in an imagined dramatic tableau:

– seated sideways in a chair in a frilled morning-dress, face cocked on an angle with an expression of impudent boredom

– stealing into the wood away from her sleeping governess, an expression of delicious mischief in her eye

– as a runaway, climbing out of a bedroom window onto a white ladder decorated with a garland

– frolicking in the forest, her dress in tatters and flowers in her hair

– as a beggar girl, palms together, with one bared shoulder and a coquettish look of supplication.

Bracebridge Hemyng presented these images to him as part of a proposal to publish a sentimental picture-book entitled, *The Runaway: Tale of a Prodigal Daughter,* a cautionary fable designed for the drawing-room tables in Manchester. Naturally, Danbury is expected to underwrite the initial printing.

What a superb model she makes, and what a captivating face and form! And to think that these pictures were taken by the insufferable prig Boltbyn! Who would suspect that his tastes ran in that direction? With some adjustments in costume, these very pictures would arouse the most ardent sentiments in the viewer, and the highest prices on the market.

How does a photograph attain such clarity yet appear as if the subject has been caught in an unguarded instant, frozen in time?

Danbury thinks of his own compositions, always stiff and clumsy. Even with the forced co-operation of the subject, the results are about as life-like as a mannequin. He has neither the sensibility nor the skill of a Boltbyn, and must discard far more plates than he uses. Bissett Grange would be solvent by now, were he possessed of Boltbyn's skill – or better yet, Boltbyn himself . . .

His ears begin to buzz like an extended cat's purr, and the girl before him recedes into cloud. *Ah yes – the powder.* Feeling slightly queasy, he pours eau de Cologne upon his handkerchief, wipes the perspiration from his forehead, leans back, closes his eyes – and another face appears, covered by a thin white hood, wet with rainwater.

At the age of fifteen, Harry Godwin, for reasons understood only by boys of that age, once attended the execution of a woman. The event was heavily covered in the press. Her relative youth, her fine form and features (engravings were sold, with varying authenticity), added a prurient component to the excitement over her approaching death.

A sight not to be missed.

Harry played truant by counterfeiting an ague then bribing the servants with his tuck money, then took a cab to Dorchester in the early morning to claim a spot with a view of the square. Hundreds had already gathered by the time he arrived; but he was able to creep within twenty feet of the gallows, as if the whole universe were co-operating with his desires.

A massive intake of breath issued from the mob as the woman appeared upon the platform; followed by a silence so profound that the future Duke of Danbury could actually hear the rustle of her black silk dress as she mounted the scaffold.

She was a housewife from Beaminster, condemned for killing her husband with a hatchet after he had striped her face with a tantor's whip during a quarrel. The circumstance surrounding the act might have brought a reprieve had she not attempted to conceal the crime by claiming that he had been kicked by a horse. Having lied to the authorities, she earned no credit for her subsequent confession and her fate was sealed.

Her head was covered by a thin white hood. A light but penetrating rain had been drizzling since dawn, and the white fabric soon clung to her so that one could almost discern her features, like a marble statue, so calm and so lovely that even Calcraft the executioner appeared uncharacteristically distracted; only after he ascended the iron stairs did he remember to tie her dress around her body, so that her limbs would not be indecently exposed.

When she dropped, the burly tradesman standing next to the future duke fell to the cobbles in a swoon; yet young Harry's eyes remained open, greedily taking in the sight as though it were the last wine left in Europe, to be savoured in memory ever after.

Since then, Danbury has since witnessed a good deal of death – the death of children, the death of his only friend – as necessary, mundane evils, for the greater good. None had the effect of that first experience. You never forget your first.

A SCENT OF SPITE
by
Henry Owler
Special Correspondent
The Falcon

Not since the capture and hanging of the fiend known as Chokee Bill have rumours and reprehensions swirled about the city at such a rate as they do presently. Grave doubts are voiced in all quarters following the disappearance of Edmund Whitty, correspondent for The Falcon. *Of particular concern are revelations which cast a shadow upon the Metropolitan Police, together with a suspicion that certain members of the police imagine themselves, not as public servants, but as vigilantes in some penny dreadful in the colonies.*

Your correspondent has learned that Mr Whitty was arrested at the scene of the murder of Dr Gilbert Williams, that he was duly charged, and that he was seen to leave Buckingham Gate in the back of a police van.

Since then, Mr Whitty has vanished from the face of London.

There is no Whitty present in any prison – this we have ascertained by painstaking effort. Nor has a record of the charges against Mr Whitty yet appeared in the itinerary of the Magistrate's Court. When questioned on this matter, Inspector Salmon of Scotland Yard replied: 'Charges are being prepared and the accused is in process. Beyond that we cannot comment upon the case.'

Finding this explanation unsatisfactory due to the uncertain meaning of 'in process', we enquired further; at which point it was revealed by a trustworthy source that Mr Whitty has been confined in Millbank.

Notwithstanding, in all of that vast institution there exists not a single prisoner by the name of Whitty. Further enquiries of the governor were referred to the Ministry.

The entire affair remains steeped in the supernatural – a murdered medium, a voice from the dead, and now a disappearing correspondent. Yet one detects more earthly concerns at work.

We do not suggest that Inspector Salmon might undertake a false arrest, in retaliation for criticisms that have appeared on these pages following the Chokee Bill affair. Nonetheless, to your correspondent, the narrative seems to exist more in the realm of scoundrels than spooks.

Crouch Manor, Chester Wolds, Oxfordshire

The Right Honourable the Duke of Danbury
K.G.C.V., K.G.C.S., K.C.A.J., (H.)O.L.J.
Bissett Grange

Cordially Requests the Company of
The Reverend C.G. Lambert and Family
On Friday next, for Dinner at Eight o'Clock.

Carriage Provided
R.S.V.P.

Admiring the invitation (Could he actually have written it by hand?), Birdie Lambert smooths a blank sheet of writing-paper upon the leather surface of the desk, opens an inkwell, and pauses with pen in mid-air. How does one properly address a duke? A formidable question when one has had little schooling, and has never in one's life attended an event involving an R.S.V.P.

What should she wear? How should she wear it?

As a last resort she could fall ill, a tactic which has served in the past. Yet, for a storekeeper's disgraced daughter to visit Bissett Grange would be a triumph of staggering proportions; to enter a world which has existed only on the page and in the mind – how can she resist?

Birdie turns her attention to the pale woman in the mirror above the writing-table: she has lost weight again. With her cheeks so hollow, her eyes appear large and liquid, like the eyes of her elder daughter. This can be worked with. It has its appeal. And her hair is still good.

She takes a few drops of laudanum from the little silver spoon she keeps in the pocket of her apron, along with her volume of George Eliot. She places the invitation in a drawer, leaving the reply for another time.

When Emma is informed by Miss Pouch that the family has been invited to dinner with the Duke of Danbury, she experiences an odd mixture of feelings.

Her first encounter with the duke occurred at church, when he honoured the congregation with his presence – and a presence he surely was.

He seemed to inspire a more lofty atmosphere, in which prayers were deeper and hymns more fervent. While conducting the singing, not once did Father avert his gaze from the solitary man in the princely pew – screened to protect its inhabitant from the prying stares of the congregation, and cushioned so that even a muttered 'Amen' remained a private affair between the duke and the Almighty.

It was the first time his Grace had bothered to attend church since the Lamberts' arrival. Miss Pouch later explained that the date, 23 April, coincided with the Feast of St George; that the Duke of Danbury was fiercely patriotic; that an ancestor fought alongside Richard the Lionheart and saw the ghost of St George appear before the king.

Having been warned of the duke's intention to honour St Swithan with his presence, the Reverend Spoole devised the entire proceeding for Danbury's benefit – the cumulative point being that, should the duke continue in his profligate ways, this ancient earldom will collapse in ignominy. The sermon was based upon the text, *Great men are not always wise* (Job xxxii, 9), and might have verged on the discourteous had not an ill-fitting set of dentures prevented Mr Spoole from making his point clear.

Emma occupied herself by examining the pillars on the either side of the nave, carved with the distorted faces of villagers: to the left, goggle-eyed men leered, tongues extended, towards the opposite pillar, itself adorned with grotesque women, with hooked noses, crooked teeth and squinting eyes.

As the postlude sounded its triumphal blast, the congregation did not immediately flock behind the Reverend to the door as was the usual custom, but remained seated, heads bowed, to await the duke.

After a long pause, Danbury rose, stepped into the aisle and passed through his subjects, looking neither to right nor left, displaying his regal profile, the elegant side-whiskers, the thoroughbred flare of his nostrils, the planate bridge of his nose, the finely shaped, slightly receding chin.

Her mother having departed for the vestry to await her husband, the girls and Miss Pouch were the last to leave the church.

Curtsying before Reverend Spoole, Emma inhaled the fresh air as she descended the foot-worn stone steps – and was astonished beyond description to see the yellow phaeton in the road before them, with the duke standing beside it, one boot upon the carriage step, stroking his side-whiskers with thumb and forefinger.

'Rather a ragged lot,' she heard the duke whisper to his companion, a wire-haired gentleman who looked to Emma like a burrowing animal.

She had never in her life seen a man with so little anxiety in his bearing. Compared to the duke, her father and Mr Boltbyn lived in a perpetual twitch of nerves.

Before the goggle-eyes of the remaining congregation, Danbury stepped forward, executed a barely perceptible nod to Miss Pouch (who turned crimson in reply), inclined his head to Lydia (who was looking at his shiny boots and did not notice), then turned to Emma. When he looked upon her it was as though estimating the price of an item of jewellery. The silence between them did not bother him a bit, though it made her feel most awkward.

'Do you like roses?' he asked at last, in what was surely the most beautiful pronunciation of four words she had ever heard.

'Yes, sir,' she replied with effort.

After another pause he bowed again, extended one hand to receive a red rose handed him by his companion, and placed the rose in Emma's hand. 'Pray oblige me, miss, by accepting this bloom as a token.'

She felt the tawny softness of his glove against her palm, and the smooth stem of the rose, its thorns carefully clipped.

Whispered the duke as though telling a secret: 'On St George's Day it is traditional for a gentleman to furnish a lady with a red rose, and for the lady to repay him with a book. It is a curious custom, but tradition must be respected, as I'm sure you agree.'

Emma made no reply, but could only stare, saucer-eyed, at the gentleman hovering above her; it seemed as if some splendid tropical bird had swooped down and offered to fly her away to another land. Yet when her eyes finally met his, they met the unblinking gaze of a hunter.

15

Millbank Prison

'Dear, dear! How queer everything is today! I wonder if I've changed in the night. Let me see – was I the same when I got up this morning?
  I almost think I can remember feeling a little different. But if I'm not the same, who in the world am I? Ah, that's the great puzzle!'

It was during his latest confinement in the dark cell that Whitty felt himself actually to disappear – or rather, felt the self in his mind replaced by various others. No night, no cellar, no crypt is so dark as the dark cell at Millbank. To Whitty it seemed as if the air was made of black wool. At unpredictable intervals, however, a tiny opening in the door would slide open, and – he may have imagined this – a bright eye would appear, like the eye of a huge wading-bird, a crusher no doubt, confirming that the prisoner had not crushed his head against the wall or hanged himself.

Whitty's most recent seclusion followed two counts of speaking aloud, compounded by blasphemy, insulting an officer, and by his conduct at his audience with the governor, at which he denied his own name.

At some point he remembers pretending to be mad, howling like a dog and proclaiming hallucinations – a spider in his soup, a corpse under the cot; later, he remembers raving in the same fashion – in all sincerity. Still later, when the heron's eye flashed in the window, the prisoner could have been Whitty, or Willows, or Fido for that matter, for the being he was before entering the dark cell no longer existed.

Yet *someone* continued to pace his cell. This party would career from one wall to another, back and forth like a snooker ball, hour after hour, eyes shut tight, shoulders hunched. At one point in his mind he actually transformed into a rhinoceros, which has notoriously poor eyesight; he could feel the weight of bony growth on his forehead and a shell envelop his shoulders like a brittle cloak, while in his mind a childhood rhyme played itself over and over:

To consider oneself a rhinoceros
Might to some seem a loss to us
But to think one is born
With a nose, not a horn
To us is a prospect prepocerous . . .

After several days, or they might have been weeks, he was taken from the dark cell and transferred to the refractory cell, in which healing rays of light were to be reintroduced by degrees.

Hours later, his eyes, let alone his mind, have only begun to adjust.

Shafts of light slice through the slits in the window, like blades, stinging his face. When he ventures to open one eye, the bricks seem to pulse with energy as though breathing; when he opens both eyes, the entire room seems to undulate, so that he must grip the sides of his cot to avoid toppling onto the floor.

After several minutes (or hours, or weeks), he struggles to a seated position against the wall, presses one eye to the crack in the window – and beholds a series of triangular, needle-like structures, spewing smoke and fire, like an Egyptian temple, to a god like the sound of a stutter. In what is left of his rational mind, he knows it to be the Lambeth gasworks; yet he is just as certain that he has been transported to another world.

How long has he been here? Has he become an old man?

The metallic snap of a deadbolt causes him to cry out in alarm and to cover his ringing ears. A metal door grinds open. He opens his eyes – too suddenly, for he must shut them tight until the pain subsides. From somewhere in the room a stentorian voice ricochets against the walls – sharper than the voices in his mind. Nearby, someone is weeping. It may be himself.

'Yor, Prisoner Willows, on yer feet, sharp now, mon, cease yer snivelling, let's see yer!' Upon reflection, the sound is not a deafening bark but an urgent whisper. 'Move yer arse, mate, d'ye want out or not? . . .'

By squinting carefully, he can discern the shape of a man in the doorway – the screw probably, whose bull's-eye is pointed, not into the prisoner's face as usual, but onto the stone floor, creating a patch of light like an egg.

'Step up, mon, get moving! There be seconds ta spare!'

To spare for what? wonders Whitty, standing upon legs of butter, trying to focus upon the yellow egg cast on the floor. Abruptly an impatient, muscular grip imprisons his arm, and the egg begins to move before him with the speed of a comet.

'Are we in a hurry?' he asks.

'Shut up,' comes the reply – the usual requirement here at Millbank.

By the hollow splat of footsteps and the mortifying smell of ammonia, Whitty guesses that they are in the broad corridor leading to or from the central hexagon. A glimmer of distant light reflects upon the wet stone floor, causing it to heave like a sea of treacle. The vice-grip on his arm tightens, and there comes a whisper like a blast of steam in his ear:

God's blood! Face the wall, mon!

Whitty is shoved directly into an alcove, smashing the right side of his face against the brick wall. Immediately thereafter, a flash of something like sheet lightning illuminates every square inch of the corridor.

Whitty has heard tell of this device, which makes ingenious use of mirrors, reflecting off one another at complicated angles so that nothing escapes. The brilliance is astonishing; with eyes tightly closed it seems to illuminate the inside of Whitty's cranium, like lightning, or the spotlight in the window of the dark cell . . .

'Christ,' whispers his invisible companion. ''Tis the Guv up there.'

'Governor Whidden? Up where?'

'Middle tower. Roams the floor with spy-glass and mirrors, all hours of the night, focusing without warning. Gets to inspect every man in spike, and waken and blind 'em in at the same time.'

'Are you taking me to see Governor Whidden?'

'Yer be taken to avoid him, ye dunce.'

Suddenly Whitty is lurched out of the alcove, and frog-marched further down the heaving corridor, black as a mine-shaft, with no egg of light to follow – and therefore no warning when he is stuffed into a low, narrow doorway, cracking his head in a shower of sparks.

'Watch yer head, mon.'

Bent double, clutching his pounding head, Whitty stumbles, or is pushed, down a low, narrow passage, which reminds him of a London sewer-pipe with its rounded ceiling – and, to go by the rustling and squeaking, the rats.

'Where the devil are you taking me?'

'Up the governor's arse, mon.'

Not an implausible journey, thinks Whitty, for the omnipresent ammonia has given way to the odour of damp earth, rotten wood, spoiled potatoes – and, more strongly as they descend, sewage.

They are up to their knees in liquid when his escort comes to a halt and relaxes his grip.

'Here I leave yer, mon.'

'I beg your pardon?'

'Yer s'posed to wade to the end of the tunnel.'

'Wade to *where?*'

Whitty can discern a small, round, dimly lit hole somewhere in the distance – an unpromising prospect at best. 'And what the devil am I to do when I get there?'

'Keep to the shadow and the high grass. And keep yer head down – the screw's a crack shot with a carbine.'

Grass, sewage, carbines. 'I would prefer to return to my cell, please.'

'Suit yerself. Yer as easily shot coming as going.'

As easily shot coming as going?

With no more rational thought than a moth entering a candle, Whitty lurches forward, ignoring the thick, foul liquid now up to his waist. He cares not how deep it might become – such is his level of courage, or lack of an alternative. As he moves towards the illuminated, circular opening, the muck thins, until by the time he reaches it, he is knee-deep in a drainage ditch.

His mind wonders what to do next; a voice some distance away removes all doubt:

'Get over here,' hisses the voice.

'Who the devil are you?' Whitty hisses back.

'Shaht up,' comes the reply.

Whitty sees a pair of gorilla arms silhouetted against the night sky, and recognises the officer who escorted him into this peculiar hell in the first place. 'Mr Clive, I presume,' he whispers.

'I said shaht up.'

'Quite.'

Maintaining a wary silence, the escaper and his companion wade through a swampy clearing with the smell of a horse-pond, then down a slender tongue of land between two monumental buildings shaped like pentagons. Crouching double, they scurry across this opening, which leads to a desolate black sentry box, whose officer stands outside by the root garden with a carbine over his shoulder, taking a piss.

Keeping to the shadows, they reach a similar tongue of land between two other pentagons, where they make their way through a crop of swamp grass, thick and tall, undulating like a field of corn.

Crawling on his hands and knees through a maze of prickly vegetation, Whitty can make out the yellow brick walls of the prison itself, lit by the lights of Lambeth. Thankfully, the pain in his eyes has diminished and he can now open them fully. He catches sight of the Millbank pier, its deep red lamps glowing like bloodshot eyes, and behind it, the inky Thames; and on the far shore, the Gothic biscuit-ware of Parliament.

'There's the boat,' whispers Clive. 'Stay below the gunnels. And shaht up, fer sound will travel across water an' the crushers is listening.'

'Why is this happening? Who must I thank for this?'

'Not the Lord, that is fer certain.'

The ironwork of Vauxhall Bridge stretches above him like the legs of an enormous grasshopper as Whitty clambers out of the boat and onto the landing. Rising awkwardly to his feet, he looks behind him to see that the silent oarsman has already headed the boat back across the river. Climbing the stone steps in the silent dark (not so dark as the dark cell), he recognises the smell of Lambeth – its bone-crushing factories, plants and potteries, whose combined effluent spreads sickness and suffocation for a mile on either side.

Whitty inhales with gusto, for it is the smell of freedom.

Given that he lacks the means to pay for a cab (and stinks to a degree that would bar him from one in any case), and given that he is wearing a prisoner's uniform, he sets out on foot, by the shortest, most discreet route to the Alhambra Baths.

Keeping to the alleyways behind Regency Street, he notes that his mind has not fully recovered from the programme of cleansing at Millbank. For one thing, it seems unwilling to stick to any one topic, preferring to bounce laterally from one mental exhibit to another as one does in a dream. Approaching Vincent Square, it flits and darts promiscuously between present and past, legend and fact, giving equal weight to what he knows, remembers and imagines (*Playing-fields of Westminster School; prison-camp for Scots; plague burial-pit; hunting-ground for rhinoceros . . .*), and wonders whether he must adhere to fiction-writing in future.

Keeping to the perimeter of the playing-field, he becomes so absorbed in the history and myth and other associations brought on by Vincent Square that he fails to notice the two footpads in ankle-length coats, leaning against the trunk of an ancient oak. They, however, do not fail to notice him.

Eyes locked upon the quarry, the smaller and more barrel-shaped of the two reaches inside one of the many pockets in his voluminous garment and produces a length of telegraph wire, with pieces of dowelling tied to either end, for grip. He is about to spring horizontally at Whitty's throat, but is restrained by an outstretched arm like a length of transatlantic cable.

'Not the ticket, Norman. Remember what the Captain said.'

'You are right, Will,' answers the smaller man, putting away his weapon. 'Seize but do not mangle. Them was the Captain's orders.'

'He will be an easy mark to trail.'

'If only by the stink.'

Insensible to the foregoing, Whitty keeps to the shadows to avoid the police courts on Rochester Row, then turns in the direction of the Royal Horticultural Society; seeing his course, the two footpads break into a smooth trot across the darkened field, like two athletes, taking their midnight exercise on the playing-fields of Westminster School.

16

New Scotland Yard, off Parliament Street

Turning down an insignificant street, then up a narrow lane in the pre-dawn mist, Constable Stubb enters into a little paved court, where a number of helmeted, great-coated policemen are drawn up in a line, smoking, and enters the outer office of Scotland Yard.

Surrounded by whitewashed walls tapestried with ragged police-notices, he reaches a cubicle containing a dock, with a height-gauge behind. In this cubicle sits a sergeant, writing beneath a tallow candle. Beside the sergeant's cubicle is the office of Inspector Salmon, into which Stubb must now enter, by appointment.

The constable heaves a sigh. In the life of a public servant there is nothing more debilitating than to be taken under the wing of a superior one does not like.

The inspector's room is an extension of the outer office, notable only for its utter absence of personal memorabilia. One might think it was a common area for the force as a whole, though Salmon alone has occupied it for twenty years.

The inspector looks up from his desk, with the pensive look of one who has been pondering weighty matters. Defying his normally dour disposition, the corners of his mouth turn upward, like little hooks. 'Hello, Stubb. Good of you to come at this early hour.'

'Good morning, Inspector Salmon. It is a duty and an honour to do so.' Stubb listens to himself speak this twaddle, cursing his own sycophancy.

'It concerns Mr Whitty, the murderer – or the correct thing would be to say, the *accused* murderer.'

'Yes, sir. Mr Whitty: why he has not been located is a great mystery. Saw him off to Millbank myself, I did.'

'It appears that clerical errors were made.'

'I understand, sir.'

'No, you do not, Stubb. You do not understand any of it.'

'Of course you are probably right, sir.'

'His whereabouts in that institution are irrelevant. The problem is that the prisoner has escaped.'

'That is a new development, sir.'

For the life of him, Stubb does not know why Whitty was arrested in the first place; only last week he said so to Mr Owler, over a pint at the Tooth and Claw.

'We are given to understand that he received assistance from within,' says Salmon, darkly.

'Turnkeys are notorious for bribery, sir.'

'But in whose service? By whose order? Who had the means and the motive to penetrate Millbank and to spring a fecking journalist?'

'That is a deep question, sir. In any case, Mr Whitty's haunts in London are well known. It should be a simple matter to fetch him unless he is off to Canada.'

'Not as simple as you suppose. Thanks to the aforementioned clerical error, the escaped prisoner goes by the name of Willows.'

'I see, sir. But do we not know otherwise?'

'We cannot be seen to know otherwise. None of the affair can be traced to shortcomings in this office. I am trying to protect you, Stubb, do you not appreciate that?'

'We does our duty, sir.'

'Good.'

'Where do you wish to take it from here, sir?'

'Cast your mind back to the murder itself. The suspect is not a burly man, and is a degenerate besides. How might Whitty have overcome the victim, single-handed?'

'Perhaps he did not, sir.'

'An unacceptable conclusion. Envisage, Stubb, a conspiracy of interest between the sensational press and certain criminal elements of society. The criminal enriches himself through crime, the journalist by pandering to the public's fascination *with* crime. The two support one another – don't you see?'

'Sir, are you saying that the London underworld is made up of people in the newspaper business?'

'That is up to you to discover. First you will find Edmund Whitty, under whatever name. And when you find him, you will arrest him. I am putting you in charge, Stubb. Does that not excite you?'

'Indeed, sir, it is most exciting.'

'Of course you will not breathe a word of it – not to your colleagues, not to your associates, not even to members of your own family.'

'My lips is sealed, sir.'

'And it should be obvious that you will perform your duties out of uniform.'

'Obvious indeed, sir.' *The Sunday clothes.*

'Carry on, Stubb. When this is resolved, I shall put you up for a commendation.'

WIDESPREAD ALARM AT WHITTY DISAPPEARANCE
by
Henry Owler
Correspondent
The Falcon

The disappearance of Edmund Whitty of this newspaper following his arrest on spurious charges has raised a general fear that he has met with some misadventure at the hands of certain parties. The possibility that these malefactors are members of that service entrusted to the protection of the public has caused alarm from several quarters, including the United States Consul, Mr Tucker, who has taken a personal interest in the case.

Mr Algernon Sala, the distinguished author and editor of this newspaper, observes: 'The issue goes deeper than the disappearance of one man. The question as to the policing of the police has acquired significance beyond our borders. It speaks to the integrity of law, government, and Empire.'

17

The Alhambra Baths, Endell Street

Morning light the colour of mercury has begun to drip through the lattice shutters and trickle across the Turkey carpet. Swaddled in an ankle-length *dishdasha* and a triangular headcloth secured with a black wool rope, Khali bin Sai-ud applies a handkerchief soaked with cologne to his upper lip, while Mr Whitty gingerly peels away his soiled prison clothing

'I sometimes wonder,' remarks the proprietor of the Alhambra, 'at the stink the English can produce from the person. In the Sudan, we would smell a Briton at many paces.'

'It must be the food,' replies Whitty. 'The pity of it is, we are not insensible to smelling ourselves.'

'Mr Whitty, you remind me of a saying: *Despiseth not the reek, for it is thine own nose that contains it.*'

'There is truth in that remark. Who said it?'

'Humbly, it was myself. I have another saying as well: *To antagonise an Inspector of Scotland Yard is to balance a sharpened dagger upon the end of one's most intimate member.*'

'Enough oriental wisdom for the moment if you please, Khali. I need to cleanse myself of recent events.'

'Cleansing is advised. Given your unpopularity in certain quarters, may I ask what occasioned your release from the demons of Millbank?'

'I am at a loss to explain it – but expect that the price will not be cheap. You may think me psychic, Khali, but I believe myself to be at someone's mercy, and he is licking his lips.'

'A remarkable phenomenon, British commerce,' muses the proprietor. 'Supply and demand in the most unlikely quarters. Blessings be upon it.'

With one towel around his waist and another about the shoulders, Whitty pads across the damp marble floor of the sitting room to the bathroom, while gloomily assessing his position: on the run, penniless, under suspicion for murder, and indebted to an unknown party. Thus continues the downward spiral, with a fresh cellar beneath each seeming nadir; between periods of moist contemplation in an inferno of sweat and steam. Is he in Hell? Is this the life to come?

Wracked by uncertainty, he lies underneath a hot mound of soapy froth in a state of utter surrender, while young Ahmed silently hoes away his burden of noxious dross. A haze of herbal steam drifts lazily upward to the rounded ceiling; through its small skylight appear the shadows of surrounding buildings, and a small patch of blue. Despite the rearrangement of his brains at Millbank, he has managed to work the events of the past weeks into a plausible though superficial narrative: his persecution by a rival; his betrayal by a colleague; the psychic hanging in the window; and that beastly photograph; and their connection, however ephemeral, to the rumoured circumstance of David's death. Yet, if blackmail is to be discounted as the over-arching principle (a prisoner at Millbank being a poor source of ransom), what remains? What is to be gained, and to whose benefit?

The hideous picture of his brother infects his imagination like a worm. In despair, he closes his eyes and puts his mind to more pleasant mental pictures – of gin, pharmaceutical preparations, and Mrs Plant . . .

He hears a sound like a thickened hum. He opens his eyes and discovers that the steam has become as thick as London fog, containing stripes of coloured light as though from a stained-glass window. He wonders if he has been moved to a church, for the sound is that of a pipe organ. He rises and steps barefoot into the fog – and can see the back of the organist, a thin man in elegant black clothes. Sensing his presence, the organist turns and rises to his feet, smiling.

Somehow Whitty knows that he is confronting something unspeakable and vile. The organist approaches him with gloved hand outstretched; he turns to flee but is rooted to the spot. As the organist begins to laugh, his eyes and mouth loom larger as though distorted by a lens. The mouth yawns like a black, fetid void – the emptiness of a grave whose occupant has rotted to nothing; a warm, damp, foul emptiness pours over him; he hears someone cry for help . . .

'You were muttering in your sleep again, sir. Life is nothing but misery, deprived of restful sleep.'

This face wears a moustache and a goatee in the shape of a T – the style affected by officers in the American West who murder Red Indians . . .

The American.

This cannot be happening, thinks Whitty. It is a product of his abused, confused mind.

'Good morning Mr Whitty, sir. You are in good health, and I am very glad to see it.'

'Is that my name?'

'It is. And when you have awakened fully, you will recognise Julius Comfort – at your service once more.'

'Are you certain my name is Whitty, and not Willows?'

'Mr Willows was a pseudonym, sir. It was I who supplied it to you.'

'A pseudonym for whom?' Whitty asks, and instantly forgets the question, for a door in his mind has abruptly opened to admit an alarming sequence of events. *The seance: the Brother: the hanged man.*

The American.

'Damn you, sir, how dare you speak to me after what has occurred?'

'I see that you hold me responsible for your recent unpleasantness. I was afraid of that.'

'Do you have another "scoop" to offer me? If so, pray let me refer you to Mr Fraser of *Dodd's*.'

'A clever remark, sir. A tribute to your native resilience – what you English call *pluck*.'

As an Englishman Whitty would like to pluck out the fellow's eyes, but his susceptible mind becomes momentarily fascinated by the American's long forefinger, with a fingernail the colour of amber, pointing at his face.

'Listen to me well, for I am come for your benefit. I congratulate you, sir. You have confirmed your reputation as a man of action, and have roused the admiration of my employers.'

'And how came I to deserve this honour?'

'You rid the world of a dangerous fraud. You are a Christian soldier, and my employers salute you.'

'Good heavens. You bloody well think I murdered the man?'

'*Murder* is scarcely the correct word in your case, sir. Let it be rather said that you meted out justice where justice was due.'

Whitty lunges at the American – to be foiled by a quick sideways movement that nearly sends him sprawling onto the floor. 'I suppose it was your "employers" who effected my "escape",' he says, picking up his towel from the floor and returning it to its proper place. 'What am I to do now – emigrate to Kansas?'

The American appears about to speak, but thinks better of it. To

Whitty's surprise, he rises to his feet as though responding to an unseen command – 'You have other business, sir. I respect that.'

A quiet word, Edmund?

The voice enters his ear like the breath of a dog. A set of calloused fingers encircle his throat like a wrench. Whitty is staring at a set of black teeth, displayed in what he supposes to be a smile.

'Good morning, Norman,' he croaks. 'You seem to have found me.'

'The Captain sends his best, Edmund. His spirits were weighted by your absence. The Captain has taken some trouble in that quarter.'

'I trust your associate Will is not very far away?' Whitty struggles to articulate against the pressure on his windpipe.

'Will is with yer Arab friend. Ensuring his co-operation, like.'

Norman's grip remains firm, and Whitty must endure the fetid breath while a great weariness pours over him, for he is well and truly finished. These two gentlemen have been on his tail, on and off, for seven years. The sequence to come is as predictable as the rising sun: he prepares himself for a blow to the belly and a neddy to the noggin, the usual opening statement in a parley with the Captain's man-bashers.

Comes a familiar voice off to the side: 'All is satisfactory with the Mussulmen in back.'

Now it is Will who looms above him – Will, whose nose has been broken so many times that it is not a ridge but a flap, bone and cartilage having been pummelled to dust.

'Good to see you, Will. Surely there is no need for violence. Long-time associates – colleagues really, when you think about it . . .'

Will's hand closes over his voice-box as he takes over from Norman. 'The Captain is upset, Edmund. Cherishes his serenity, the Captain do.'

This Whitty knows to be true. To recover his serenity over an overdue obligation, the Captain once locked a man in a cage with a hundred half-starved rats for three days. For the rest of his life (about five years), the unfortunate man refused to eat rabbit, howled at the sight of any animal smaller than a dog, and was a fanatic for punctuality in all things.

'Look at him, Norman. See how he wriggles like a fish.'

'That's fear for you, Will. It turns men into the lower animals.'

'Shall we put him to sleep?'

'Yes.'

Whitty prepares for the blow, but it does not come. Instead, Will presses to his face a rag soaked with a liquid. The fumes are not altogether unpleasant, and presently he is wafted through space to an enchanted land . . .

He does not struggle. Glorious, the modern era. No need for a neddy to put a man to sleep.

A few minutes later, the larger footpad, with his naked cargo draped over one shoulder, pauses in the vestibule of the Alhambra, while the smaller man opens the door for 'Employees and Trade' slightly and peers outside.

'Sod it, Will, I see a crusher.'

'Surely not, Norman. The Endell Street patrol is not due for another ten minutes.'

'I knows that. Yet it walks like a crusher, and it gapes about like one, so it is a crusher.'

The taller man peers over the head of his colleague and out the crack in the door. 'Bloody hell. It's Inspector Salmon's bumboy.'

'So it is. I did not recognise him in plain-clothes.'

Gently closing the door, they light the ends of their cheroots and proceed to talk things through.

'Them is good clothes he has for a copper, Will. A real Sunday suit, I'll warrant.'

'This one here could use some clothes. Lord knows how he'll pay for them, tho'.'

'Aye. And yet, when such an opportunity pops up, it is a spitting on one's luck to refuse it.'

Nodding agreement, the larger man unceremoniously drops his burden: Whitty's inert body flops onto the marble floor like a wet sheet, head meeting stone with a soft thump. At a nod, Norman opens the door and the two men proceed casually down the lane to Endell Street without a glance at the figure opposite; proceeding further down the walkway, they nod good morning to the milkman as he passes, then turn down a lane in the direction of the Care Ward, discussing race results in muted tones.

Constable Stubb fidgets uneasily in his Sunday clothes as the milkman passes by, two covered pails hooked to a yoke about his shoulders. Stubb would feel much more self-assured were he in uniform, though he has brought with him his neddy and his policeman's rattle – a kind of ratchet which, when swung, will attract every Peeler in the borough.

He eyes the milkman's burden hungrily. He would not at all mind a bowlful of that fresh, wholesome liquid. It is likely to be a very long time before he has another chance, this being but the first of several localities he is to inspect for signs of Mr Whitty – his club, Plant's Inn, the family seat in Mesopotamia . . .

As the milkman's receding back approaches High Holborn, Stubb turns to hail him; at that moment, and with the improbable speed of a wild boar, a stocky figure in a long coat pounces upon his unsuspecting back, wraps a garrotte about his neck and pulls it taut, precisely above the Adam's apple so that no sound may escape. At the same time, a larger man thrusts a brine-hardened fist into Stubb's belly, then another, and proceeds to remove his coat.

This being the constable's Sunday best, the garrotting does not proceed entirely without resistance; by wriggling, pig-like, the victim manages to free one arm and to deliver a punishing blow to Will's kidney. As Norman tightens the garrotte further, the constable's fingers grip the sleeves of his coat with remarkable tenacity, so that it takes several more blows of Will's fist to persuade him to accept the loss.

'A pity to die for a suit of clothes, Jimmy,' Norman whispers into his ear, as the constable is undressed like a child and left naked in the lane, grasping feebly for his rattle, a testament to the disadvantages of plain-clothes work.

Having cleared the field, the larger footpad returns to the trade entrance of the Alhambra, while his partner proceeds to the corner to look for a cab. In the vestibule, Will heaves the insensible corre-spondent over one shoulder, then returns to the lane – where he meets with unexpected resistance from, of all things, the British Army.

'You there,' speaks the officer with white hair. 'I command you to surrender Mr Whitty and withdraw at once.'

'You are mistaken, sir,' replies the ex-pugilist, one smashed face confronting another. 'You are making a very serious mistake.'

'No mistake, sir. We have been on reconnaissance at this location for several days, with standing orders to seize that man. Our orders come from the highest quarter.'

'Be on yer way me bucko and go frig yerself.'

The lieutenant-colonel turns to the corporal. 'Good God, Mr Weeks, the fellow takes us for dirty *diddiki* like himself.'

'Native mercenary or I'll be whipped, sir.'

'Keep a watch for the stocky one while I teach this oaf a lesson.'

'Yes, sir. *Hazar*, sir!'

Advancing upon the big man with neddy raised, Robin executes a vicious swipe at the man's temple; Will dodges the blow easily and, with the economical movements of a professional athlete, taking full advantage of size and skill, promptly executes two piston-like jabs straight into Robin's face with his left fist; this he does while still carrying the unconscious Whitty over his right shoulder.

'Oh! Mr Weeks! I am down!'

Unhappily, the corporal is otherwise engaged, as Norman's forehead smashes into his face with the momentum of a cannon-ball.

'It is good that your uniform is red, sir,' Norman says for a joke, as they step over the two bleeding soldiers in the lane, heave their limp cargo onto the floor of the waiting cab, clamber inside, and shut the door.

18

Crouch Manor, Chester Wolds, Oxfordshire

Must he then only live to weep,
Who'd prove his friendship true and deep,
By day a lonely shadow creep,
At night-time languish,
Oft raising in his broken sleep
The moan of anguish?

The day having been set aside for games and photography, Boltbyn arrived at the nursery with a collection of false noses, constructed from papier mâché and of every conceivable type: the freckled snout of the Nordic, the Roman ridge of the Iron Duke, the velvety dumpling of the sot. These proved a resounding success with both Emma and Lydia – not to mention Boltbyn himself, who almost did himself damage from laughing, as all the morning a succession of grotesques paraded through the room, superimposed upon the exquisite form of a little girl.

An hour before luncheon, he brought out the puzzle of the day, in which the girls were challenged to rearrange the words NOR DO WE into one word. With the girls consumed with puzzling, Boltbyn prepared his rosewood camera, glass plates and chemicals, in order to be ready for that precious hour when the sun tips into the longer light of afternoon.

A short while later, sunlight streaming through the window in columns, he photographed the girls. They posed as wood-nymphs in white dresses with garlands in their hair; as country maids with bare shoulders and impish visages; and as the most charming beggar girls ever.

The sitting ended naturally as the sunlight entered the red end of the spectrum and then faded. By this time Miss Pouch lay slumped in her chair as though boneless, having grown drowsy from sandwiches and tea, not to mention the ether fumes that attend the preparation of every plate.

How time flies!

Suddenly it is dusk. The day is over. In a reverie of sweet regret, Boltbyn puts away his chemicals and his portable darkroom as though packing up after a picnic, while the two sisters settle luxuriantly into velvet cushions on the big couch, like angels nestled in clouds, while a gentle fog of ether wafts dreamily through their clever little minds.

He joins them on the couch, in his customary spot at the opposite end, seated upright – if anything *more* than upright – with his pocket watch, as usual, open on one knee.

Story time.

'I expect you ladies have grown accustomed to the particulars of our setting; but in case some detail escaped your attention, I shall sum up.

'Treacletown is a small, sunny settlement in the uppermost branches of an extremely ominous forest. Though constructed of the lightest building materials, the town is populated by the darkest of citizens – which became immediately evident, you will recall, when a hedgehog subjected our Emma to a bad-mannered display, about which the less said the better . . .'

'That is when I fled back down into the forest,' pipes up the older girl, unexpectedly.

'I do not recall that having been the case, Miss Emma.'

'It was. You implied it yourself. You said the magical talking tree functioned like a mechanical lift. Therefore it must have been capable of transporting a person down as well as up.'

'You seem to know a good deal more about the conveyance than I do. Would you care to continue the narration from here?'

'You don't have to be snippy. It was just a suggestion.'

'I am not being snippy. Please continue.'

'Mama says you are deaf in one ear, Mr Boltbyn,' says Lydia, who wishes to change the subject. 'Is it true?'

'I see no need to discuss either one of my ears, Miss Lydia. Miss Emma, if you have a contribution to the story please make it now.'

'It is not so much an addition as an unforeseen character.'

'And who might that be?'

Lydia groans, theatrically. 'You are diverting the story again, Emma.'

Boltbyn hesitates, sensing that Emma has begun to find the story childish and seeks to complicate matters.

As though reading his mind, Emma hops onto the floor, marches to Boltbyn's end of the couch, deposits her chin upon his knee (he must rescue his watch from falling to the floor), and looks directly into his eyes.

'Emma has a twin,' says Emma, watching the vicar's response carefully.

'How extraordinary. And what is her name?' Expecting a long detour, Boltbyn closes the lid of his watch and drops it into his waistcoat pocket.

'I do not know anything about her. At least not yet,' says Emma.

'Is it me?' asks Lydia.

'Certainly not,' replies Emma. 'You may be my sister, but you could never be my twin.'

'Tell us more about this twin,' says the vicar. 'Where did you meet her?'

'I didn't meet her, I dreamt her up. She is the subject of some verses which I wrote down and learned by heart. Would you like me to recite them?'

'Please do.'

The prospect of a poem elicits another groan from Lydia, for the story is now postponed indefinitely. She settles resignedly into the pillow while Emma recites:

> *A girl inside my looking-glass*
> *Presumes to be my twin;*
> *Tho' she is plain and I am pretty,*
> *She is plump and I am thin.*
>
> *She has freckles, I have dimples,*
> *She is tall and I am short;*
> *Her eyes squint close together,*
> *Mine do nothing of the sort.*
>
> *She insists we shared a womb,*
> *Tho' we were borne by different mothers;*
> *Yet no argument will serve*
> *To warrant one side or the other.*
>
> *So I call upon my sister dear*
> *To settle the affair,*
> *But when she peers inside my looking-glass,*
> *My twin is never there!*
>
> *Thus without a witness,*
> *My solution is no nearer;*
> *Must I forever live with*
> *An impostor in the mirror?*

The vicar nods and scratches his chin while his eyes grow moist. Emma the little girl is disappearing or, rather, is assuming a different form. Is it any wonder she imagines a twin – the grown-up Emma, whom she no longer recognises as herself?

'Very good, miss. And . . . and . . . and what inspires you to apply these admittedly fine verses to Emma's Adventures in Treacletown?'

'Perhaps the story is all a dream. Anything can happen in a dream, you know. The question is, which Emma is the dreamer, and which Emma is the dream?'

'I'm afraid I do not follow.'

Emma is not certain she understands it herself, yet she cannot resist an opportunity to tease. 'Why do you find it puzzling, sir? You once told me that the greater part of your own life is a dream.'

'Did I say that?'

'Yes.'

'Be s-so good as to sit upon the cushion and give my leg a rest.'

'Very well. Is that better?'

'Somewhat.'

Lydia stirs drowsily in her cushion, wishing to make her point before falling asleep. 'It would be nice if I made an appearance to some extent,' she says.

Having taken the floor, Emma continues the narrative in a parody of the vicar's rhetorical style. 'Encouraged by the presence of someone who might be a stranger but is at least friendly, Emma accompanies her twin up the tree to Treacletown, which, as we remember . . .'

'Yes, yes, I remember,' replies Boltbyn, somewhat snappily.

Curled up like a dormouse, Lydia has fallen into a sound sleep while her elders bicker, and Miss Pouch snores on.

'Upon their return, the two sisters meet with a quite different reception from the hedgehog, for it is a superstition in Treacletown that twins possess superior powers.'

'That is thought to be true in some quarters. But wait a moment, if you don't mind: if the girls do not resemble each other as your poem suggests, how is it that the hedgehog takes them for twins?'

Emma gropes for an answer to this reasonable caveat. 'Perhaps someone has cleverly disguised one of them to make her appear like the other. Only by looking very closely can one tell which twin is real and which one is in disguise.'

'That – that – th-that is indeed a most curious circumstance.'

'Why does it bring out your stutter, sir?'

'It does not. D-do you have an explanation for this – a reason for the deception?'

'Not yet.'

'I am trying to see where you are headed, without success. Yet Emma's Adventures can surely accommodate your presumed twin.'

'You are patronising me, Mr Boltbyn, and I do not like it.'

Lydia jolts awake: 'What is happening? Has the story gone on without me?'

'No, Miss Lydia,' replies the vicar, with an inexplicable feeling of relief, 'we have been patiently awaiting your return.'

Rising from her pillow, Lydia studies him closely. 'Mr Boltbyn, you have grown red and I fear that you are vexed.'

'Indeed, Miss Lydia, I – I – I am vexed, and I have been saving a particular item of amusement for just such a vexed occasion. Miss Emma, that was a singularly fine poem, an excellent poem, and one fine poem deserves another.'

Rising from his seat, the vicar rummages among his noses and masks and other materials until he produces two sheets of paper, and returns to the couch. After cleaning his spectacles with his handkerchief, and after clearing his throat, he reads aloud the following poem, which he wrote the previous night as the clock chimed a sleepless three.

THE BADGER AND THE MAID
by
Wallace Beverley

The brittle badger means to bite
The maiden of the moor,
With morganatic pride his wattles laden;
O forswear thou from force majeure,
Barbarian or blackamoor,
Nor shall falsely thou adjure
An aplanatic maiden!

O Maid, be not content, secure
In Innocence's sin-o-cure!

His smile is like a garden-snake,
His tongue an asphodel,
As opens he the mandibular maw;
Now tolls a ghostly gloaming bell -
O hear the phantom philomel!

Behold, foretold, the hinds of hell,
Now blooms the devil's claw!

Be chaste, the bitter-cup untaste,
Be ever-green! Be ever-graced!

'If you please, Mr Boltbyn,' mutters a groggy Lydia, 'I do not understand the meaning of *aplanatic*.'

'Spherical perfection, Miss Lydia. Perhaps you should have looked it up. That would be the s-s- – the intelligent thing to do.'

'Am I unintelligent?' Lydia turns to her sister for support.

'I said no such thing!' the vicar protests. 'Have you made any headway with our puzzle?'

In a sudden temper, Emma rises to her feet. 'Lydia's intelligence, sir, does not reside in her ability to solve your childish riddles!'

Feeling the charmed afternoon begin to disintegrate around him, he dabs his eyes with his handkerchief, replaces his spectacles and, with a sudden flourish, produces from his pocket a mechanical tortoise.

'D-do you see what this is? What do you suppose it calls itself? See how it s-sticks its neck out, wags back and forth, s-s-s-see how its little feet thrash about as though scrambling to an invisible sh-shore!'

Emma and Lydia exchange glances, for it is clear by the vicar's stutter that they have ventured upon tender ground.

'What time is it?' asks Miss Pouch – who, having awakened, gathered her knitting together and positioned herself as though that was what she was doing the whole time. 'Oh, dear, have we fiddled away another afternoon? Mr Lambert will not be pleased.'

'Not so, Miss Pouch,' replies Reverend Boltbyn, putting away his tortoise, which has not been a success. 'The afternoon has been full of s-s-surprises.'

'I'm afraid I have made Mr Boltbyn rather cross,' says Emma. 'And vice-versa.'

Boltbyn is about to make a sunny reply, a funny reply, when Emma abruptly leaves the room.

'Emma, come back this instant!' calls Miss Pouch.

'*NOR DO WE* spells "new door",' says Lydia. 'But you said it was to be one word!'

19

The Hen and Hatchet, Houndsditch

Lying in a semi-conscious state, Whitty's mind turns to the Book of Job, in which an industrious man, having led an exemplary life, is arbitrarily impoverished and infested and infected as a test of his subservience to God, so that the Creator might win a celestial bet. Which, being omnipotent and all-seeing, He won – God always does, with the exception of the Fall of Man, depending upon your catechism, or the Fall of Satan, depending upon your Milton, or the Fallen Woman, depending on your . . . *Where am I?*

Millbank Prison . . . abducted by ratters . . . assisted escape, indebted, indebted, indebted . . .

Oh dear God. His body shivers in the foetal position, naked as a newborn, draped in two damp towels, with a most adult headache.

His mind returns to Job, whose absurd outcome at least gives reason for hope. For his suffering, Job's possessions were not only restored but doubled, and he lived another hundred and forty years. From which we might draw a moral such as: *When on the receiving end of a thrashing from above, lie still and await compensation.*

The room is nearly as black as the dark cell, unless he has been struck blind. He starts to roll out of his cramped position and nearly falls over the edge of some sort of precipice. Is the squeaking coming from below?

Not to dwell upon his future, he reflects upon the past: not so many years ago, he was attacked by a rat, named Rodney, if memory serves . . .

Looking on the bright side, Whitty does not expect that he will be murdered, if only because a citizen of the next world retains no obligations in this one. Nor is the Captain likely to have him damaged in a way that will impede the practice of his profession. Injuries to the brain, eyes and fingers are unlikely; on the other hand, he can earn some sort of income without his legs or teeth.

Oh if only he had not made that one ruinous wager, committing his fortune and his future to a dog. How mortifying to admit that no loss of a loved one, no childhood horror, no spiritual crisis has ever burdened his soul so much as the money he owes to the Captain!

To some, the title 'Captain' might evoke a picture of hearty paternity, yet the reality is quite different. Any man addressed as Captain has overseen unspeakable punishments, while commanding a class of men for whom the fear of punishment is all that stands between order and bedlam . . .

Whitty clears his mind of this. He is sinking into despair when he must rise above it all.

Ecclesiastes. *All is vanity and vexation of spirit.* To every thing there is a season: a time to mourn, and a time to dance, a time to fight – and a time to lie still and await compensation.

These comforting catechisms form a small yet sturdy paper boat in which he drifts back into a half-sleep. As his mind retreats into its own dark cell, he smells shit, and spilled ale, and wet fur, and blood.

He awakens in a puddle of gaslight. What he had presumed to be a subterranean dungeon is in fact the main ratting theatre of the Hen and Hatchet, with its horseshoe-shaped, whitewashed arena, enclosed by a high wooden wall and railing: the scene of his downfall, unchanged but for its emptiness, with neither patrons nor employees present, nor the usual *mélange* of scarred, yapping mongrels and their fevered, desperate owners. He notes a six-foot cage nearby containing some two dozen rats, his serenaders of the evening – Embankment rats by the look of them, the same unwholesome breed that brought about the demise of Tiny, Whitty's terrier, the most promising ratter in the city, once the focus of his worldly hopes.

The Captain once painted a man's bare arm with lard and held it in a similar cage full of the creatures, for an hour. It is said that the gentleman now wanders the drinking-places with a hook for a hand, the sight of which turns the most brazen toff to introspection and melancholy.

Someone is watching him. It is not a rat.

In deep shadow at the far side of the arena, the watcher is seated in the high chair from which the signal is given for a small dog in a fit of excitement to be dropped among fifty rats, to kill as many as he can . . .

Rising upon one elbow, Whitty conjures up the memory of rats in the scarred wooden arena, scratching frantically at the walls, forming themselves into small barricades against the approaching monster. Having no longer any stomach for the sport, he lies back and his mind retreats to its dark cell . . .

Now it is Whitty who is standing within those arena walls scarred by claws and teeth, having shrunk to the size of a terrier, while the rats remain the size of wharf rats.

Let this be a dream!

He opens his eyes: some of it is a dream, but not all.

It is the Captain sitting over there. It must be. The high chair is, after all, his customary position – a pilot's-chair captured during the Battle of Copenhagen – from which he oversees the betting, the level of competition and the tallies, without stirring his bulk.

Whitty can discern his distinctive silhouette – like the body of a spider with a set of massive whiskers – and the glow of his meerschaum pipe. Now the figure turns sideways, drinks from a pint of liquid and wipes his beard with the back of his sleeve.

Brass it out.

'I don't suppose . . .' Whitty begins, clutching his precious towel and curling tighter into the foetal position. 'I don't suppose that a sincere apology will suffice.'

Silence. Only squeaks from the cage nearby.

'I thought not. And I expect that my heart-rending tale of misfortune and hardship is unlikely to raise a tear.'

Another silence. Whitty continues, if only to hear his own voice for the last time. 'Sir, your muteness is positively medieval. I beg you to cease the dramatic pause and proceed: bring out the whips and the pincers! Do your worst!' Having exhausted his supply of brass, Whitty begins to weep.

'Cease yer bleating, boyo, it be not manly.' The voice is ominous – how could it be otherwise?

'Confound your manliness,' Whitty replies, not being in a masculine frame of mind.

'Yer misread the position, ye glock. It does yer mind no credit.'

Whitty hears an unfamiliar note in that dreaded voice that he is at a loss to interpret. 'Are we at a tea-party, sir? Cucumber sandwiches? Scones and jam?'

'Yer be warmer there.'

'In what possible way can I be warmer?'

'Yer in luck, boyo. On the pig's back, yer be. On the sunny side o' the hedge.'

'I'm not certain I catch your meaning, sir. I'm not sure I wish to, for I suspect you are toying with me.'

'*What a fortunate man be Edmund Whitty*, I says to meself directly yer hove in view.'

'I feel somewhat less than fortunate to be frank, sir. I was hove into view by force. The evidence is before you.'

'That be the odd thing about evidence. It is an unsteady glass for seeing what is.'

For an interminable moment, the Captain refills his pipe, lights it with a lucifer, and continues:

'For an instance, I allows that a man in a suit of fashionable clothes, with a good dinner in his belly and a filly on his arm, might see yer situation in an inferior light. On the other hand, boyo, I see no fish-hook sticking out of yer eye; nor be yer fingers broken like chalk. It is true that yer be situated on a hard surface, sticky with spilled lager; but yer be not in yonder cage – which would be stickier, I expect.'

The correspondent turns sideways and permits the meagre contents of his stomach to splash upon the floorboards.

'Something 'as disagreed with yer?' The Captain partakes of another quaff of ale.

'It has been a week of disagreements, sir.'

Here the Captain raises his voice to an unseen audience. 'Lads, I believe she be time to usher Mr Whitty to his quarters.'

Recalling the Captain's penchant for understatement, Whitty thinks of the rat cage, and vomits a surprising amount of additional fluid.

'Relax, boyo. I did not pluck ye from Millbank just to feed ye to the little fellows.'

Whitty uses one of his towels to wipe a film of feverish sweat from his cheeks and brow as Will comes nearer, with his long coat and his flap for a nose, followed by his stocky companion. Both men are wearing grey wool gloves, like undertakers.

'Sleep well, boyo,' says the Captain, raising his tankard as though proposing a toast. 'In the morning we will all awaken as better men.'

The cloth descends, and Whitty re-enters the enchanted land.

20

Crouch Manor, Chester Wolds, Oxfordshire

And cannot pleasures, while they last,
Be actual unless, when past,
They leave us shuddering and aghast,
With anguish smarting?
And cannot friends be firm and fast,
And yet bear parting?

'Mr Boltbyn, I beg you to forgive Miss Emma's conduct.' Miss Pouch clings to the Reverend's favourable opinion of her like a woman overboard; Mr Boltbyn has behaved courteously and attentively to her since their first meeting; he is the only man in her memory who has seen fit to do so.

'I should check her for fever, Miss Pouch, there is a lethal ague about the district.' The vicar dons the paper nose of the Iron Duke, then abruptly whirls about and glares down its tubular bridge at Miss Lydia, who starts with fright, then giggles.

Miss Pouch backs away from the doorway. 'Of late she has become headstrong and difficult. I have requested that Mrs Lambert call Dr Briars.'

The vicar expects that Dr Briars will recommend the same tincture he gives to Mrs Lambert, and every other woman with an inexplicable nerve complaint. 'Never mind the doctor, Miss Pouch. I shall speak to her.'

So saying, Boltbyn rises from the couch and, still wearing the false nose, marches out of the nursery and downstairs.

Seated in the breakfast room (unused at this time of day and therefore a good place for a quiet moment), Emma nibbles at a leftover scone while watching Mrs Rusk count the knives on a tea-towel at the buffet. Emma cannot prevent herself from staring at the cook's sore, chapped hands.

So absorbed is Emma in the thought of how they must feel, it is the cook who takes note of the vicar's silent presence in the room. 'Hello, Mr Boltbyn, sir. May I fetch you a nice cup of tea?'

Emma does not look up from her scone, for she expected his arrival. Of late, she can predict Mr Boltbyn's responses as accurately as she can predict what will happen if one pulls the tail of a cat. Without looking up, she expects, knows, that he will have entered the room in some sort of disguise, and that he will put on a funny voice, to ease the tension.

'Explicate, young lady, the meaning of such an inelegant withdrawal.' The vicar speaks in the nasal honk of a cartoon commodore. She knows without looking that he has chosen the Wellington nose.

She also knows that the point of the performance is to reveal, and yet *not* reveal, that she has hurt his feelings. Soon the strain will get the better of him and he will stutter. It seems that this defect has appeared more often, of late. Likewise, the air between them is frequently brittle and thin. Emma wishes she understood what is happening.

'I left, sir, because you snapped at my sister, when you should have snapped at me instead. For it was I who vexed you.'

'Wh-which . . .'

There, thinks Emma.

'What you say may or may not be true,' Boltbyn replies. 'Yet I wonder: who vexed whom?'

Emma catches the metre and replies, 'Why did the maiden shirk the groom?'

'Did the vicar . . .'

'Start to snicker?'

'Will she beat him with a broom?'

It does him good to see her laugh at his rhyme, though it was rather weak. 'We were saying,' he continues, 'something about being vexed.'

'I was perplexed by your poem, sir. Was there something in particular you wished to say to me through it? Am I in some sort of danger? If so, why do you not simply say it?'

'No, it was only a p-p-p- . . .'

'A piece of fancy?'

'Yes.'

Boltbyn removes his spectacles to make use of his handkerchief. After a pause, Emma gets up from her chair, walks to his side and puts her hand upon his sleeve, with an almost maternal expression on her face. 'Don't be troubled, Mr Boltbyn,' she says. 'Don't be sad.'

'I do not know you any more.' (How absurd he feels, babbling like a rejected swain, with a pathetic smile as a brace for his lip.) 'I have watched you change week by week, each change more startling than the last. Now you are nearly a-a-a woman.'

'You are a mathematician, sir. Surely you have a knowledge of numbers, and can count.' Emma smiles teasingly. 'Don't you remember my eleventh birthday? You came to my party, and we ate cake, and you brought me an acrostic poem.'

> *Elastic as a bouncing ball,*
> *Momentary as a rhyme;*
> *Memorable as summertime,*
> *Ageless as a waterfall –*
>
> *Emma shall defy the beast,*
> *Lick it with her biting tongue;*
> *Abiding it in one mind at least,*
> *Maiden shall be ever young;*
> *Beaming from both West and East,*
> *Even past when even sung,*
> *Radiating without cease,*
> *Thro Winter's fall, till summer's sprung.*

'My goodness! You remember it still!'

'Of course I do. In the first verse my name is spelled both down and up. Then my last name, with my first name in-between the two, like a fence. It was ever so clever of you.'

'I should not have gone to such bother were you named Hyppolita.'

'You gave me a Chinese chess game. It is in the study. Would you like to play?'

'No Chinese chess at present, thank you.' Emma's face has become blurry again. The vicar takes off his spectacles and cleans them with his handkerchief.

'I think I shall find thirteen an uncomfortable age,' she continues. 'Some people want you to be a grown-up woman, while others want you to remain a little girl.'

He replaces his spectacles – much clearer now. 'I confess myself to be of the latter persuasion. If you'd asked my advice I'd have told you to leave off at eleven.'

'One should never ask advice about growing up,' Emma says.

'Do you mean that one should be whatever one has become – notwithstanding?'

'I mean that one cannot help growing older, and one must make the best of it.'

'That is true. But even so, I think it is a mistake,' says the vicar, and at last removes his nose.

'Here is your tea, sir,' says the cook, setting the cup and saucer before him. 'A nice cup of tea is the very thing.'

'The very thing,' replies Boltbyn.

Emma looks at Mrs Rusk's dry, reddened hands – will they be her hands, one day?

The Hen and Hatchet, Houndsditch

He is in a bed. Under an actual blanket, though it is a rough one. Oh the luxury of it! *But where are my towels?*

Rigid with panic, Whitty gropes about the mattress, and is pathetically relieved to lay his hands upon his souvenirs of the Alhambra – his friends, neatly folded beneath his pillow.

Now that his eyes are open, he looks about the room, only to encounter the ruined features of the brawnier of the two man-bashers, drawing closer, and arranged in what Will seems to think is a pleasant expression. Will holds a tray before him containing a teapot and a mug; there is a napkin draped over one arm.

Obviously, Whitty is in a delirium.

To his right, he hears an unmistakable rustling sound. Turning his head, he spots two examples of *rattus norvegicus,* gliding along the wallboard as though mounted on tiny wheels. They disappear through an improbably small aperture in the cracked plaster and it occurs to him that rats have a collapsible skull . . .

Where did he learn that?

Of course, rats were bound to enter his dream at this point. Rats, or snakes, or the two together.

'Do not mind the rats, Edmund. An amount of escapers is inevitable. Nothing to be done I fears – poison will find its way to the main stock, don't y'see.'

Will sets the tea-tray upon a small dressing-table; brushing away a tangle of cobwebs with his napkin, he exposes a mirror.

'Quite,' Whitty hears himself reply, as he contemplates Will's reflection. So realistic, this dream, one could stay in it for life.

'I'll warrant ye slept well. Nothing like a whiff of the chemical for a sound sleep.'

'It was much appreciated, sir.' Whitty humours the apparition, to keep things pleasant.

''Tis enfeebling to lose one's sleep. Life loses its lustre.'

'That has been my experience as well.'

Will hands him a mug of tea, on which he scalds his lips and tongue . . .

O heavens! I am awake!

Seeing his horrified expression, Will executes a travesty of a smile.

Frantically, Whitty peers about the room, while waiting for his mind to clear. 'I do not see your colleague, sir. Surely not a falling-out between you?'

'Nothing of the sort, Edmund. Norman is on an errand concerning a welsher – a Scotsman by the name of Menzies. Slip a rat down his trousers and it will set him right.'

'A rat named Rodney, I presume.'

'They is all named Rodney when used to that express purpose.'

'A sort of pun, I suppose.'

'A pun? How so, sir?'

'Spare the Rod and spoil the child, sort of thing.'

'Very good, sir! Good cut!' The big man explodes with laughter, disturbing the flap on the front of his face, and affording Whitty an unwelcome glimpse of two small holes, firing like a fowling piece.

Shifting his gaze hastily to one side, he observes a suit of clothes draped upon a three-legged chair next to the dressing-table. A small rat reclines on one shoulder, like an epaulet.

'That is a fine suit of clothes, Will.'

'A real Sunday suit,' replies the man-basher. 'Its owner fought hard to keep it.'

The Sunday suit does not fit, most notably in the area of the crotch – which binds intolerably, so that he must reach back to retrieve the rough moleskin from between his buttocks, or suffer the torment known to Napoleon as the ring of fire. The adjustment is in itself an uncomfortable procedure, for the armholes of the jacket have been cut too high, imposing an unnatural limit to his reach. The collar smells of macassar, a cheap pomade combining orange peel and sheep fat, while the underarms smell of old cheese. He does not wish to know what the trousers smell like. Overall, he much preferred his towels.

Seated at the opposite end of a black table, the Captain smokes his yellow meerschaum pipe, no doubt contemplating Whitty's future. It has been years since their last encounter in daylight, yet it seems to Whitty that our man has aged well beyond that. The eyes glitter with moisture and are shot with tiny red rivulets. This is not a well man.

'I see the lads found yer a suit, boyo.'

'They did, sir. It was most appreciated.'

'The cost will be charged to yer account.'

'Only to be expected.'

The two men contemplate each other in a silence which stretches like a slingshot aimed at Whitty's forehead. Were he to look into a mirror he would not be the least surprised to find that his hair has turned white. Yet in this cavernous silence, a curious thing happens: terror, pushed past its limit, is superseded by curiosity.

The Captain did not go to the expense of retrieving him from Millbank, solely in order to punish him. And he spoke of an 'account'. Unless, of course, Whitty was dreaming at the time . . .

In a pause with an adversary, never break the silence. The advice enters Whitty's mind unexpectedly; he has no idea who said it.

He peers about this narrow, low-ceilinged room, the private quarters of a man of the sea, whose far wall is entirely covered by a ragged, sun-bleached man-of-war flag. As well, the dark wooden shelves are filled with models of ships in astonishing variety, from sloops to galleons, white with dust, all headed in the same direction like a squadron of ghost ships. Above them, a number of brass storm lamps hang from the black ceiling beams.

Every other horizontal surface is stacked high with books, and more piled on the Turkey carpet; though Whitty cannot read the titles, this unexpected love of literature casts the Captain in an unfamiliar light.

Behind every object in the room he senses movement – a nervous rustle beneath piles of newspapers, an industrious rattle in the coal-box, and a sound like an army of tiny charwomen, scrubbing. As his eyes adjust to the murky light, the creatures assume an all too familiar shape – the arched back, the hairless tail . . .

The Captain gestures to a chair by the table. 'Come closer,' he says.

Whitty sees the holes in the chair's upholstery, and the movement within. 'Thank you, sir, but I prefer to stand.'

'Ah, the rats. They be part of the establishment. Yer can't poison 'em . . .'

'Or the poison will find its way into the stock. This was explained to me.'

'And bringing in cats would interfere with the dogs, don't ye see. We trap the vermin as best we can, but the buggers breed remarkably.'

Whitty attempts no reply, nor is he any more inclined to take a seat.

'Now we stow the banter and hove to our purpose,' the Captain says, turning his gaze to the back of the room. 'Dermot! Come and speak up, boyo! Yer be in the discussion now.'

Shocked that there has been a third individual present without his knowledge, Whitty turns, to face a tall, thin, silent gentleman standing immediately behind him. He flinches, half-expecting to be felled by a neddy; instead, the figure extends a hand at the end of a thin, hairless wrist. Whitty shakes the hand, whose fingers are surprisingly strong, like the tentacles of a squid.

'Good day to you, sor.'

Everything about the man is long. Even his head seems attenuated, as though shaped by a potter, then topped with a thatch of hair, and the body reminds Whitty of a stoat on its hind legs.

'This be Dermot, boyo. Dermot Abbott of the Mint. Downy Dermot, as familiars knows him. And a knowing card I warrant, best snakesman in London, best hand with a rook or jemmy, enter any toff-ken with ease. Runs in the family, am I not correct, Dermot?'

'Aye, Captain, that is so. And coal-mining, a narrow occupation as well.'

'More danger and less pay, I'll wager.'

'That may or may not be so, sor.'

'In any case, you have made use of your bloodlines to good effect.' Whitty notes that the Captain seems genuinely impressed by the fellow.

'Conceptably so,' replies the snakesman.

If only to keep things chummy, Whitty joins in. 'Permit me to introduce myself, sir. Edmund Whitty of *The Falcon*.'

Dermot breaks into a smile, and again grasps Whitty's hand in a tangle of strong fingers. 'Mr Whitty, sor, it is with memorial gratification we make your reunion in the flesh.'

'Excuse me, but have we met?'

'Perhaps not. Yet I am obligated to you and your coverage of the Bertram case in '56.'

'Please remind me. I write many articles about court cases and they blur in my memory.'

'Summer of '55: we was nibbed for lifting the analytical engine from Mr Bertram's offices on Chancery Row. A machine of great value, said to calculate at a devilish velocitation.'

'You stole a machine?'

'Perhaps so, perhaps not.'

'I appreciate your caution, sir. Continue.'

'Would of been fourteen years cut and dried for us, if not for yer Amateur Clubman notating that Mr Bertram sold the machine before we was said to have stole it.'

Whitty now remembers – vaguely, for he was deeply into the

laudanum in '56. 'Bertram. Ah, yes. Are you referring to Chauncy Bertram, known for defrauding assurance companies by means of bogus thefts and fires? I believe he was transported to Van Diemen's Land, so it seems justice was served.'

'Excepting that we did steal the machine.'

'I beg your pardon?'

'We stole it. Yet we stole nout from Mr Bertram.'

'Are you telling me that I helped to convict an innocent man?'

'Oh no, sir. We stole the machine *for* Mr Bertram, and substituted it for the one he himself sold, don't you see. A variety of the bait-and-switch.'

'In other words, you replaced the original engine with a machine of no value.'

'No, the original engine were not worth the metal it were made of to begin with. We was the intended victim, sor, of that you may be sure.'

Whitty heaves a sigh. The thing keeps convoluting – complicated by the distorted vocabulary of an intelligent illiterate, who envisages more than he can express.

'It is the very devil for an independent operator these days,' offers the Captain. 'A city operator will top him every time. Dermot were victimised on an assurance flam, but he be safe with us, now. And we have the benefit of his uncommon mind.'

'Congratulations, Mr Whitty, sor,' says Downy Dermot. 'With the Captain you has retinued yorself with an employer what is firm but fair.'

'Excuse me, sir, but I am not aware of having been employed by anyone.'

'Nobody ever is,' says the snakesman.

'One moment, gentlemen,' interjects the Captain. 'We be getting ahead of ourselves. Dermot, report to Mr Whitty what we has discussed.'

'Certainly, sor. It concerns the operation at the Monkton Milnes establishment, 37 Holywell Street, on Tuesday last. The work took six assistants and a preparation of three months twelve days.'

Whitty recognises the address as that of a pornography establishment which was raided last year. Peelers confiscated near a thousand books, and four times that number of prints. The loss kept Wynyard out of business for all of one week. This and other seizures inspired Parliament to pass the Obscene Publications Act, in which any magistrate can order the destruction of an 'obscene publication' at will.

'Mr Abbott, if I may interrupt, how have prices for the commodity stood this season?'

'Mr Whitty, you are a discernible one. Indeed, the Obscene Publications Act is a windfall for the industry. Retail prices has tripled – and photographs? One issue of *The Exquisite* fetches as much as a guinea.'

'Smutty pictures are more valuable per pound than most jewellery,' adds the Captain.

Whitty knows this to be true – in fact, last winter he tried to profit from it himself, by dashing off an item for *The Boudoir* (under a pseudonym of course). As with other attempts to stoop for easy money, he discovered how the skills essential for one trade – literate English prose – can be a detriment in another. 'Lacks spontaneity and gusto,' sniffed the editor, by which he meant that the story was told in complete sentences and not a series of grunts and groans.

Raped on the Railway having received the same response from several others, Whitty consigned it to the fire one draughty night when he was out of coal, along with an epistolary romance, rejected as insufficiently heart-warming. Huddled over the small flame, he consoled himself that, contrary to criticism received, the work was worth the paper it was written on.

'Should we continue, Captain?' Dermot enquires, as though broaching a touchy subject.

'Do so.' The Captain's face takes on the hollow look of a man bereaved, whereupon the snakesman proceeds to recite a full account of the stolen inventory, with the prodigious memory common among men who cannot write memoranda.

'The operation at Monkton Milnes yielded, in quantities of printed matter, 247 volumes – sorted according to Sodomy, Incest, Buggery, Rogering, Rape, Flagellation, as well as the fashionable French Vices. It were a singularly profitable run.'

'Profit,' echoes the Captain, bitterly, and downs a quantity of rum.

'*Tales of Twilight* alone fetches two guineas at competing establishments,' continues Dermot. '*The Jesuit and the Nun* fetches six, being illustrated.'

Whitty has begun to grasp the magnitude of the spoils – clearly, nothing short of robbing a bank might yield such value. He examines the captain's newly-acquired library, scanning the titles, leafing through volumes at random, with a sense of wonder at the variety with which a man can accomplish such a simple, animal objective.

'To what proclivity does this one appeal, Dermot?' he asks. '*Sub-Venus – or Sport Amongst the She-Noodles?*'

'Four guineas it fetches among the poofsters what dress as Chinese.'

The Captain interrupts: 'Go forward to the main point, Dermot, what leads to Mr Whitty's presence today.'

'Begging pardon, Captain?'

'The photograph, Dermot!'

'Very well, sor. To begin, the photographs represented the greatest value, congregated as five gross at two guineas a print, many smuggled from France in Embassy bags . . .'

'The *photograph*, boyo! Must I say more?'

'Begging pardon, sor,' replies the snakesman. 'As you knows, gentlemen, of all products with that class of appeal, the photograph is the most precious. Only in a photograph may the buyer be assured that the thing depicted were actually carried out, don't you see, that he has not been duped by fiction nor sleight-of-hand. Whether it be rogering or buggering or what-have-you, in a photograph it is a fack that the thing has been done –'

'Enough!' The Captain rises from his seat like a tottering Colossus. 'Only *one* photograph need concern yer! Listen the both of ye! Only one picture! Downy Dermot Abbott, present the thing to Mr Whitty at once!'

Nodding solemnly, the snakesman reaches into his coat pocket and hands Whitty a postcard.

A naked girl lies on a couch, spread out in such a way as to leave no doubt as to what is expected. From the spectator's assumed point of view, the position is unambiguous, though the face is set in an expression that is anything but a welcome. The background is a painted wall, a study in oriental pretentiousness.

'It is part of a series,' Dermot observes with a professional aspect, retrieving a bundle of photographs. 'Must of arrived at the shop recently by our reckoning, for they was stacked at random and was not yet classified.'

Whitty rifles through the stack of photographs quickly as though it were a deck of cards: the images appear to move, as though they depicted a single, continuous act, performed by a girl of between ten and twelve, partially or wholly naked, in various situations both predictable and bizarre.

'Clearly it is the work of an amateur photographer,' observes Whitty. 'The lighting is mediocre, and the focus slightly off . . .'

'The photographs be of my niece.'

Whitty takes in this information, then turns to the Captain, whose eyes glitter with tears. 'I am very sorry to hear that, sir,' he says. 'It is a great pity when a young girl enters that sort of a life.'

'The girl were kidnapped,' Dermot corrects him. 'That is the problem, don't you see.'

'What the devil do you mean, *kidnapped*?'

'Ye glock, is there more than one meaning?' cries the Captain. 'My Eliza be stolen from me and her body made into a . . . a privy, for . . . O Jesus!' The Captain finishes his rum and pours another. 'That is why you, my delinquent Mr Whitty, have not been kneecapped and put in the cage with the stock. Because yer be of use to me, boyo, d'you wish it otherwise?'

'Not in the least, sir. I am entirely at your service.'

'Good.'

The Captain calms somewhat, while his new employee examines the photographs more carefully. They were taken by the Archer process, with not a daguerreotype among them – hence, they are not French.

Notoriously difficult to execute, the Archer, thinks Whitty, requiring a higher level of expertise than this particular photographer possesses. Reluctantly he turns his attention from the background to the subject, avoiding as best he can the naked body of the captain's niece. Though lacking in expression, the face is quite beautiful – a real English rose, just beginning to bloom, intelligent eyes and a smooth brow beneath the dark curls . . .

Now the realisation comes: *It is she.*

She. The same girl. The girl in the picture with David, the same hair, the same brow, the same expression, the same girl . . .

'Dear Jesus.'

'Well said, boyo, it is a shocking thing.'

Whitty looks closer at the face, and now he is trembling. He cannot speak, he can only stare at the girl, for it is the same girl. He inspects the other pictures in the stack – the girl, the focus, the oriental wallpaper, are all the same, exactly the same.

'When did you last see your niece?' he asks.

'Two weeks ago.' The Captain's face starts to crumple like a leaf.

Two weeks ago, thinks Whitty. And David in his grave these six and a half years.

MORE QUESTIONS IN THE WHITTY AFFAIR
by
Henry Owler, Correspondent
The Falcon

The disappearance of Edmund Whitty of The Falcon *grows more mysterious by the day.*

Having been at last located in Millbank Prison, where he was held captive on spurious charges amid a tangle of 'clerical errors', upon investigation it appears that one of two things has occurred: either he was never there at all, or he has vanished once again. As ever, Inspector Salmon of Scotland Yard has proved singularly unhelpful.

After questions were raised in Parliament, Inspector Salmon has been excused from duty with pay, pending a resolution of the matter.

In the meanwhile, the Whitty affair appears to have acquired international significance.

Concern has been expressed by the Consulate of the United States, alerting Britons to the presence in their midst of a colonial celebrity. In the years following the Chokee Bill affair, Mr Whitty has become a hero of what is known as the 'penny dreadful' – a species of periodical more fanciful than the sensational monthlies, but which has nonetheless assumed a position of serious influence in colonial affairs.

'For many Americans Mr Whitty has become a symbol of the best of our race,' attests Mr Julius Comfort, an American businessman with close ties to the Consulate. 'Mr Whitty is, in a way, an unofficial ambassador. Should his loss be attributable to some official malfeasance, it could invite an inauspicious response overseas, and a chill in the good relations between our two countries.'

The Hen and Hatchet, Houndsditch

He has thoroughly examined the photographs of the Captain's misfortunate niece. He now knows Eliza with an anatomical intimacy he has never aspired to with any woman, and has made liberal use of the Captain's bottle in the process.

He has even retained one of the dreadful images for purposes of identification; after all, it would be the height of imprudence to reveal the existence of another photograph in his possession – of David and Eliza, obscenely linked, years after his death. He resolves to keep this matter to himself for the time being.

To Whitty, the notion that one might derive satisfaction from a photograph is a puzzle. Not that he is unmoved by a well-turned ankle, or the swelling of a bosom over a fringe of décolletage. Nor has he lacked curiosity as to what lies beneath the layers of wool, lace, whalebone and cotton. Yet it has never occurred to him to ask Mrs Plant to show him an intimate part of her anatomy. Not that she would comply; on the contrary, she might take the coal-scuttle to him.

He imagines the relation between a photograph and a living woman to be akin to a dream. As Downy Dermot indicated, a photograph is not like a painting or etching, which depicts an image in the mind of the artist; rather, its purpose is to create an event in the mind of the spectator – a dream, bought and paid for by the dreamer.

The picture of naked Eliza in David's company has the quality of a dream, not least because it could not possibly occur in waking life; yet Whitty saw it with his own eyes, visible evidence that the thing was done.

On the bright side, he has shared the Captain's bottle; on the dark side, he has had to endure the dismally common tale of his wayward niece.

Still, it is an incalculable relief to be, for the moment, without fear. Dermot having left on other business, relations between the correspondent and the Captain have assumed the quality of old comrades-at-arms.

'Eliza be the youngest girl of my brother Tom. Tom were into the horses at Tattersall. Took a fall over the Running Rein affair, pickings very lean. Eliza be given me for raising – Tom thought me well suited, Eliza having much spirit and mischief in the eye. Thought I might steer her on a safer course, avoid the worst. Which I failed to do, to my shame.'

The Captain takes a drink of rum. Whitty joins him.

'I am familiar with the type, sir,' he says. 'A pity there exists no place in society for spirited young women but as whores or actresses or suffragettes.'

'*Whore* would be the correct word in this case, I fear. The villains will have her locked in a brothel on Lewkner Lane by now.'

'It is shocking, the increase of child-brothels throughout White-chapel. It is more shocking to think that one may be acquainted with their customers.'

'Now, boyo, I have a piece of the business meself, and the clients be worthy gentlemen on the whole.'

'Quite.' Whitty chooses not to highlight the Captain's double standard at this time. 'Why are you so certain that Eliza was kidnapped?'

'Days before, she spoke of being followed – by uniformed men, she said. I put it down to soldiers on the randy.'

'Might she have gone with them willingly?'

'No, she were repulsed by the ugliness of them. In any case, were she of a mind to run off to such a life, I would know from my people in the trade. No, she were nicked, for certain. These days there are parties who will fetch a good-looker to order. I have dealt with them meself . . .'

As the Captain's face again begins to crumple, Whitty searches for an uplifting phrase. 'A good-looker she certainly is, sir. And a clever, resourceful child, I have no doubt.'

'Oh, Eliza were a bright one, that is the truth. Could read and write I'll warrant, though I cannot reckon where she learned it. And count? In the ring downstairs, the girl could compute the odds on a mongrel faster than meself – and she but a tadpole, not yet twelve! Were she a boy I'd of had him in a situation inside of an hour, off the streets and out of trouble's way. Yet I did not. And for that I let her fall into the hands of . . . don't ye see . . .'

At the memory of what he did not do, tears again fill the eyes of this terrifying old warrior, who employs man-bashers with razors in their boots in every part of the city, yet was powerless to protect his own flesh and blood.

Whitty searches for a comforting noise with which to break the silence. 'It is not possible to raise a girl as though she were a boy. Society will not permit it. Persons who live as the opposite gender face a dismal life.'

'Not so dismal as what were done to Eliza.'

'That is true.'

The old man is weeping openly now. Though unnerved by the sight, Whitty takes a deep breath and dives into the main issue. 'It is time for us to speak plainly, sir. How may I be of assistance to you?'

'Go to the bottom of it, the sorry tale of my girl, like it were one of yer reports. I'll warrant yer people will pay ye, bad news is popular and the worse the better. Sufficient is my need, that upon learning of what was done and who done it, yer debt will be forgiven. Yer free and clear, boyo, free and clear.'

Words entirely foreign to Whitty's understanding: *free* and *clear*.

'And if I refuse, or fail?'

To judge by the look he receives, there is no need to probe further. 'Quite.'

'We will absorb all reasonable expenses.'

'May I have another drink of rum?'

'Ye may.'

The Captain's offer, though compulsory, seems more than fair – and all else aside, Whitty truly wants to know; not for the Captain, for himself.

Father is in California – which is to say, on the moon. Mother is in Heaven. David's bones reside in St Marylebone, his restless soul at an undisclosed location perhaps last seen at Buckingham Gate.

Edmund the disgrace, Edmund the disappointment, is the last Whitty alive and kicking in London. And will remain so – if only to spite them all.

23

The Falcon

'Edmund! I had begun to despair! Come here, sir, and let me embrace you!' In a fit of emotion, Sala manages to pry himself out of his chair, lumber around the desk, and envelop the correspondent in a voluminous blanket of moist tweed.

'Most touching, Algy. Please relinquish me now, and give me a cigar.'

Cream watches the spectacle with revulsion, and says nothing.

Whitty accepts a light, seats himself on Sala's desk, and puffs his cigar. It is a moment to savour; the year has contained few such moments.

'You must reveal all, old trout. Everything you endured must appear on the pages of *The Falcon*. Name your price, sir . . .' Sala pauses, thinking twice about that last statement; while doing so, he notes Whitty's appearance.

'That is a novel suit of clothes, Edmund. Ill-smelling and ill-fitting at the same time.'

Whitty selects a second cigar from Sala's humidor, which he puts in his chest pocket for later. 'It is the latest fashion – the accustomed look. The line of the jacket and trousers have been redefined by the French.'

'One never knows with fashion,' Sala muses, cleaning his monocle with the tail of his shirt. 'I have yet to understand what my wife means by the sentimental look, other than fabric draped over everything living and dead, in ruinous abundance.'

Cream peeps over his copy of *Dodd's*. 'Perhaps Mr Whitty is attempting to emulate his colleague, Mr Owler – the costermonger look, in preparation for his next occupation.'

'Shut your cake-hole, Mr Cream,' says the editor.

Whitty leans over the desk and speaks in a confidential tone, sufficiently loud for the sub-editor to overhear. 'Actually, old chap,' he whispers, 'I am incognito.'

'What the devil do you mean, *incognito*?'

'If one is to infiltrate the criminal classes, one must appear as one of them. You're an old hand, Algy, surely this is obvious.'

'Yes, I suppose it is.'

'Linger in the Hen and Hatchet with the clothes and manners of a newspaperman, and you will likely get a shiv in the belly.'

'The Hen and Hatchet? Not gambling on the rats again, surely?'

'Certainly not. However, past experience with that odious sport has put me in touch with certain parties.'

'What sort of parties?'

'Can I depend upon your discretion?'

'Really, Edmund, you affront me with your suspicions. My God, we rowed on the same eight!'

'Please keep your voice down, sir, my life would not be worth a shilling if this reached the wrong ears,' whispers Whitty.

'Quite,' the editor whispers back. Sala's leonine head is now so close to his face, Whitty can smell the kipper he had for breakfast.

'I have established a connection between the affair of Dr Gilbert Williams (in which I found myself entangled, to my cost), and a notorious pornographer on Holywell Street.'

'The devil, you say!'

'Again, Algy, I must ask you to keep your voice down.'

'Sorry, old chap, but if what you say is true, it is a stunner of the first water.'

'I quite agree. For it appears that blackmail lies at the heart of it. The medium in question had managed to entice members of the upper classes into his circle. In due course, the prospect of scandal loomed over several parties.'

'By Jove, that might be a motive for murder, I should say.'

'Indeed, you have got to the crux of it.'

'Please continue your narrative, old chap, my heart is in my mouth.'

'First, there are practicalities to discuss – if I may assume this to be of interest to *The Falcon*. I beg you not to feel pressured by our friendship; other publications have expressed keen interest.'

'Believe me, Edmund, *The Falcon* stands foursquare behind your project.'

'To the tune of, shall we say, a £30 advance?'

Sala grows pale. 'Are you jesting? Have you taken leave of your senses?'

Whitty well knows that every shilling invested in a narrative must be defended before Mr Ingram and his corps of little shits. 'Twenty-five is the lowest I can manage. At that price, I forgo a more generous offer from *Lloyd's*.'

'Fifteen.'

'Twenty. And expenses.'

'On approval.'

'Not to be unreasonably withheld.'

'Done. I pray, Edmund, that you come up with something more than a shell-game of miscellaneous facts. This has occurred before, might I say.'

'To set your mind at rest, I am prepared to reveal that in three days' time – Thursday afternoon to be exact – I am to meet a gentleman named Will at the Hen and Hatchet, to whom I shall present myself under the name Menzies. I am then to ask for a Mr Rodney – a gentleman who has plumbed the very depths of that filthy industry, and is prepared, for a price, to reveal its inner workings in stunning detail – including the involvement of our deceased medium, and his subsequent demise.'

'I say, old chap, that sounds absolutely splendid!'

Behind his copy of *Lloyd's*, Cream takes copious notes: *Thursday Afternoon. The Hen and Hatchet . . .*

Fraser will pay well for the *nom de guerre* of Menzies, and for access to the party by the name of Rodney.

24

Bissett Grange, Oxfordshire

Sister, do not raise my wrath
I'll cook you into mutton broth
I'll kill you easy as a moth.

Since the move from Upper Clodding, Birdie has rarely been out of the house except to go to church. As a result, a carriage ride at a gallop is an unnerving experience. She can barely look out the window of the brougham as it rattles up the long driveway to Bissett Grange, for the elms are a blur and she must sometimes hold her breath not to cry out. Turning her head to the left, she beholds the equally unnerving sight of her husband looming above her; the air in the carriage is sticky with clove oil, an ingredient in the emulsion he rubs into his gums for the toothache.

Seated opposite, Emma watches her mother for signs of panic. It is the first time since the move that she has forgone use of her veil. Certain of Father's disapproval, Mother enlisted Emma's help, and together they wound the veil of transparent muslin into her hair, so that it appears as an adornment and nothing else. 'It need not cover my face,' she said. 'But I need to know it is there.'

'Mother, will I be as beautiful as you?' asked Emma.

'Yes you will,' said her mother, 'and you will manage it much better than I have.'

Emma hopes so, for she does not wish to live the way her mother does. If it is true that one is a combination of both forebears, she wonders where in her do Father's traits reside. With Lydia it is obvious, having Father's long, straight nose and, it seems to Emma, his impatience with description and poesy. Emma, on the other hand, is a dreamer like Mother, with what Mr Boltbyn calls the power of fantasy.

'Lydia,' she whispers to her sister. 'I just looked out the window and I saw a ghost.'

'You did not,' whispers her sister. 'There are no ghosts.'

'Look for yourself and see.'

'I don't believe you,' replies Lydia, who cannot resist looking out the window nonetheless. 'But I see two deer by the copse.'

'Where?' Emma must admit that her sister has the sharper eyes, though whether they come from Father or Mother she cannot tell.

Meanwhile opposite, Birdie shuts her eyes, the better to drift from one thought to the next and to ignore the smell of clove oil.

The entire village of Upper Clodding turned against her when she married the Rev. Lambert – including, it must be said, Lambert himself. It seems that, for a man of the cloth, female beauty is best appreciated in the dark of an empty church. The memory of her fall from grace is entirely without a visual component – just the feel of his hands upon her, the scent of sweat as he removed his wool coat, the snort at the end . . .

In the Bible, the greater sinner was Eve, who not only succumbed to temptation, but sided with the serpent to tempt Adam. Not entirely fair, Birdie thinks, given that the serpent was *attached* to Adam. She stifles a giggle with a cough.

'Are you not well, Mrs Lambert?'

'I am well enough, thank you, Mr Lambert.'

'Do you expect to be coughing at dinner? Otherwise it might be better for you to rest at home.'

'I have no intention of coughing.'

'See that you do not, madam, or I shall regret having brought you.'

'I think you regret it already.'

Emma listens with eyes closed, or she will get a lecture on eavesdropping. She feels as though, for most of their lives, she and her sister have acted as spectators at a fencing tournament. Between matches, Father works on improving his game, while Mother rests in her bedroom.

'You are intoxicated, madam. You have taken opium, have you not?'

'I took some Godfrey's Cordial. You yourself said it would calm me and that I should.'

'Not half the bottle. How much have you on your person?'

'None. Do you wish to paw through my things, for reassurance?'

Emma knows that a gentleman would never stoop to opening a lady's purse, therefore Mother has won the round.

Birdie smiles to herself, for she has become better at answering back – a result of her increased reading. At first, her husband confined her to the Bible and editions of the great sermons; when she turned to poetry he would want to know what it was, as though a poem must be sniffed for poison before one ate it. But the reading did her good, and he grew weary of screening her selections.

The coach comes to a halt; after a short pause the carriage door swings away, the step is lowered, and a uniformed, powdered footman hands down Emma and her sister, while in the dark of the carriage Lambert gives his wife the benefit of some last-minute advice: *Do not touch a utensil in advance of the host. Do not speak unless spoken to. You are not excused by your ignorance of proper manners . . .*

Standing on the magnificent portico, Emma and Lydia stare up at the house, eyes wide in disbelief. It is a dream-house – a knight's castle and a theatre and a haunted mansion all in one. It is the most wonderful house Emma has ever seen and she would like ever so much to explore it.

Climbing the steps, Birdie stumbles on her unaccustomed heels; a footman's gloved hand steadies her, while Lambert springs smartly forward to take her arm.

When the family has gathered at the front door it swings as though of its own accord and, before them, framed by the open doorway and back-lit by gaslight, stands the most high-born gentleman in the shire, with the most land and the most money and the purest, most precious blood, who gave Emma a rose in front of everyone.

'Good evening, your Grace,' Emma says, as instructed. 'I have brought you a book, as you requested.' From the pocket of her dress she produces an edition of the sermons of John Henry Newman, wrapped with a blue ribbon.

The duke accepts the book with a cordial smile and hands it on to a footman. 'Extraordinary girl,' he says, to no one in particular. Behind her, Father murmurs agreement – after all, the book was his selection.

Now the Duke of Danbury's attention turns to Mrs Lambert. Birdie tries not to flinch as he moves forward and extends a tailored arm to the wife of the most prominent guest. 'Mrs Lambert. My compliments to you.'

The Reverend relinquishes her arm to the duke, and the nobleman conducts them into his house. Birdie notes how he remains focused entirely upon on her, as though she were all that mattered, and she basks in the unaccustomed warmth of his attention. To avoid committing an indiscretion, however, she confines her own gaze to the maroon carpet. Only when they enter the reception room does she dare look at his sculptured profile. To think that, if she dared, she could plant a kiss upon that cheek!

'Is there something you find amusing, madam?' asks the duke.

'No, your Grace,' she replies, returning her gaze to the carpet, covering her mouth with one gloved hand as though to stifle a cough. She can feel the skin above her bodice redden and her cheeks flush.

Behind her, the girls are giggling about something or other, and behind the girls, there being no hostess to take his arm, Lambert enters in the company of Boltbyn. Birdie smiles to herself, knowing that Mr Lambert tolerates Mr Boltbyn for the prestige he brings the house, when in truth he cannot stand the sight of him.

'I am given to understand, sir,' she hears her husband murmur to the vicar, 'that we have you to thank, in part, for the honour we are about to receive, praise God.'

'How do you mean, sir? I cannot think how I can have been responsible for your dinner.' For some reason the sight of Mrs Lambert on Danbury's arm gives Boltbyn a peculiar chill.

Lambert continues, oblivious to everything but his status and his toothache: 'It is well known that his Grace is an ardent student of photography. Is it not true, sir, that one of your photographs of Emma elicited the admiration of a certain prominent person?'

'No, I don't think that is what happened at all.'

'You are too modest, Mr Boltbyn. I myself have seen your photographs of both my daughters, and they display the children to excellent advantage.'

'That is true.'

'Which is why I have you to thank for our good fortune.' Lambert raises his voice as though speaking to the deaf. 'I have it on good authority that our Emma has attracted the notice of his Grace. He, in his turn, has taken a warm interest in the welfare of the family.'

'And you suppose me to be the matchmaker?'

Passing through the door into the central hall, Emma senses Mr Boltbyn watching her. When she turns to him, he appears vexed.

As Birdie enters the reception room with her hand in the warm crook of the noble elbow, she detects a peculiar smell, incompletely masked by the heavy sweetness of hyacinths. As well, she sees two liveried servants across the carpet, standing with silver trays balanced on the tips of their gloved fingers – *facing the wall*. She would like to ask the duke about these things, but fears appearing ignorant.

The servants turn away from the wainscoting to serve the company; as a further challenge to her powers of concentration, she must now endure introductions to several strange gentlemen. A painter named Crede, with a limp, feverish handshake and a woman's wrist. An architect whose name escapes her and whose buildings she has never seen. A literary gentleman whose essay on Blenheim Palace she once tried to read, with an abnormally narrow chest, so that his shirt-front appears stuffed with a small pillow. Also among the company is the estate manager, Mr Lush – a wire-haired gentleman with a common demeanour but an accent nearly as refined as his employer. Following introductions, all except Boltbyn revolve about the duke like the moons of Jupiter.

So many men in one room! More than she has encountered at one go since she was a child, when her father's friends, storekeepers and tradesmen, would hoist her onto their aproned laps (covered with the dross of their calling), to make jokes she did not understand, while fingers like sausages would pinch her cheeks and, when her father left the room, accidentally open the top button of her dress.

Wandering about the gloomy reception room with its black wainscoting and beams, Birdie believes herself to be the only grown woman in the house. Nearby, under the Buhl clock, Lydia watches intently while Boltbyn (on his knees) demonstrates a puzzle he has brought – a polished, wooden egg which, when dropped onto the floor, disintegrates into a tangle of oddly shaped pieces. With a voice intended to approximate Humpty-Dumpty, the vicar defies all the king's horses and men ever to put him together again, a challenge Lydia eagerly accepts.

Sensing Birdie's eyes upon him, the vicar struggles self-consciously to his feet. 'I thought to b-bring a little something for them to enliven the evening.'

And for yourself as well, she thinks – observing, not for the first time, that there is something of the arrested child in his appearance: his pageboy-length hair has been slicked down, his necktie placed as though by his governess, and his cheeks appear to have been pinched.

'Emma does not seem to have joined the game,' she says, noting that Emma is nowhere to be seen.

'That is true. She has little patience for me these days.'

'That is only to be expected, given her age and development. Where has she gone, then?'

Mr Boltbyn's cheeks redden. 'She said something about wishing to explore.'

> *The wandering phantom broke and fled,*
> *Straightway I saw within my head*
> *A vision of a ghostly bed . . .*

Crouched beneath the banister to avoid detection, Emma climbs swiftly up one of two enormous staircases in the central hall. Reaching the upper gallery, she takes a moment to examine the portraits of the duke's gloomy ancestors, then wanders down a long dark hall, its ceiling somewhat oval, with everything carpeted and papered in such a way that she imagines it as a sort of tunnel. Keeping one hand to the wall for guidance, she creeps along the muffled passage until her progress is stopped by a rope, presumably meant to prevent visitors from progressing further. Here she hesitates, for it is often the case that such ropes are warnings of danger – a collapsed floor or unfinished construction – and she would hate to fall down a hole and have to call for help. Finding an open door to the left, she decides to explore here instead.

The room is even darker than the passage outside, and Emma cannot see so much as her hand in front of her face. Nonetheless, she can feel the velvet curtain that covers the wall next to her, and she recognises the faint smell of ether. She is in no doubt that this is where photographs are taken by Mr Boltbyn and his club. Having explained things satisfactorily to herself, she exits the room, then stops, wondering which way should she go. Does she dare proceed beyond the rope barrier to find out what lies beyond? Or should she retrace her steps back to the dreary gathering in the reception room and Mr Boltbyn's silly puzzle?

Her moment of uncertainty is rudely terminated by a frightened voice to her right: *Jesus, Mary and Joseph save us!*

The gentleman standing at the top of the stair is clearly a servant, and in a state of the utmost alarm. Seeing him gape at her like that, eyes agog and mouth open, Emma almost lets out a scream herself. The moment freezes in the way such moments do, and between the Irish servant and the girl in the white dress, an observer would be hard-pressed to determine who is the more terrified. Finally, emitting a little squeak, the servant turns tail and clamours pell-mell downstairs, calling for assistance.

No longer in a state of indecision, Emma slips quickly under the barrier, hurries further down the dark passage, and up a narrow stairway.

At the top of the stairs she finds another unlocked door, which opens on to a room which is the smallest she has seen. It is somewhat brighter than the hallway, thanks to a small casement window fitted with iron bars, much like the nursery window at Crouch Manor – excepting that the room it illuminates is monastically spare, no carpet or pictures or mirror, with only a bed and a table for furniture.

Continuing down the short hallway, she tries a second door, likewise open, expecting another spare bedroom just like its neighbour, but this room is filled with a darkness so deep, one can almost touch it with your hand.

O'Day, this is most inopportune . . .

She hears the voices below; momentarily a feeling of panic wells up in her breast, for there will be no end of bother if she is caught snooping. Having no obvious alternative, she hurries back to the bedroom, drops to her knees, and crawls underneath the bed – a poor and childish hiding-place to be sure, but the only one in evidence.

A moment later, four legs appear in the doorway, lit from above by a candle. Without knowing to whom the legs belong, she lies very still and listens.

'I swear to Jesus, Mr Lush, me on the stair and it pops up, the very picture of – what was its name, sir?'

'In any case, as you can see, there is no ghost present.'

'True, Mr Lush, yer right there. Yet I did see something by the Christ.'

'No doubt you did. I have my own suspicions as to the identity of your ghost.'

Holding her nose not to sneeze (the floor beneath the bed is extremely dusty), Emma watches the legs turn and then disappear, thinking that it is all very peculiar. Who is the ghost O'Day thought he saw? Why has she been taken for one? Who is the man with the fine accent? Whom does he suspect? What is in the darkened room? So many questions, all of a sudden!

The footsteps recede down the staircase, then the two voices fade down the hall, murmuring back and forth. Even so, Emma counts to fifty before she ventures out from underneath the bed – and with difficulty, for it is uncommonly narrow and low. Rising unsteadily to her feet, she puts one hand against the wall for balance – and feels something in the surface of the wall. It is an impression, or rather, a curved indentation, engraved deeply into the wallpaper with a blunt, hard object such as a spoon.

Convinced that a word has been written into the wallpaper, by using her fingers like a blind person, Emma traces each letter until it spells out a name.

Eliza.

Rising to her feet, she looks down at the bed where Eliza must have slept, after having written her name into the wall, like a prisoner in a dungeon.

Emma sits upon the edge of the bed to think. What can it all mean?

At the tinkle of a small silver bell, the duke's guests are directed across a wide hall into the dining room, identical to the reception room but with maroon walls, whose fittings seem built for a race of giants. A massive black buffet nearly fills one end of the room, behind a dining table whose legs would support a meal of elephants. In one corner, Birdie observes a cage of stuffed birds – as does Lydia, who is joined by her sister. Emma appears slightly out of breath; a blotch of dirt mars the front of her dress.

'I see that Emma has chosen to honour us once again with her company,' Lambert whispers into Birdie's ear. 'I had hoped you might control her a bit more firmly.'

'She went exploring. I see no harm in it – nor does his Grace, I expect.'

Meanwhile, having secured the attention of both girls by standing between them and the cage, Boltbyn begins to imitate various feathered creatures, causing the Reverend Lambert to roll his eyes as if to say, *Will somebody please do something about him?* In the meanwhile, two footmen conduct the girls to places of honour on either side of the duke.

For her part, Birdie takes a seat between Boltbyn and the pigeon-shaped literary gentleman, whose name she forgets. She determines to engage the latter in conversation, if only to be spared the vicar's riddles and games.

The table setting, like the furniture, is a model of hideous solidity, with everything made to look as ornate as possible and to take up as much room as possible and to display the Danbury crest as conspicuously as possible. The silver seems fashioned to taunt the user with its exaggerated weight, as though to say, *Wouldn't you like to melt me down?*

At her place lie no fewer than twenty-four utensils, whose names and functions are a mystery. Each knife nestles in its own rest, next to a butter pick and a set of game shears. Eight pieces of stemware are arranged in two rows, only one of which, the water glass, appears the least bit familiar. In the centre of the table stands an elaborate floral arrangement for which the gardener must have denuded half the conservatory.

The Duke of Danbury rises with wineglass raised to deliver the obligatory speech of welcome. 'Ladies and gentlemen,' he begins. A keen silence follows, as upwards of ten pairs of eyes turn to the head of the table.

'We who undertake our duties at Bissett Grange welcome you to Bissett Grange. We extend an especially warm welcome to the Reverend Charles Grantham Lambert, together with Mrs Lambert, their daughter, Miss Lydia – and above all, to the young lady on my right, who stands at the threshold of her majority, who adorns our table as might inspire the flowers to wilt in shame.'

Birdie extends an inquisitive glance at her elder daughter, who executes an almost imperceptible shrug in reply. She turns to Boltbyn beside her, who appears decidedly troubled, then back to the duke.

'Reverend Charles Lambert. Pray, be so kind as to honour us by delivering the grace.'

Taking his cue, her husband rises and clears his throat, in that modest way he affects when he feels important. As he says the grace it occurs to Birdie that he and the duke must have met beforehand: and if so, what other subjects were discussed?

> *Come Lord Jesus, be our guest,*
> *May this food by thee be blest,*
> *May our souls by thee be filled,*
> *Ever on the living Bread . . .*

Grace complete, amens muttered, Birdie surveys the table and is puzzled to see that the bread in evidence, living or not, is but a single thin, unbuttered slice, resting on a napkin to the left of each plate, with its own potbellied salt cellar close by.

As dinner proceeds, it becomes clear that the fare is a good deal more meagre than even a supper at Crouch Manor: a consommé as thin and as filmy as rose water, a haunch of mutton whose graininess suggests an uncertain vintage, and tiny portions of ice cream and sweetmeats.

The four magnificent silver wine coolers hefted by the servants and stamped with the unavoidable crest contain wine that has been noticeably watered-down; indeed, the only substance the house is pleased to serve in quantity is water.

While thin coffee is poured, their host rises, tapping his glass gently with a coffee-spoon. The sense of moment causes Birdie to suspect that what is about to transpire will constitute the point of the entire affair:

'Ladies and gentlemen, it is not without satisfaction that I stand before you to make an announcement of the highest importance. We live in a time of moral uncertainty; a degenerate time, alas, when mankind seems to have forfeited, through our sins, the gospel gifts as vested upon us by Jesus Christ our Lord.'

'Amen,' mutters Lambert.

'Therefore, after earnest deliberation and prayer, I wish to inform you that, at services this coming Sunday, it will be announced to the parish that the Reverend Charles Grantham Lambert has been appointed to the position of Spiritual Adviser to the Danbury estate.'

As astonished as anyone by this news, Birdie joins in the ovation, noting a peculiar silence to her left. When she turns to Boltbyn, his large, shallow-set eyes are as wide as the butter-plates.

As the applause subsides, Mr Lambert rises from his seat to undertake a response, which Birdie knows to be both well crafted and well memorised.

'Your Grace, my family, my dear friends. It is with humility and deep gratitude that I accept this high honour – to serve he whose steps on the path must be sure, who must stand firmly upon the Rock of Ages, whose house must be the Holy House on the Hill, like the Holy Church which Almighty God hath established for ever, in Jesus' name . . .'

At a nod from the duke, the new spiritual adviser to the House of Danbury resumes his seat, leaving his Grace to bring the moment to its conclusion.

'We have designated rooms at Bissett Grange for use by the Reverend Lambert. Bissett Grange is at his family's disposal. We are glad to report that already Miss Emma has agreed to join us on Saturday next, together with her sister and her governess – and her mother, should she so choose – for tea, croquet, and photography . . .'

The moment is broken by a soft cry to her left, followed by a crash. Birdie turns to face the empty chair previously occupied by Boltbyn, who lies at her feet in a swoon. A cry escapes her lips, she starts up from her chair – and bumps the server hovering over her shoulder, about to pour from his enormous silver ewer: a veritable waterfall drenches her with such force that her hair becomes undone and her veil falls, clinging to her face and rendering her temporarily blind. Immediately, shadows scurry about her wielding towels, while others drop to their knees and in urgent whispers attempt to revive the fallen vicar, and another voice calls for brandy . . .

Removing the film of wet muslin from her face, her cheeks burning with embarrassment, Birdie turns to the head of the table, and her eyes meet those of the Duke of Danbury, who is staring at her with the most peculiar expression.

After an evening notably lacking in amiable conversation, the company makes a hurried, hushed exit from the house, at the end of this odd dinner – so pleasing to the duke and his new spiritual adviser, and so oddly disturbing to everyone else. Given the strange tenor of the occasion, as she and Lydia pass through the front door Emma is startled but not exactly surprised to find Mr Lush, standing on the portico as though waiting for her, with the tight smile adults wear when they are cross and don't wish to show it.

'I trust you enjoyed your evening, Miss Lambert?'

'Very much, thank you, sir,' she replies, while thinking that two of the legs in Eliza's doorway surely belonged to him.

'And how was the exploring? Did you find that pleasing as well?'

Seeing no point in lying, Emma decides not to bother thinking up a plausible denial. 'Quite pleasing,' she smiles, as though he were asking about the sherbet.

He glares at her with watery eyes. She observes his round body and wiry hair – very much like a hedgehog, actually. 'I am glad of it, miss,' he says, smiling again. 'Yet I would caution you against such expeditions in future.'

'Why, sir? Did not his Grace say that Bissett Grange is at our disposal?'

Smiling down at that angelic childish face (with a most adult gleam of defiance in the eye), Lush's feelings for children undergo a radical alteration for the worse.

Like most people of humane disposition, he has always regarded children as sweet, innocent creatures. He does not share the duke's cavalier ruthlessness, born of breeding, and cannot think upon the doomed creatures employed over the past half-decade without a sense of remorse, if not horror. Were they not innocents themselves, once? Yet without them there would have been no business to undertake, and Bissett Grange would now be in the hands of its creditors, forevermore. True, the enterprise can turn a profit for years based upon duplicates. But there must always be an original – a subject which must remain quiet.

So beastly, and so necessary. Yet in the case of this cunning little witch, should such action become necessary it would be a painful necessity as always, yet somehow satisfying all the same . . .

The silence between Emma and the estate manager contains sufficient tension for even Mr Lambert to take note. 'What has my daughter been doing, now? Has Emma said something rude?'

'Not at all, sir. A perfectly lovely little girl.'

The Hen and Hatchet, Houndsditch

The day's ratting is done, the dead rodents have been cleared away and the U-shaped arena thoroughly whitewashed. Yet the gamblers and spectators have by no means lost enthusiasm for the sport. This they express in various ways, so that the room practically undulates with swearing, spitting, sweating, biting, farting males, yapping simultaneously like mongrels, requiring the barmen to bellow like town criers in order to make their way through the heaving throng. The room is a festival of drink going down a hundred necks, whether in celebration, solace, or the simple desire for oblivion.

So popular is the Hen and Hatchet at this time of day, it takes Fraser several minutes of crab-like insinuation to cross the floor to the long bar, where he secures a place for himself with the help of two sharp elbows. Leaning forward upon the mahogany surface, he scans the company to either side with his small, shrewd eyes, and he has no difficulty recognising the party named Will – described by the waiter as a giant in a long coat, with a face seemingly smashed by an omnibus.

Will is nursing a pint with a group of ratters, some of whom hold bull-dogs under their arms, while others clutch their Skye terriers to their chests like wet-nurses. The only dogs not asleep are the sharp-nosed English terriers, which squirm to get loose from their neat black leather collars, having smelled the rats in the room above.

Behind the bar, above several tiers of luminescent bottles, hangs a bright silver collar which will be the prize in a coming match. On either side of the trophy hang a series of worn leather collars, stamped with the names of deceased champions and their owners. One of these belonged to a dog named Tiny, owned by an Edmund Whitty, Esq. The sight of it causes Fraser to smile inwardly, as a monument to his rival's decline and fall.

'A glass of the out-and-out, my man,' Fraser calls to the barman, affecting a working-class accent to go with his tattered corduroy suit. In truth he needs a drink badly, for though he has steadfastly claimed otherwise, he has never in his life gone anywhere incognito. Fraser is not a journalist who seeks things out for himself; rather, his skill or gift is the ability to synthesise and re-tell, in a morally committed, indignant voice, what other journalists have uncovered in the field.

Adding to Fraser's discomfort is a morbid fear of rats. While a child on the privy outside a strange cottage at night, he once nearly sat on one, and the memory has clung to him for life.

Not until he has downed a second glass of gin does he summon the courage to inch his way down the bar towards the gentleman in question. But just when he takes his place beside and below the quarry, before he can open his mouth to introduce himself, Will is joined by a short, barrel-shaped fellow, with whom he conducts an anxious exchange.

'That is a right sour look you have on you, Norman. Another day gone for nothing?' It has been half a week since the Captain's order, and Menzies the welsher is not yet located, and the Captain takes a dim view of failure among his staff.

'The same fecking story, so help me Christ,' says Norman, bitterly. 'At his work they says he is taken sick; at his rooms they says he is at his club; at his club they says he is abroad. His drinking companions forget ever knowing the sod.'

'It is most worrying,' says Will.

'Most worrying,' agrees Norman, signalling the barman for a large of the usual.

'Excuse me, gentlemen,' announces an unfamiliar voice to the right.

The gentleman standing beside them is a stranger with a Glasgow accent and a corduroy suit. 'How do you do, gentlemen,' he continues, smiling. 'I am instructed to present myself to a party by the name of Will.'

The eyes of the two man-bashers narrow at once. The larger man plants his feet in the stance of a boxer, as a precaution. 'And what might your business be with that particular gentleman?' asks Norman.

'I am told I should speak to Will. I am told that, through that gentleman, I might meet another gentleman named Rodney.' Fraser executes a conspiratorial wink.

A pause follows, as Norman and Will exchange puzzled glances. Never in their lives have they entertained such a request.

Norman takes the lead: 'And who might you be, sir? Who is it what wishes to see Mr Rodney?'

'My name is Menzies,' replies Fraser, taking a cigar from his pocket and lighting it, to show confidence.

'You are Mr Menzies?' asks Will, softly.

'I most assuredly am. And I have been given leave to speak to Mr Rodney by parties on the highest level.'

'I believe you, sir,' says Norman, and looks sternly at his associate. 'Will, did you not hear the gentleman? Go now, and fetch Mr Rodney. Tell him Mr Menzies awaits.'

'Certainly,' replies Will.

As Will pushes his way through the crowd to another room, Fraser orders another gin. On inspiration, and in a most extraordinary departure, he requests a glass for Norman as well.

'Most kind of you, Mr Menzies. To your health, sir.' Norman raises his glass, displaying a row of brown teeth.

'Mr Rodney is an extraordinary individual, I am told,' says Fraser, thinking to capitalise upon the goodwill he has secured for the price of a drink.

'Indeed so,' replies Norman. 'I have never known anyone like him.'

'I am told that he is a party with unique knowledge of the lower depths of London.'

'That is also very true, sir,' replies Norman. 'It were his home for much of his life.'

In the mind of the correspondent for *Dodd's*, headers appear in coloured lights: *Born in the Sewers of London. Bred for a life of Crime . . .*

By this time Will has returned with one hand in his coat pocket. 'Well now, gentlemen,' he says.

'Will,' says Norman, 'have you been after speaking to Rodney?'

'I have,' nods the larger man.

'Then please introduce him to Mr Menzies without delay.'

So saying, Norman takes a sudden grip of Fraser's waistband and pulls smartly – whereupon, in a surprisingly deft movement for such a large man, Will produces a sleek, wriggling, furry object and inserts it straight down the front of the trousers; in almost the same motion, he lifts Fraser into the air, barges through the crowd to the arena, and tosses him over the railing, where an eager crowd gathers to see what follows.

'Do you see, Will? He is dancing! Do you think it is the highland fling?'

'Aye, Norman. And he makes the sound of the bagpipes as well.'

Crushed against the arena railing, dog-owners break into peals of laughter, awakening their animals, who join in with barking until the room is ringing with merriment, and squeaking as well.

26

Crouch Manor, Chester Wolds, Oxfordshire

It is late at night – or, to be precise, very early morning, and the house is long asleep. Lydia listens to the big clock in the parlour, which she never hears at any other time, and turns her head to the window. Outside, a cold sliver of a moon appears to impale the top of the tree on the front lawn.

Lydia's sister is likewise awake, excepting that, having no window next to her bed (the result of a coin-toss upon their arrival), her eyes remain closed. Imagining there to be a set of windows behind her eyelids, she dreams up stories that might explain the curious events of the previous evening: the name *Eliza*; the announcement that sent Mr Boltbyn into a swoon; the water spilled on her mother; the warning from the unfriendly gentleman. Surely these events must be connected in some way, if only because they all happened in the same evening, involved the same people, and had the same peculiar quality . . .

'Emma? Are you awake?'

'When you ask me that, Lydia, it *always* wakes me up.'

'So you *are* awake.'

'I am. What is it you want?'

'The man who was cross with you on the verandah?'

'How odd! Do you know, I was thinking about him just now.'

'He is quite odd. I think he would make a capital hedgehog – do you think? For Mr Boltbyn's story.'

'Do you mean with his wire hair sticking up?'

'Yes, that and . . . and his form in general.'

'Do you know, Lydia, that precise thought occurred to me as he spoke.'

'Why was he cross with you, Emma? Was it something you said?'

'No. I think it was something I saw.'

'Oh? What could that have been?'

'I'm not certain what it was, but it was all very queer. Would you like to go and see for yourself?'

'Will there be danger?'

'Mortal danger.'

'Oh, splendid!'

'For one thing, we could be seen. For it will have to be done by daylight.'

'Why?'

'Which do you mean, Lydia – why will there be danger, or why must it be in daylight?'

'Both, I expect. After all, the duke as good as said we had the run of the house.'

'That is what I told the hedgehog. It made him cross. I don't think he likes children much, and he certainly doesn't want us exploring.'

'Should we ask Mr Boltbyn's opinion?'

'Mr Boltbyn is unwell, as you saw. Best not upset him.'

27

Plant's Inn

Whitty awakens in pain, for the bone of his cheek is mashed upon an unyielding surface: a familiar circumstance of late. He is beginning to view the act of waking as a cruel motif. Where the deuce is he now?

Ah, yes. The rear snug at Plant's – dark but for a few dim embers in the fireplace. Though he cannot immediately bring to mind the circumstance of his arrival, it is clear that he has fallen asleep while drinking. Should that be the case, it is a depressing thing that he has not been awakened by whomever remained at table – or, if left on his own, assisted from the premises by the barman, placed in a cab with the address of his club, and sent on his way. Heartless, just to leave a man like this . . .

Hello. Someone is seated at the end of the table.

To judge by the shape and the dimensions of the shadow, it is not the Captain. Nor is it Inspector Salmon, nor a man-basher of one kind or another. This is a different shape, that of a member of the fairer sex.

It is Mrs Plant. Momentarily he is suffused with pleasure at the sight of her – and relief, that she is not gone from him for ever.

On the other hand, she must now be faced. A discernible chill radiates from the figure opposite, distinguishable from the clammy coolness of the room itself. As his vision adjusts, he thinks he can make out her green eyes, which nearly glow in the dark.

'How do you do, madam?' he says, glad that he succeeded in trading in the Captain's cock-chafer for a different, if second-hand, replacement.

'Well, don't you have a bluster on you, Mr Whitty. Gone for weeks and you march in like butter wouldn't melt in your mouth, and there I was thinking you went over to the Mollies Club.'

Whitty bridles at the mention of that notorious establishment for inverts, shut down during the last century after a scandal whose nature escapes him for the moment. What does she mean by it?

'The Mollies Club, madam?'

'Heard of it have you?'

'Indeed I have but . . .'

'Perhaps the Mollies Club is where they should have looked when your disappearance was the talk of London.'

'I am at a loss as to your meaning, Mrs Plant. Yet I am very glad to see you at last, and delighted to see you looking so well . . .' His mouth continues to operate along these lines while his mind scurries about for scraps of information. Meanwhile, his eyes become distracted by her copper hair, some of which has turned ruby in the light of the coals as though lit by stained glass, while the skin of her forehead and neck glows in the way of the moon. He notes the colour of heat splashed upon her cheekbones, an ardour which he has experienced before at first hand, at close quarters – if rarely, and upon conditions of secrecy that might better suit relations between a Frenchman and his mistress.

'Tell me, Mr Whitty, did you study Greek in your fancy school?'

'And Latin, for most of the school day. At Eton we learned little, but we learned it accurately. May I ask about your sudden interest in my education?'

'You are not a sailor, nor a man of the theatre, and you are certainly no athlete.'

'I make no claim to any physical capacity, madam. I am primarily a spiritual being.'

'I have often wondered what you are, sir. Recently I have wondered what circumstance necessitated that you should become what you are. Many blame public schools such as Eton.'

'True, and I was poorly served at Oxford as well – monstrously served, if the truth be known. A matter I prefer not to discuss in the presence of a lady.'

'Indeed, sir, the presence of a lady must have been a rarity in your case.'

He has no intention of discussing his expulsion from St Ambrose College, nor does he intend to thrash out the events of recent weeks and months. Where the devil is she headed with this?

'Mr Whitty, have you fallen asleep again?'

'No, madam. I was thinking.'

'Might one ask if the condition is beyond your control?'

'The human condition, you mean? Or do you refer to certain indulgences to which I am occasionally prone? If I could control either, madam, I assure you that I would do so.'

'I am not familiar with it beyond mention in the sensational press. Are you apt to become violent?'

'Far from it, madam. Unlike most Christians, I do not do to others as I suspect they would do to me.'

'I have heard that the condition runs in families.'

'I beg your pardon?' Does she mean to bring up the matter of the brother, he wonders? By now, all of London surely knows of the rumours around his death – does all London know about the photograph as well?

'I beg your pardon, madam, but what aspect of my family do you mean?'

'I mean to say that many hold it to run in the blood.'

'Blood, madam?'

'Your affliction.'

My affliction? Certainly that is one way of putting it, thinks Whitty. When a member of the family descends to the level depicted in the photograph, the name itself is stained by implication, a suspicion that the corruption, like syphilis, may infect the entire family.

'Madam, I assure you that my reticence on the subject is but the normal consideration a gentleman extends to a lady.'

'Sod your consideration, Mr Whitty, I want to know the truth.'

Mrs Abigail Plant watches the elegant, dissipated figure at the far end of the table with her stomach in the usual knot. Having reached her present position in life, she has no more intent to marry than a released convict might wish to construct a new cell for himself. As a consequence, she has no moral claim upon any gentleman with whom she might maintain an association; if he requires heirs, he is free to seek elsewhere.

And yet, upon the sixth day, did God not declare that He did not wish loneliness on anyone? This alone might account for her uneasy attachment to Edmund Whitty, whom she loves, with whom she sins, of whom she then repents, about whom she then makes confession; for it is not easy to discard one's religion. This is especially true when in a foreign country, where *sin* and *forgive*, spoken in one's native language, provide comfort far beyond their literal meaning.

> *Sé do bheath' a Mhuire, atá lán de ghrásta,*
> *tá an Tiarna leat.*
> *Is beannaithe thú idir mná agus is beannaithe*
> *toradh do bhruinne . . .*

Now the war within her breast has found a new battleground: Mr Whitty's purported sexual inversion; odious and unnatural if true, depicted with obscene relish by his colleagues in journalism – led, of course, by Mr Fraser. At first she scoffed at the very idea, with her memories to defend him. But memories fade, and then came his weeks of absence from her establishment and her bed, followed by reports of his frequency at the Alhambra Baths. With no competing explanation, she lies awake at night with a bad stomach, wondering: Is he done with her, then? And if he is, why does it matter?

The truth will make you free, or perhaps not. Either way she must know, so that she may determine her course with open eyes.

Pride, is it?

At the same time, she has known this gentleman long enough to understand that a direct question will rarely produce the truth, especially when it concerns an intimate matter. Taking a generous swallow of her whiskey, Mrs Plant sets the glass sharply upon the table, rises from her chair and straightens her bodice.

Whitty knows this gesture – it indicates a decision taken.

Is she about to strike him with the coal-scuttle? Should he protect his head? Closing his eyes, he hears the rustle of her skirts; now he can detect her lavender soap, the warm musk of her Irish whiskey, and herself.

When he dares open his eyes, she is seated directly across from him, well within his customary zone of comfort. He would return to a state of feigned unconsciousness, but it is too late. Her eyes have already drawn him in. As though responding to the pull of gravity he inclines forward, while at that same instant she chooses to do the same.

When a woman and a man kiss on the mouth, especially after a long absence, in that moment no other thought is possible – unless somebody is feigning a sentiment he does not feel. Not true in this case.

Their lips touch ever so lightly, in the way that a thirsty man attenuates the pleasure of that first sip of cold water. Now they go deeper, mouths slightly open, lips moving slowly and softly together, a sensation felt by both, controlled by neither, an electric magnetism that operates by its own rules.

'Let your hair go,' he whispers into her ear.

She looses the fastening and it all rushes down in a torrent of sudden tresses, heavy and radiant over her shoulders and arms and bosom, and she draws his face up to her own with her hands and kisses him with all her strength, throbbing from head to toe.

A woman possesses more layers than does a man, both in mind and dress. Whitty's fingers struggle with a wide variety of tiny buttons and hooks, attached at maddeningly close intervals and unexpected locations. His hands tremble from the unaccustomed assault upon his nerves while she laughs teasingly in his ear, until at last he can feel her flesh with his hands and explore the unseen mystery of her soft woman's body.

Lacking the patience and the breath to undertake the journey upstairs, they remain in the rear snug – and to how much better use do they now employ the long table than ever before in its long, battered, gin-soaked life!

And when they are done they lie together upon the table at which the most published minds in England have debated and dissected the issues of the day, two dishevelled, tender, subtle bodies, refuting every argument, every position, every postulate, in the way that a master of chess vanquishes a table of opponents in a single move.

'I congratulate you, sir.'

'For what, madam?'

'For having refuted your critics.'

'What are they saying now?'

'You don't know?'

'Upon my soul, madam, state your meaning and be done with it.'

'Mr Whitty, they say that you are a pouf.'

'What on earth do you mean?'

'A nancy boy. A marjory. A mollie. A practitioner of Socratic love.'

'The devil you say!'

'The devil I do say!'

Here Whitty's mind experiences a kind of seizure, for he feels the enormity of the charge even more keenly than she does – and to think this monstrous assumption has gone unrefuted for weeks. *The deuce!*

'I'll warrant that Fraser has something to do with it,' he says, having regained the power of speech.

'True, but the others were eager to take up the charge.'

'Blast!'

'Try to remain calm, sir. You are trembling and it is beginning to worry me. One might think you were accused of murder or theft.'

'The stigma is far greater, madam. The Miss Grundys have taken up the cause and will have no satisfaction until some prominent wretch is crucified for it. Then they will move on to the next vice that catches their fancy.'

'Did I not say that I acquit you of the charge?'

'Perhaps, madam. But I am dismayed that you gave it credence in the first place.'

'You are not steady, Mr Whitty – indeed, I should say that you are a distinctly wobbly individual. I never know what to expect from you, and expect I never shall.'

'I concede the point, madam. I never know what to expect of myself.'
She presses her lips onto his. Silence follows.

'The room is grown chilly, sir. Let us undertake your defence in the upstairs room.'

Bissett Grange

The girls have planned the expedition carefully – eluding the attentions of Miss Pouch by affecting a need to visit the water closet. 'What do you see, Lydia?'

They crouch inside the front door while Lydia (having the sharper eye) scans the vicinity for signs of movement. 'It is safe I think,' she says, voice quivering with excitement. 'Which stair should we take?'

'Either one, but we must crouch at the top while we reconnoitre.'

'Agreed. Shall we proceed?'

'Let's.'

With a delicious sense of exposure they dash across the front hall and up the left staircase (Emma goes first, being the faster runner), then up a second staircase, then into a spare room which looks very like a nursery.

Lydia is somewhat disappointed. 'It is only a bedroom.'

Emma has to agree. In daylight, the room looks entirely different – a perfectly sensible room for a servant, or a visitor taken in out of pity.

'Come with me,' she says, 'and feel the wall.'

Next the bed, Emma takes Lydia's hand, and traces with her fingers the name indented in the plaster: *Eliza*.

'Who is Eliza?' asks Lydia.

'I don't know. Now let us go to the room next door.'

As with the bedroom, the door is unlocked – for the duke to order a room locked would be to question his own authority. Thanks to the time of day, when she peers inside this time, Emma confronts a darkness which, though deep, is not absolute.

At first she thinks it might be a bathroom, for she can make out the gleam of white porcelain; or perhaps it is a laundry where bed-linens are washed – excepting that there are no hampers. As her eyes adjust she can make out the shapes she has never seen before: A medical apparatus? A small pump?

Having superior night-time vision, Lydia makes her way to the opposite side of the room, where she stands beside a kind of bookcase.

'What is over there, Lydia? I can't see.'

'I am not sure,' says Lydia, who disappears into the gloom, then emerges holding two pieces of paper. 'Look,' she says. 'Do you suppose this is Eliza?'

Emma looks at the naked girl in the photograph and it is as though she is in front of a mirror – not a real mirror of course, but the mirror of her poem, in which the girl in the glass is like her and not like her at the same time.

The second photograph confounds her utterly, for it is like a portrait of a ghost, shadows – shaped like a human being, yet shredded by some overwhelming light.

Unaccountably, it looks familiar.

'Emma,' whispers Lydia. 'There is somebody coming, I think it is the hedgehog.'

And so it is.

'Good evening, ladies,' Lush says, remaining as calm as he can, for he did not expect two of them. 'And what is it that has taken you upstairs upon this particular occasion?'

'Curiosity, sir, nothing more,' says Emma, holding up the two photographs for inspection.

Lush examines them, and is greatly relieved that the second is so poorly focused. 'These photographs are the duke's private property,' he says. 'To be frank, ladies, I am shocked by your impudence.'

'We were to have the run of the house, you know,' Emma says. 'I thought you knew that.'

'That is true,' Lydia agrees. 'He said it at the big dinner.'

Lush would like to strangle them both immediately, if such a thing were physically possible. But at this age they can be quite strong and very quick, and should they escape he will have tipped his hand disastrously.

For it is a fact that the imp named Emma has been on the mind of the estate manager, ever since they spoke on the portico. Quite apart from the danger she presents to his future she reminds him of other young women, in his youth, the disdain in their eyes when they would find themselves in his presence, their carefully hidden hostility – a sentiment he has returned ever since, with interest . . .

'Excuse me, sir, but I think Mr Boltbyn is expecting us,' Lydia says, once the flinty silence has attenuated beyond endurance.

'Yes of course,' he says, smiling, executing a little bow.

29

The Pith and Paradox

The events of the previous evening have awakened sentiments Whitty thought he would never experience again. The memory of Mrs Plant lingers like an imprint on his skin, a desperate tenderness which has put a new tone and colour to his life – for the time being.

If only it would last. If only a moment could be stopped altogether when one is certain that time has nothing better to offer. If only the rest of the world would tactfully withdraw.

Having banished himself from the Eden of Mrs Plant's upstairs room, her bed and her whiskey, Whitty must begin his own dark crossing in search of various truths – regarding the Captain and his unfortunate niece; regarding his brother and, by association, regarding himself. If he stands acquitted of uranism, there remain other allegations to refute.

As to his intermittent association with Mrs Plant, doubts began to plague him the moment he stepped onto the street this morning. After all, what can compare with a drinking-place as a hothouse of artificial sentiment? And who is better trained than a publican in the production of warmth and laughter? What is he, really, to Mrs Plant? Does their personal association, lacking the normal rituals of courtship and marriage, bear any relation to normal life? Or does its value reside as a work of mutual fiction, an alternative to life?

On the other hand, given the life he leads in her absence, such questions are both idle and moot.

Having taken leave of her warm body, fragrant without the need of perfume, her eyes in a delicious half-sleep, Whitty's first act is to head for the Pith and Paradox, to redeem the dreadful envelope. At her post behind the bar, Phoebe Owler meets his greeting with a quizzical tilt to her brow.

'Your mother's letter is spicier than I expected.'

'You saw it, then?' Whitty feels his face redden.

'You said I should destroy it if you failed to return. I thought I had better see what I was destroying.'

'And what did you conclude?' asks Whitty, torn between panic and relief.

'It raised certain questions in my mind.'

'I should be surprised if it did not.'

'You are not a man with the taste for much younger women. At least that is what you said to me.'

'It is the gentleman I am interested in. Have you not heard the rumours?'

'The gentleman in the photograph resembles you more than a little.'

Whitty can never lie when Phoebe looks at him in that way.

'He is my brother.'

'I think I understand,' Phoebe replied, handing him the envelope. 'That will be 7 shillings, please.'

While attempting to hire a cab outside the Pith and Paradox, Whitty reminds himself that the universe was designed so that one must travel through darkness in order to reach the light; one must assume the existence of light, without evidence to support it. Nor can one be certain that the clarity of the light will compensate for the darkness of the dark.

Nestled in the privacy of a hackney coach, he pulls the envelope from his pocket, removes the photograph, and examines it, in the faint hope that it will prove to have been all a mistake, that the male in the picture is not David but some unknown roué from France.

Not so.

His own brother! Whitty slides the photograph back into its envelope, joined by the picture of Eliza which was given him by the Captain. He returns the envelope to his coat pocket (he will wash it out with lye soap, when and if this ordeal is finished). Eliza and David, Whitty cannot discover one fate without unlocking the other. Eliza and his brother now form a single narrative, beginning and ending with these photographs. For practical purposes, it is as though two spectres have married in Limbo and sent wedding pictures to the relatives.

Such a dangerous emotion, curiosity, when it leads one to unveil the dirty secrets of one so close to oneself.

The hackney shudders and dips over the uneven pavement, to the London district known as Mesopotamia, which contains the Whitty residence on Machpelah Square. At this location, the Richard Whitty establishment grew, thrived, withered, then uprooted itself and disappeared. Thereafter, the Whitty town-house fell into an abyss, pending the outcome of a dispute over the disposition of its owner's debts. A resolution remains as remote now as it was five years ago, when its principal subject sailed for America, leaving his assets in a legal Gordian knot that has confounded the Chancery ever since.

In the years since, the residence has remained idle, sealed-up, decomposing, a senile maiden awaiting the return of her elderly prince.

Whitty peers out the window of the cab. Twilight has fallen already. It is a known fact that, owing to an accumulation of plane trees and gloomy architecture, darkness falls upon Mesopotamia more readily than in other neighbourhoods. Or that may be Whitty's perception of it – the dismal prospect of a visit home.

He disembarks on cheerless Machpelah Square, whose name denotes the biblical burial-place of Sarah, as well as the Whitty family fortunes. In the houses along the street, the blinds have been pulled down; the walkways are, as always, deserted. As Whitty paces the empty square awaiting his dreaded appointment with the past, he attempts without success to avert his gaze from the sagging town-house on the opposite corner, the embodiment of slow ruin. The stacks of the chimneys have begun to look down, as though calculating how far they will have to fall. Any windows which are not broken and boarded are the colour and transparency of smoke.

'Good-day, Mr Whitty, sor. Your arrivance is well timed.'

The voice so close at hand gives Whitty a start. Turning cautiously, he sees that Downy Dermot has insinuated his elongated form into the crook of a Lombardy poplar, so thoroughly as to simulate a branch of it himself.

'Dermot. Good-day to you, sir, it was most generous of you to come.'

'It is a dooty, sor, to assist a Captain's man in any way one can.'

'I await your guidance. Have you examined the premises already?'

'One may or may not have done so.'

'Dermot, though it is clearly not in your nature, I beg you to speak plainly.'

'Please to excuse, Mr Whitty, but in a profession where the mere possession o' the instruments is sufficient to five years' transportation, one grows wary of too much plain speaking.'

'An understandable position.' Whitty pauses to rephrase his question. 'Might the premises yonder be in any way familiar to a certain snakesman standing in the vicinity?'

'Indeed, sor, a crow has been installed on the street for the day to that purpose.'

'A crow, did you say?'

'I might have.'

'And what is the next stage in the enterprise?'

'A canary might arrive presently.'

'A canary?'

'Perhaps.'

'I emphasise, sir, that caution and discretion are as essential on my part as they are to you. I am as much an intruder as you are, and am open to criminal charges as well.'

'Ah, Mr Whitty. Who knows what is an intrusion and what is not?'

'For a start, I expect that there is a constable in the vicinity.'

'The officer in question walks a twenty-minute beat, sor. At this moment he is lighting his pipe on Oxford Street, at the far end of his route.'

'Still, does it not seem imprudent before dark?'

'Nout could be farther from the fack, sor. At this hour the wives and servants are all a bustle, preparing for the master of the house. The children be learning their lessons. At this time of day, nout is minded to peer through the window at suspicious parties in the street.'

'I defer to your professional judgement.'

Abruptly the snakesman sets out across the square with long, smooth strides and a preoccupied expression, straight towards the house – just as a nanny with a perambulator turns the corner onto Machpelah Street.

Struggling to keep up, Whitty grasps Dermot's arm. 'I advise caution, sir, for I see someone approaching.'

'That is our canary,' replies Dermot without breaking stride, and it occurs to Whitty that the snakesman has deliberately set the pace so that they will encounter the nanny at the front gate (its rails so rusted, one could peel the metal like bark from a tree). The nanny, who has the florid, fleshy countenance of a thousand other nannies, neither slows her pace nor accords them so much as a glance. At the precise moment of her passing, Dermot deftly reaches into the perambulator and extracts a carpet-bag of some weight, simultaneously giving the gate a sharp shove with his other hand. The two men are on the other side of the closed gate in seconds.

Having been left to itself for over half a decade, the front garden has deteriorated into a state of primal abandonment, a tangle of vegetation whose brambles coil and uncoil like the feelers of insects. Yet Dermot glides through the bushes to the front door as though the walkway still existed; when Whitty attempts to follow, thorns seem to reach for him, picking apart his clothing and raking his skin.

By the time Whitty arrives at the front door, Dermot is at work on the bars of a ground-floor window. Having circled two of the bars with a piece of reinforced rope he inserts a jimmy and proceeds to twist, so that the bars, already weakened by rust, are squeezed together, widening the opening. After wrapping the jimmy in a piece of cloth and replacing it and the rope in the carpet-bag, he produces a glass-cutter's stone with which he extracts a piece of window-pane. Reaching through the opening, he unlatches the window. Turning sideways, he slips through the improbably narrow opening and disappears. No more than a half-minute has elapsed.

Whitty waits on the front step, amid an inundation of memories – of a time when the door was his to enter, and the house was a world unto itself.

The lock is released, the latch turned, and the front door abruptly swings open, emitting a gust of air thick with mildew. Standing in the entrance as though he were the householder and Whitty come to call, Dermot seems strangely surprised to see him. He raises his hands in a gesture of surrender, his eyes cast slightly above Whitty's right shoulder.

Blast.

Whitty turns with a sigh of resignation. No doubt it is the constable, having passed the house ahead of schedule, as he feared.

Seemingly not.

A familiar, not unpleasant odour infuses his brain as a rag is pressed over his mouth and nose by a white-haired gentleman in dark glasses and a military coat. Yet again he is transported into an enchanted land . . .

30

Bissett Grange, Oxfordshire

Lush's nerves are worse than usual. And he suffers from fatigue, having to endure night after sleepless night, fraught with worry. And during the daytime, hour by hour, various areas of his skin itch, as though taking turns, and in progressively unreachable places.

Now it is the middle of the night, and he writhes between linen sheets that might as well be made of sandpaper, for all the comfort they afford.

In purely theoretical terms, of course, his mind explores various imaginative means of dealing with this unprecedented situation – absent the creative strictures of conventional morality.

Lush wonders: What is unique about the position in which he finds himself? Not the danger of exposure – always a given, to be carefully managed but never denied; nor is it that the threat is of the female gender, for all females are potential threats; nor is it that the female happens to be under the age of majority. What makes this threat special is that it is a young woman widely known in the county, and with established ties to the Duke of Danbury.

Whose absence will be noticed, and will have to be explained.

An accident in the woods? Possibly. Perhaps a drowning, like the unfortunate mishap which felled David Whitty?

How easy it is to imagine a precocious child, with an impetuous nature, wandering unaccompanied in the wood, only to become lost. Days later, after a frantic search led by the Duke of Danbury (whose entire establishment has been put to the task), their worst fears are confirmed, and the body of the unfortunate child is discovered, having slipped while attempting to cross the brook, fallen onto a rock, and drowned.

A believable narrative, sufficiently obvious for the local constabulary, Lush thinks.

But what is to be done about the younger one – especially should it display the same gift for meddling, the same cheekiness, the same animal cunning? Oh for half a century ago, when village children disappeared willy-nilly, and it was assumed to be the work of witches or gnomes!

Tormented by an unreachable spot on his spine, Lush sits up in the bed and scrubs his back against the headboard like a dog. Now he settles back under the covers, closes his eyes, and endeavours to count – not a line of sheep, but a procession of little girls, tripping through the woods one by one, across the meadow, and over a cliff . . .

Being in an excited state thanks to their adventure of this afternoon, Lydia is awake yet another night, staring out the window at the moon, which has grown from a sliver to a crescent, like the white part of a fingernail.

'Emma? Are you asleep?'

'No.' As with Lydia, Emma's brain is boiling with the discoveries and mysteries of the day.

'What did you see in the picture, Emma?'

'Do you mean the picture of Eliza?'

'We don't know that it was Eliza.'

'Do you think she looks at all like me?'

'Perhaps she does, but only a little bit. But I didn't mean that photograph. I meant the other one.'

'It was nothing but shadows and light. There was nothing to see.'

Shadows and light, thinks Emma, one in the shape of a loop, the other like the ghost of a woman. What is it that transforms a muddled fog into distressing and evil? Is it just her imagination?

'Is that all you saw, Emma?'

'Yes.'

'I don't believe you.'

'Let's not talk about it now. It would only keep you awake.'

3 1

Machpelah Street

He lies splayed out upon the worn Turkey carpet he crept upon as a child. Even in this dim light he recognises the wainscoting of the Whitty dining-room – the chandelier, the mantle, the festoons of flowers carved in the wood panels, all rendered a ghastly grey by fungus and dust. Just beyond his peripheral sight, Whitty hears two voices in discussion.

'Did I not tell you that the chemical is best? They do not struggle and kick like the mystic of Buckingham Gate.'

'Had we used it on that one I should have more teeth in me head than today.'

'Pish-posh, Mr Weeks, you are better off without them and have nobody to blame but yourself. It was you who insisted upon hanging the chap, when a bullet would serve as well.'

'It is not in me to fire on my own race, sir. I should feel like a traitor. I am already bothered with the girl what was done for.'

'Yet you do not hesitate to top an Englishman, nor pulverise him with your fists.'

'Regimental discipline, sir, is the heart and soul of the force.'

'Quite, Mr Weeks. Very good.'

By straining his eyes in a downward direction, Whitty discerns the insensible form of Downy Dermot, wearing what appears to be a noose around his neck.

'*Hazar, jawan,* Mr Robin. That one is awakening.'

'The chemical is not new to him, it seems.'

True, thinks Whitty, who is a walking history of modern drug-taking. Cautiously he lifts his head to observe his most recent attackers, and immediately faces the white-haired soldier in dark glasses, at close range.

'Lie still, sir, and you need not stain the carpet.'

Whitty opens his mouth to argue, but is prevented by a constriction: it seems that, like Dermot, he too wears a noose about his throat. Thinks Whitty: *What a ridiculous way to die.*

'He seems to be choking already, Mr Robin.'

'That is the whole point is it not, Mr Weeks?'

Bissett Grange

In a Wonderland they lie,
Dreaming as the days go by,
Dreaming as the summers die.

The girls, their mother and their governess have set a tea-table upon the clipped lawn in between the round room of the house and the conservatory; by the time Boltbyn arrives, the tea-cosy is on the pot and the tea is about to be served.

Birdie makes welcoming noises in an abstracted tone of voice and without meeting the vicar's gaze. After listening in silence to the usual pleasantries between Boltbyn and the girls, without taking tea herself, Birdie mentions a need for fresh air, opens her parasol, and sets off for an afternoon stroll.

It is the first time Boltbyn has seen her take any sort of exercise. He pretends to admire the cakes while she places the children under the supervision of Miss Pouch.

Lately he has been conscious of a lack of sympathy between himself and the mother of his angelic friends; whenever he visits the girls he feels he is tolerated, like a distant, deeply uninteresting relative. This has been the situation since that appalling dinner, when he was literally overcome by a sense that something dreadful is happening, without the faintest notion what it is, or to whom.

Miss Pouch having settled into the sermons of John Henry Newman, he turns his attention to the girls (who have already put away a surprising number of cakes), determined to make the best of what might be, for all he knows, their last afternoon together.

'Very well now, ladies. Pay close attention, for you are about to receive an extraordinary lesson in mathematics and logic. The question is this: if six cats kill six rats in six minutes, how many cats will be required to kill a hundred rats in fifty minutes?'

Emma is not listening, but is still looking in the direction her mother took to the wood. Unusual to say the least, thinks the vicar, for a woman to enter the wood unaccompanied while her husband is seeing a dentist in London.

'Miss Emma, what is your initial response to the question?'

Emma turns to him, suppressing a yawn. 'Repeat it if you please, Mr Boltbyn.'

Boltbyn does so, and is rewarded with a shrug. So he turns to the younger sister, who is blossoming into a charming young lady. 'Miss Lydia? Do you have something to contribute?'

'It is simple enough, Mr Boltbyn,' says Lydia – unlike her rude sister, she seems to thrive on mathematical problems. 'At one cat per rat per minute, the second group of cats is killing rats at double the rate. That would require twice as many cats as there are rats.'

'Very good, Miss Lydia – on the surface. But your assumption – that each cat kills a rat by itself – ignores other possibilities. For example, it might take all six cats to kill an especially large rat – which they do in a minute, while the other rats await their turn.'

'Or,' says Lydia, counting on her fingers, 'it might require three cats to kill a rat, which they do in two minutes.'

'Well done. Now consider: if a cat can kill a rat in one minute, how many cats will be needed to kill it in a thousandth of a second?'

After a long pause, Lydia replies: 'Sixty thousand.'

'Capital, Miss Lydia!' exults the vicar, for she really is a clever little darling.

'But that is absurd,' says Emma, rising to her feet. 'Surely it is plain that if so many cats were to set upon a single rat, at least fifty thousand would never see the rat at all.'

'I see you have lost patience with us,' he says, cleaning his spectacles.

'I am going to look for Mother and perhaps draw a picture.'

Replies the vicar, somewhat stiffly: 'But with Miss Pouch to accompany you, surely.'

'Well, Miss Pouch?' she says. 'Are you coming or not?'

Torn between the prospect of an arduous walk and her comfortable situation, Miss Pouch replies: 'I do not see the harm in your following your mother. But you are to keep to the main paths.'

'And especially avoid the woods and grazing-fields, where mantraps and ha-has await the unwary,' Boltbyn adds.

'You have given me that warning a hundred times,' replies Emma, tossing her napkin upon the grass and taking up her drawing-book. 'I am not a little girl, you know,' she says.

Boltbyn's cheeks flush as he watches her retreating back, then turns to his remaining audience. 'Miss Lydia, since you have been so patient (unlike certain others), would you like it if I were to take your picture in the guise of a wood-nymph and a goddess?'

'May I wear horns?' asks Lydia.

'Indeed, I have brought horns – and a costume that will make for a charming wood-nymph. And a halo for Miss Pouch.'

'Oh yes, Mr Boltbyn!' Lydia claps her hands, grasps Boltbyn's arm and endeavours to pull him to his feet. 'Let us do so at once – and I might give you a kiss on the cheek!'

'Now, Lydia,' cautions the governess. 'You are being presumptuous.'

'That is all right, Miss Pouch,' replies the vicar. 'A kiss on the cheek is always welcome.'

Emma wanders in the general direction her mother seemed to take, without at all expecting to find her. It is enough to escape the tedium of Mr Boltbyn's games and puzzles – and, truth be told, his photography. (Of late, she has become aware of changes in her person that alter the significance of baring a shoulder as a beggar-girl, or showing one's legs in the costume of a nymph, wading in a stream.)

She might be more amenable to taking pictures were the duke behind the camera and not the vicar. Danbury speaks to her as a gentleman to a lady. In fact, he once mentioned a vague possibility of photography – with Father's permission, of course.

By following the narrower path at each fork, she finds herself in a delightfully wild and neglected part of the estate, not unlike the Adderleigh Forest she used to imagine, with the roots of ancient, knotted hardwoods clutching its slopes and levels. For drawing, she settles on a picturesque clearing, with wild flowers peeping out among the rocks, and a soft sward growing in the shadows of russet, thorn and oak.

In the lap of this pleasant dell she finds a sun-warmed, flat-topped rock, near a patch of wild strawberries amid the tall grass. Here she can eat the delicious, pea-sized berries, while drawing some thin birches beside a fragment of an ancient stone wall.

As she basks in the dappled sunlight, her sketch forgotten for the moment, she becomes aware of approaching voices – of a man and a woman. She would rather not be discovered by strangers, if only because it is so much better to watch them; so she retreats further into the cave-like shadow of the bushes.

As the sounds come nearer she recognises her mother's voice, but not the male whisper. Then she hears her mother laugh – a rare sound in her experience. She peers beneath the boughs just as the pair step into the sunlight, her mother with her parasol, and the Duke of Danbury, in tweeds and boots and a floppy hat, carrying a thick blanket of the type used to warm horses.

They stop, regard one another, and laugh again. Never before has Emma heard her mother laugh twice in such a short period.

What transpires from that point as she watches from her hiding-place is confusing, but not so confusing as she would like it to be.

The duke spreads out the blanket as though for a picnic and the two sit down together. After an inaudible exchange, he leans forward and kisses her upon the mouth – a gesture she has never witnessed between her mother and father. She assumed, from her acquaintance with Mr Boltbyn, that the practice was restricted to the cheeks and hands. Nevertheless, such kissing cannot be all that unusual or uncomfortable, for Mother and the duke continue in this position for so long that she begins to suspect their mouths to have become stuck together. Now he seems to be nuzzling her throat and they lie down in the long grass, as though resting. Shortly his head reappears, hatless, kissing her bosom, while his hands loosen her bodice so that he may kiss her further down. Now his hands unbutton the front of her dress all the way to the waist, and his head disappears. After a pause, her mother makes an unfamiliar sound, something between pain and delight, and again they seal their lips together for a very long time.

She sees a blur of white stockings, garters, white thighs and other bits of flesh, and a momentary glimpse of a patch of dark hair. She hears a tearing of light cloth which must be her mother's chemise; the sound continues until the stays stop the fabric from tearing further.

Emma has forgotten to breathe, torn between the urge to run for her life, or to stand up for a better look.

It is as if they are dancing, but in a horizontal position. Both begin to moan softly, but with increasing urgency. Now her mother begins to moan as though from some deep ache – and yet something tells Emma that her mother is not in pain, that what is being done is entirely deliberate. Carefully she cranes her neck, in time to see her mother cry out aloud with eyes shut tight. Now the duke draws down the veil from her hair, the veil she brought to the dinner, and he covers her face with the white muslin, and kisses Mother through the thin fabric. After some urgent rustling, he makes a succession of sounds so disturbing that it is all Emma can do not to run down and rescue her mother – excepting that Mother does not protest. On the contrary, she seems to co-operate until, after an extended shudder, they fall limply onto the blanket together.

They remain still. Emma, trembling with fear and excitement, reviews the events in her mind, this strange, dark story, sensing that her mother is in some danger but that none of it can be mentioned to anyone.

Mother and Danbury reappear above the grass, adjusting their clothing, cheeks flushed as though with fever. Mother neatly folds the blanket, gives it to her companion, retrieves her parasol, and together they walk through the tall grass the way they came, while Emma hides in the bushes. They cannot be more than a yard away when they pass; Danbury pauses to pick a wild strawberry, puts it in her mouth, and Mother laughs a third time.

Emma counts all the way to five thousand before leaving her hiding-place. Clutching her drawing-book and pencils, she walks to where the long grass lies flattened, to search for clues as to what they were doing. In the corner of her eye she catches sight of a crumpled wad of paper, which must have fallen from someone's pocket. This she picks up, and after smoothing it upon her knee, reads the elegant script:

> *Who is it that hath burst the door*
> *Unclosed the heart that shut before*
> *And set her queen-like on its throne*
> *And made its homage all her own*
> *My Birdie.*

She feels what she suspects to be a flash of jealousy – of her own mother! The duke was to have been *her* protector, *her* special friend, now that she has outgrown Mr Boltbyn. Yet if what she just witnessed is a requirement for a special friendship with a gentleman, perhaps she is better off the way things are.

She places the poem between the pages of her drawing-book and decides to find her way back by a different route, for if she were to overtake her mother and the duke she would simply die of embarrassment and shame. So she picks her way along the ruined stone fence, reasoning that it must lead somehow or other to the main part of the estate; she lifts her legs high with each step, not to ruin her hose on the brambles which cover the stones as though to prevent intruders.

At length she reaches a stile that straddles the ruined wall and, crossing over, finds herself on a well-worn path. Further along she is surprised to discover a tiny, ancient churchyard – but with no church in evidence, nor even the foundation of one; just a rusted fence containing a strong, spiked gate, ornamented with skulls made of stone, like severed heads impaled by the iron spikes. In the late afternoon light they grimace down at Emma as though to say, What a pretty girl! Off with *her* head as well!

She wants to flee this unwholesome spot at once, but first she peers through the rails into the graveyard, where a sparrow, perched upon a broken, lopsided tombstone, chirrups away as though it were the most pleasant place in the world.

The gravestones have crumbled and the mounds have lost their shape from centuries of rain, with many collapsed into little valleys – excepting a row of more recent graves near the rear fence, whose overturned earth has sprouted a thick layer of weed-cover. Indeed, one of the mounds appears as though it were dug very recently – how peculiar that none contains a marker of any kind!

She glances at the skulls on the opened gate. In the long light of late afternoon they seem to wink at her in conspiratorial fashion, as though to say: *If you knew who is sleeping here, you would be surprised.* They put her in mind of haunted places and ghosts – although she does not believe in ghosts, unlike the servant who took her for one.

A ghost named Eliza?

An alarming sensation follows: that someone is watching. And it is not the skulls. It is someone alive.

Lush has spent the best part of this afternoon at the window in the round room, smoking the duke's cigars, and observing the elder daughter in action, as it imitated the behaviour of a normal child.

Naturally the fool Boltbyn, being a counterfeit child himself, not once detected the undertone of malevolence, the flinty contempt in the eyes, the barely concealed groan whenever he initiated one of his infantile games.

Not long after the mother made her exit (an assignation with the duke, no doubt), the elder daughter gathered sketch-book and pencils, and left the company for the wood, alone.

An unanticipated opportunity – to do *what*? In truth, Lush cared not a fig whether or not the daughter stumbled upon her mother, *in flagrante* – in fact, such an event might prove an advantage, if only the threat of imminent scandal might stifle the affair.

What worries Lush is that the girl might find the cemetery; should that occur, the creature would present a serious threat to the estate and, most important, to himself.

Run of the house, indeed!

Accordingly, while Emma wandered down a path to the right, Lush took a more circuitous route to the spot he now occupies, in the graveyard, awaiting the moment of truth – and the resolve required to do what must be done.

Inside his coat pocket, he feels the barrel-shaped bottle and the handkerchief he will use, for he is not a beast. As with the others it will be done painlessly, and with a heavy heart.

How is it possible, Lush wonders, for a mere child to uncover, in the space of a few days, secrets which have remained secure for half her lifetime? Not a normal child to be sure, and certainly not an innocent one.

Childhood fables come to mind about the changeling, the demon child, who can be saved from the clutches of the devil only through torture, or by causing it to laugh.

Lush has no stomach for torture, and no hope of making Emma laugh.

She sees in her peripheral vision the unmistakable hedgehog shape, beneath a hawthorn tree, in a corner of the cemetery, beside a lichen-green obelisk with a barely discernible symbol of the Freemasons.

A feeling of dread comes over her – that this hedgehog is nothing like the one in Mr Boltbyn's story.

She wishes her sister were with her now – which is odd, for it is difficult to imagine Lydia providing any special protection against the ill-behaviour of a fully grown adult. Then again, she is not certain what she needs protection *from* – having the duke's protection. He said so himself, and Mr Lush is in the duke's employ.

Unless the duke himself means to do her harm.

Emma recalls their first meeting – the soft gloves, the rose, the eyes of a hunter. She was afraid of him then, and is afraid of him now. She does not have the least idea why this might be, for it is clear that he and Mother – and Father as well – are on the closest possible terms.

Inexplicably, the photograph comes to mind – the mysterious pattern of shadows and light that caused her to shudder.

Resolving to return to the safety of Bissett Grange at once, Emma thinks it will take twelve walking steps to reach the gate, at which point she will casually turn in the opposite direction from Mr Lush –

whereupon, she will run just as fast as she can, until the hedgehog is out of sight, and then she will hide until it is safe.

As soon as she starts for the gate, however, she hears footsteps behind her – a man's heavy boots scrunching through the overgrown lawn. When she quickens her step, so does he. As she struggles through the tall grass, in Emma's mind he is catching up. Now she can feel his presence at the nape of her neck, and cannot resist turning sideways, and beholds the hedgehog, even closer than she had imagined, with a white object held out in one hand. Biting her lip not to cry out, she breaks into a run, pell-mell, through the tall grass, past the skulls, along the iron fence, jumping over uprooted sod and exposed rocks, until at last she summons the courage to look behind her – and there is the estate manager, far behind, leaning against the gate, seemingly tying his shoe . . .

He was not chasing her after all.

Soon thereafter, Emma happens upon an undulating sheep-walk which leads to a wide glen, and from there to the conservatory and the main estate. Now the picnic things are in sight, near the round room; there, a worried Miss Pouch sits alone at the tea-table, her book closed in her lap.

By this time, Emma has decided not to mention the incident to anyone. What a silly goose they will think of her, running away from a gentleman armed with a handkerchief!

'Emma, you are flushed and out of breath. I hope you have not given yourself a chill.'

'No, Miss Pouch. I hurried back because I did not wish to worry you.'

'Mr Boltbyn is photographing Lydia among the flower-beds. He asks that you join them.'

The cramp in his side having subsided, the estate manager rises to his full height, to face the grinning skulls on the gate: *Thought you could run it down did you – like the lion and the gazelle?*

How foolish. Lush has taken no exercise since university; even then, it was only so far as to meet the quota demanded of a well-balanced Oxonian – *Mens sana in Corpore Sano*. Meanwhile, in the intervening years he has taken on several stone, smoked ten cigars per day, drunk a bottle of claret and a half-bottle of brandy – the burden of responsibility here at Bissett Grange.

Now Lush realises he faces a deeper menace: the speed and

determination with which the girl ran away indicates the canny little demon, whatever it might suspect, knows Lush to be an enemy. It will be Christmas in Hell before he catches her alone again.

A pity, and a worry.

Stuffing his handkerchief back into his pocket, Lush proceeds painfully along the rusted fence to the sheep-walk, thinking that the girl will be taken care of, one way or another, and not necessarily when asleep.

Emma finds her sister amid the flower-beds, trying to prance through the blooms in the guise of a sprite – a difficult assignment when one is required to stand on one foot as though in mid-prance. Once, Emma recalls, she was compelled to stand at the top of a very high ladder, one foot on the rung, as though she had just climbed out a window, for nearly half an hour, as the sunlight did not meet with Mr Boltbyn's approval.

'Mr Boltbyn, I do not know how long I can remain in this awkward position,' Lydia complains.

'Only one more minute,' pleads the vicar, about to insert the glass into the camera. 'Imagine yourself as a tree.'

'I do, but the tree keeps waving in the wind.'

'Then you need to be a bigger tree.'

'Here is Emma,' says Lydia. 'She is much better at being a tree.'

'Ah, Miss Emma, we missed you,' says the vicar, relieved. 'Your sister has not yet mastered the art of stillness.'

'I took a walk. I was thinking about the girl in the mirror, the girl in my poem who claims to be my twin, and I have decided to give her a name. Do you know what it is?'

'I haven't the faintest notion. Please tell.'

'She is Eliza.'

'That is an exceedingly pretty name. Did it appear in the mirror?'

'No. It was written on the wall of her prison.'

'I see. Do you know, there is a book in which something of the kind happens. It is called *The Count of Monte Cristo*?'

Emma thinks, inexplicably relieved: He does not know about Eliza, or he would surely have stuttered.

33

Machpelah Street

Whitty is standing upright now, on the dining table at which he once ate dinner, with a noose around his neck.

There is no doubt in his mind that the medium suffered the same fate, at the hands of these same peculiar pillars of empire. To the psychic's credit, he must have acquitted himself well, for the face of the taller officer is badly smashed, while the corporal rasps when he takes a deep breath, in the way of a man with broken ribs.

The rope chafes Whitty's neck as he turns his head in the direction of his fellow victim, who appears to be saying his prayers.

England expects every man to do his duty!

Issuing the above proclamation, the corporal delivers a forceful kick to the table, causing it to roll upon its side, and Whitty finds himself swinging from the chandelier, with his feet a yard above the Turkey carpet.

Reaching desperately, he grips the chandelier with both hands, to lessen the pressure of the noose – a short-term solution to be sure, for already the sharpish metal-work is cutting into his fingers.

Says the officer in dark glasses: 'We have hanged many fellow Englishmen, sir. An English soldier may be hanged for losing his weapon, for cowardice and for many lesser offences.'

'I am a civilian. Release me at once.'

'Civilian hangings serve to restore public order,' replies the officer. 'Especially in cases of looting and profiteering.'

Whitty is beginning to lose his grip. Turning his head as far as possible to the left, he glimpses the form of Downy Dermot, similarly attached to the chandelier.

Having nothing better to do, he cries out at the top of his lungs, 'Help! Murder!'

'You will have to do better than that if you want to be heard from the street,' says the white-haired officer, moving to the door. '*Shebash*, sir. Face it like an Englishman; not like the last fellow, kicking and screaming like a woman.'

'Your qualms are specious, sir,' rasps the correspondent. 'You are murderers – and smug murderers, which is all the worse.'

'Might we stay and watch the death struggle, sir?' Of all the forms of entertainment, the corporal has a special regard for traditional army discipline.

'That is not our way, Mr Weeks. When the 2nd Infantry secures a noose to a man's neck, it remains secure.'

'True for you, Mr Robin. An efficient hanging is the thing.'

> Let him wiggle on the branch,
> Take not a backward glance,
> And we'll hang the more in Delhi in the morning!

At the door, the two soldiers address the two hanged men as though for the conclusion of a court-martial. 'Britain, India and St George!' cries the superior officer, heels clicking smartly. '*Hazar!*' cries Weeks, his salute marred by the missing thumb – whereupon the two wheel about in tandem and make their exit.

In the sudden silence of his family dining room, Whitty turns in the direction of his companion.

'Dermot, have you done with praying?' he rasps.

'I may have,' comes the strangled reply.

'How goes it, then?'

'As voluble as can be expected, sor.'

Whitty looks down upon the great mahogany sideboard, grey with dust, which bore witness to lavish dinners. 'They have pushed the furniture out of reach, I'm afraid.'

'Oh they have fer certain. Knows their business them two. Queen's Indian Army, you know.'

'You flatter them outrageously, sir. They are mercenaries for the East India Company – killing natives so that the trains run properly.'

'Veterans o' the mutiny, true. The most feared man-bashers on the Embankment. Prefers for hanging 'cause it saves ammunition.'

Having no patience for conversation in the circumstances, Whitty's attention turns to the ceiling beam – and curiously, at that instant he experiences a memory of the brother . . .

A quarter-century ago, David persuaded his younger brother Edmund that they might enjoyably swing from this very chandelier, as though it were a merry-go-round. The two boys climbed upon the table and enjoyed a merry time of it, until they began to detect the sound and feel of splitting wood . . .

'Do you suppose, Dermot, there might be dry-rot in the roof?'

'I breaks into houses, not builds them, sor. Yet any kind of rot would be most welcome.'

'Dermot, I wonder what would happen were we to swing ourselves back and forth in a concerted manner?' By now, the sound coming from Whitty's mouth is like air escaping from a hose.

'Knowing the alternative, sor, we concurves.'

The two men begin to swing their legs back and forth in unison – tentatively at first, from the knees, then the torso, until the chain supports in the ceiling move sharply back and forth. The I-bolts in the ceiling appear discouragingly firm at first, but after four or five cycles the two hanged men are rewarded with a light, delightful sprinkle of sawdust upon their heads. Thus encouraged, they begin to chant a unison 'heave-ho', in the manner of sailors, though it hurts the throat damnably. With each syllable, one man kicks forward while the other heaves backward, and now their heads are covered by a thick layer of sawdust, as welcome as manna. By craning his neck backward, Whitty can now see that the bright iron shaft of one of the I-bolts is now visible, that two others are moving slightly. The two swing wider and wider, until they hear a familiar cracking sound from the beam, followed by a sudden, joyful crash, as the entire apparatus smashes down upon their heads, together with a dense shower of sawdust, followed by an entire colony of carpenter ants in a state of utmost agitation.

For a long while the two men lie upon the carpet, buried in tarnished metal and coiled chains, breathing in great rasps, spitting dust and ants from their mouths, scraping their eyes with their throbbing fingers, and wondering what to do next.

'An auspicious outcome, it seems,' Whitty remarks, at length.

'Seemingly,' replies Downy Dermot.

What Whitty has in mind is a speedy retreat, followed by a dose of medicinal snuff, followed by several jars of spiced gin, then a bath and a change of clothes. After that he intends to peruse the shipping news for imminent sailings to Canada. 'We had better vacate the premises immediately, is my view,' he says, rising to a seated position and removing the noose from his neck.

'It is a rare murderer, sor, who returns to inspect his work. As well, the Captain takes a low view of those what fail to complete a dooty. By my reckoning, the danger is the greater in retreat, and we had best continue.'

'Sir, you were to assist me in entering this residence. That accomplished, you are free to undertake a discreet exit, with my thanks.'

'Perhaps, yet an attempt on one's life pikes the curiosity something marvellous.'

'Quite,' Whitty snaps, who may be curious also, but holds discretion as the better part of valour.

Untangling himself from the knot of chandelier and chains, it occurs to Whitty that he is about to probe his brother's private life, in the company of an employee of the Captain. Can this be wise? Does he have a choice?

'If I may speak frankly, Dermot, as we continue on our journey, is it your intention to report to the Captain everything that you see and hear?'

'I have no notation as to what you infer,' says Dermot.

'I mean that we are in my former home, sir. There are issues of privacy.'

'We must retrieve our tools, what are also private,' says the snakesman, who disappears into another room.

Reasoning that if he cannot pry a direct answer from Dermot, neither will the Captain, Whitty makes his way to the staircase leading to the brother's chambers on the uppermost floor – stairs he has not climbed in years, to a room he has never entered at all, even when his brother was alive.

Dermot returns with the heavy carpet-bag under one arm. 'Appears a fine house,' remarks Dermot. 'A person were extremely fortuitous to be raised in this house.'

'That may be so,' replies Whitty. 'Yet one must take into account what went on in it, and what has gone on thereafter.'

'Possibly,' agrees the snakesman. 'Still, it is a fine house.'

The treads groan as though in pain as the two house-breakers proceed from one landing up to the next. Each level opens onto a series of melancholy, tomblike orifices that were once cosy bedchambers, sitting rooms, dens, now with their window-shutters closed tight. Each floor emits a stronger pong of mildew than its predecessor. On the top floor, the rooms are tinier and rougher than any of the chambers below, having been designed for the armada of servants required for such an establishment a generation ago. From here they climb a queer, steep little stairway to David's chambers, really just a turret at the back of the house.

Dermot puts down his carpet-bag to catch his breath and to extract an ant or two from under his collar. 'Some might find it queer, sor, that the first-born of a fine house such as this would choose such a remote and inconvenient bedchamber.'

'My brother was of an intense, studious nature. When at home he preferred seclusion. This is the first time in my life that I have ventured here.'

In fact, when David took the upstairs room, it seemed as though his brother sought refuge from having to breathe the same air as the rest of the family. 'I expect that the door is locked,' he says.

'That is no great problem if you would stand clear.' So saying, the snakesman turns his back to the door and takes hold of the railing with both hands. Using the leg furthest from the door, he suddenly kicks back in the manner of a mule, so that the heel of his foot strikes a spot next to the key-hole, causing the door to snap open with a sharp crack.

'Very impressive,' remarks Whitty.

'It is a question of aim and follow-through,' Dermot replies. 'And practice.'

David's room, while in use, was clearly as spartan as Whitty would expect it to be, consisting of a simple bed, writing-table and chair, and an easy chair upholstered with what Whitty remembers as green velvet, now the colour of dead skin. Under the low gable is a fitted bookcase. These furnishings, however, lie buried beneath the contents of David's Oxford rooms: rotting leather volumes of the Greeks, piled waist-high, manuscripts containing treatises and translations, now the texture of oat cakes left in the rain, and piles of clothing – all coloured a rotten greenish-grey. Heaped carelessly in the far corner is David's photo-graphic equipment, also mouldy but for the glass and metal, on top of a heavy oak cabinet with two wide drawers, of the type used by clerks in the City.

'Were we on regular business,' confides Dermot, 'we would regard this here as a paucitous return for time and effort.'

Whitty has sunk to his knees and now struggles unsuccessfully to open one of the drawers, afraid of what they may contain.

'It is locked,' observes Dermot. 'You might as well pound your head upon it. Move aside, please.'

Crouching beside the correspondent, Dermot pulls open his carpet-bag and extracts a number of small tools, individually wrapped in cloth to prevent the clanking of metal against metal. From among these he chooses a set of instruments of thin steel, like something a dentist might employ to probe a toothache. Now he produces a lantern which, when lit, trains a narrow, intense spot upon the lock. From a bundle of metal picks he selects a flat-headed instrument, which he inserts into the keyhole and turns like a miniature key. Leaving the instrument inside, he selects a pick whose end curves upward, and inserts it next to its flat-headed cousin. With his ear all but touching the lock, he now undertakes a series of small, deft movements in the way of a watchmaker, then abruptly rotates the flat-headed instrument and opens the drawer without difficulty. He repeats the process with the second drawer. The process, all told, requires about a minute.

'Examine at leisure, sor.'

'Thank you.' Whitty leans forward with more apprehension than gratitude and begins to explore.

The top drawer contains, as expected, hundreds of photographs, mostly landscapes taken during the brother's travels: trees silhouetted in the Cotswold mist; noble gardens and walks that create a study of perspective near Cheddar Gorge; the Bowder Stone in Barrowdale; as well as various other scenes of the Oxford region – the Thames River, Blenheim Palace, the White Horse of Uffington and the Roland Stones – eminently predictable subjects for the seeker of Mystic Britannia.

The second drawer contains not landscapes but portraits. Leafing through with thumb and forefinger, Whitty encounters what appears to be a series of worthies and colleagues at St Ambrose, dressed in gowns and caps in cloistered settings, or in sporting clothes at picnics and boat-races.

From a theme of Prominence, both geographic and human, David's photographs now turn to the theme of Innocence – mostly portraits of children, all female, with parasols on their shoulders and smiles upon their faces. Gradually, the pictures begin to alter in theme and in tone, until the young women appear as allegorical figures from the Greeks, whose costumes display rather more skin surface than before. One of these women is depicted sleeping in the bath – an image made famous by William Nixon Crede.

At the back of the drawer he discovers a sheaf of portraits depicting David himself, alone and with various companions. Of particular interest to him is a scene depicting the rowing team in which David acted as coxswain, to an eight led by none other than the Duke of Danbury, the same noble who presided over the brother's last seance. He poses, oar aloft, with one hand upon David's shoulder. A note on the back indicates that the picture was taken by William Boltbyn, a fixture of the college – who, Whitty recalls, achieved a sort of fame as an author of children's books, and as a portrait photographer.

Still further inside the drawer, he uncovers another photograph which, to judge by the equipment at its centre, depicts the photography club of which his brother was a member – as was, it seems, the Duke of Danbury, the same nobleman who presided over Bill Williams's last seance.

Attached to the picture of the photography club is a sheet of paper containing the sort of contrived pastiche Oxford men create for casual amusement, having little better to do:

> *Under a spreading camera-tree*
> *The Picture-taker stands;*
> *A sharp-eyed, patient man is he,*
> *With steady arms and hands . . .*

Putting aside the photograph and its accompanying doggerel, he searches the rear of the drawer and pulls out another sheaf of photographs, one of which causes him to gasp aloud.

David, naked, in circumstances identical to the obscenity Whitty now carries in his pocket – from the luxurious divan to the scar upon his shoulder; from the mark upon his naked thigh to the painted screen and the oriental wallpaper in the background.

The resemblance is not lost upon the snakesman. 'I say, sor, were that one from the Hollywell job?'

Whitty ransacks his mind for an answer. 'No, as you can see, it is from my brother's personal collection.'

'I knows that, sir.'

'Indeed you do. You might as well have a look at this.'

Whitty pulls from his pocket the envelope and extracts the two photographs containing Eliza. 'Do you see the background, Dermot? And the gentleman accompanying her?'

'Indeed I does, and I am not surprised that you are leerish of telling the Captain.'

'I am counting on your discretion in the matter, Dermot.'

'I know nout of what matter you mean, sor.'

The correspondent holds two photographs in Dermot's bullet-lamp for comparison: in one the brother stands alone, as though gloating over his own perfection of form; in the other he is joined by naked Eliza, as though they are about to participate in an unspecific sexual act. In the third, Eliza sits alone, in the same surroundings.

'Dermot, I appeal to your experience with this sort of material. Does anything strike you as unusual or suspicious?'

'Indeed, sor. The gentleman in the picture is, shall we say, in repose.'

'In repose?'

'There is no evidence of excited tumescence, if you take my meaning.'

'Quite.' That had not occurred to him. Sometimes Whitty is appalled by his own *naïveté*.

'As well, sor, if you hold the pictures together it is plain that the girl is somewhat ill-focused, while the gentleman is sharp and clean. From this it is my belief that it is a combination print.'

'A combination of what?'

'Where the glass plates is stacked one upon the other.'

Of course, thinks Whitty. A mongrel technological oddity, the technique was a highlight of the Manchester Art Treasures exhibition two years ago – a piece of unimaginative trickery which thrilled the queen.

He could shout for joy on David's behalf, would not the sound, if heard outside, earn him ten years' transportation.

'My thanks, Dermot. You have taken a weight from my mind.'

Whitty returns his attention to the cabinet and the remaining pictures of David. Who took them, he wonders? Which member of the photographic club? Despite the oriental wallpaper, the impression is undeniably Greek, and undeniably vain – a man in the prime of life, holding himself up to be the Platonic ideal of manliness.

'Note, sor, how the background of the two is the same – rather Chinese unless I am mistaken, who knows nout about art.'

On the back of the photograph, as with the rowing club, someone has written a commemorative poem.

'Might you read that, sor?' asks Dermot. 'We has a interest in poems but no knack for reading.'

Whitty complies:

> *A is for Angley in anger to dwell,*
> *B is for Boltbyn and Bracebridge as well;*
> *C is for Crede, the cock in a cage,*
> *D is for Danbury, shocking the age,*
> *And for David Whitty, stalking the stage . . .*

'That is a deepish one,' mutters Dermot, scratching his chin. ''Tis a bundle of rhymes.'

'What is your sense of it?'

'Seemingly they is a sort of club. 'Tis a clubbish thing to make a joke of one another's character.'

'You are correct – it is the Oxford Photographic Club.'

'That would explain the nature of the photographs themselves,' says Dermot, taking a picture from Whitty's hand and indicating David with one long finger. 'Look at your brother, sor; by the looks of him, he be very much on stage.'

'Dermot I salute you,' says the correspondent, 'for you have cut to the heart of it. I must search out the Oxford Photographic Society.'

'Perhaps, sor. Yet if it was me, I would search for the wallpaper.'

3 4

Crouch Manor

LOSS of TEETH
Dr Gunter Eisler, the dental surgeon,
of 17 George Street, Hanover Square,
announces production of an entirely
NEW DESCRIPTION of ARTIFICIAL TEETH,
without springs, wires or ligatures,
which so perfectly resemble natural teeth
as not to be distinguished from the originals.
They will never change colour or decay,
nor does the method necessitate painful extraction.
Interested parties should avail themselves of this discovery.

The most bitter misfortunes in life are those one brings down upon oneself, while on the quest for happiness.

How often has the Reverend Lambert longed to have his teeth pulled out – to put an end, once and for all, to this constant torment, these demons infesting his mouth. Yet as a man with a calling, a man destined to lead, Lambert would consent to worse tortures before surrendering to a set of rattling, hissing dentures like those of the Reverend Spoole.

Recently, however, Lambert has been eagerly following, in the press, news of a remarkable advance in dentistry thanks to a Dr Eisler, a dentist of Swiss descent and training, credited with bringing to London the most modern European developments.

Maintaining a sceptical frame of mind, Lambert took an exploratory trip to London, to seek out Dr Eisler's offices. Not only did the doctor himself present a most impressive figure (and a set of excellent teeth), but an entire wall of the consulting-room displayed photographs of previous patients, dozens of them, smiling for the camera, row upon row of perfect, white, painless teeth.

The Reverend made his decision there and then.

A week thereafter, having informed the house of his intention (if not the cost), and after informing Mr Spoole of an unspecified medical necessity, once again he took the train to London.

Instead of pulling the teeth, in the Eisler method they are sawn flat to the gum, after which the roots are scored with tiny wire brushes, leaving a secure foundation, to which an ivory bridge is anchored by means of steel pins. The result, according to the literature, is 'exactly like having one's own teeth for life, and without pain'.

The latter claim could not be made for the operation itself. In Lambert's case, only direct applications of chloroform enabled him to withstand the sawing, and the chemical burnt his mouth abominably. After what seemed like an eternity in Hell, it was over, and the patient was able to stagger out of the surgery with his new teeth, minus several months' salary.

After a sleepless nightmare in a rented room, delirious with opiates, he made the return journey to Crouch Manor with the lower part of his face covered by a scarf, whereupon he immediately took to his bed, there to await what Dr Eisler termed 'the healing process of nature'.

The healing process has been slower than expected.

Lambert and his teeth have remained festering in his bed for two weeks now, drugged with morphine and under constant attendance by Lizzy, the maid-of-all-work, whose own face is becoming increasingly drawn with fatigue and distaste.

Meanwhile, in the rest of Crouch Manor life goes on.

Emma, whose own teeth are excellent, has observed recent events in the household with interest, if not engagement. It is a sad truth that, while she respects her father as the head of the house, she has no clear picture of him as a person. While she hearkens to everything he says, the state of the mouth itself is of little consequence. It is her mother she worries about more, especially in light of recent events.

For of late there has occurred a curious reversal of position between her parents, in which Mother, who rarely ventured outside the bedroom before, now spends hours out-of-house, at the dress shops, or off to Bissett Grange by private coach, while it is Father who remains closeted like an invalid.

Mother's stated reason for visiting Bissett Grange is as an intermediary for her husband's spiritual counsel during his illness. The lessons must be subtle indeed, for Emma has not heard Father utter an intelligible syllable to anyone.

Meanwhile, Mother has acquired a new, almost feverish vitality; upon one occasion, when Emma entered her dressing room for the ritual kiss and to watch her mother braid her hair before retiring, Birdie suddenly took her daughter into her arms in a frenzy of joy, and recited a nursery-rhyme:

> *If her father's cottage*
> *Turned into a palace,*
> *And he owned the hilltops*
> *And the flowering valleys,*
> *She'd be none the happier,*
> *Happy little Alice!*

'Oh, my darling, I am happy!' Mother cried out. 'I am happy at last, and you shall be too!'

Emma didn't know what to think of that.

35

Crouch Manor

So passed they on with even pace:
Yet gradually one might trace
A shadow growing on his face.

There was a time when the nursery seemed a magic place to Boltbyn, a safe haven of innocent wonder. Not so today. Now it is a place of inchoate menace, and the picture by William Nixon Crede fills him with such inexplicable revulsion, he would like to tear it from the wall and trample it to pieces. Likewise, the bars in the window no longer represent protection but imprisonment – again, he does not know why.

Worst of all, while it has always been his practice to encourage the imaginative flights of his little friends, no matter how nonsensical, for some reason he cannot bring himself to follow Emma's train of fantasy concerning a twin in the mirror named Eliza. What comes to his mind is the subject of the last photographic session, and the insinuation in Danbury's aspect, in that moment, standing above the sleeping girl who looked like Emma . . .

'Mr Boltbyn!' cries Lydia from her place on the couch. 'Are you going to begin the story or not?'

'Ah yes. In fact, there has been a change of course: Rather than return to Emma's Adventures, we turn our attention to Miss Lydia – who, while waiting for Emma to come home from Adderleigh Forest, has encountered a hedgehog, who is able to provide Miss Lydia with important insights which will surely be of benefit in later life. With this in mind, we turn to the Song of the Hedgehog:

I'll say the little that I can,
Confinèd to my set;
Pondering on Afghanistan
And points of etiquette:
"What badge of hedgehog be thou?"
To the mirror me I said;
"I see thy malady now
You've been eating peas in bed . . ."

'Excuse me, Mr Boltbyn,' interrupts Emma, though he wishes she wouldn't. 'Lydia and I have decided something about the hedgehog.'

Boltbyn sighs.

'The hedgehog is Mr Lush. Have you not observed that he looks like one?'

'It is true,' says Lydia. 'I was the one who first noticed.'

Boltbyn finds himself in agreement. 'It is true: Mr Lush does indeed correspond to the shape and the prickliness of a hedgehog. Yet I do not see how this advances our story.'

'That depends upon how one looks at hedgehogs,' replies Emma. 'Hedgehogs are neither friends, nor pets. A hedgehog is a sniffer, who lies in wait.'

'Miss Emma, I don't have the slightest purchase on your meaning.'

'She is always doing this,' says Lydia. 'She should make up her own stories rather than ruin ours.'

'I sympathise,' replies the vicar, patting the blonde head of this remarkably pretty and intelligent girl.

Emma remains undeterred. 'I mean that it is a curious thing to encounter a creature whose desires are not the least like one's own, it can take one by surprise.'

'That is true,' replies Boltbyn.

'Which is what happened to Eliza.'

'What on earth do you mean?'

'Eliza is a ghost.'

'I see.'

'Eliza has entered the other world, yet there is something she must accomplish in this one.'

'And what might that be?'

'Did you once tell me that the savages refuse to have their picture taken?'

'True. There is a belief among the natives that it will steal one's soul.'

'That is how it was with Eliza: The hedgehog stole her soul, and she wants it back.'

Unaccountably, the vicar succumbs to a bout of stuttering. 'Th-th-th-the story cannot progress f-further. Please forgive me, I am f-f-feeling ill and must retire.'

'Mr Boltbyn, what is wrong?' asks Lydia.

'Something has upset him,' says Emma.

36

The Thames

Easily the most efficient way to Oxford nowadays is by train. However, Whitty has not forgotten Governor Whidden of Millbank, who will surely have put crushers onto the case of the escaped murderer named Willows. Thinking it best to take an unorthodox route, Whitty consulted the Captain, who suggested (of all things) a canal-boat. The craft in question now awaits him at the Paddington arm of the Union Canal, ready to transport him to the Thames and north to his destination.

Holding a handkerchief over his nose and mouth, Whitty grimly regards the *Endeavour*, easily the most dissipated hulk at the dock, packed to the gunnels with wooden kegs.

Other than its fugitive passenger, the *Endeavour*'s obligation is to transport the handiwork of Dr Uriah Pegg, the 'drink-doctor' who can double the volume of a keg of gin with the drinker none the wiser, other than to remark that it is a signal vintage of the Out-and-Out. A sure winner for the myriad drinking places catering to the sailors, longshoremen, porters and watermen who populate the Thames, and a gold-spinner for the Captain who controls the distribution.

The boat-horse, a lumpy animal with a wiry coat like a pig's, is in the process of being harnessed by a small, leathery horseman of indeterminate age, of the Islamic persuasion, whose task is to direct, feed and water the lumbering beast through upwards of sixty locks, all the way to Birmingham.

'How do you do, sir?' Whitty addresses the keg-shaped man at the stern. 'Are you Mr Neffici?'

The gentleman rolls his eyes towards the bow, where Whitty encounters another gentleman, also keg-shaped but with a wedge-shaped beard, who lifts one palm upward, shrugs, and makes a mysterious clicking sound with his mouth, as does a third Mussulman at the stern.

'Quite. Gentlemen, I believe I am expected. Edmund Whitty, correspondent for *The Falcon*. I bring greetings from our employer.' The correspondent heaves his carpet-bag onto the deck and stumbles aboard, having received neither greeting nor a hand-up.

According to the Captain the three Mussulmen once served the Sultanate of Shihr and Makalla, of the protectorate of Aden. While in command of a naval ship, the Captain moved guns and opiates on the sultan's behalf. For this, he was given a generous stipend, and three slaves.

Given that slavery is, to a Briton, an evil to be expunged from the earth (without harming British interests, of course), the Captain was not about to parade around London with a contingent of slaves; neither could he simply turn them loose: such an insult to the sultan, even in London, could earn him *khukuri* in the back. Knowing that the three once piloted a dhow in the Red Sea, the Captain opted to utilise them in transporting Dr Pegg's prized cargo to the thirsty mouths of Middlesex – with the assurance that Mussulmen abstain from alcohol and would not deplete the stock.

Having apparently taken his arrival as the signal to depart, the two boatmen busy themselves with the tie-line and tow-line, while the horseman mutters a syllable to his unlovely steed, inspiring the beast to trudge methodically along the narrow path, ankle-deep with steaming turds, at a steady pace of three miles an hour. In a little while Whitty feels a slight tug, and the *Endeavour* is on its way.

There being no roof, furniture, nor any other accommodation upon the vessel, the hold being filled with kegs to the gunnels, Whitty settles down on his carpet-bag and proceeds to view the passing cavalcade of London's seediest architecture, her flimsiest bridges, her poorest neighbourhoods.

Soon the *Endeavour* settles into its accustomed rituals, a regimen of coffee-drinking, *ghat*-smoking, sullen contemplation and intermittent prayers to the East, as the vessel lumbers on past Bulls Bridge, past the Railway Works, forty-five locks to Marsworth. In that time, not once does the horseman lift his gaze from the shit immediately ahead of him – clearly our man takes no solace in the English countryside. Or perhaps he is in prayer, drawing on some ancient legacy of camel trains plodding through the Sahara.

Nor does an intelligible sentence emanate from the beak of Mr Awad at the stern; and as for Mr Neffici at the bow, the English language exists as a series of *non sequiturs*, with smiles and nods at either end.

As the *Endeavour* passes the Grand Junction Canal, a gentle shower moistens Whitty's head and neck for an hour, then turns to sleet – another whimsical turn of the weather on a summer day in Britain. By the time the barge makes its way through Ealing it is early evening and the sleet has become a gentle drizzle, warm only in comparison to what came before.

By the third day, Whitty finds it possible to breathe the air without an intervening handkerchief, the *Endeavour* having penetrated deep into the countryside – a rolling vista of rectangular fields coloured various shades of green and yellow, like a nonsensical game-board, dotted with thatched cottages, each containing a country family, cuddled up with the pigs. At regular intervals they unload a portion of their cargo, at night and in eerie silence, as the lumbering shadows of local workmen appear and disappear like ghosts . . .

'Lock hoo!' Mr Awad cries out.

Awakened from a feverish slumber, Whitty faces the prospect of a set of lock-gates, green with slime, groaning as if in pain. The gates open slowly before him, and their vessel slides into a dark pit smelling of rotten fish; now the mournful lock gates close, leaving the *Endeavour* floating in rubbish.

The level slowly rises until he glimpses a lock-keeper, whip-thin and as dry as an old pocketbook, moving the blunt wooden levers of the windlass. Now the second set of gates opens in front of them and they re-enter the Thames, as grey and as flat and as heavy as slate . . .

Nothing can be seen but the spoiling effects of water: discoloured metal, rotten wood, dank deposits of loathsome vegetation, suggesting a potential story – *Through the Belly of Britain*, sort of thing. While musing on the prospect, Whitty is startled when Mr Neffici, apropos of nothing and with the peculiar discourse of his race, speaks, and at surprising length.

37

Bissett Grange, Oxfordshire

'I don't understand, Harry. I don't know what it is you want.'

'I would wish for a clear focus for once. Therefore please oblige me by remaining still and by closing your mouth.'

'Please do not use that voice to me, Harry, I don't like it.'

'Forgive me, my dear, but the procedure is difficult enough as it is.' The duke is beginning to wonder if he needs spectacles, for it takes him ages to focus, and even then the result is at variance with what he thought he saw through the lens.

Even more irksome is the artistic difficulty. Though the face beneath the muslin hood, and the undraped form beneath (exactly as he imagined beneath the skirts of the condemned woman so many years ago), are sufficient to arouse in Danbury the most passionate sentiments, Birdie cannot seem to capture the expression, the cool defiance on that statue-like visage.

Still, if he continues to badger her about it she will weep, and the session will be ruined.

'Listen carefully, Birdie, while I explain it to you once more. First, lift your chin slightly – no, a bit more, and to the left. Now purse your lips, and allow your eyes to drift upward to the rope, while assuming a proud expression, full of defiance.'

'But wouldn't a person be frightened, Harry? Standing before the hangman, unclothed? I certainly would,'

At her pronunciation of the word 'unclothed', Danbury struggles to contain himself. 'But that is just the point, my dear. You are not simply *anyone*. Alone and – and – and *naked* before the beastly throng, and yet you defy them – with your lack of fear and your . . . nakedness . . .'

'Are you all right, Harry? Your face is very flushed.' Birdie regards him curiously, having no idea why he should want such a picture, yet wishing to please him in the way that he pleases her. 'Harry, I think I am running out of patience with this – indeed, I must say that I find it most peculiar . . .'

'Yes! Yes, that is the expression. That is it. Oh, yes indeed. Hold very still now. Do not move. Perfect!' And the Duke of Danbury takes his photograph, satisfied at last.

The Thames

'Hail ho, Mr Whitty, and you honour my house. Peace be to you on this narrow path to the sea, like the path to the vastness of Heaven, down which all travel! *Allah Akbar!* God is great!'

So saying, the Mussulman exhales a puff of smoke, which is not the usual *qat*, more like fragrant clay. Now he removes the mouthpiece lips and extends it to Whitty, while performing a foreign gesture with the other hand.

For politeness' sake, Whitty inhales the musty smoke from the tube, then repeats the operation, for the flavour is not unpleasant . . .

After a certain amount of time he finds himself, and Mr Neffici, staring upward in wonder – at the greatness of God, the vastness of the universe, and the frangibility of human existence . . .

If thoughts are chemicals swishing about the skull, thinks the correspondent, does it follow that chemicals are thoughts? Can a chemical produce, not just an effect, but an *idea*? A treatment as innocuous as coffee will induce not just wakefulness but a wakeful sense of purpose; ale will create hearty thoughts, while gin can be wild or indecent, depending upon the brand . . .

Whitty looks at the Mussulman, only to discover that he has enlarged considerably, especially the head, while beneath his little beard there seems to be no neck at all.

Who are you? asks the Mussulman, meeting his gaze.

'Odd that you ask, sir, for the question has been much on my own mind. Father was incognito, it seems. Mother so subsumed her life to his, I cannot imagine her, beyond the word *Mother*. If one does not know who one *was*, how to know who one *is*?'

What do you mean by that? demands the Mussulman with the tube dangling from his mouth. *Explain yourself.*

'I mean that leading one's life is rather like piloting a rowboat. Propelling oneself forward while facing astern, don't you see.'

I do not see.

'One sees everything, except where one is going. It is very confusing.'

It isn't.

'Maybe not to you, sir. You are a foreign race with primitive, simple beliefs. Were your child to attend Balliol, he would see things with less certainty.'

Not a bit.

The Mussulman blows a puff of purple smoke in his direction, and Whitty feels his spirit rise out of his body like a hot-air balloon, and now he is looking down at the canal, like a grey serpent far below, writhing and twisting through the fields of Oxfordshire, and the *Endeavour* is a match-box containing three tiny animals, moving with comic slowness towards Oxford, the heart of the civilised world, where lies the answer to everything.

39

Bissett Grange, Oxfordshire

From the sickbed of
The Reverend C.G. Lambert,
Crouch Manor,
Oxfordshire

Your Grace, the Duke of Danbury,
Please excuse the script in which this document must needs be
communicated, as I am indisposed and rely upon my children's
Governess, by whose hand I communicate herein.
Circumstances beyond my purview have effected a disruption of that
intimacy which, as Spiritual Adviser to the House of Danbury, I had
hoped to effect. A misfortune, which is God's Will, deters me from
providing such advice as may be within my ability to convey. It comes as
a comfort that my dear Wife has willingly undertaken this ministry in my
absence.
It is natural to one blessed with the gold of distinguished elevation not
to soil one's ears with the base coin of the rabble. Notwithstanding, it
would be a relinquishment of my duty to remain silent. I must, painfully,
inform your Grace that Rumours have reached my ears of Improprieties
which I shall not dignify by name.
These rumours, were they to spread, would cause Great Harm, not
only to the Danbury name, but to those who look to Danbury as a moral
beacon in a confused world.
In the grace of our Lord Jesus Christ, and the fellowship of the Holy
Spirit, I remain
Your loyal and obedient servant,
the Reverend Charles Grantham Lambert

'I say, of all the impudence!' cries Danbury, crumpling the letter into a
ball and tossing it into the fire.

Lush moves quickly to save the paper from burning in order to get
the gist of the message. 'I beg your Grace to look at the situation
calmly. After all, you did appoint him your spiritual adviser.'

'What the devil has that to do with it? Surely it is a given that when
I want advice I shall ask for it.'

'Harry, the lady under discussion is his wife. It has been many years since the nobility enjoyed *droit de seigneur*. Surely you can appreciate that.'

'I promise you, Lush: if you continue in this supercilious vein I shall not be pleased.'

'Very well, your Grace,' replies Lush.

'He is threatening me. It is as simple as that. It is tantamount to blackmail. It cannot be permitted. Next thing you know, the villain will be demanding half my estate in return for his silence. Well, I won't have it, and there is an end to it.'

'Truthfully, Harry, this business with the Lambert family has gone altogether too far. First the daughter, now the mother – why not simply confiscate the entire family?'

'An interesting suggestion. I shall take it under advisement.'

'No, Harry, it is not interesting. I beg you *not* to think about it.'

'I'll think about what it pleases me to think about. In the meanwhile, I feel a need for personal protection. Go and fetch your brutes, will you? They cost me a small fortune, they should be eager to come.'

'What is it you want them to do?'

'I shall announce my wishes upon their arrival.'

'I must warn your Grace that these are not ordinary men, either in character or appearance. I have gone to great pains not to associate them in any way with your name and estate – and with good reason.'

'I certainly won't allow them on the grounds, if that's what you mean.'

'I mean that it is imperative that they avoid the vicinity of Bissett Grange. There is simply too much risk involved, Harry, I will not have it.'

'If you think I give a damn about what you will have or not have, you are very much mistaken. As the estate manager of Bissett Grange, your function is to do my bidding. And I will not have my Christian name bandied about in my own house. I find that our association has taken on an inappropriate familiarity, and I want it stopped at once.'

'Yes, your Grace,' replies the estate manager. And as they stand side-by side before the fire, it is as if an invisible door between them has closed.

About time, Lush thinks.

40

Crouch Manor, Chester Wolds, Oxfordshire

The condition of Lambert's mouth has not improved. Desperate letters to Dr Eisler, dictated in agony to Miss Pouch and mailed twice daily, have gone unanswered. He cannot take anything but consommé without pain, nor speak coherently for the swelling; his morphine dosage would kill another man and has begun to produce alarming side-effects – hallucinations, lack of impulse-control, and a complete inability to sleep.

Upon discovering what was clearly a love-poem while inspecting Emma's drawing book, it being beyond the Duties Description of a governess to speculate upon the hand that wrote it, Miss Pouch's response was, purely and simply, to do her duty. Indeed, for her not to act upon such a shocking document would be grounds for instant dismissal. Therefore, without delay and with a clear conscience, she proceeded upstairs to present the offending document to the head of the house, and to request instruction.

Only after observing her employer's alarming and excessive response did the specific content of the document, and the fact that the script could only have come from one hand, sink in. Miss Pouch had no wish to possess such inappropriate knowledge; indeed, it put her in a profoundly awkward position, pressed into service as confidante and secretary to the Reverend.

At his insistence she was made to fetch writing materials, whereupon her employer dictated a letter – which took the entire afternoon to accomplish, due to the swelling of his mouth and consequent difficulty in speaking. Once accomplished, Mr Lambert took a medicament and proceeded to become quite unhinged, uttering words and phrases of such shocking indecency (especially from a man of the cloth), that Miss Pouch came to bitterly regret her dutiful disclosure.

Thereafter, for the sake of the family and her position in it, she destroyed the offending verse, and determined never to mention its existence, ever again.

Having destroyed the evidence of one disgrace, Miss Pouch had begun to fear one that was far more dangerous to everyone concerned: for if there is anything more socially damaging than to lose one's reputation, it is to go mad. Suffer a betrayal, and you receive a measure of pity; go mad, and you become infected with an incurable, contagious disease.

Miss Pouch's fears, and those of the rest of the household, are confirmed when Mrs Lambert orders the closure of the topmost floor of Crouch Manor, where Lambert can be heard wandering from room to room at all hours, talking to himself, swearing atrociously, and threatening to murder anyone who summons a doctor. Of course there can be no question of calling a local physician: the congregation of St Alban's would hardly seek spiritual guidance from a man who has gone out of his mind. It would not be an exaggeration to say that, should it become known that Mr Lambert has succumbed to mental disease, the resulting scandal will put his entire household in the poorhouse.

As for Birdie, she soon sought out her one source of assistance, the Duke of Danbury.

The Duke responded with sympathy and concern: in particular, he worried that Crouch Manor might have already become an unwholesome place for the children, and proposed a plan. 'I assure you,' he said, 'that you are under my protection.'

Later, relieved of her worry, Birdie dropped her veil of her own accord at the height of their exertions, to Danbury's evident delight . . .

It is an hour before dawn, when even the maid-of-all-work is asleep. The house is silent but for the clock in the parlour, and the muffled footsteps of Mr Lambert upstairs, pacing the floor and moaning at the moon. Abruptly, urgently, the Lambert girls are awakened and commanded to remain silent. It is Miss Pouch, who hurriedly drapes them in dressing-gowns, then shoos them out the door and downstairs, where Mother awaits them at the front door.

Outside, the four women scurry down the elm-avenue to an awaiting carriage – which, they are informed by Mother, is to transport them to temporary quarters in a wing at Bissett Grange.

'What about Father?' asks Lydia.

'Your father is very ill,' replies Mother.

Emma finds it all very peculiar, and very sad. She glances back at the receding shadow of Crouch Manor, and for the first time in her life she feels pity for her misfortunate father, and for what he has lost, in addition to his teeth.

*

Mother tucks her into a bed several times larger than her own, while Miss Pouch arranges their clothes for tomorrow. Though the room is scarcely lit, by the echo of their whispers Emma knows that it is much larger than the nursery at home. Now the four of them join in a good-night prayer and Miss Pouch proceeds to blow out the candles.

'Leave us just one candle, please,' says Emma. 'For I am afraid of the dark.'

'Now, Emma,' says Birdie, 'I should think you far too grown-up to be afraid of the dark.'

'I'm afraid too, Mother,' whispers Lydia from her side of the room. 'And I'm not so grown-up as Emma.'

'Very well,' says Birdie, placing a candle on a stool in the middle of the floor, safely away from the curtains and bed-linen. 'You may keep one candle. But it must not be touched except to blow it out. We don't want to return his Grace's kindness by burning down the house.'

'We promise.'

Snuggling beneath the weightless luxury of down and cotton, watching the shadow of the candle dart to and fro upon the ceiling, listening to the muffled rhythm of footsteps marching back and forth in the hall (so many servants!), Emma thinks about this new situation, and their furtive flight from Crouch Manor. Her mind turns to the room upstairs where Eliza once slept, to the servant who mistook her for a ghost, and the graveyard in the forest, and her peculiar encounters with the hedgehog. Lastly she thinks about the room containing the picture she believes to be Eliza, and the one she could not decipher but which disturbed her, nonetheless.

That is why she has made up her mind to return to the other room with the candle; for there must be many other photographs inside, in addition to the two they were able to glimpse (before they were interrupted by the hedgehog), and who knows what they might contain?

Some time after the footsteps in the hall have ceased, Emma and Lydia slip out of their beds, Emma claims the candle, and the two proceed unseen and unopposed out the door and to the main stairs; no doubt the servant named O'Day who received such a fright previously would be doubly shocked at the sight of two small ghosts in white nightdresses, one holding a candle, gliding through the darkened halls of Bissett Grange, up the stairs, past Eliza's room and into the dark, chemical-smelling room next door.

'I still think it looks like a laundry,' says Lydia while Emma holds her candle above the basins on one wall. 'It smells like one too.'

'Do you see the wood-and-brass machine in the corner? That is where they make the photographs.'

'How?'

'For that you must ask Mr Boltbyn,' Emma replies while searching one corner, where she locates a wood-and-brass rack divided into compartments and containing photographic plates. She holds them one by one in front of the candle, finding it curious how the light part is dark and vice-versa . . .

'Do you think it was Mr Boltbyn who took the photograph of Eliza and . . . and the other one too?'

'I don't know,' replies Emma, gazing wide-eyed, at one of the glass plates. 'I *hope* it was not Mr Boltbyn.'

'Why?'

'Because . . . because they are not very well done.'

'You look surprised,' says Lydia. 'Are you looking at something surprising?'

'No. They are just pictures of Eliza, and . . . and someone else.'

'Who is it, Emma?'

'Nobody you would know,' Emma says, and blows out the candle.

Emma opens her eyes. She cannot believe she slept a wink, yet morning sun is pouring through the enormous arched window and sparrows are singing outside. As she lies drowsily in the sunlight, gazing at the cracks in the plaster ceiling, the smell of rising damp reminds her of where she is, and how she came to be here, and what she saw last night . . .

'I am vexed with you, Emma. I think you are very naughty.' Seated on the floor in a corner in her nightgown, Lydia is in the process of arranging the many pieces of her Noah's Ark.

Rising on one elbow to look about the room, Emma sees her favourite dolls on the prayer-stool beneath the window – porcelain blonde Alice with the prim snood, and Nell, the French *poupée* with eyes like marbles of blue ice; both are arranged in attitudes of prayer, which is just the sort of thing Miss Pouch would do.

'How, Lydia? How have I made you cross?'

'Because you refuse to tell me who it was in the picture. That is *so* mean of you, Emma.'

So it was not a dream.

'It was nobody familiar.'

'You're fibbing. I know when you are fibbing.'

So I am, thinks Emma. Lydia would want it explained, and she is scarcely able to explain it to herself except that it was an alarming situation in which to see one's mother. She is still puzzling over the incident in the wood and the strange sounds and movements under the blanket. What can it mean? What was he doing to her?

Their new room, the dolls, the photograph upstairs, the hedgehog, the scene in the wood – could it be that the peculiar events of past days, taken together, are all part of some sort of plan? If so, is it the duke's plan? The hedgehog's plan?

Shrinking from the thought without quite knowing why, again she lies back and gazes up at the road-map of cracks in the ceiling, until she hears the muffled slap of hooves upon the hardened earth of the carriageway. The rhythm is a dactyl, she thinks – or is it an anæpest? Now the squeal of springs as the carriage rattles to a halt; the passenger does not wait for the driver to open the door, but climbs out immediately, and crosses the carriage-sweep at a run.

Something has happened.

Footsteps two floors below – urgent, adult footsteps, joined by others. She recognises the voice of Mr Boltbyn, uncommonly serious and businesslike, almost harsh, followed by a long, primitive wail that could only come from Mother.

She is about to say something to Lydia when Miss Pouch bursts into the room with reddened eyes and cheeks, her thin, nervous fingers rubbing an imaginary piece of cloth. 'Girls, you must dress immediately! There has been a misfortune!'

'What sort of misfortune?' Emma asks.

'Do not question me! There has been an accident and that is all there is to be said!'

The urgency with which Miss Pouch pulls Lydia to her feet suggests that the house might be on fire. And what did Mr Boltbyn say downstairs that so upset Mother?

Reverend Boltbyn has never experienced a day such as this, and fervently hopes he never will again.

Upon his arrival at Crouch Manor for morning tea, equipped with the usual games and puzzles, he could hear a great wailing within, so unnerving that he was tempted to return to the carriage and go home.

When repeated knocking went unanswered he pushed open the front door and entered, to discover a house empty of servants and family, and that the keening sound was coming from upstairs. Reminding himself that it is part of his vocation to offer solace in desperate situations, with his heart pounding at the speed of a rabbit, he climbed the stairs to the top floor, where he found the maid-of-all-work in a state of the utmost alarm.

Upon entering the bedroom he saw the cause of her disarray: Mr Lambert, in a half-seated position, hanging from the neck by a noose which had been tied to the curtain-rail of the bed.

His face! The black, protruding tongue! Beyond the paintings of Brueghel and Bosch, the vicar had never seen anything like it.

Not until the maid-of-all-work had calmed somewhat did Boltbyn ask about Mrs Lambert and the girls. Receiving no satisfactory reply, and with a gloomy sense of duty, he took the carriage to Bissett Grange, there to pass on the melancholy news and to ask what is to be done.

Boltbyn was not in any way prepared for the role of spiritual counsel, as his meeting with Mrs Lambert revealed. Running from the carriage, he barged into the hall like a fireman and blurted out the terrible news the instant she appeared, with his stutter performing in all its attenuated glory. Then for the first time in his life (outside a theatre or carnival-ride), he heard a woman scream – or perhaps the word is *howl*. He was unprepared for the galvanising effect such an utterance can have at close range, and for a minute his mind ceased to function.

Viewed in retrospect, he should have immediately assisted the lady to the divan, providing her with a comfortable place to swoon. Instead, as the poor woman fell into a faint, his first impulse was to avert his eyes from the sight of her legs, so that he failed even to break her fall – and heard the poor woman's head crack upon the mahogany floor!

Nor was Boltbyn prepared to wrap his arms around a lady's upper torso in order to raise her to a seated position, to have his face in such contiguity with hers, thus receiving the full benefit of her soaps, perfumes and creams . . .

Now, thank Heaven, Miss Pouch has taken charge and is applying a cold compress to Mrs Lambert's forehead, while the vicar endeavours to calm down.

Satisfied that all that can be done is being done at present, Boltbyn has just begun to find refuge in a mathematical conundrum he has under construction, when out of the corner of his eye he sees Emma and

Lydia, in their nightdresses, side by side, standing beneath the archway that divides the hall from the reception room.

Presented with the two little girls whom he loves more than his own life, Boltbyn must now deliver the most dreadful news.

Somehow he finds the strength to rise and cross to the archway. Sighing deeply, he looks down at his two little friends with a gentle, sad smile, crouches down to Lydia's height, and speaks.

'E-E-Emma and Lydia, your f-f-f-f–'

'Take your time, please, Mr Boltbyn,' Emma says.

'Your f-f-f-f-father . . .'

'Slowly, now.'

'Has had an, ah, ah . . . accident.'

The sight of a pair of riding-boots stops him in mid-falsehood; his gaze travels upward to the face of the duke, wearing a dark brown riding-suit, with a blue bird's-eye handkerchief around his neck, carrying a riding-whip and gloves.

'What has happened?' asks the noble face above him. No fish could maintain a more unwinking stare than the duke does in this moment.

Boltbyn feels uncomfortably like a dwarf. His knees crack disconcertingly as he struggles to his feet – too abruptly, for he must brace himself against the archway until the dizziness subsides.

'What has happened, Mr Boltbyn?' repeats the duke.

'I b-b-b–'

'Sir,' offers Emma with a curtsy, 'it concerns our father.'

The duke bends down to pat her upon the shoulder with one gloved hand. To Emma he smells of leather and horses and other male smells: scents she never detected on Mr Boltbyn, nor on her father, on the few occasions when they were sufficiently close.

'Whatever has occurred, Miss Emma, permit me to assure you that you and your mother are under my protection and have nothing to fear.'

To which Emma executes another curtsy, for there is no question that they require protection.

The duke turns to the vicar: 'Sir, oblige me with a word in private.'

Boltbyn nods his assent, reflecting that no bullying superior could exercise the spell Danbury does, with so little effort. Without exception, new members of the photographic society begin by vowing to tell him to go to the devil, and end by obeying him like footmen.

'Come into the library, then.'

Boltbyn returns his attention to the two girls. 'Miss Emma and Miss Lydia, I must withdraw momentarily to speak to his Grace. P-p-p-lease comfort your mother. Miss P-P-Pouch has something important to tell you.'

Iffley Lock, Oxfordshire

The lock-keeper swings the windlass and the upper gates part like a pair of hands to reveal a stretch of the undulating river Whitty knows all too well.

It is a perfect day for boating, with a fresh breeze blowing across the stream, barely enough to ruffle the waters. Standing at the bow of the *Endeavour*, he prepares for yet another assault on his mind and memory.

Iffley Lock is where it happened; the bottle-nosed lock-keeper with liver-coloured jowls may well be the same party who opened the gates for David on his last paddle. Whitty recognises the tidy inn behind the lock-house, frequented by boatsmen in-between laps, and remembers the blackened Norman church across the roadway, whose baptismal font is ringed with severed heads, each wearing a surprised expression, as a severed head might.

Each year in springtime his parents brought him to Oxford to watch his brother run the boat-trials and races. Since David inevitably excelled in the event, the trip took on the character of a family rite – a symbolic quest with an assured outcome and the prospect of renewal.

While Mother and Father joined the other spectators at the start, Edmund preferred to walk to the turning-position at Iffley Lock, to await the St Ambrose eight-oar. There he would crane his neck to spot the boat, first a speck in the distance, then a shape like an eight-legged insect, skimming along to the last reach. How he would thrill at the magnificent sweep and life of the stroke against the green water, with a fresh breeze ruffling the stream just as it is doing now. Long before he could distinguish the individual rowers he would recognise his brother's voice piercing the air: *Two, well forward! Time, three, don't jerk! Four, you can get another pound on!* as the marvellous sliver came hard-on up to the pool below the lock, the coxswain standing at the stern holding a tiller-rope in each hand, then shipping oars . . .

This is the point where Whitty's memory defers to a mental picture, not of what was seen but of what was heard from others, yet equally vivid: not the eight, but a single oarsman in a boating coat and St

Ambrose cap, handling the sculls like an old hand, out for a gentle paddle, about to meet his maker.

How well Whitty remembers accompanying his distraught father on their grim journey back to Oxford while Mother remained home under a doctor's care. When they arrived, father proceeded to grill each witness like a prosecuting council, as though by finding fault in their story he might undo David's death. Not once in that time did Father acknowledge the presence of the boy by his side. To Whitty it seemed that it was he who had become a ghost, and not his brother.

'The river was rather high,' the manager said, a warning he issued to all rental parties that day, for heavy storms up Gloucestershire way had swollen the stream, and the Thames was as full as could be without overflowing. 'I assure you, sir, that I warned him to especially mind the millstream at Iffley Lock, and pull the right-hand scull at Berkshire.'

The lock-keeper recalled having issued a similar warning: to stay well out before hugging the Berkshire side, and to mind the small lasher (a kind of wooden trough feeding the millstream by the river), which created a narrow funnel of concentrated current that could draw a man off-course and out of control.

Only now does it begin to dawn upon Whitty how each account melded so seamlessly with the official version. Does life really occur with such neatness?

Equally, the official account of David's death has remained as clear in his mind as anything he might have witnessed in the flesh. Standing to the stern of the *Endeavour*, he can almost see his brother round the bend and, rashly choosing left scull, hug the Berkshire side when he should be well out – at which point the current from the lasher catches the bow of the boat, which whirls around, turns on its side, and shoots the brother's skiff onto the planking and down the steep descent as though it were caught in a waterfall. The algae-covered boards would have been as slippery as ice as he frantically clawed them, while the boat rolled over like a piece of driftwood into the still pool below, to disappear beneath the black water, leaving a grave-marker of scattered sculls and bottom boards turning gently on the surface.

By the time of the funeral, David's demise had assumed the familiar mythic pattern of similar tragedies in sport: the expert swimmer who unaccountably drowns; the experienced hunter who shoots himself through some elementary error – always with an ironic moral which might be summed up as *Death By Over-confidence*.

But now another more recent memory comes to Whitty: *I did not die as you think I died.*

What did David mean? he wonders – then stops himself, for there is no reason to assume that the message was not a parlour trick. Nonetheless, the sentence itself begins to poke holes in the accepted mythology – the fact that some unknown person put him through a great deal of trouble, immediately after he heard it. For there can be no doubt that the atrocious picture of David was concocted in order to turn him away from the journey he has undertaken, and the truth about what happened to him.

If someone would have Whitty murdered over David, it suggests that he, or someone close to him, probably murdered David as well.

Looking back, Whitty notes that other than half-remembered warnings, there was no eye-witness to the event itself. Though the rentals manager and the lock-keeper described a handsome gentleman, a Fellow and not a mere student, neither identified him as David.

I did not die as you think I died.

Whitty begins to laugh, a frequent reaction when something startling occurs to him. The laughter builds until he must wipe away the taste of salt with his handkerchief.

Watching him curiously from the bow, the Mussulman extends the tube of his *hookah* as a possible remedy.

'No, thank you, sir,' Whitty replies. 'On this occasion I am just going to have to think.'

A mile and a half distant and just south of the town, they pass the boat-builders' establishments on both sides of the river; soon after, they reach Christ Church Meadow on the Oxfordshire side, where cows continue to graze and where the spectators' barge containing Mother and Father would moor for the races.

The crew of the *Endeavour* and Edmund Whitty of *The Falcon* must now part company, each as puzzled by the other as when they set out. Still, Whitty feels it is he who has benefited most from the journey. The eternal rhythm of the river, the slowing of time, not to mention the curious dreams emanating from Mr Neffici's wonderful tube, have given him a new perspective on what he is about to undertake. If nothing else, for the first time he is able to face the photographs in his pocket without flinching at their contents, and to recall past events in detail without self-pity

Still, he could certainly do with a drink, having spent part of a week squatting on the deck of a barge filled with gin, like an alcoholic Ancient Mariner, without a drop to drink.

As for the Mussulmen, having delivered the last of their doctored gin, they will continue up the waterway to a livery in Heyford, and an agent who deals in young women from the Midlands-bound, in most cases, for the London brothels eager for green fruit.

For a long moment the correspondent stands on the pavement next to the canal, wondering how best to bid farewell to his fellow sojourners. Mr Neffici seems similarly at loose ends, stroking his wedge-shaped beard with an expression of befuddlement. Out of nervousness more than anything, Whitty reaches into his coat pocket – and discovers a cigar he must have scooped from his editor's cigar-box.

'Please accept a cigar, sir, with my compliments.'

Mr Neffici takes the cigar, gives it a sniff, and replies: 'High-ho, sir, you adorn my mouth with your gifting.' With that, he reaches into his pocket, extracts a wedge of brown putty the size of a *bon-bon*, and extends it to the correspondent.

Whitty accepts the gift with appropriate ceremony, though he doubts he will make use of the substance, which seems to produce the most unnerving insights.

The Mussulman at the stern, while untangling some rope, favours him with a nod, while for his part, the horseman acknowledges Whitty with a complicated motion of his right hand. For a suitable reply, Whitty gives the fellow the Oxford salute – the upraised thumb of old-boy encouragement; at this, the horseman appears startled, then offended, then articulates a long, bitter reply in what Whitty assumes to be Arabic.

Without further ceremony he hurries across the meadow, eager for a clean bed, some nourishment other than bitter coffee, a mug of gin, and a companion who speaks in complete English sentences.

Halfway across the meadow he stops, transfixed by the castellated outline of St Ambrose College, seen in the long light of afternoon it is medieval in appearance, like a tiny outpost of civilisation in a Dark Age.

Given that it could well be someone connected with St Ambrose who wishes him ill, in choosing his lodging he decides to favour Town over Gown, though it will require him to endure the stink from the central market: in London one's handkerchief turns black whenever one blows one's nose; in the town of Oxford to breathe the air is like attending a convention of slaughterers.

To avoid being recognised for the time being, he keeps to the lanes below Broad Street, past the Twelve Philosophers and down the back alleys; past a medieval churchyard as black as if it had been charred; past townsmen in their peculiar, anachronistic clothing (like the third-hand offerings near Waterloo Bridge), until he can see no evidence of a university presence, other than a lone proctor fluttering down the road in search of gownsmen who have gone missing at roll-call.

Threading his way through a series of courts, he reaches the dark entrance of the Grass, a quiet little inn whose occupants pay by the week or the month and are therefore unlikely to spread word of his return, being at one or another stage of delirium tremens. In the little bar he recognises the proprietor, a stout woman with spectacles as thick as telescopes, whose age is no clearer to him than it was nearly a decade ago, in her greasy armchair, stitching plain work for her grandchildren.

'Bless us if it isn't Mr Whitty of St Ambrose! Weeks it has been since you were with us,' she exclaims, with a publican's eye for a patron and a publican's imperviousness to the passage of time.

'Whitty it is indeed, Mrs Wafer. And a good evening to you. I trust that you still draw famous ale.'

'The Grand Medallion is it not?'

'Quite right, Mrs Wafer. Let us have a jug of that excellent substance, please. And you'll take a glass with me, won't you?'

'Duncan!' she cries, exhibiting the publican's capacity to speak with a velvety murmur for the clients, and a glass-shattering shriek for the staff.

For the professional seeker of information, the regular clientele of a small inn comprises a virtual encyclopaedia of the city. It is a curious fact of life in such drinking establishments that, however addled the individual brain may become, the room as a whole remembers everything.

The ruling spirit in the drinking-room of the Grass is a former advocate named Egerton Prawn, an octogenarian in a shiny, snuff-coloured frock coat and slippers. According to Mrs Wafer, the human eye has never seen him otherwise attired.

Should Mr Prawn mistake himself on some point or other, he will receive speedy correction from his constant companion, Mr Ellington – a man of about fifty, with a tumour growing upon his left ear which hangs from the lobe like a fig.

Mr Prawn represents that most valuable journalistic commodity, the Failure who Watches. Whitty therefore cultivates Mr Prawn with generous lashings of brandy and ale, to be repaid with local facts – especially concerning the university. For while it is true that the masses in Town may be reflexively disregarded by Gown, the reverse does not apply. A fierce preoccupation for Town, is Gown.

'Thangs be a bit calmer since ye left, Mr Whitty,' begins Mr Prawn, in that flattened Midlands accent which can drive any fellow Briton to strong drink.

'And yet I should expect more than one rat in the wainscoting, sir.'

'True, sah – a good deal more than one . . .' Mr Prawn places a finger beside his nose, signalling the confidentiality of what he is about to divulge to a relative stranger.

The narrative proceeds, with Mr Ellington acting as a kind of editor, his tumour swinging one way or another as a verdict of accuracy. By the time Whitty staggers up the stairs to his bed, he has gathered an inventory of the scandals and controversies of the term, as well as the various rumours circulating like leaves come autumn – it being characteristic of academic life that only rumours are to be believed. He now knows which gentleman commoner has been paying for his grades; which published eminence has lost his mind and drools over his notes; which don's wife is up to no good with the tutor-assistant; which servitor has become independently wealthy as a procurer of women and opium; which comely townswoman has ensnared a besotted proctor . . .

After the scandals came the suicides. As always, Oxonians have been hanging themselves and poisoning themselves, or stuffing their pockets with stones, hopping off a bridge and making a hole in the river. These incidents are recorded as 'accidental death', in the interests of both the family and the university, with the result that every untimely death, even genuine accidents, leaves a scattering of suicide rumours circulating in its wake. In this respect, David's death was no exception. Unhappily, nothing in Mr Prawn's litany of scandal stands out as having any possible connection to David or the Captain's niece.

The most recent rumoured suicide, expressed in the alarming vowels of Mr Prawn, 'be the precentor Mr Lambert, said to die of fever when the truth is he hanged himself – so say the servants. Poor Miss Lizzy discovered him hanged from the bedstead wi' the teeth hangin out, be so shocked she not out of bed since.'

This one will bear investigation, Whitty thinks, having acquired a special suspicion of all hangings outside the prison-yard.

Whitty opens the door to his room with his latch-key, reflecting that the evening has been by no means a failure, if only because he is happily drunk for the first time in days.

The garret-room assigned to him – rarely swept, frightfully dirty and with a low, slanted ceiling – affords a splendid view of the surrounding chimney-pots and slate roofs, as well as a relatively clean, if damp, bed.

Whitty sinks into the luxury of a horizontal, comparatively soft surface, reflecting that, as usual, his quest is that of a near-sighted hound, who will recognise the fox, if at all, when it is literally in front of his nose.

Excepting that in his case the hound is himself hunted by armed men – and possibly by the fox as well.

All afternoon the two retired soldiers in shabby reds have been wandering the streets of Oxford, which seems to them as dusty and desolate as any village in Bengal or Lahore. At last the sky has grown sufficiently dark for the lieutenant-colonel to remove his sun-glasses and determine their position by means of an area map of the town, purchased at the train station by his subaltern. It is the first time they have ventured out of London. They have done their duty, and should be on their way back to London had not Mr Lush ordered them to remain, to carry out a second assignment when called upon.

In the meantime they remain at liberty and on their own – a singularly disorienting experience.

'Do we have our bearings at last, sir? Do you make our position?' Weeks has been jittery and out of sorts since their arrival. He is unnerved by the creatures in black gowns who sweep back and forth in the streets, some with gold tassels dangling from their flat hats. To the corporal it is as if they have entered a coven of wizards.

Looking up from the map, the lieutenant-colonel speaks in a controlled manner, not to undermine the morale of the company. 'Mr Weeks, are you aware that this map you purchased is in *French*?'

'What?'

'I cannot read our position, because it is not in English.'

'I do not understand, sir. Are we in another country?'

'When we alit from the train, sir, I sent you to the stationmaster's wicket with a shilling, to obtain a map of the town of Oxford. This map what you purchased is in French.'

Wouldn't you know, thinks Weeks. Besides the mysterious gowned figures, another alarming discovery while wandering the streets has been the presence of people speaking in French, standing in small groups in the older parts of town, discussing statuary and pointing at the architecture.

'Mr Robin, you know I do not read. Reading is not in my line. And we was in a dead hurry with Mr Lush waiting for us up the road.'

'I am aware of that, corporal. Still, the bloody map is no use to us in a foreign language, is it? How are we to find our bearings without a bloody map to go by?'

'Point taken, sir. Request instructions.'

'We will obtain directions from a local civilian.'

The corporal contemplates a gentleman-commoner from Balliol flying past in his silk gown, chased by a number of other gentlemen, similarly attired and with cigars in their mouths, emitting high-pitched laughter.

'Ask directions from that lot? Sir, do you think they can be trusted?'

'Probably not. Devil take it, Weeks, why did you not ask for a bloody English map?'

'Well, I spoke English when I asked for it, didn't I? One would think that sufficient. And there is nothing French about the uniform, tattered though it is.'

Robin and Weeks stop to think about this, and come to the same conclusion.

'Mr Robin, sir, I believe it was the man behind the wicket. He saw that I was new to the region, that I do not read and would not know the difference. He sought to make a fool of me, sir. And being blind in the daylight, you were at a similar disadvantage.'

'I quite agree. By the voice he had a superior way about him.'

'Shabby treatment for the heroes of Lucknow I should say, sir.'

'It calls for a punitive expedition, in memory of the brigade – *Hazar!*'

'Indeed, sir. For those who died for England on foreign soil – *Hazar!*'

Robin places his sun-glasses in his pocket and leads a brisk march in the direction of the train station. Without his glasses, Robin's eyes glitter like the scales of a fish.

'The more I see of the country, Mr Robin sir, the more I pine for the old days – *O for the pipeclayed belts and the pillbox hats, and the smell of beer and oats and horse-piss . . .*'

Robin produces his flask. 'Tot, corporal.'

'Thank you, sir.' Weeks takes a long draught.

'Beware of romanticising the brigade, Weeks. Butcher and bolt is what we did.'

'Yet we is Englishmen, sir, as British as any *h'ramzada* on this stinking street!'

The lieutenant-colonel stops to administer another dose from the flask to his subaltern, as the corporal's eyes are beginning to glaze over. 'Speak more quietly, will you? You are attracting attention.'

Weeks continues to reminisce over army life in India, albeit in more moderate tones, while they trace their way back to the train station for a meeting with the clerk.

REQUIESCAT IN PACE

Lambert, CHARLES GILBERT, 43 years. On Saturday 3rd June, at a private funeral, shall be consigned to earth the Mortal Remains of Reverend C. G. Lambert, precentor for Church of St Swithan Church, Chester Wolds, Oxfordshire, and trusted Spiritual Adviser to the Duke of Danbury. For an extended period he had been labouring under severe disease of the mouth; notwithstanding the unceasing efforts of the members of his devoted family and his able physician, he was at length prostrated and, after a few days of extreme weakness, his existence terminated. His death, unexpected and lamentable, occurred on the previous Wednesday and was marked by a placidity of mind and kindliness of feeling for all around him. The Reverend Lambert is survived by his devoted wife, Euphemia, and two beloved daughters, Emma and Lydia.

Services at Church of St Swithan, Reverend Jeremiah Spoole officiating. Photographs of the deceased, prepared by the Reverend William Leffington Boltbyn of St Ambrose College, Oxford, to be presented to family and friends.

Whilst in this world I did remain
My latter end was grief and pain;
But when the Lord he thought it best
To take me to a place of rest,
My time was spent, my glass was run,
And now, sweet Jesus, I am come.

42

Oxford

Over morning tea in the drinking-room of the Grass, Whitty peruses the morning's edition of the *Oxford Times* through a fog of stale tobacco smoke. 'I see, Mrs Wafer, that Oxford has taken to the practice of photographing the dead.'

'Aye, Mr Whitty, it is much in demand by the mourners.'

'As a memento, I suppose. In London, no parlour is complete without a family Bible and an album of cadavers.'

'Seems right morbid to me.'

'Still, to have one's photograph taken by Mr William Boltbyn is a signal honour, even if one happens to be dead.'

'True for you, sir. Mr Boltbyn seldom photographs anything but little girls, is what I am hearing.'

'You don't say, Mrs Wafer?'

'Aye, in particular the Lambert girls, whose father they're burying today, poor things.'

Circling the item on the Reverend Lambert with a pencil, Whitty scans the list of Oxonians who will be attending the funeral, and recognises not only Boltbyn, but his Grace the Duke of Danbury as well. *Hello*. He resolves to set out for the church at once, that he might arrive in advance of the funeral and have a look around.

He remembers St Swithan as a minor chapel about two miles north of the city, a small, mean building, funded in perpetuity by the lord of the manor in the early part of this century, at the end of a pointless life chasing the hounds and the chambermaids.

Putting down his newspaper, he reflects upon the strange route his own life has taken, from his downfall at St Ambrose to his current position with *The Falcon*, from a disgraced theology student to a chronicler of disgrace; from articulating what should be to dealing in what might be, in the hope of telling what is.

Whitty tucks into a full breakfast of kidneys, haddock and pudding, followed by a healer of gin and water, followed by a healthy dose of Acker's Chlorodine. Ready to face the challenges of the day, he folds the paper, with hardly a glance at the other news.

A SHOCKING ASSAULT
by
Oliver Crabtree
Senior Correspondent
Oxford Times

Following an enquiry from his wife in the late hours of yesterday evening, Officers of the Oxford Constabulary discovered stationmaster John Butty, near death and in an unrecognisable state, having been beaten and thrown upon the railway by persons unknown. Robbery is the suspected motive, for an amount of Railway property was taken. Adding insult to injury, a foreigners' map was discovered in the victim's mouth.

Foreign visitors to the shire have been summoned to the constabulary for questioning.

'A singularly vicious assault upon a public servant,' commented Inspector Watkins of the Police. 'Caution is advised among the citizenry.'

43

The Roland Stones

Wouldn't you know, just when the price of images rivals the price of jewellery, a bell has rung on some invisible clock, and it is time to begin anew.

On his way to set the course that will secure his future, Albin Lush puts his mind to the logic of the situation, rather than succumb to a sensation of giddy nausea – that the normal parameters of risk and profit no longer apply; suddenly the risk side of the equation has expanded to infinity, which no amount of profit can balance.

In short, he is plagued with fears that require decisive management.

He has not slept in three nights; the moment he closes his eyes he sees a black, infinite maw, opening to swallow him up, and next thing he is sitting bolt upright in the bed, gasping for air.

With careful planning, however, he will soon be free – and high time, for the effort of remaining steady has taken its toll; witness the burning rash now itching his scalp and hands.

First off, his vocation in the service of the Duke of Danbury is over.

In hindsight, Lush sees his original error: in forming his attachment to Bissett Grange he placed too little significance on the fact that children of the Quality do not mature at the rate of other Englishmen.

The full extent of the duke's capriciousness has only now come to light. At first, Danbury's orders concerning the Reverend Lambert seemed in the realm of the rational, given that impudent letter with its stench of scandal.

Who might have imagined that removing an enemy was but an incidental bonus? That his Grace's primary intention was to indenture an entire *family* in the way that Macbeth acquired the throne of Scotland – by murdering the head of the house?

Lush had thought that the duke had learned his lesson in the David Whitty affair: when conducting business at the risk of ruinous disgrace, it is people who create problems. When there are no people, there is no problem. Now Bissett Grange is simply swarming with eyes and ears, with the risk of bringing *everything* to light, right from the beginning. The mere thought of it turns his bowels to jelly.

As the carriage rattles off the main road, past the Roland Stones and over the rise to the Wayland Smithy, in his mind Lush reaffirms his second decision: the daughters therefore must go. Both of them. In the face of such risk, one errs on the side of caution.

Moreover, he has decided that the best plan would be for the brutes to accomplish the task – at a time when Lush will be miles away. It is as clear as a mathematical proof.

Yet not quite as certain.

Goodness knows they made enough fuss over the last girl. Soldiers are like hunting dogs in that respect – bred in the bone to tear some to shreds, and others, not.

Yet they will not refuse. They will do what he needs them to do. Reaching into his coat pocket, Lush produces the small pistol from the duke's study, feels the satisfying weight of it – neater than hanging, quicker than gas.

Reason, self-interest, and the prospect of the hangman will prevail. For have they not already crossed the Rubicon in their own minds? Do they think more than one Hell awaits? If so, he will shoot them both, and then they can see for themselves, while he does the work himself. As he climbs down from the carriage, he feels the pistol in his pocket. It has capacity for two rounds – adequate for his purpose, one way or the other.

Grinding his teeth behind a congenial smile, the estate manager greets the two dishevelled officers standing in the mouth of the cave. 'A very good day to you, gentlemen. My apologies for the accommodations.'

'Only the dark is sufficient,' replies Robin.

'A field trench would be an improvement,' says Weeks.

'Permit me to remind you that it is your own rash actions that have put you in a cave, and not in a comfortable bed. When you arrived, you said nothing about beating the stationmaster half to death. The entire city is up in arms, and conspicuous foreigners are especially suspect.'

'We're every bit as English as them,' says Robin. 'Even more so.'

'It were an affair of honour,' adds Weeks.

'My employer is extremely displeased. He demands that you vacate the area as soon as it is safe to do so.'

'We done our duty,' says Weeks.

'And expect to be paid accordingly,' adds Robin.

'His Grace has authorised a generous stipend, of that you may be sure. Moreover, he ensures your safe conduct back to London – provided that you perform one additional duty . . .'

44

Oxford

Swinging his walking-stick with a new sense of purpose, Whitty makes his way past the walls of Balliol, past the metal cross commemorating the heretic Cranmer, and past the quadrangle of St John's – a stately edifice in whose chapel, Whitty remembers, it is the practice on a Sunday morning for undergraduates with hang-overs to vomit into their hats.

The dust that pervades the air at this time of year softens everything; a mile further, however, and the air clears to an unprecedented freshness. Indeed, he may cover his nose with his handkerchief, for the intake of oxygen is making him giddy.

At length he finds himself amid large open fields, scythed by stocky, red-faced men in leather breeches and shapeless felt hats; soon he approaches the village of Fordlow, a quaintly desolate collection of thatched cottages, up to its fetlocks in greenery, with no post-office, constabulary or railway station. Its public buildings consist of a school, a poky little inn called the Bricklayer's Arms, and St Swithan – squat and ugly, without spire or tower, crouched at the back of a churchyard whose graves accommodate so many generations as to form a hill several feet above the road.

As he approaches the church, a clamour of rooks rain upon him a volley of negativity and discouragement, their feathers gleaming like shards of black porcelain. Removing his hat, he pushes open the heavy door, enters the church, and pauses while his eyes adjust to the dim interior.

Before the altar lies the corpse, uncovered from the waist up, in its Sunday clothes, nestled in a fine mahogany coffin with brass handles and ivory inlay, upon a sturdy table designed for the purpose. Curiously, on either side of the deceased, the pillars are carved to depict medieval grotesques – a succession of half-wits with broken teeth, sores and warts, japing at one another across the coffin. Surrounding the cadaver, bouquets of flowers create a stage setting for a recumbent leading man – who will, at the proper moment, sit bolt upright and burst into song.

Between Whitty and this fragrant tableau of death is the rear end of a gentleman, bent over a rosewood camera, which is set on a three-legged stilt. Before Whitty can adjust to this unusual spectacle he is dazzled by a flash of magnesium, and must sit in a nearby pew while the spots fade.

Removing the plate from the camera, and with the poise of a waiter with a bowl of soup, the photographer transfers it to a portable darkroom – a wooden frame draped with black velvet – into which he stoops, so that once again only his bottom and legs remain visible, framed by coat-tails of mourner's black.

In the interval between camera and darkroom, Whitty recognises the profile of the most illustrious member of the Oxford Photographic Society – older by precisely the number of years that have elapsed since David's death. And yet, other than a noticeable thinning of his hair, the man does not seem to have aged a day; his smooth, rosy cheeks can scarcely have felt a razor, while his slender physique is that of a boy of fourteen.

He watches as Boltbyn examines the developed plate, inserts it into a portable cabinet made of brass and rosewood, then extracts a fresh plate, all with admirable dexterity. Returning to his camera, he inserts the plate, replenishes the tray of flash powder, and adjusts the focal length of the lens by minute degrees, turning a brass knob. On this occasion, Whitty has the presence of mind to cover his eyes in advance of the flare.

With Boltbyn once again shrouded in the velvet of the portable darkroom, Whitty rises from his pew and steps briskly to the nave, to inspect the corpse.

The gentleman in the coffin is straight-featured and blandly handsome, but with a certain puffiness about the mouth, as though having suffered an injury to the face. The effect is of a man who died with his mouth full of food, while trying to smile.

Taking a closer look (with the usual odour of chicken gone bad), he notes the artificially pink make-up – thick enough to mask the rich purple of a hanged man; and when he inserts a gloved finger between the high, waxed collar and the neck, he uncovers the welts left by a wide cord or a knotted sheet.

'Excuse me, sir, but I do not believe you are the undertaker.'

Whitty removes his finger from the dead man's collar, turns, and smiles genially: 'Edmund Whitty of *The Falcon*, sir. I am at your service.'

'The name is familiar, somehow,' says Boltbyn, standing with a plate delicately balanced on five fingers. 'I did not see you enter the building.'

'I did not wish to disturb you. Photography is a delicate business, even for an expert such as yourself.'

'True. Even under ideal circumstances, not one plate in five is satisfactory.'

'I have often wondered what happens to glass plates which are not up to standard. There must surely be a good many of them.'

'Indeed, I have seen them used to construct greenhouses . . .' Abruptly, the photographer hesitates; it has begun to occur to him that this is a rather peculiar situation.

Whitty continues blithely on the subject of photography, though he knows nothing about it: 'I suppose that is one advantage of photographing the dead – they will hold still.'

'Why are you here, sir?' asks Boltbyn, sharply. 'Were you acquainted with the deceased? Or are you one of those journalists who like to mock the feelings of other people?'

'The fact of it is, I came to observe a master at work. You would be the Reverend Boltbyn, I presume – unless you prefer your *nom de plume*.'

The face brightens with sudden interest. 'Sir, did you know that you just rhymed?'

'No. Did I?'

'*Presume*, and *nom de plume*. It's really quite good.'

'Blast! So I did.'

'And you scanned as well – with a triplet in the second line.'

'Completely accidental, I assure you. Perhaps it is the landscape.'

'How could it possibly be the landscape?'

'A gnomish aspect to the country. Like pictures in a book of rhymes for children.'

'Oh. I see.' Boltbyn's face returns to its original expression of watchful alarm. 'Have we been introduced?'

'As I told you, I am Edmund Whitty of *The Falcon*.'

'Quite. Of course. Whitty of *The Falcon*. The Chokee Bill affair, the near-hanging of an innocent man – shocking.'

'I too was shocked, at the time.'

'What brings you to this part of the country, sir? Surely nothing as nasty as that.'

'One never knows what nastiness lies about; however, I am here for the memoirs.'

'Whose memoirs?'

'My own, of course. In which, Mr Boltbyn, you seem to play a role. You may or may not remember that I was once, however briefly, a student at St Ambrose.'

Boltbyn's eyes widen with comprehension. 'Ah – *that* Mr Whitty. You exhibited a proficiency with provocative rhymes, if I remember correctly.'

'Indeed, sir. And speaking of rhymes, what do you think of this?'

Whitty withdraws a sheet of paper from his pocket and reads aloud the piece of club doggerel based on Longfellow:

> *'Under a spreading camera-tree*
> *The Picture-taker stands . . .'*

'Did I write that?' asks the vicar. 'By Heaven, I think I did! Where did you find it?'

'I believe we have a mutual acquaintance in my deceased brother David, who was an avid photographer like yourself.'

'Th-that would be . . . oh yes. Good heavens. David Whitty. A remarkable talent for the craft.'

'Further on, the verse refers to various members of the society, I believe. It is all quite clever:

> *A is for Angley in anger to dwell,*
> *B is for Boltbyn and Bracebridge as well;*
> *C is for Crede, the cock in a cage,*
> *D is for Danbury, shocking the age,*
> *And for David Whitty, stalking the stage . . .'*

'Oh,' exclaims Boltbyn in a soft voice, and the negative shatters on the floor.

'I beg you, forgive me, sir,' says Whitty, looking at a spreading puddle filled with shards of glass, and the smell of ether is overpowering. 'It was my express wish not to disturb your work – and look what has happened!'

Whitty looks up, and is surprised to see the vicar's swallow-tailed rear, heading for the door.

'Mr Boltbyn!' he calls. 'Shall we say this evening, then? At your rooms for tea? Excellent!'

Seated in a rear pew, between an elderly woman with the palsy and a gentleman with a boil on his neck, Whitty focuses upon the face of the

Duke of Danbury as he makes his way down the aisle – the receding chin, the side-whiskers like wisps of angel's hair, the same air of unruffled assurance he displayed to such effect at Buckingham Gate. As the nobleman passes by, Whitty notes a slight flicker in the eye, suggesting that he has been recognised, but not quite placed.

At Danbury's side is a sobbing women in full mourning (well-favoured, from what he can see beneath the white veil), followed by two girls of contrasting but equally striking aspect: the younger is in tears, while her dark-haired sister eyes the congregation with an expression of anxious enquiry. There is something slightly familiar about the older girl, Whitty thinks.

As the mourners file past the corpse, Whitty notices Boltbyn's camera, still assembled and leaning the wall; seemingly Boltbyn, the corpse photographer, has not attended the funeral.

The organ gasps out a series of sombre chords as the vicar, a Reverend Spoole, mounts the pulpit, and extends what Whitty assumes to be the invocation, for the man seems to suffer some kind of speech impairment. Eventually, the amen is sounded, whereupon the choir erupts in the bellowing of a hymn he particularly dislikes:

> O generous love! That he, who smote
> In Man for man the foe,
> The double agony in Man
> For man should undergo . . .

Leading the singing is a nervous young man who may well be conducting his first service, as an audition, in the hope of replacing the precentor in the coffin.

As the congregation rises to join together in praise, a small figure in black squeezes out from behind a line of legs, exits the duke's pew, and dashes down the aisle and out the door, unnoticed. Overcome with grief, Whitty expects. Even so, a short word with one of the bereaved cannot cause her additional harm, and goodness knows he has had his life's fill of country death rituals.

Murmuring vague apologies amid the din of off-key singing, he slips quickly past the gentleman with the inflamed neck, out of the nave and out the door, where the rooks greet him with another round of scolding.

As he heads down the steps to the churchyard, he hears the sound he was expecting, of a young girl weeping for her father. A quick turn around the cemetery and he places the small figure covered in black, seated upon a horizontal gravestone like a crumbling dining table, her head buried in her little hands.

'Excuse me, miss,' he says. 'I do not wish to intrude.'

'Then why are you doing so?' she asks, without looking up.

'Only to offer my sincere condolences at the loss of your father. I am certain he was a fine man.'

The girl meets his gaze and, yes, it is the older sister, with the smooth brow and severe demeanour – softened by sorrow, yet a sceptic all the same. 'How do you know he was fine? Were you acquainted with Father?'

'I regret to say that we never met. Yet I understand he was a man of character and substance.'

'He had trouble with his teeth.'

'Oh. That is unfortunate.'

'And Mother as well.'

'Do you mean to say that your mother had trouble with her teeth?'

'No. I mean that Father had trouble with Mother. And she likewise with him. And now we are under the protection of the Duke of Danbury . . .'

'Under his protection, do you say?'

'Yes. So we must be perfectly safe, and yet I am afraid of, of . . .' She looks down at her fingers, which are all in a knot. Her dark hair obscures her face. A tear falls, unchecked.

'What is it you are afraid of, miss? Is it the duke?' With an effort, Whitty maintains a calm aspect.

'No. Yes. Well to be perfectly truthful, I am at sixes and sevens. I do not know whom to trust or not trust. Whom to believe or not believe. I do not know who is good and who is evil . . .'

'And so you are afraid.'

'Yes.'

'I know that feeling. And I highly recommend it.'

Emma's brow furrows slightly. 'Why?'

'It has been my experience, miss, that it is not something one fears that pounces upon one, but something one would never expect. That is why it is best not to be too sure of oneself.'

She looks up at him with a quizzical tilt of a perfect eyebrow. Whitty could swear he saw a trace of a smile. 'So if one is afraid of falling upon one's head . . .'

'Then it is likely one will land on some other part of the anatomy.'

'And if one is afraid for one's mother, then it is likely that . . .'

'That the real danger is to somebody else.'

She thinks about this idea, then shrugs her dismissal. 'Sir, you sound like one of Mr Boltbyn's nonsensical stories.'

'You are correct, miss, and I apologise.'

'Do you know Mr Boltbyn?'

'I am familiar with his work.'

For a long moment she looks him directly in the eye, as though discerning friend from foe. 'What is your name?'

'Edmund Whitty of *The Falcon*, at your service.'

'Are you a falcon? I know someone who is a hedgehog.'

'No, I am a journalist – a man who searches for facts,' he replies, lying outrageously.

'And what facts are you seeking at my father's funeral?'

A sharp questioner, thinks Whitty. Would make a fine solicitor, but for her sex. 'Again, my condolences, miss . . .'

'Emma.'

'May I sit down?'

'You may, but only for a short time, and only if you tell me what you are about.'

'I am here to discover the fate of a young woman named Eliza.'

At the mention of the name, Whitty knows he has struck a chord. A long silence follows.

'Eliza, did you say?'

'Yes.' Feigning disinterest, Whitty traces the inscription on the tombstone with a forefinger. *Sacred . . . Memory . . .*

'There are photographs of Eliza. I have seen them.'

'Oh really? Can you tell me where I might find these photographs?'

'Certainly I can. And I can tell you who it was took them.'

Emma tells Whitty the whole story. When one doesn't know whom to trust, one might as well trust a stranger.

45

St Ambrose College, Oxford

In his mind Whitty struggles to unravel Miss Emma's account of her adventures, which ranges from the familiar to the unexpected to the fantastic – bizarre photographs, a ghost named Eliza, a sinister hedgehog. And yet she left no doubt that the location, Bissett Grange, is very much of this world. Nor that it is a matter of some urgency, for Emma is clearly not the sort of girl to be frightened easily.

As a first step, he has resolved to pay a visit to David's old school (and his own), and to a certain prominent member of the Oxford Photographic Society, as promised.

St Ambrose is a gracefully crumbling collection of buildings which house seventy or eighty undergraduates, a high percentage of whom are gentlemen-commoners – scions of noble families who live as they wish and dine at the head table, in exchange for double fees. In David's day it was not unknown for a gentleman-commoner on the level of the Duke of Danbury to graduate with full honours without ever having entered the quadrangle.

Pausing in the gateway after taking a portion of medicinal snuff, he raps upon the window of the porter's lodge and almost recognises the face of its potbellied occupant, a double for the porter Whitty remembers in his day – perhaps it is the same man.

'Edmund Whitty to see the Reverend Boltbyn. I am expected.'

The porter shows no sign of interest, nor does he query the visitor further, his function being not to keep intruders out but to keep students in. 'That is fine, sir. Carry on.'

As the Whitty family fortunes underwent their decline in the years before David's death, the younger brother had no option but to follow the path of his brother, at what was termed 'compassionate rates'. Edmund's position in the school differed from David's, who was by then a Fellow of the college, like Mr Boltbyn; still, his brother was able to introduce him to a smart set of clever young men. When the younger brother took to writing with an audacity beyond his station, however, David could do nothing to ameliorate his disgrace . . .

He pauses on the familiar quadrangle, overlooked by little saw-tooth gables and mullioned windows, carpeted by an expanse of grass. By tradition, first-floor residences at St Ambrose are reserved for the ordained Fellows, dropped among the undergraduates as a kind of ballast, and the Reverend William Boltbyn occupies one of these.

After climbing a short wooden staircase in the north-west corner, the correspondent faces an oak door with 'Boltbyn' painted on it; following a period of persistent knocking, the door opens a crack, revealing a face with pink cheeks and a nervous demeanour.

'Mr Whitty. How do you do? To what do I owe this visit?'

'We arranged for a meeting, sir. Before the service at St Swithan's.'

'Did we?'

'It has to do with my brother David, and later developments in the art of photography.'

'Ah, the art of photography.' The face in the crack relaxes a touch. 'Has it not to do with memoirs?'

'Indeed, sir, the memoirs were my primary object. So you do recall our arrangement.'

'I suppose I must.'

'May I come in?'

'Is that what you wish to do?' Alarmed, yet wishing to appear amenable, the Reverend Boltbyn opens the door a bit wider. He is still dressed for the funeral, in a long, black coat topped by a waxed butterfly collar, and has taken great care in the way his side-curls fold over the ears.

'A pitfall of the profession, Mr Boltbyn, is that once one reaches a certain age, one is expected to write a memoir – whether one has any memories or not. You will be writing your own memoirs soon, I expect.'

'I doubt that, sir. I prefer not to dredge up the bad memories. And today's readers relish the bad memories most.'

Whitty follows his host down a dark hall, past a dining room stuffed with books, into a sitting room with green wallpaper and a red couch and settee. In the centre is a round deal table, on which have been set a half-dozen jelly crèmes and a tea-set.

'I was about to take tea in any case, so you might as well join me.'

The walls are almost entirely hung with photographs of little girls. Some have taken the form of fairy pictures, arranged around what appears to be a painting, or a reproduction of a painting, by William Nixon Crede, whose saccharine *œuvre* Whitty avoids for fear of tooth-rot. This particular daub depicts a young woman in classical guise, sleeping – as are all Crede's women – on a rock, having dropped a box . . .

Eliza.

Calming himself with an effort, Whitty turns to his host, who is leaning against the mantel, beside the coal-scuttle, apparently deep in thought. After a pause, the vicar turns and delivers a speech concerning David which sounds, to Whitty's ear, thoroughly rehearsed:

'David was a leading light in the photographic society – as in everything else he attempted. He was the sort of man one admires, but whose presence discourages familiarity. None of the members felt himself to be David's equal, on so many levels – except for his Grace, of course.'

'Are you referring to the Duke of Danbury?'

'Our patron, yes. The duke thought a great deal of David. Had he not met a tragic end, I have no doubt Danbury would have found him a position on the estate.'

'So the duke is a photographer as well?'

'Unfortunately, his Grace lacked a gift for the craft. Your brother spent hours instructing him, but the results were never more than mediocre. Not so with David, of course. Nobody at Oxford matched him in combining the technical and the artistic aspects of the process.'

'Excepting yourself, sir.'

'Perhaps so. Yet David excelled in so many other areas of university life. The boating set, the reading set – I can safely say that his passing cast a pall over the entire college for many weeks . . . Your disgrace was hard on him, you know. As a Fellow of the college, it cast a shadow on his reputation.'

Whitty is about to speak in his own defence, but thinks better of it and downs a second jelly crème instead. Then he turns his attention to the painting of Eliza. It is time to introduce a narrative of his own.

'Mr Boltbyn, I am grateful for your kind words concerning my brother. And it is a privilege to make your acquaintance. I only regret that we were brought together on such a sad occasion – over the remains of Mr Lambert. Such a tragedy, to lose a dear friend by hanging.'

'It would be in-in-in–'

'Sir, though I had no acquaintance with the Precentor at St Swithan's–'

'–inconceivable, to allow s-s-s–'

'Yet I am sufficiently acquainted with the symptoms of hanging to know that his journey to the next world was not as described. Mr Boltbyn, do you agree that suicide is a mortal sin?'

'God is the master of life. We are stewards of life. Life is not ours to discard.'

'Well put. Yet there are ambiguities, surely. Life is not kind to some people.'

'It-it-it is, sir, a t-t-tragedy that I trust, as a gentleman, you will keep in confidence if-if-if you feel a shred of regard for the welfare of the family.'

'You may be assured of my discretion – not from altruism, but because such a scandal would hardly cause a ripple in London. *Maddened by Dental Problem, Man Takes Own Life*, perhaps; or *Hanged by the Neck to Spite His Teeth*. What does the sad tale of Mr Lambert amount to, compared to a narrative such as, say: *Country Church Abets Atrocious Murder*? Or even better: *Eminent Children's Author at Centre of Oxford Outrage*?'

'I do not understand your meaning at all, sir. And if I did, I suspect I would not like it.'

Whitty examines the picture he knows for certain to be Eliza, under the agitated stare of his host. 'I am curious about this picture, sir. The artist is, I believe, William Nixon Crede.'

'Mr Crede makes his paintings from photographs. He would prefer that this were not generally known.'

'A reproduction of a reproduction, then.'

'That is Mr Crede's method. More praise, for less effort.'

'Of course. *C is for Crede, the cock in a cage*.'

'Correct.'

'And did Mr Crede take the photograph?'

'No, it was I who took the photograph. When it comes to the apparatus, Crede is all thumbs.'

'It appears to be a depiction from the Classical repertoire.'

'Psyche, actually. A myth having to do with lost beauty.'

'The face is familiar.'

'A m-mythical figure. You can look it up if you wish.'

'I mean the sitter. She is an intelligent girl. A perceptive girl, in my estimation.'

'You-you have not touched your tea, sir, though the crèmes seem to have met with your approval. Would you care for something stronger?'

'Whatever you have.'

The vicar fetches a bottle and two glasses. 'Mr Whitty, are you fond of mathematics?'

'Numbers depress me unbearably.'

'Riddles, perhaps?'

'Please proceed.'

'Here is a good one. Because cigars cannot be entirely smoked, a derelict who collects cigar-ends can make one complete cigar out of every five ends that he finds. Today, he has collected twenty-five cigar-ends. How many cigars will he be able to smoke?'

Replies the correspondent, at once: 'Six cigars. He will make five cigars from the twenty-five, and another from the five ends that remain when he has smoked them. I have seen derelicts perform just such a manoeuvre.'

Disappointed at the quick response, Boltbyn pours Whitty a glass of brandy, and more tea for himself. 'Your answer displays an unbecoming familiarity with the smoking habits of derelicts.'

'Permit me to repay one conundrum with another, sir,' Whitty says, and presents the vicar with the photograph of David, alone. 'This is a photograph I found among David's things. Like the picture on your wall, it seems to depict a figure in the Classical style.'

Boltbyn glances at the photograph with mild interest. 'Ah yes. I remember this as one of a series – as you put it, in the Classical style.'

'Did you take it?'

'No. David took it himself.'

'He took it *himself*?'

'By means of a bulb beneath his foot, which he would squeeze and thereby expose the plate. An ingenious manipulation of the equipment, and a testimony to your brother's skill. And to his vanity, if I may say so.'

'Which brings us to another riddle: having explained one photograph, what do you have to say about this one?' Whitty places on the table the photograph of David and Eliza – and waits.

Producing a gold-rimmed *pince-nez*, the vicar examines the photograph of David and Eliza as though it were a text in a foreign language.

'As you can see, Mr Boltbyn, the two figures had to have been photographed at different times – the evidence is on your wall.'

Continuing silence.

'Was it a trick in the development? You are the expert, sir.'

'Yes. A t-t-trick . . . two glass n-negatives, one on top of the—'

And for the second time today, Whitty hears the satisfying crash of glass shattering upon the floor. He dared not hope for such a reaction; a simple gasp would have sufficed.

'Her name is Eliza,' Whitty says.

The vicar stares down at the shattered teacup, at the tea splattered upon his boots and trousers, at anything but the photograph in his hand, which he holds at a distance as though it were in flames.

Continues Whitty: 'Or perhaps I should say that her name *was* Eliza, for she was taken by persons who murder at their convenience.'

Boltbyn sets the photograph gently upon the table, face down, and stares at the blank surface for several moments. He nods, not in the way of agreement but of a terrible finality; now he turns, crosses to the window overlooking Adera Street, opens the casement wide, leans outside as though taking the air . . . and leaps out the window!

For a moment Whitty fears he has driven the man to suicide, until he remembers that Mr Boltbyn's rooms are on the first floor. He is about to leap out the window in pursuit, when it occurs to him that he has been left alone in the gentleman's private rooms. Of course only a cad or a journalist would exploit this opportunity to rummage through another man's private life.

Whitty closes Boltbyn's window, puts the photographs back into his coat pocket, pours himself an ample measure of brandy, and sets to work.

What the correspondent had assumed to be bookshelves turn out to be a frame for a series of secret compartments – which, when opened, reveal child-objects of all sorts.

The playthings are remarkable for their extent and variety: a glass-topped music box, through which one can view its inner workings; an organette that produces music from perforated cards; a compartment fitted with mirrors, creating a *trompe-l'œil* doll's house extending in all directions. At one point Whitty opens a small door and a severed clown's head springs out at him, in a way that is most alarming. From other apertures emerge mechanical walking bears, singing tops, talking cats, climbing monkeys, a smoking railway engine, a flying bat, a singing dog, a clockwork bank – not to mention a library of picture-books and games.

An oddly touching collection, thinks Whitty. Its owner actually *thinks* as a child, knows at first hand what surprises and delights. He has never tired of childish things – therefore desires to be with children in the way that a native desires to be with his own kind.

At last he locates the one spot in the room which has been put aside for Boltbyn the adult – a cubby containing a desk, lamp and bookcase, whose every horizontal surface overflows with books, manuscripts, correspondence, publisher's enquiries, drawings, design notes, mathematical problems; and, piled upon a shelf, a series of diaries, year by year, continuous from the age of ten.

Mr Boltbyn's diaries are consistent with the genre, self-absorbed and self-aggrandising, distinguished by two curious tendencies.

One is to underline important words, like an over-wrought schoolgirl; the other is the addition of white stones to the text – pebbles really, never more than a half-inch in diameter, glued with white paste at the edge of the page, beside a date whose entry is blank. Nor do the entries above and below the stones reveal their significance, being an account of people spoken to, food eaten, the weather – the normal events of a repetitious, insular life.

What do the pebbles mean? Clearly, the use of stones in place of written language indicates a message from the diarist to himself – a private code. And there exists the obvious symbolism in which white stands for purity, and a stone implies permanence. Whitty cannot dismiss such a simple-minded interpretation out of hand – especially given the cloying sentimentality of the man's serious verse.

Working from the present to the past, all of the writing is original, and all of it is bad:

> Between the green brine and the running foam
> White limbs unrobed in a crystal air,
> Sweet faces, rounded arms and bosoms prest
> To little harps of gold.

In other entries, the diarist notes his philosophical speculations, with typical overemphasis:

> There are <u>sceptical</u> thoughts which uproot the firmest faith; there are <u>blasphemous</u> thoughts which dart unbidden into the most reverend souls; there are <u>unholy</u> thoughts which torture by their presence the fancy that would fain be pure. This is the battlefield upon which I fight my tormenters.

Such tortured admissions are inevitably followed by a mathematical problem and its solution, as though he were seeking escape.

> A triangular billiard-table has 3 pockets, one in each corner, one of which will hold only one ball, while each of the others will hold two. There are

3 balls on the table, each containing a single coin. The table is tilted up, so that the balls run into one corner, it is not known which. The expectation as to the contents of the pocket is 2s. 6d. What are the coins?

In other entries, again and again the writer sounds a note of petulant complaint: *Miss Pouch has dictated that I may not kiss the girls more than <u>once</u> each half-hour. The impudence.*

Leading to the same melancholy conclusion:

> *I'd give all wealth that toil hath piled*
> *The bitter fruit of life's decay*
> *To be once more a little child*
> *For one short sunny day.*

All men are egotists in Whitty's opinion, yet the condition takes specific forms. Some dream of an impossible greatness; some dream of an impossible holiness; Boltbyn's egotism takes the form of an impossible innocence – a childhood no child ever knew.

46

Bissett Grange, Oxfordshire

Emma can see that her governess has been in a vexed frame of mind since she absented herself from Father's funeral. Therefore it would only aggravate the situation were she to mention her chat with the falcon – for it is really not the thing, to speak about one's private life to a stranger. And yet, when an adult lends his full attention to what one has to say, the occurrence is sufficiently rare that it is a close-mouthed child who refrains from telling all.

Now Miss Pouch has decided that the two of them must take the air, with a stroll around the magnificent flower-beds that decorate the carriage-sweep, before retiring to prayers. (Lydia has gone to bed with a fever – the entire episode has been too much for her.)

To Emma it seems that, whether in a garden or a funeral, flowers are an important part of life and death. Tomorrow, she will suggest to Mr Boltbyn that they stage a contest in flower arrangement, for the imaginary services of people they know. She is about to mention it to Miss Pouch, when the governess fixes her nose towards an emerging puff of dust – a hackney coach, rattling up the elm-avenue.

'Who would come to call at this hour – and at such a speed?' asks Miss Pouch.

'I hope it is Mr Boltbyn,' says Emma. 'He might brighten things up.' If nothing else, she would ask him about her father's funeral.

She has always found it tiresome, making solemn conversation on solemn occasions, and this is the most solemn occasion she has experienced. Looking ahead to the months of compulsory mourning, she wonders how she will endure it: mornings at catechism, afternoons with the Book of Common Prayer, and the in-between moments contemplating the exemplary life of the father she never really knew.

The coach pulls up the carriage-sweep and stops abruptly amid a cloud of dust, a groaning of axles, and a chorus of whinnying from the horses as the reins are pulled taut. Immediately the door opens and a gentleman climbs down hurriedly – it is Mr Boltbyn; yet Emma's delight quickly gives way to concern, for his expression is not one that she has seen before, and when his eyes fall upon her they contain none of the usual warmth.

'Mr Boltbyn! I am ever so glad to see you, sir, and expect that Miss Lydia would agree, though she is in bed . . .'

'That is very well, Miss Emma, but this concerns another matter. Please excuse me.' And before she can reply, he is halfway up the steps.

'Sir, I have always thought we were friends, and ask that you explain this curtness,' Emma calls after him.

The vicar stops with one foot on the top step: 'I shall explain it, Miss Emma, when I understand it myself.' With that, he proceeds to knock upon the door forcefully with his stick. While a footman unlatches the door, he turns to her, and his taut expression has become downright grim.

'Mr Boltbyn, your face is like that of a ghost,' she says.

'Have you seen a ghost?' comes the rejoinder. 'Somehow I think that you have.'

Before she can reply, the door opens and the footman glowers down upon them; the vicar pushes past him without a word.

'I find Mr Boltbyn's behaviour most singular,' says Miss Pouch.

'Perhaps *he* has seen a ghost,' replies Emma.

She lies swaddled in a rosewood bed, with an enormous eagle perched over her head, and crowns on all four posts that would suit an oriental emperor. The ceiling has been decorated with painted dolphins, and there are similar fish made of plaster over the door-frames.

In an alcove across the room, is a bath shaped like an enormous coal-scuttle, supported by marble cupids with trumpets in their mouths, set upon a Turkey carpet. In the bath is her lover, asleep.

Why, she wonders, are the fish in the sky and the cupids on the bath? Shouldn't it be the other way around?

And how innocent he looks! Curled up like a child, under a sheet, stretched across the bath to keep in the heat. She could love him always, if he would only remain in that state.

Watching him, she recalls the French revolutionary Marat, who died in his bath, and under a sheet. How vulnerable he too must have appeared, though in his waking hours he murdered thousands. And for Charlotte Corday, what a test it must have been, to slay the man and the child at the same time.

When a woman forms an association with a man, it is understood that she sleeps when he does, wakes when he wakes – a scarcely noticeable concession for most people; yet how different it is, to accommodate oneself to the schedule of a nobleman. Danbury wakes

233

when his eyes open, sleeps when he is tired, and in-between he does precisely what he feels like doing – and his entire establishment patterns itself accordingly. Including his mistress.

It is barely sunset, and the duke is sound asleep, and Birdie must pretend, though she is no closer to sleeping than she is to the moon. But if she were to stir, and he awoke, it would be tantamount to treason.

At first, he seemed a miracle of supernatural proportions. His breeding, dignity, manners, the luxury of his surroundings, his effortless power, enveloped her like a laudanum dream, a delirious pleasure she never dared imagine.

In her dream, they stood in a chariot side by side, while he drove the plunging horses into eternity. Now the giddy sense of limitlessness has begun to affect her in other ways.

The photographs. At first she thought it was an artistic whim; a matter of indulging a taste peculiar to his class, a harmless indulgence like spanking. But as she stood there in her nakedness, with a rope about her throat, while watching his ardent response, she began to suspect something deeper. What did he see when he looked at her through that lens – was it she? Was it anyone like her? Why would a man wish to see his lover with a rope about her throat?

Beyond the photography and play-acting, he does not appear to enjoy anything much. When she attempts to talk to him about one thing or another, he becomes stony and dignified; and looks straight through her as though she were made of water.

Despite a tendency to dreaminess, by nature and upbringing Birdie's mind turns to practical matters. Now that Mr Lambert is dead, who will care for her daughters and herself?

'Of course there is the probability that one day I shall have to marry,' he once said, as though it were an afterthought to a casual conversation.

'These days, some do not see the necessity,' she replied, as though she ever knew anyone who did such a thing.

'But I must. For the line, you see. For the house and the land.'

'Of course.' In truth, she had no idea how these things connected.

'Don't look cross. You and the girls shall be provided for.'

'But when they are grown and I am old and withered, why should you provide for me then?'

'Because – and I have said this to you before – you are under my protection.'

This answer satisfied her, for the moment; yet what does it mean, to

234

be under someone's protection? What does he wish to protect her from? And who will protect her from him?

Mr Lambert was at least predictable. She knew what he was capable of, and what he was not.

Absorbed in these uneasy thoughts, Birdie at first does not hear the knocking upon the door, then assumes it to be a servant's mistake. Eventually, the knocking becomes so insistent that the duke begins to stir, causing an uneasy rippling beneath the sheet.

'*Your Grace! Harry! There has been an unforeseen development! You must come at once!*'

It is the voice of Mr Lush; but not the unctuous purr he normally affects – in fact, it is almost a command.

The duke opens his eyes. 'What sort of development?' he calls back. 'And why the devil are you bothering me with it?'

'Boltbyn has arrived, in a deuce of a snit.'

'Why should I give a damn?'

'He is claiming all sorts of rubbish. He demands to see you at once.'

'Turn him out. Set the Irish on him, they do little enough as it is.'

'I think you should speak to him, Harry. I really think you should.'

It is the first time Birdie has heard Danbury's familiar name spoken aloud by Albin Lush, and she wonders what gives him the right.

Seated at his drinking-table wearing his red silk dressing-gown, Danbury takes a measure of medicinal powder to counter the impudence of his estate manager, then turns his chair to face the windows overlooking the lawn. Swinging his left leg over the arm, he trims a cigar and puts it in his mouth; instantly Lush supplies a lucifer.

'An unfortunate detail seems to have come to light, your Grace. It has to do with the name Eliza.'

The estate manager scratches the backs of his hands, noting that the rash, like the danger, appears to be spreading. What a relief it will be when he is out of this for good!

'The name means nothing to me, I am afraid. Why?'

'Is your Grace certain of that?'

'Confound it, are we to play guessing games?'

Lush enunciates carefully, as though addressing a halfwit. 'Think back, Harry, it was not so very long ago. The subject of the last lot of photographs went by the name of Eliza.'

'Ah yes, nasty business, best forgotten. Why the deuce are you bothering me with it now?'

'Somehow or other, Boltbyn has got wind of the name Eliza, and he is in quite a state. I advise you to . . . cheer him up.'

'He can go to the devil. Cheer him up yourself.'

'Your Grace's cavalier bearing is, if I may say so, inappropriate to your position. Whitty has taken a room in town. After the incident in London, he is set on uncovering the business of his brother. In doing so, he seems to have taken an interest in the late precentor – and Mr Boltbyn as well. This trend must be stopped at once, Harry, surely you can see that.'

'Confound it, you were to have seen to the newspaperman ages ago. I paid out a small fortune on that score.'

'That is beside the point now, Harry. The point is, the danger, now that he is in Oxford – especially after what happened to the Reverend Lambert.'

'How so? The Reverend is dead. I attended the funeral.'

'Rumours linger to the effect that the precentor died by hanging, that it was a case of disguised suicide. Well and good, but Whitty might well see it otherwise – given what he witnessed at Buckingham Gate. He is unlikely to see it as a coincidence, don't you see? He is bound to dig in.'

'Shoot him, then. Have you no imagination? Bring him here and shoot him as an intruder. An instance of mistaken identity.'

'Yes, your Grace – and shall we shoot Mr Boltbyn as well? Try to remember, Harry, we are not in London. And the situation is further complicated by your enthusiasm for the mother. Now is not the time for a scandal.'

'Don't make yourself more disagreeable than nature obliges you, Lush. For one in my position, rumour and speculation are a fact of life.'

'Damn you, Harry, do you think I care about your reputation? It is Whitty I am talking about.'

'Your impertinence is staggering, Lush. The proper thing for you is to take my wishes as a matter of course – and my wish regarding Whitty is clear. You may go.'

Lush speaks to Danbury as though to a child – one whose head he would like to place in the fire.

'Harry, I want you to imagine a magnificent house, with good riding horses, good dinners and good brandy, supported and maintained with the least possible effort. That is your situation, sir, we have created it together. But the house is under threat. A rodent has entered the premises, a rat with a purpose, a persistent nature, and sharp little teeth . . .'

'Oh, stop it, will you? Really, this is the most inane conversation in the world.'

'Harry, I demand that you speak to Mr Boltbyn, immediately. Otherwise I shall have no more to do with the business, do you hear me? I shall take myself elsewhere, and your Grace will be on your own.' Indeed, thinks Lush, that is exactly what he intends to do.

Danbury stands and crosses to the window to survey the grounds. He takes so long to reply that Lush wonders if he will speak at all.

Feigning indifference, Lush moves closer to the hearth and gazes up at the Danbury ancestor over the mantel, while his fingers probe an itchy spot in the nape of his neck. Everything has become damnably complicated. He feels like a juggler, with one too many knives in the air.

The duke's cigar-end lands in front of him in a shower of sparks. 'Very well, damn you. Show him in. But you will oblige me by remaining close at hand, in case he becomes a bore.'

Pouring himself a second brandy with his free hand, Danbury examines one of Boltbyn's photographs – Emma as the beggar-girl, in a dress that has been torn to reveal her small white shoulder. A brilliantly suggestive piece of work. In fact it was this picture that inspired Danbury to envision a kind of repertory company in which he would act as impresario, with a secure cast of subjects and photographers, a steady stream of profit – and no bodies to dispose of afterward.

Of course, nobody would dream that William Boltbyn, the poet of childhood, might harbour the sensibilities of a Ruskin, or any of the stunted legions who favour girls of that age, in that way. But Danbury understands Boltbyn – more, he expects, than Boltbyn does. He understood Boltbyn the moment he looked at the photograph.

Cheer Boltbyn up? What the man requires is to be put in his proper place.

Placing the photograph back in its drawer, he turns to contemplate the portrait over the fireplace: no Danbury in history has deferred to the will of anyone short of a duke. The duke is not about to defer to a vicar.

Knocking softly upon the door, the estate manager appears. 'Will your Grace see Mr Boltbyn now?'

'I say, Lush, there is a pistol missing from the wall.'

'O'Day took it out for cleaning, sir.'

'Bring it back at once. It looks like the devil with one missing.'

Rather than continue on the subject, Lush steps aside to admit a dishevelled and trembling Boltbyn, then retires to the bookcase, to scratch his neck and watch the proceedings.

For a full minute, Danbury regards the vicar as though he were an animal at auction, and not a particularly valuable one at that. For his part, the vicar stands unsteadily in the middle of the Turkey carpet, looking for all the world like the famous French lunatic, released after forty years in a windowless cell.

Unable to withstand the silence, the vicar attempts to speak. 'It is m-m-m-m-m-m-m-m-m-m-m . . .'

Danbury undertakes no response; he merely lifts his eyebrows slightly, as though to say, *If you can't spit it out, why are you bothering me?*

Giving up on that particular consonant, Boltbyn stares wide-eyed at the floor, as though he were looking past the multiple jaws of Cerebus, down to the River Styx.

Danbury strokes his side-whiskers with an expression of mild concern. 'I beg your pardon, sir?'

'M-m-m . . .'

The duke crosses and uncrosses his legs, then takes his handkerchief from his waistcoat and trifles with it elegantly, while the motor of consonants attempts, and fails, to produce a clear sentence. To Lush it is clear that when Boltbyn entered the room to stand before that serene, confident presence, he fell into a place where life as he knows it does not exist, and none of the rules applies.

After another excruciating pause, Danbury clears his throat gently, and addresses his visitor in an almost ethereal whisper. 'Mr Boltbyn, if only as a way of lubricating the conversation, might you oblige me by explaining the purpose of your visit?'

'The young, the young, the p-p-p- . . . It is like a terrible dr-dr-dr- . . .'

'Mr Lush, perhaps it would help if you gave Mr Boltbyn some water.'

'Throat trouble, Mr Boltbyn?' asks the estate manager. 'Will you take water?'

'I c-c-cannot s-s-speak of it,' replies the vicar, miserably.

'Water it shall be, then,' answers the estate manager, while giving the duke a look as if to say, *Do not push him too far.* For the fact of Boltbyn's stammer, the scrambling of a mind to find its bearings, does not make the situation any less serious. Upon entering the house, the vicar's speech was audible, though confused, and Lush distinctly heard the words *obscene* and *horror*, and, most important, *Eliza*.

'Pray, what is it you cannot speak of, sir?' asks the duke, as though moderately intrigued.

'It is unsp-sp-speakable. I-I cannot speak of it.'

'Then perhaps it had best remain unspoken.'

'M-m-madness!' The word explodes in a bellow and the vicar appears to fall into a sort of seizure, not unlike a man the duke once witnessed choking at dinner, whose gaping mouth had the stupid, agonised appearance of a fish.

'It is beyond c-c-comprehension. I am in a s-state of . . . I am s-s-stunned.'

'What an odd coincidence. Do you know, I was just thinking about stunning a fish.'

'You are mad, sir. You are a m-madman.'

'I suppose that is true. Everyone is mad in a way. If we weren't mad, we wouldn't be here.'

'Your water, sir,' offers Lush.

Upon swallowing his water and after a series of sighs, the vicar collapses into the duke's ancestral chair. Lush silently cautions the duke to overlook this impudence, for the man is pretty far gone.

'Mr Boltbyn,' says the duke, 'I was only trying to remind you that madness is an omnipresent, necessary part of life. Madness is God-given and must be accepted.'

'How you can s-speak of such a thing, and the h-hand of G-God not crush you to dust!'

'Well, if it is that awful to think about, my advice to you is not to think about it.'

'You c-c-cannot make light of it, sir! It is be-be-beyond imagining that you would make light of it!'

'Make light of what, pray?'

'I-I-I cannot . . .'

'You cannot what? Jump a horse? Skip a rope?'

'I saw the ph-ph-photograph, sir! Of D-David Whitty and, and – Oh, monstrous! It is too horrible! . . .'

The duke and his estate manager exchange a significant glance in which the latter asks: *What shall we do now?* and the former replies, *Oh just leave him to me, damn you!* For awhile, the two look down upon the wretched spectacle of a man who believes he is too sensitive for the real world, only to discover that the world is infinitely worse than he imagined.

The duke clips another cigar and leans into the flame supplied by Lush, who can see that Danbury is finding the conversation rather interesting, in the way that it is interesting to dissect a frog.

'Have you been to London, Mr Boltbyn? Have you visited the theatre? The music hall?'

'W-what is that to you?'

'Are you at all acquainted with the personal services on offer on every street in the city? Or did you spend your time at church?'

'W-w-what are you implying?' Boltbyn does not wish to listen, yet he must, compelled by the duke's voice and bearing, his perfect aplomb.

'Dear fellow, I say only that in London life is no more or less mad than it is here at Bissett Grange. For example, by taking the trouble to walk along the Embankment, you will find parties who may be put to work for a few shillings, who have tied Mussulmen to the mouths of cannon – is that not so, Mr Lush?'

'Indeed, your Grace. Dismissed servicemen are accustomed to the most appalling cruelty. Understandable, I say, given the cruelty invested on them. Is your Grace suggesting that we may need such assistance in this case?'

'No, Lush, what is required from Mr Boltbyn is a degree of realism.' Danbury bends close to the vicar, who is making a careful study of the water in his glass. 'I am told that in Whitechapel there are brothels filled with children, where a gentleman may carry on in whatever beastly fashion he likes, also for the price of a few shillings. An appalling business, but there you are.'

'I do not understand your m-m-meaning, sir. Why tell me this?'

'I am explaining to you why there is no point making a fuss. We live in a brute of a world. One is always running into objectionable things. People with manners don't make a fuss. It isn't done. An unpleasant business takes place, one accepts it as part of life. It is childish to bite one's lip over it.'

A peculiar calm descends upon the vicar, like the air after a thunderstorm, and he speaks in surprisingly clear syllables:

'This is not about what people do, sir. It is about what you yourself have done. I think that you are mad, sir. I marvel that you place your conduct in the human realm, that you put yourself on a scale of human b-b-behaviour, and not the beastliness of wolves.'

'Ah yes, of course. So sensitive, so touchy. You who cannot face life have chosen the path of fantasy. You choose to dream – for it entails no risk. Your little mind is strewn with roses, their thorns clipped, little girls holding them in their dimpled hands. Nor does age or infirmity wither your imaginary garden, nor the base, carnal things of this world. Yet your heart knows what you think, what you really dream in your sleepless bed. Are you so shocked to discover that others are capable of action?'

'It is l-l-life and death that I speak of, sir! Of ch-children, for that is what they were, no matter how low-born or fallen! The value of a child's life is not a matter for discussion!'

'Sir, if I may speak frankly: is anyone to believe that you actually thought the girl you yourself photographed, this Eliza, to be *asleep*?'

'I-I . . .'

'You did the proper thing. You kept your place, and followed the lead of your betters. I advise you to do the same in future.'

'You are an aberration, sir. You are deformed.'

'And by what authority do you say such a thing, you overgrown child? You are an aberration, but that is your privilege. Still, if you suppose I care a damn for the moral pronouncements of a ten-stone infant, you are mistaken.'

'I will expose you, sir! It is m-m-m . . .'

'Yes, yes, yes, monstrous and all that, but of course everything is monstrous to you. Unlike you, I accept my duty, which is to safeguard the house and what it stands for. Wars have been fought over it, sir. Thousands have given their lives – not a few Whitechapel urchins.'

'So you murdered them. You murdered them all.'

'It is the great families who provide leadership through war, death, pestilence, and – who was the other horseman, Lush? I can never remember.'

'Famine, your Grace.'

'Famine. That is correct. Get me a brandy.'

Lush obeys.

Calmer now, and with an air of finality, Boltbyn rises to his feet. The duke does likewise, in order to look his prey in the eye, before dealing the killing stroke.

'You allude, Mr Boltbyn, to a terrible secret you feel honour-bound to expose. I applaud your sense of moral purpose, sir, your unflinching determination, at the price of your reputation, your freedom, even your life.'

'What you do is beyond thinking. It is monstrous.'

'Monstrous, yes, you used that insult before. And it would indeed shock the parish beyond measure should something so monstrous as you imply have occurred at Bissett Grange. Yet, with the advantage of hindsight, one can see the potential for such an abuse. And it would not be the first time such a monstrous deception were played upon a member of the aristocracy. Given sufficient audacity, it is conceivable that a photographic society might be corrupted into taking liberties with children. Especially when some of its members have already exhibited a dubious interest in photographing little girls, in indecent postures and states of undress. To my shock and shame, I have with my own eyes witnessed such pictures of Miss Emma Lambert, whom I have taken under my protection.'

The duke crosses to the side-table, opens the drawer, and produces the photographs, one by one. 'Here we see Emma, supposedly as a beggar-girl. Note, Mr Boltbyn, the bare shoulder, the insinuating aspect, the coy angle of the head – all of which is to remind the viewer of the true nature of child-begging in London streets. Having been to the city, I don't have to remind you of the filth which can emanate from the mouth of a Haymarket child.'

The duke produces another picture. 'Now note the artist's depiction of our dear Emma as a runaway, about to climb from an upstairs window, forsaking the family which has raised her and cared for her, to join her lover in an illicit affair. I ask you, sir, *Who is that lover, if not the photographer?*

'People will wonder what blindness kept me from discovering such filth in my own house. Put it down to the naïveté of an overgenerous fool, who sought to devote his property in the service of progress and art, and was monstrously deceived for his trouble!

'Report it, sir. Throw dirt upon the Danbury name – and upon the name of Wallace Beverley. For who will fail to recognise your most recent subject – victim, if you will – as a virtual twin of your Emma? Are we to believe it is a coincidence? And are we really supposed to accept that you believed the model to be *sleeping?*'

'You said it was for r-r-realism. I-I accepted your, your—'

'Of course you did. It is only natural to take the word of one's superiors. I strongly suggest that you continue to do so – in which case, I shall forgive and forget. Like the Lambert woman and her daughters, I shall take you under my protection, and you need fear nothing. You are a superlative photographer, capable of exceedingly lifelike effects. You and Miss Lambert share an admirable rapport.

'Speaking of the Lamberts, I have something to share with you: after a suitable period of mourning, I shall ask for Mrs Lambert's hand in marriage. When I do, I will instruct my daughters to call you Uncle.'

The vicar rises unsteadily and speaks in a hoarse whisper. 'D-do I understand you, sir? You expect me to remain silent – even to *co-operate?*'

'Silence is golden, Mr Boltbyn. By the way, there is a lovely silent spot in the wood not far from here. You are welcome there any time.'

'And so is Miss Emma,' adds the estate manager, as he ushers the vicar to the door.

47

Oxford

Whitty makes his way through the throng of townsmen and gownsmen milling about the centre of Oxford on a Friday evening, taunting one another between puffs of tobacco. It seems to him that the town has grown darker than when he last walked its streets. The buildings are sootier than he remembers them, they intensify the sombre severity of the stone façades on Radcliffe Square and the Broad. Burdened by this oppressive, medieval atmosphere, plastered with ash and perfumed by cow manure, Whitty recalls how much of Oxford belongs to the Dark Ages – from the Prince of Darkness to Henry the something, who should not have murdered the Archbishop of Canterbury, to King John, who put his nephew in gaol without food until he died, having eaten his hands . . .

By the time he settles into a heated gin at the Grass, even the drinking-room seems to have taken on a sinister aspect. Prawn and Ellington (whose tumour seems to pull his ear sideways) scowl into space like stone gargoyles, while Mrs Wafer, busy with her knitting, resembles that well-known feature of the French Revolution, seated by the guillotine, cackling merrily with each drop of the blade, and never dropping a stitch.

'Bless us, Mr Whitty, and weren't there two visitors asking for you not a quarter-hour past.'

'Thank you, Mrs Wafer, and another warm glass of the out-and-out if you don't mind,' he replies, wincing at the possibilities. 'By any chance, were the two visitors dressed in the reds of the Indian Campaign?'

'Poor fellow, you looks pinched as a rooster.'

'Setting aside my mental state for the moment, madam, did you recognise the gentlemen as soldiers?'

'No, the first one was an Irishman in livery. As to t'other, I'd be blind not to peg the Reverend Boltbyn – he of the books and such.'

'Mr Boltbyn was here? With the Irishman?'

'No, he came on his own.'

'Do not forget the pitures, Mrs Wafer,' adds Prawn, whose hearing has survived age and dissipation. 'Be making pitures of the daughters of the late precentah . . .'

'Be talk of them pitures,' mutters Prawn's asymmetrical companion. 'Talk what they be scarcely decent.'

'They are works of art, Mr Ellington. Like paintings and the like.'

'Not the same at all, Mr Prawn.'

'Mr Boltbyn did look a caution,' comments Mrs Wafer, refilling Whitty's gin and adding the price to his bill. 'Jabbering with words as would break his jaw coming out . . . Oh, bless me, I forgot the letters!'

Rummaging through her voluminous garments, she produces two small envelopes with Whitty's name inscribed upon them. The first he opens and proceeds to read, first in silence, then aloud to the company, for it is gibberish to him:

> *BEYOND OSIRIS' ROILING STONES*
> *I' THE RIBWORT LIES SHE STILL*
> *SUNLESS, SOULLESS ARE THE BONES*
> *SOBER, CRUEL WAS THE KILL*
> *END HER SLEEP IN NAMELESS EARTH*
> *TAKE NO NAME FOR NOBLE BIRTH*
> *THAT DECLARES HER NOTHING WORTH.*

'Does this make sense to anyone here?' Whitty asks.

'It is a poem,' says Egerton Prawn.

'Indeed, I have established that for myself, but thank you anyway.'

'By Mistah Tennyson, by the sound and sentiment. Be always on about grand ladies in tombs.'

'Swinburne, more likely,' counters Mr Ellington, with contempt.

'It is dismal and modern, whoever writ it,' adds Mrs Wafer.

Whitty leaves the drinking-room while the poetry discussion continues, no wiser than when he entered, while opening the second envelope and extracting a card of thick vellum:

The Right Honourable the Duke of Danbury
K.G.C.V., K.G.C.S., K.C.A.J., (H.)O.L.J.
Bissett Grange
Cordially Requests the Company of
Mr Edmund Whitty Esq.
On Saturday next, for Luncheon at Twelve o'Clock.
R.S.V.P.

Trying to fall asleep between sheets with the texture of wrung-out dishcloths, Whitty wishes he had never encountered Mr Boltbyn and his damned riddles – in particular, the one he delivered this evening. What the devil is Boltbyn's intention? Surely not to communicate: how damnably perverse (and damnably English at the same time) to require the recipient of a personal message to decode it, before any response is possible.

The normal combination of depressants and opiates has done nothing to pacify Whitty's roiling brain. *Roiling Stones?* As he settles into a restless slumber that is to sleep as gruel is to mutton, again and again the picture of David appears, posing for a photograph in an unclad state, with that self-satisfied smile, silently proclaiming to the world, *Look at me! Admire me! See how pleased I am with the meat of which I am made!*

Whitty falls into a whirlpool at the centre of a gigantic puzzle, then wakens abruptly, rigid as a stick, soaked in sweat. He returns to slumber again only to watch upon the lids of his eye the most disquieting nonsense phrases, spinning about, which repeatedly arrange themselves into the text of Boltbyn's verse, with its hint of a forgotten corpse, a buried woman, a cruel nobleman, and a call to end her anonymous sleep:

> *BEYOND OSIRIS' ROILING STONES*
> *I' THE RIBWORT LIES SHE STILL*
> *SUNLESS, SOULLESS ARE THE BONES*
> *SOBER, CRUEL WAS THE KILL*
> *END HER SLEEP IN NAMELESS EARTH*
> *TAKE NO NAME FOR NOBLE BIRTH*
> *THAT DECLARES HER NOTHING WORTH.*

Whatever is the fellow trying to say? And if he has something to say, why does he not say it?

From his Oxford years, Whitty recalls that Osiris was the Egyptian god who judged the dead – but where does that get him?

As he lies in this mud-hole of a bed, at the mid-point between sleeping and waking, the lines of verse projected upon his eyelids grow larger and smaller, then whirl and fragment, so that some letters appear to have more significance than others, revealing hidden words within the text, writhing downward and upward in the manner of an acrostic poem:

B Y O S
I R B R
S U S O
S B C R
E N E R
T A N O
T D E H

Blast! Whitty springs into an upright position, cracking his head upon the rafter just above the headboard.

Bissett. Danbury. Obscene. Horrors. Were these words consciously buried within the text? If so, how the devil would Boltbyn expect anyone to solve it? Or does he expect no such thing – protecting himself from harm while remaining morally superior? Or has Boltbyn determined that anyone who cannot solve the riddle cannot solve the larger enigma? Or is it the only language he speaks – life being such a conundrum in his mind?

He opens his eyes to behold the bleak promise of first light, as the gables and the tottering chimneys reappear as shadows, then as forms.

As he consciously steers his mind to a more rational framework, Whitty ponders the invitation for luncheon with the duke. Of course, he will accept by first mail, yet he has also determined to arrive well in advance of the appointed time. For as the saying goes, *He who arrives late is guilty of tardiness; he who arrives early is capable of anything.*

Bissett Grange, Oxfordshire

When midnight mists are creeping,
And all the land is sleeping,
Around me tread the mighty dead
And slowly pass away.

She dreams about Eliza now, ever since her visit to the graveyard. At times she see a falcon hovering overhead. Her mother too appears in her dreams, and she sometimes encounters a hedgehog.

Though the dreams vary, their inspiration remains stubbornly consistent: her discovery of the name *Eliza*. That she was mistaken for a ghost. Mr Boltbyn's odd reaction to the name. The hedgehog in the graveyard – all remain equally fresh in her mind, yet with nothing to unite them but a suspicion she is at a loss to articulate.

As Mr Boltbyn once said, when one finds oneself at a loss, the thing is to shake things up generally and then have another look.

For this reason, and because she can think of nothing better to do, and because she is beginning to think there might be such a thing as ghosts, Emma has decided to take her investigation further, beginning with another visit to the graveyard – which, she suspects, contains Eliza. She will undertake this exploration in the dead of night. She will include Lydia, whose eyesight is particularly sharp.

Having formed their plan on Friday afternoon, the two sisters lie awake until the hour when the house is utterly silent, then slip out from under their sheets, creep out of the room, and fly silently down the halls and stairs in their white nightgowns, like puffs of cotton. Squeezing through the big front door into the night, they keep low to the ground until they are in the shadow of the old clock turret; now they break into a run – past the quadrangle and stables, around the greenhouse with its roof of glass plates, past the paling onto the footpath, which narrows into a sheep-walk beneath the chestnut trees.

'This is the way to the graveyard,' whispers Emma. 'See how it was worn down by skeletons, on their way to the Roland Stones? These are quite recent.'

'Emma, you said nothing about ghosts when you proposed this

adventure. You know there is no such thing as ghosts.'

'That is true. But there are skeletons – you have seen them in picture-books, surely.'

'What do the skeletons do at the Roland Stones?' asks Lydia, trying to maintain a grown-up tone of voice.

'They meet at the Knight Stone and dance the Skeleton Dance,' replies Emma.

'Oh,' says the younger girl, for Emma pronounced the words in such a matter-of-fact way that she feels she really *should* know about the Skeleton Dance, everyone else in Oxfordshire does.

'Come, Lydia, let us proceed quickly. But watch how you go, for the path is uneven. Bony feet have been puncturing the mud.'

Puncturing the mud, repeats Lydia to herself, then hurries after her sister, for it is unthinkable that Emma should wander out of her sight.

'I am not fond of graveyards, Emma. I hope we are not going to see skeletons there.'

'Not this time. Tonight we are going to visit Eliza.'

'Eliza? Do you mean, the girl in the picture?'

'That is the one.'

'What is she doing in the graveyard?'

'That is what we must find out.'

At the entrance to the ruined cemetery, the rusted gate pierces the darkness with its sharp spikes, while the skulls, grinning in the uncertain illumination of the moon, alternately appear as rough stone and as sallow skin.

Hello, they say to Emma. *We have been waiting for your return.*

'You said there would be no skeletons, Emma,' Lydia whispers, clutching her sister's arm. 'I am as frightened as ever I wish to be.'

From a nearby pond, a frog voices a reply – *gibbet, gibbet, gibbet . . .* Holding Lydia's hand, Emma draws her sister through the graveyard to the grave-mounds at the rear. Thin grass covers the fresh soil like the hairs on the back of a man's arm; however, Emma is surprised to discover that someone has scattered dozens of tiny white stones upon the most recent mound, in the way that people litter rose petals upon the grave of a loved one. Peeking out from between the blades of new grass, they seem to glow in the dark.

Lydia stoops down, picks up one of the pebbles and rolls it between her fingers. 'Where do you suppose these came from?'

'I have no idea,' Emma replies. 'I am certain they were not here before.'

'It *is* a mystery,' says Lydia, who is glad she came after all.

'We must speak to Mother about it.'

'And not Miss Pouch?'

'No,' says Emma. 'I do not think Miss Pouch will do.'

Danbury has chosen to sleep alone tonight, for he has come down with a headache. In his estimation, his headache stems from two causes. For one, the mental exertion during Boltbyn's visit the previous day tired him damnably. For another, he no longer finds Mrs Lambert's physical presence such a pleasure. Notwithstanding a degree of animal rapport between them, she has begun to tire him with her damned questions, her ongoing enquiries as to what he is *thinking*.

From a drawer in his bedside table he retrieves the photograph – to Danbury's eye at least, a masterpiece, and well worth the effort; in fact, increasingly he has come to prefer the photograph to the woman herself.

It has been two hours since he took a sleeping-draught, and still his headache pounds with an almost martial rhythm, yet eventually he sinks into a restless doze, so that it takes him a moment to distinguish the pounding in his head from the pounding upon the door.

'Who the devil are you? Name yourself!'

Lush's distinctive shape appears, silhouetted in the doorway. 'It is about Mrs Lambert's daughters, Harry.'

'Confound it, what the devil do you mean, disturbing me at this time of night?'

'They are running willy-nilly about the estate. They have seen the graveyard.'

'Why should I give a damn?'

'You do not see it, do you, Harry? People are not quite as stupid as you suppose. Fortunately for us both, I have arranged that they be taken care of.'

'Put on a light, damn it, I'm not conducting a discussion in the dark.'

'Put on the light yourself.'

'What the devil do you mean by that?'

'I have come to extend my resignation,' says Lush.

'Don't talk such rot.'

'Contrary to what you think, your Grace, there are men who lead an existence independent of you; men who don't give a tinker's damn about Bissett Grange. As of tonight, Harry, I am one of them.'

Before the duke can come up with an appropriate reply, Lush turns his back and exits, slamming the door as hard as ever he can.

49

The Roland Stones

Local legend has it that an invading king and his retainers once stood upon this ridge, which commands a view of two counties, and were met by the witch of Lower Shipton; when they threatened her with their lances, she turned them into stone. Having made her point, the witch turned herself into the elder tree that still stands at the crest of the mound near the King's Stone, with his men in a circle some distance away. Since that time, witch, king and retainers have become friends. In the dead of night, they are said to walk down the hill together, to drink from the spring.

These spectres may have settled their differences, yet a malignancy remains. The neighbouring farmers, it is said, cannot keep their cattle penned on certain nights, for the gates will be open come morning. While clearing nearby fields, oxen refuse to pull certain stones from the ground, for fear of an unseen presence below. Occupants of homes and taverns trace lines with yellow chalk around the hearth and along the edge of the floorboards, so that spirits may not enter through the chimney or cellar. Whitty dislikes puns, but the term 'roiling stones' in Boltbyn's rhyme is rather apt.

He has always avoided places such as this – superstitious locations which attract credulous visitors from all over; yet this is the only practical way to approach Bissett Grange. According to his consultants in the Grass, the Danbury estate fairly prickles with mantraps, silence-trained mastiffs and armed game-keepers. Only the Roland Stones, being in public trust for the local tourism, provide an approach across the lawns.

Lawns were created by noblemen so that an approaching enemy could be spotted far away. Hence, Whitty's pre-dawn excursion.

He pays the fare to the elderly driver in his heavy black cloak; the man resembles a rook perched upon a ledge, seen against the faint, reddish clouds – *red sky in the morning, sailors take warning*. Therefore it is going to rain – an unpleasant prospect, for Whitty has no umbrella.

He watches the vehicle clatter across the grass and down the road back to town. As the silence of the countryside closes in, he becomes aware of a presence, or a number of presences – angular giants in cloaks of stone. Having no heads to speak of, they appear balefully non-committal. Feeling rather spooked, he walks to the crest of the ridge overlooking the lawns of the estate, a series of undulating rises, bordered on either side by thick woods. Everything has been shaped as though it were designed to be viewed at only one angle – from the eye of the House of Danbury.

Again he feels a presence, as though someone is watching.

It occurs to him that he has no idea what he is looking for. Indeed, that is the Whitty way – to stumble into the unknown, then to blindly crash into objects willy-nilly, with no means of stopping or steering himself other than to throw out his face as an anchor. It can get a man in trouble. It can leave him open to unexpected attack.

In the distance, the window-panes of a round room at the rear of the house glitter in the low morning light as though beckoning him to *come down*. And what is he going to do when he gets there – peer into the windows? Prowl about until luncheon?

You there! Halt! Stand as you are!

The voice appears to issue from the mouth of the cave known as the Wayland Smithy, which is thought to contain the ghost of a blacksmith. Once the correspondent's heart has returned to its proper place in his chest, he is appalled but not altogether sur-prised to see the tall, blanched form of the lieutenant-colonel, followed by Corporal Weeks, emerge like newly risen corpses in their ragged reds.

Run! shrieks the voice within, but Whitty chooses to ignore it, in the hope of brassing it out.

'Lieutenant-Colonel Robin. And Corporal Weeks. Good day to you both, gentlemen. A splendid morning for a ramble in the country, don't you think?'

With heightened unease he observes the percussion pistol held in the thumbless hand of the better-sighted but less stable of the two. He has no doubt that its possessor, despite his disability, is a dead shot.

'Prepare to fire,' says Robin, whose dark glasses and white hair give him a spectral cast.

My good sir,' says Whitty, as calmly as he can, 'I was led to believe that you were above shooting unarmed Englishmen. How extremely inconsistent of you.'

'Pish-posh, sir. Are we inconsistent, Mr Weeks?'

'We is not, sir. We follows our orders to the letter.'

'Of course you do,' Whitty replies. 'You slaughter women and children on demand.'

'Women and children?' asks Weeks, lowering the pistol slightly.

'Explain what you mean,' says Robin to the enemy prisoner. 'Explain what you mean by that statement.'

'I refer to the murder of innocent girls, sir. *English* girls, at that. Wayward ones I grant you, but hardly monsters like yourselves. I wonder that you keep up the pretence of Englishness at all. Good heavens, you are no more English than a Sepoy at Cawnpore! Did you bury them, when your superiors had their fill of them? Or did you cut them to pieces and throw them down a well? *Women and children in pieces, like a ghastly puzzle of flesh!*'

Like a ghastly puzzle of flesh! the corporal echoes, in an altered voice, as though transported to that faraway location.

'Tot, corporal!' says the lieutenant-colonel, flask in hand.

As Weeks drinks deep from the flask, the voice in Whitty's cranium reasserts itself – *Run!* – and is obeyed with vigour.

'Stop him, corporal! Can you see him? Shoot on sight! *Hazar!*'

'Yes, sir! I have him, sir!' With the instinctive surge of concentrated focus that follows the receiving of an order, the corporal aims, fires – and wounds the air.

'The enemy has disappeared, sir! He was in my sights, and disappeared!'

'Where, Weeks? Can you see him now?' The two men scan the field, which glows in the long morning light, like green glass, cracked by the long, angular shadows of the Roland Stones.

'He began to run, I had him sighted, and he vanished! This is an evil place, sir, a place like nothing I have ever seen. Since we arrived in this place, I have not slept an hour!'

This much is obvious to Whitty: he has fallen into a ha-ha. He might have seen it in advance, but the shadows confused him; it is some comfort that, had he responded in a more capable manner, he would have been shot in the back.

Long ago, a series of narrow ditches were dug across the field to contain the sheep that occasionally graze here, eliminating the need for fences, which would spoil the view from Bissett Grange. Thanks to the ha-ha, the lawn appears as a picturesque, unbroken expanse. To a pedestrian who might wish to wander the field, however, it is as if an enormous axe has chopped several deep wedges straight across – trenches with steep slimy walls and a hazard to be sure, especially if the pedestrian is running headlong from the barrel of a gun.

Lying at the bottom of the ha-ha, Whitty takes stock. On the bright side, he has broken neither legs nor arms – though he has turned his ankle, which is already beginning to throb.

His moment of reflection is interrupted by a voice above and behind him – *After him! Forward! Seize him!* – in the distinctive bellow of an officer on parade, and disconcertingly close at hand.

In a state of animal panic, Whitty scampers on three limbs in the manner of a crippled stoat down the length of the ha-ha to the woods edging the field. Only when he finds himself in deep shadow does he dare climb up the side and assess the danger. He barely manages to scale the ha-ha and to poke his head over the edge when his foot slips, and he finds himself tumbling right back down again.

Hazar, Weeks! There he is! Sight him in the shadows by the wood! Shoot at will!

Above his face, a white wound appears in the trunk of a beech tree where his head was a second ago, followed by the crack of the corporal's pistol. Twice in as many minutes he has saved his life by falling down a ha-ha. Again Whitty struggles to his feet and breaks into a run, with poor success, for the ankle pains him badly.

There he is! Reload! Shoot or capture! Seize that man! Seize him!

After scrambling up the slope at the end of the ha-ha, leaning upon a willow for balance, he assesses his options: he can surrender and be killed face to face, or crawl away and be shot in the back. For the most part, that covers the field. He therefore resolves to be shot as late as possible and with maximum difficulty, and at maximum cost to his executioner.

Glancing at the willow supporting him at present, at the level of his chest he notices a branch two inches thick, extending about six feet like a large riding-whip, which suggests a plan. No – to call it a plan would be an exaggeration. Better express it as *Things To Do While Awaiting Execution.*

Whitty is no expert on trees, yet from hard experience at Eton he knows that a willow has an exemplary spring to it, sufficient to cause severe pain. Positioning himself so that he might intercept the oncoming rumble of soldiers' boots, he grasps the branch with both hands and pulls it back as though it were a sort of catapult. Crouched in the brush, muscles straining, he waits – but not for long, as the muffled sound of two sets of boots draw sufficiently close that he can distinguish between them. Reasoning that the man of lower rank would take the lead, he waits until he hears the voice of the lieutenant-colonel a few feet away.

'Reloaded, corporal?'

'Loaded, sir!'

The corporal passes, and Whitty lets the branch fly.

'Mr Weeks! I am down!' Whitty peers around the trunk of the willow to see the lieutenant-colonel writhing on the ground just a few feet away, clutching his eyes with both hands.

'Are you hit, sir? Are you wounded?' The corporal stops and turns, torn between responsibilities.

'Carry on, Weeks! Leave me and carry on! He is in the woods nearby! After him! That is an order! *My eyes!*'

Blast, thinks the correspondent, whose hope was that both pursuers would be delayed by his attack. Now he is left with a lone adversary – the one who has the pistol and is prone to hysteria.

Retreating deeper into the forest, he suppresses a shudder at the ominous sense of enclosure, of being swallowed up by an enormous land-whale with digestion to follow. His first response is to thrash about the underbrush, but he thinks better of it. *When in Rome . . .* If you wish to remain inconspicuous in a forest, imitate a tree.

Not a difficult challenge, to imitate a tree, to stand as straight and as still and as silent as possible, breathing as little as possible. Rather like being dead, actually. Just another piece of the forest, growing up or rotting away as the case may be . . .

From the stillness of his position he can now hear that Corporal Weeks is doing a good deal of thrashing around; at one point a pistol appears in a shaft of light a short distance away, pointing at the correspondent's stomach; however, all at once Whitty hears the clumsy but alarming flutter of a thrush partridge, which alarms the soldier, who wheels about, fires twice in the direction of the sound – and steps directly into the open jaws of a mantrap.

Oh! I am hit! Oh, Mother!

A cruel device, a mantrap, it has caused many a poacher to lose a leg – even a life, should blood poisoning set in. At a minimum, with two sets of iron teeth meeting at his tibia, a man can think of little else. Upon discovering the corporal's discarded pistol (an Adams type, he notes), Whitty feels emboldened enough to inspect the wounded man lying in the foetal position on the forest floor, clutching his leg with both hands, iron jaws sunk deep into the muscle of his calf, blood soaking the ground beneath him.

'Sir, I am afraid I must leave you in the care of your superior officer. Should you bleed to death in the meantime, I invite you to think upon Eliza, whom you murdered, and who is waiting to haunt you when you go.'

'I do not know what you mean, sir,' says the corporal through clenched teeth, as he removes his belt and wraps it above his knee as a tourniquet. 'The girl died, yes, but we were not to blame, it were an accident.'

'You can be certain that it was no accident. But your employer would know more about that. Being newly arrived in London, were you under the impression that you served some sort of brothel-keeper – a slave-master who buys and sells living children?'

'Such trade is a business in the East like any other,' replies Weeks through gritted teeth, while struggling with the jaws of the mantrap. Whitty admires his ability to carry on a conversation under these circumstances.

'In Britain the trade in children is more of a scandal, especially among the gentry. One's reputation might suffer. A well-born gentleman will go to great lengths to assure confidentiality.'

'Were we tricked, sir? Into *thinking* it were an accident?'

'It would seem so, from what you say.'

'Therefore no women nor children have died at our hands?'

'That much you can lay claim to, yes.'

'Then praise be, for we was to sin again.'

As Whitty emerges from the wood into the long shadow, he sees the lieutenant-colonel on his knees, feeling for his glasses with one hand while covering his eyes with the other, and bellowing, 'Corporal Weeks! I need you!'

'Corporal Weeks is down, I am afraid,' says the correspondent. 'He is as much in need of your assistance as you are of his.' Whitty reflects on how one's confidence improves with the possession of a pistol.

'Who are you, sir? What is the nature of your business?' Having found his glasses Robin picks them up, only to discover that they have broken at the bridge, so that it is necessary to hold the lenses over his eyes in order to see.

'It is for you to understand what sort of business you have got yourselves in, sir. Have your associate look at this and report back – if you really wish to know.'

Whitty takes from his pocket the obscene photograph of naked Eliza, and hands it to the lieutenant-colonel. Puzzled, the officer attempts to decipher it, using one of his lenses as though it were a magnifying-glass.

Securing the pistol in his pocket, Whitty hobbles down the hill in the direction of the house, keeping to the edge of the wood so as to avoid any ha-has to come, and without the slightest idea what to do next.

50

Bissett Grange, Oxfordshire

Standing in the portico by the front door while smoking a cigar, the former estate manager of Bissett Grange savours this new morning like a man who has just been released from gaol.

His scalp does not itch. Nor do the backs of his hands. For the first time in weeks, he feels comfortable in his own skin.

Life at Bissett Grange has been an education in how to live like a gentleman. Most valuable is his manner of speech, painstakingly acquired – the stately, graceful, unaffected pronunciations of a member of the quality; not perfect, but good enough to impress the middle classes, and an inexhaustible coinage to invest in any situation.

On balance, Lush is a vastly improved Englishman. And a richer one, to boot.

But there comes a time when the student must graduate, must take off the old school tie and venture into the school of Life.

Thus resolved, Albin Lush will pack his valise with a change of clothing, toiletries, and a fortune amounting to approximately £10,000. (Danbury had no patience for keeping accounts.)

Throwing aside his cigar, he looks up at the dark beneath a garnet sky, and remarks to himself that it looks like rain.

'There he is! Do you see him? He has come out of the house!'

'Where, Lydia?'

'In the portico. It is the hedgehog, lying in wait for us. O Emma, I so wish we were back in the house, for I am ever so cold.'

'We must find a warm place to hide. Do you see how close the forest verges on the conservatory?'

'The greenhouse, do you mean?'

'Yes, except that in the houses of the quality it is called a conservatory.'

'Isn't a conservatory to do with music, Emma?'

'A conservatory is a place where things are conserved.'

'A place to conserve ourselves, do you mean?'

'To conserve ourselves is the whole point. We will steal alongside the wood to where it verges with the conservatory, and then we will run to the door and go inside, and hide there, and hope that the hedgehog does not see us in the meantime. We will wait there until he becomes tired of looking for us, or until the gardeners are up and about if need be.'

'And what shall we do then? Shall we speak to Mother and tell her everything?'

'Yes. But we must avoid the hedgehog first.'

Standing just inside the wood, taking the weight off his bad ankle, Whitty contemplates the conservatory: an impressive structure, clearly intended as a homage to the Crystal Palace, with a rounded glass roof in the picturesque style. Of the type designed by Paxton, who created the conservatory at Chatsworth, whose feature is a tropical tank, wherein a woman can stand upon a giant water-lily.

The impressively engineered ridge-and-furrow roof is designed to render vertical supports unnecessary within, thanks to a perimeter of hollow columns made of cast-iron – hollow, so that they can both support the structure and serve to bring rain-water from the roof, via the gutters, into the ground. Whitty wonders what range of foreign species dwell inside, what outrageous plants and creatures thrive by means of steam pipes, without which all would wilt and die instantly when exposed to the English climate.

Exotic – yet no more so than the creatures who own them.

Hello. At the edge of the wood nearer to the house, two small figures flutter past in what appear to be white gowns – in this light they seem to be in mid-air, darting furtively this way and that, first in the shadow of the wood, then in the direction of the conservatory, whose glass roof serves as a dark mirror reflecting the gathering clouds in the sky.

More eeriness, he thinks. People who reside in the English countryside must have nerves of iron.

Having crept through the woods as close as they can to the edge of the wood, having kept to the shadows as far as possible, Emma leads her sister – 'Run, Lydia, run!' – on a headlong dash for the conservatory. 'Now keep to the wall,' she whispers, 'so that we remain in shadow. The door is just ahead, we must open it quietly.'

'What shall we do then?' asks Lydia, who wishes she were in bed.

'We will take stock.'

They step into the conservatory, shut the door behind them, and instantly their faces become flushed in the steamy, saturated air – filled with heavy scents that remind Emma of the perfume old women wear at church. With a sensation that they have entered a secret, alien world, they wander past a rockery covered with giant ferns and palms, then turn a corner to face row upon row of roses, hyacinths, orchids, water-lilies – every fragrance-producing plant imaginable.

'O Emma, look! Do you see?' Lydia is not looking at the flowers; instead, she stares wide-eyed at the glass ceiling. 'Angels!'

Emma follows her gaze and sees them too – angels hovering above, looking down upon them. Lit from behind by the morning light, they seem three-dimensional, but soon it becomes apparent that they are actually photographs of young girls, each imprinted upon a glass pane. They may be insufficiently clad for a proper choir, and have assumed postures in which anyone would be hard pressed to sing, yet heavenly light pours through them, like transparent honey, turning them into angels in the eyes of the girls below. Multiplied in dozens of plates scattered high above, they form a combined picture of glowing innocence; yet each face appears singularly brilliant, beatific, and beautiful, each in its own way.

'The windows have been made from the glass Mr Boltbyn uses to make his photographs,' says Lydia. 'Do you see yourself up there, Emma? Are you there? For he has photographed you far more often than me.'

'No, I am not there – but look!' Emma points to a particularly exquisite, dark-haired angel near the top of the domed roof. 'Do you see her, Lydia? There is Eliza!'

Lydia, however, has become distracted by the shadow of a man, standing outside the glass door. Now she sees a face pressed against the glass, squashed and grotesque, its nose flattened like a pig's.

'Oh, Emma!' whispers Lydia to her sister, who is also very afraid. 'Does he see us, Emma?'

Emma puts her arms around her sister and together they kneel beneath a low stone wall, topped by a plant with huge leaves. 'If we remain very quiet,' she whispers, 'perhaps he will go away.'

By pressing so hard against the glass that he risks a nosebleed, Whitty can barely make out the two small figures in white nightgowns, far less ghastly than they first appeared, crouched near a tropical fern and looking up at the ceiling. Using the wall of the conservatory as a support, he makes his way to the glass door and pulls it open; now his lungs take in the steamy air laden with a heavy sweetness, and he hears the sound of running water.

'Ladies!' he calls out. 'I assure you that you have nothing to fear. For I am injured in the leg, and could not chase you even if I wanted to.'

After a long pause, the two girls appear from behind the rockery, both of whom he instantly recognises from the funeral at St Swithan's.

Proceed carefully. Assume nothing.

'Miss Emma,' he says, with a small bow.

'Who is he?' whispers Lydia.

'It is the falcon,' replies Emma.

'I am very glad to see you again,' he says to Emma, then turns to Lydia. 'And no doubt you are the sister.'

'I am very glad you are not the hedgehog,' says the smaller girl.

'Were you expecting a hedgehog?'

'Not as such,' replies Lydia.

'Edmund Whitty, at your service. And what is your name, if I might ask?'

'My name is Lydia,' says the smaller girl. 'And you, sir, are the falcon.'

'That is quite correct. I am a correspondent with the newspaper of that name. How did you know?'

'That is not what I said,' replies Lydia. 'You *are* the falcon.'

Whitty turns to Emma. 'I'm afraid I don't understand.'

'I am told that falcons have sharp eyes,' says Emma. 'Please, sir, look up and tell us what you see.'

Whitty looks upward. And he sees.

What am I to say?

Clearly the thrifty owner of the estate has replaced the glass panes with discarded photographic plates, just as Boltbyn suggested. Which leads to two conclusions: first, that the photographer possesses neither shame nor fear; and second, that he is not the vicar. At the same time, there is something ethereal about these ruined girls, in their desperate postures far beyond their years; in this light, despite what has been done to them, it is as though they have been consigned to the heavens.

Standing together in the middle of the glasshouse, Whitty and the two sisters contemplate the figures above, each according to his or her experience.

'Are they angels, sir?' Lydia asks.

'Not precisely, Miss Lydia. They are photographs of angels.'

'Have they died?' Emma asks.

'Yes.' Whitty lacks the capacity for lying at present. 'There are three of them as you can see – in various positions, and they have all died.'

'What happened to them?'

'For that you will have to ask your mother,' replies Whitty. His gaze has fixed upon one of the girls above, who is without any doubt the Captain's niece.

'You are looking at Eliza,' says Emma.

'How can you possibly know that her name is Eliza?'

'I met her in a dream.'

'Did you really?'

'Well, not exactly. I saw her name on the wall of a room in the house. And I know she looks like me.'

'Indeed she certainly does,' he replies.

'Look!' cries Lydia. 'It is beginning to rain!'

The clouds which have been gathering since before dawn have finally joined together to weep upon the conservatory – first in scattered, tiny droplets, which steadily grow in size and frequency until the roof is streaming with water, so that the entire conservatory seems to be in the midst of a waterfall. Whitty and the two girls watch the spectacle in silence, sharing a moment whose best expression is silence, and the sound of rushing water.

'Wait until I tell you about the white stones,' Emma says.

Entranced by the spectacle above and around them, they fail to notice the two men in soaked uniforms, limping painfully past the conservatory and across the quadrangle, towards the house.

Soaked to the skin and in an utterly miserable condition, Robin and Weeks hobble up the lawn to the carriage-sweep, the former clumsily holding his broken glasses on his nose with his one hand, while supporting his companion with the other; for his part, Weeks has been growing steadily weaker from loss of blood.

'How goes it, Mr Weeks?'

'Quite rum for the leg I fear, sir. Yet the bleeding has subsided. I recommend you go on ahead and inspect the site, sir.' The teeth of the smaller man chatter audibly, for the soaking they received has chilled him to the core.

'Out of the question, Weeks. The 2nd Infantry leaves no man behind who is still breathing.'

'Imagine, laying out mantraps with no warnings.'

'A vicious attack from a deceitful foe, corporal. But we will regroup. And exact payment in full.'

The thought of payment encourages Weeks, somewhat. 'A punitive expedition, sir?'

'With spoils to be taken.'

'It is a caution, Mr Robin, what we have seen and heard in our homeland. There seems no limit to the mantraps about.'

'Yet we fight on, corporal. *Hazar!*'

'*Hazar* indeed, sir.'

As the two ragged soldiers lurch towards the portico, a carriage has been geed-up by the stables. They hear it rattle up the hill to the carriage-sweep, where it comes to a halt. Immediately, a liveryman alights with an umbrella, opens the carriage door and waits expectantly, while facing the front steps.

'Advance with caution,' whispers Robin. 'We are about to requisition transport.'

'That would be a blessing, sir, for walking is a bother.'

Using one of the front pillars for support and concealment, they watch and wait until the door opens and Lush appears, carrying a valise in his hand. Leaving the shelter of the portico, he hurries to the carriage, hunched over in the rain, holding his coat-collar to his throat.

You! Halt! Halt or I fire! shouts the lieutenant-colonel, in a parade-ground voice. Though neither soldier has at present anything to fire with, the ring of authority stops the gentleman in mid-stride.

Lush recognises the voice and turns to face his two hired man-bashers, with a queasy sensation in his stomach, for they were not to act until much later in the day. He was to be well away – that was the entire point!

Such is his annoyance, only now does he take note of their condition.

'What the devil has happened to you?'

'We was set upon, sir,' replies Robin, shivering along with Weeks.

'Ambushed,' adds the corporal, growing faint.

'Good heavens. Well you cannot remain here. You must be off at once.'

'Indeed we will,' Robin replies. 'But first we must settle accounts.'

'Very well. You will be paid in advance, with an additional allowance for your return to London. Should my employer require you in future, you will be notified in the usual way.'

With an air of confidence appropriate to a gentleman who possesses a good deal of money, Lush places his leather valise upon the step of the carriage, opens it, and carefully extracts a small bundle of banknotes.

'There you are, gentlemen. Price as agreed upon for the precentor, and a sizeable bonus for the two remaining.'

The sky having grown sufficiently dark with rain-clouds, Robin removes his dark glasses, exposing his milky white eyes. 'You seem to have a fair amount of money on your person, sir,' he says.

'I am to make a bank deposit on our employer's behalf – part of my duties as estate manager. As a matter of fact, gentlemen, you really must excuse me, for I am late for my appointments.' Lush closes the valise and places one foot upon the carriage-step – though the rain has subsided somewhat, his coat is becoming soaked.

'Never mind the door, let us be on our way at once,' he whispers to the driver, who moves behind the carriage to the far side.

'Heading into town are you, sir?' asks Weeks.

'May I offer you gentlemen transport? That leg really should be looked at, you know.'

'First I have a question in my mind, sir,' says Robin.

'Ask it quickly, then.'

'What is it, exactly, that you have done for that money?'

'I beg your pardon?'

'Word has reached us, sir, of unsavoury doings here at Bissett Grange.'

'Most un-British doings,' adds the corporal.

'I do not understand you, nor do I see how it is any business of yours.' Lush steps into the plush sanctuary of the carriage, and prepares to close and lock the door.

'But it does concern us, sir,' replies Robin, whose eyes have the brittle delicacy of tiny china saucers. 'Does it not concern us, Mr Weeks?'

'It does, sir,' replies the latter. 'Very much so. He would turn us into monsters, by trickery.'

'Died in transit, was how you expressed it.'

'It is unacceptable,' says Weeks, holding aloft the photograph.

Lush pounds repeatedly upon the ceiling of the carriage with his stick, with no response – the liveryman, sensing trouble, having abandoned the reins and run back to the stables. He lunges forward to shut and lock the door when, in one swift, practised motion, the junior officer clutches the lapels of his coat and pulls him down from the carriage, with such force that the estate-manager's face smashes against the soldier's forehead. Lush collapses to the ground with a soft groan, whereupon the men of the 2nd Infantry Division go to work.

*

'I hear a carriage,' says Lydia to the falcon with the limp, as they exit the conservatory.

'So you do, Miss Lydia. It is heading down the elm-way, I think.'

Whitty accompanies the children to an architectural mish-mash of Greek, Gothic and Grimm, with its pillars and its grand carriage-sweep, and an elaborate flower-bed growing in the centre like a monstrous wedding-cake.

The air is clean and silent after the rain-shower, though the sky is still dark with cloud.

'There, ladies – do you see the light in the front door? No doubt it is a welcome sight, when one has been wandering through the chilly night.'

'You just rhymed, sir,' says Emma.

'Did I?'

'You did. But it does not scan.'

'Alas,' he replies.

'Nor does the light of the house seem welcoming at present,' adds Lydia. 'Not to me at least.'

'I am certain your mother will be frantic about you.'

'I doubt that,' replies Emma. 'Mother likes to sleep late.'

Whitty rings the bell, repeatedly and with emphasis. At length, an iron latch is unbolted, the heavy front door opens, and a uniformed footman appears – whose face is familiar and whose livery appears to have been darned in several places.

'A very good morning to you young ladies,' says the footman with a bow. 'Please enter, for your governess has been asking for you.' He now turns to Whitty, and with less warmth: 'Are you expected?'

Whitty, recognising the accent, thinks, Of course: the footman from Buckingham Gate, the night of the seance, seemingly ages ago.

'I am Edmund Whitty of *The Falcon*, sir. These two young ladies became lost. They requested my assistance in returning them to the residence.'

'And how did you happen to be at their service – this being a private estate?'

Whitty is about to reply when a small shriek is heard from within the house.

Oh, merciful Heaven! Praise God!

Miss Pouch appears in the doorway, very vexed and red in the face, having gone upstairs to wake the girls only to find two empty beds.

'Is this your mother, Miss Emma?' asks the correspondent.

'Not in the least, sir. It is our governess. Come along, Lydia.'

Lydia, however, does not reply; in fact, she has turned her back to the house, and is staring down at the carriage-sweep . . .

'Sir, I am grateful to you,' says Miss Pouch to the correspondent.

'Think nothing of it, madam. Please oblige me by taking these two young ladies inside, and by giving them a hot drink.'

'No, Miss Pouch, we wish to see Mother at once,' says Emma, and it is not a request but a command.

As the two girls follow their governess to the staircase, Lydia whispers to her sister: 'Did you see? There is a man lying in the flower-bed. At least I *think* it is a man.'

'Who could it be, Lydia?'

'I could not tell, for I saw only a hand and part of an arm.'

'Perhaps he fell asleep.'

'If he fell asleep, why would there be blood?'

'Perhaps he hurt himself. Perhaps he stumbled and fell.'

'Now that we have seen to the children,' says Whitty to the footman, 'I request an audience with the Duke of Danbury.'

'Do you indeed, sir?'

'I do. Here is my invitation.'

The footman takes the card and reads it. 'This invitation is for luncheon. You are about five hours early.'

'It is something I have been looking forward to. The excitement was too much for me.'

'His Grace does not accept visitors this early in the morning.'

'His Grace will see me nonetheless,' says Whitty, in a nobbish accent at least as convincing as the footman's. 'Present him with my card, will you?' Reaching into a breast pocket, he removes the terrible photograph he has carried next to his heart for far too long, and hands it over.

The footman looks at it and lifts one eyebrow. 'Very well, sir. I shall speak to the duke. You will remain here until I return.'

Seated at her dressing-table, Birdie paints the outline of her lips and eyes with a tiny red brush, and refreshes her fragrance with cologne water. She has been summonsed (once it was a plea, or a poem) to join his Grace in his apartments for breakfast.

The more she reflects upon the whole affair, the queerer it seems. Why is she more attractive to him when she covers her face, and why has his devotion evaporated since those queer photographs – as though that was what he was after, all along?

Though this inchoate sense that she is on treacherous ground keeps her in a perpetual state of anxiety, she has managed to refrain from the medicine that was so much a part of her marriage. Fully alert and on edge, she starts audibly when Lydia bursts into the room, followed by her sister. To Birdie they are a sight – her darling urchins, nightgowns covered with mud, hair clinging to their cheeks and shoulders, cheeks flushed with excitement.

Emma steps up to her mother and solemnly holds Birdie's face in both hands so that their eyes are no more than six inches apart, and in low, measured tones, proceeds to tell Birdie the most extraordinary tale she has ever heard in her life: about a room with barred windows and a name on the wall, and a grave, and white stones, and a falcon, and a hedgehog, and a glasshouse, and a girl by the name of Eliza . . .

'My dear Emma, I have not the faintest notion what you are telling me. Have you become frightened by one of Mr Boltbyn's stories?'

'No, Mother, it is true, every bit. I tell you because we cannot understand the meaning of it by ourselves. Because we are too young. That is why you must come and see it. The falcon said you must. He said you would understand what it means, and would know what to do.'

'What is it that you and your falcon wish me to see in the glass house? For I am expected shortly.'

'The angels in the roof. Especially Eliza. He said we should show you. And then I want you to see the grave with the white stones.'

'The house is called a conservatory,' corrects Lydia, standing a few steps back. 'He said that it is urgent that you should know what is happening at Bissett Grange,' she adds.

A week ago, Birdie would have sent her daughters out of the room with an admonition to confine their stories to the nursery, that she was engaged in adult business and that they should speak to Miss Pouch. Yet she is struck by the unusual gravity upon both their faces, suggesting that this is not just one of Mr Boltbyn's fantastic games.

Glancing upward, she wonders what Harry will do or say when she fails to arrive. Part of her has begun to dread the duke's summons, and knows that the association will bring her nothing but misery in the end; yet another part cannot resist him, caught in the desire of the moment, content to remain at Bissett Grange until she is wrinkled and old and he turns her out. For in her heart she knows her place, knows that she is not a lady and never will be. She is Euphemia Root of Upper Clodding and he is his Grace the Duke of Danbury. So they were born and so they will die, no matter what takes place in-between.

Emma's insistent tone of voice returns her attention to the dressing-table and her fantastic tale. 'The falcon's name is Mr Whitty. He is a newspaperman, and he said you must see and know everything. He said it is a matter of the utmost urgency.'

'Utmost urgency,' reiterates Lydia, with the word *utmost* an octave above its neighbours.

'And then,' continues Emma, 'I shall tell you all about Eliza, and about the hedgehog, and all about the white stones, and show you as well. That is what the falcon said I should do.'

'Very well, my dears. I have never heard such a story in my life, but I concede defeat. Let us go to the conservatory and see your angels. And let us see your hedgehog, if need be. And on the way, you can tell me about the white stones.'

Whitty follows the footman's coat-tail down the red carpet, past the twin staircases and along the hallway. The latter is filled with hothouse plants, imparting an earthy, jungle-like quality to the atmosphere, as though Bissett Grange were peopled with jaguars and anacondas.

They pass a series of oil portraits depicting generations of male Danburys, each seated in the same substantial chair, silently demanding of the viewer: 'And who do you think *you* are?' At the end of the central hall he is conducted into a queer, many-sided room whose tall windows overlook the lawns all the way to the Roland Stones and beyond, as though the entire county existed for the benefit of the person seated in this room.

The recipient of this honour is presently standing, or rather posing, in profile by the fire, with his left forefinger thrust into the pocket of his waistcoat while the right gently strokes his side-whisker. A long silence ensues, which Whitty is reluctant to break, for the room is most interesting.

'You are early,' says the duke, at last.

'Not by my watch,' Whitty replies. 'I shall have it looked at.'

Eyebrows raised, the duke turns to look at the speaker – or rather, to look through him. 'So you are Mr Whitty, the journalist. I believe you went under another moniker when we met at Buckingham Gate. Pray, take a seat and accept a glass of brandy.'

'I believe I shall remain standing. And no brandy, thank you.'

'That comes as a shock, sir. I shall wager that this is the first occasion in many years on which Edmund Whitty has failed to accept a free drink.'

Whitty inspects the Duke of Danbury's immaculate coat and velvet waistcoat, while fending off the horrifying urge to defer. He notes that the reddish hair has been artfully combed to conceal a spreading bald pate: there is nothing noble about a man who will consent to such a manœuvre.

'Your Grace has examined the photograph, I trust?' he says, affecting casual interest.

'Indeed, sir, it was I who had it sent to you, through my agent Mr Lush, following that remarkable encounter with the spirit of your brother.'

'What were you attempting to achieve by it?'

'I wished to spare you, Mr Whitty. And to spare David's memory as well.'

'Most considerate of you. In what way was I spared by possessing an obscene photograph of my brother?'

The duke takes the photograph in question from the mantel, holds it to the light with thumb and forefinger, and turns to Whitty with an expression of bemused regret.

'Whether or not you give credit to such phenomena as we both witnessed, your brother's utterances upon that occasion were all too true. David did not die as he was said to have died, nor did he live as he was thought to have lived.'

'Please continue, your Grace. You interest me.'

'David Whitty was my friend – perhaps my only friend while at Oxford, for in my position one chooses one's intimates with care. We rowed on the same eight. He was a founding member of the photographic club, sponsored by this estate. And he excelled at the medium, sir, not even Mr Boltbyn could match his ability – in all ways but one.'

'Was his flaw technical or aesthetic?'

'Neither, sir. It was moral. It is with the most profound regret that I tell you that your brother acquired an enthusiasm for the kind of photography associated with the French and sold under the counter at bookstores on Holywell Street. It became a material obsession with him – to the point where he sought to *appear* in such photographs. To that end he perfected an ingenious technique involving an apparatus beneath his foot – a remarkable achievement, if only it had been applied to a different result.'

A shrewd customer, thinks Whitty, who knows that the most successful lie is that which snuggles close to the truth.

'If I understand you correctly, you are saying that my brother took this picture *himself*?'

'Indeed he did, and many worse as well – long destroyed, I am thankful to say. Eventually, of course, word spread as word always will in a college, until it seemed that exposure and ruin were in plain sight. It was only a matter of time. That was why your brother chose to do what he did.'

'So you suggest that my brother's death was not an accident?'

'That is so, sir, and it pains me to tell you. Nonetheless, though he stood a ruined man, a man given over to degeneration – a commitment with no provision for escape – your brother remained my friend. Though I could not save him from his fate, I could rescue his name from permanent ignominy. I therefore contrived a scenario, at some personal risk, which would cause the world to make a determination of accidental death. If I could not save David's life, I could save his family's good name.'

'A gripping narrative, sir. My compliments to you. And yet, as anyone who reads the newspapers is aware, the sin of suicide makes capital cover for a death of another sort.'

'What the devil do you mean by that?' Danbury's eyes continue to look through him, but not in the same way; the emptiness has taken on the quality of twin pistols.

The acidic flush of sudden anger that arises in Whitty at this moment is as much directed towards his instinctive acquiescence to class as to the elegant fiend himself. Though he does not remember having produced it from his pocket, he suddenly seems to be pointing a pistol at the man – the Adams which belonged to Corporal Weeks.

'Good heavens,' says the duke, more offended than alarmed. 'What the devil are you doing with my pistol?'

'I intend to shoot you, sir. When a party murders one's brother it seems the most obvious thing to do.'

'Murdered your brother? Wherever did you get that idea?'

'The wonderful thing about a lie is its capacity to reveal the truth. The young man in the picture you hold in your hand is indeed David Whitty, who possessed unusual intelligence and spirit, and was much admired – yes, by himself as well. The young woman is named Eliza, beloved by the gentleman who employs me. Eliza was not yet born at the time of my brother's death, sir. Which facts, you understand, establish the creator of the picture, and the liar as to its contents, as the fiend who murdered both.'

The duke laughs. Whitty has never heard laughter so lacking in mirth.

'You are ridiculous, sir. Not only is your conclusion preposterous, it is the word of a degenerate scribbler – attempting, no doubt for money, to blacken one of the great names of Britain.' With a quick, efficient motion of the wrist, the duke tosses the photograph into the fire. 'There, sir. Where is your story now?'

The correspondent makes no effort to rescue the photograph – indeed, he is very glad to be rid of it. In silence, the two men watch the border turn brown, until gradually a similar brown blot appears in the centre of the photograph, in the space separating the brother and Eliza; the blot expands quickly until it consumes the both of them, then yellow flames appear through the blackened hole, and David and Eliza are gone, and all is gone.

'What do you intend to do now, Mr Whitty? Shoot me and hang for murder?'

'You are a remarkable man, sir. You take living girls and turn them to dead pictures. Then they become windows for your conservatory, where flowers are grown to die. Your whole house reeks of death. You disgust me, sir – as I believe you disgusted my brother. Did you look at his portrait of himself, naked, and imagine you had a confederate? Did you take his friendship for a rapport of another kind? Was that your mistake – imagining that you were not entirely alone? That you were something other than a solitary freak?'

'Upon my soul, I do not need to listen to such impudence in my own house,' replies the duke, giving the bell-cord next the mantel a sharp tug.

'Point taken,' replies the correspondent and, almost without thinking, pulls the trigger.

51

The Wood

Standing between her mother and sister, Emma looks down at the grave with its young grass and its white stones, then back at the gate with its skulls, then around at the surrounding wood, its leaves and grass glistening thanks to the morning rain-shower; and all at once she understands how the fantastic superstitions and legends that permeate the county came to exist.

Here they are, the three of them, taking part in a perfectly reasonable gathering, after all that has happened. Yet imagine if a passer-by, even in broad daylight, were to come upon the Lambert women standing in the abandoned cemetery, two of them wearing muddy nightgowns; imagine how easily he might take hold of an ancient interpretation, that the three were engaged in some unnatural custom. Nor would it be surprising if, upon recalling the sight later, he remembered that the birds went strangely silent at the time; then he might recall the sound of a woman intoning in some arcane language. Thus, another legend might take root in the county, and it would be only a matter of time before people in nearby villages began to avoid these three women, to take to the other side of the road at their approach while crossing their fingers.

Emma no longer believes in such things, nor does she take pleasure in them, for it seems to her that such stories are like threads, made into a cloak to disguise all kinds of meanness.

She knows she will never entirely cast aside Mr Boltbyn's fantasy world, in which nameless fear turns to wonder by a leap of the imagination. Life is filled with terrible things that can only be explained in a made-up story. But there is no need for this graveyard to be haunted by anything other than the sad stillness of its occupants.

To Emma, who is nearly grown-up, one thing remains clear: she and her sister and her mother are together, alive, here and now, and they share the same story, and the same responsibility for what is to be done.

'Her name is Eliza,' says Emma to her mother. 'And I will tell you what happened to her.'

Bissett Grange, Oxfordshire

Face-down on the floor of the library, Whitty reflects upon the drawbacks of a policy of playing a situation entirely by ear – especially when one's theoretical knowledge of a thing so outstrips one's practical experience.

Guns, for example. While it took no great effort for him to identify the pistol as an Adams, he had never before touched one of the instruments in his life, and retained only the vaguest notion how to fire it – let alone whether it contained ammunition. With his nose buried in the luxurious nap of the carpet, he grimly recalls the lieutenant-colonel's command as he ran pell-mell down the lawn, away from the Roland Stones: *Reload!*

The meaning of that command, was lost upon him at the time, fleeing on three legs like a wounded stoat.

Neither should it have taken a stellar intellect to realise that the duke would scarcely choose a *tête-à-tête* with a declared enemy without protection near at hand. Nor is it surprising that the Irish are efficient with a neddy – for which the correspondent is grateful, for it takes considerable practice to put a fellow out without killing him.

Not that the end will be different in Whitty's case. No doubt he is about to join Eliza, or perhaps he will become fertiliser for the conservatory. Will Danbury take pictures of him as well? Will he become a windowpane? To take his mind off the prospect, he turns his attention to the whispering voices overhead, one a thinly disguised Irish brogue, the other a derisive upper-class drawl.

I must be reporting some serious trouble, your Grace.

Close the door, O'Day. We have a more pressing problem here, which must be dealt with at once.

Sir, ye must come out at all speed and see. It is very bad indeed.

Damn your impertinence, get out! Find Lush and tell him there is something he must deal with at once!

Mr Lush cannot, sir.

Nonsense. I have not accepted his resignation, and he still works for me until I do. Tell him I want him.

That is the very trouble I was coming to, sir. Mr Lush has been beaten to death. Ye'd best come and look, the liveryman be after losing his breakfast over it.

What the devil? Are you certain?

More than certain, sir, that it is a corpse and that it is Mr Lush – although many would not be recognising him now. Sure, and it were not an accident, nor the doing of anyone here. Should we send for the police?

Out of the question. We will deal with the matter ourselves, do you understand?

Before we do, sir, ye'd better see the photograph what was stuffed in his mouth.

Whitty remains motionless, playing dead with his face in the carpet, barely breathing until the footsteps recede down the hall and out the front door. After a slow count to ten, he opens one eye to make certain he is alone, then lifts his head – too quickly, for the pain in his skull is like the blow of a picaroon. Rising carefully to his knees by the side-table, he downs the remaining brandy from Danbury's glass, which gives him strength. On his feet at last, he leans upon the mantel for support – and before his face is an ebony box, of a type often used to store medicinal snuff.

Capital.

His condition having much improved thanks to the indulgence of his host, Whitty regards the worthy in the portrait over the mantel, whose stern expression would turn downright grim at what he plans to do to the Danbury reputation assuming, of course, that he survives, and assuming that the duke has not removed all trace of what has gone on by the time Whitty convinces the police to pay a visit. Graves are quickly dug up by a crew of strapping Irish, and the roof of a glasshouse is easy prey to a slingshot.

Exiting the library, he moves quickly down the hallway towards the front door – but then remembers what is in the flower-bed outside. Turning abruptly, he climbs the staircase at speed, resolving to remain discreetly out of sight until darkness affords him an opportunity of escape.

He makes his way down the dim, suffocating hall, Paladin arches dripping like stalactites overhead, until he reaches a thick rope stretched across the hall, reminding him of the rope in the office of the governor of Millbank Prison and no doubt existing for a similar purpose. Before stepping over it and exploring further, however, he tries the door to the left – and finds it open.

He enters a large, utterly dark room which might have been a drawing-room, before the windows were sealed shut and painted over. As his eyes adjust to the darkness (owing to the slight illumination from the doorway), he can make out the shape of a wall-sconce and a tallow candle. This he lights with a lucifer.

In the resulting patch of uncertain illumination he catches sight of another wall-sconce nearby, which he lights as well; after lighting a third candle, the room is adequately bright for him to recognise the photographic apparatus in the centre, and the stands containing lighting equipment along the periphery, and the dark velvet curtain covering the walls. Pushing aside the curtain next to the door, he exposes the plaster wall, not covered with wallpaper but hand-painted in the oriental style, in the same pattern as in the photographs, and every bit as ugly.

He turns to the centre of the room, and in front of the camera in his mind he sees the ghost of his brother David, in the prime of his life, naked as Michelangelo's David, intoxicated with all the pride of the English and the glory of the Greeks, freezing his image against time and deterioration and, without knowing it, choosing death.

For a photograph of a naked human being can be many things, depending upon the viewer: to one it might signify perfection and innocence; to another, licentiousness and depravity. Clearly, when it came to David the duke assumed the latter. Assuming a similar nature, different only in that David possessed the photographic skills Danbury lacked. David seemed the ideal collaborator for the beastly enterprise Bissett Grange was about to undertake. And now Whitty can imagine the scene that must have taken place when Danbury made his proposal and David responded – possibly with a fist to the jaw. Realising his mistake, the duke or his servants saw to David with a blow from a neddy perhaps, followed by an apparent death by drowning.

And in his mind Edmund Whitty says goodbye to his perfect, dead brother, and walks out of the room.

But what to do now? Will he simply hide in some crevice like a rabbit or will he search further? Deciding upon the latter course, Whitty climbs over the rope barrier and up a narrow stairway, which leads to a landing containing two doors. One is open, and looks into a small, spartan room with bars in the window. The other door is locked.

The second room is utterly dark; but after lighting a candle in the wall-sconce next to the door, he can see that it is a twin to its neighbour – the difference being that the window has been painted over. At first he takes it for a bathroom or a laundry, for there is a basin on a counter to his left. Over the basin, however, are chemicals in wooden racks which, by the light of a lucifer, he recognises as sodium chloride, silver nitrate, silver iodide – ingredients necessary for the making of photographic prints. Nearby is a stack of fine writing paper, and beside that a wood-and-brass apparatus containing a lamp, and a rack for holding a glass negative. Further into the room, on another table in one corner he finds a case divided into slots for storing the negatives.

When he holds a plate up to the light, he sees the face of an angel.

A MYSTERY DEEPENS
by
Oliver Crabtree
Senior Correspondent
Oxford Times

Oxfordshire remains in shock and in mourning at the passing, arrectis auribus, *of Harry Godwin, the Duke of Danbury, having succumbed in his bath on the night of Wednesday last. Physicians have determined beyond doubt that his death was the result of an inflammation of the heart – an inherited ailment known to have cut short the lives of the Fourth and Sixth Dukes before him, in what was once known as the Danbury Curse. Ergo, the conclusion that the duke suffered a seizure in his bath, after which he drowned.*

This explanation having proven satisfactory to the authorities, and having taken into account the lack of any sign of a struggle in the bathroom, rumours of death by misadventure have been put to rest.

Other mysteries, however, remain – having to do with a number of missing items from Bissett Grange, chiefly items of precious metal, as well as the entire contents of the wine cellar.

A number of household servants are sought for questioning, as is the Estate Manager of Bissett Grange, Mr Albin Lush.

Bissett Grange, Oxfordshire

Child of the pure unclouded brow
And dreaming eyes of wonder!
Though time be fleet and I and thou
Are half a life asunder.

William Leffington Boltbyn disassembles his photographic equipment for the last time, having waited a week since the death before returning to the estate, for decency's sake. He performs his task with a sense of ceremony, carefully rolling each piece in wool, then tying the bundle with ribbon.

Without the settings of Crede and Angley to create an illusion of glorious antiquity, the photography room is like the empty stage of a theatre; with neither actors nor audience to give it life, it is as though the room has itself expired. Surrounded by funereal black curtains, with no trace of natural light to indicate the time of day or the century, Boltbyn imagines that he has died and gone to some shabby approximation of Heaven – a spurious Heaven for souls who risked little, whose sinful deeds were not terribly sinful and whose good deeds were not terribly good, who chose to dwell in a state of artificial innocence, deliberately insensible to the evil in view.

In thinking through the events of the past few weeks, it has become clear to the vicar that at some point in his life he made a fundamental error. He does not know when or how but, as with a mathematical problem, the sum is inarguable. An unnatural, idyllically sweet childhood perhaps, whose memory left him with no taste for the bitterness of real life. Yet who in his right mind would willingly exchange the life of a coddled child for that of an adult? Who, given the option, would agree to a procedure in which you begin with perfection, then undergo a steady process of putrefaction until you sicken and die?

As he reduces the photographic apparatus to its component parts – rosewood and brass and thick, highly polished crystal, beautifully precise – Boltbyn wonders whether he was overly hasty in agreeing to sell the lot to, of all members of the club, Bracebridge Hemyng. The man is certain to make dreadful pictures with it. It seems almost a betrayal to consign his precious camera to a man with the imagination of a literary critic. Could he not simply keep it for himself, unused, to be contemplated as a beautiful *objet d'art*? Being one of the first Scott-Archer models sold to the public, the camera must surely have historical significance; perhaps one day he would donate it to a museum, which would be far more satisfactory than to recoup his original investment of £20.

No. All of it must go. That part of his life is over. There are no white stones pasted in his diary now, and there will never be again, for they would have an entirely different meaning, as would the practice of photography itself.

'I thought you would be here,' says the familiar, welcome voice of Emma, who has been watching from the doorway for heaven knows how long. 'Did you take a picture of the room? It will be a very black picture if you did.'

Boltbyn turns to the love of his life, framed in the doorway as though in a picture. 'Perhaps I will call it, *A Coal-Mine at Night*.'

'Or *Blenheim Palace, with Eyes Closed*.'

'I thought it best to leave the apparatus in a readily transportable form. We don't want him damaging it straight off and then blaming me. Mr Hemyng is a stupid man.'

'*Who summers in Afghanistan*.'

'*As some avouch, he has a pouch*.'

'*It's made of cat-hair and rattan*.'

They laugh, though he notes that hers is of the nostalgic kind, and that she looks fondly upon him as though he were already in the past. Only adults have that laugh and that look.

'Very good,' says the vicar, cleaning his spectacles, which have become unaccountably wet. Avoiding her gaze for the moment, he busies himself with an inventory of the accessories inside the rosewood cabinet, whose combined value is nearly as great as the camera itself. 'Let us see now: funnels, beakers, scales and weights, good, good . . . and silver nitrate, and colodon, and . . . Oh. Oh dear me.'

He looks up to see that Emma has been joined by Lydia, who stands silently by her side, watching him with sharp, serious eyes.

'How do you do, Miss Lydia. I am very glad to see you.'

'How do you do, Mr Boltbyn. I trust you are well?'

'Rather perplexed, actually. For there is no ether in my cabinet. It is the first time there has been no ether. I had a bottle and now it is gone.'

'Perhaps you ran out,' Lydia suggests.

'The bottle is not empty, Miss Lydia. The bottle is entirely missing. Here is the space for it, in the shelf right there. As you can see, it is unoccupied.'

'Oh,' replies the smaller girl. 'I do see that it is.' And she looks up at her sister for a reply.

'We borrowed your ether,' says Emma after a lengthy pause, holding Boltbyn in the beam of her dark, quizzical eyes. 'Mother said she needed it. I should have asked you first. I hope you are not vexed with me.'

'Oh. I see. Quite. Well, that explains it, then. And no, no, I am not vexed.' The vicar shuts the rosewood cabinet carefully, locks it with a brass key, and places the key in the pocket of his waistcoat.

Emma turns from the doorway and into the hall, where her mother waits anxiously by the stair, holding a chemical bottle in her hand.

'Has he noticed it missing?' Birdie asks her daughter.

'He has, I'm afraid. We were too late. And I had to tell him the truth. Mr Boltbyn and I have always been on truthful terms, and he would know if something was made up.'

'You told him the truth? All of it?'

'Only up to a point. Mr Boltbyn is not partial to detail.'

'I see. In any case, I suppose it is too late to return it.'

'No, Mother, I think you should. He would like to leave his equipment in a complete state. He is quite fussy that way.'

'But how can I simply give it back? What shall I tell him?' Her mother's voice is filled with uncertainty but not fear, being reconciled to whatever happens from now on.

'When there is nothing you have to say, it is best to say nothing,' replies Emma. 'Or you might comment upon the season, or ask him to tell you a riddle. Mr Boltbyn would prefer that. It is not in his nature to make a fuss.'

54

The Alhambra Baths, Endell Street, London

Everything's got a moral, if you can only find it.

Wearing two delightfully fresh towels, Whitty patters across the wet marble tiles of the sitting room, feeling less hunched-over than normal, thanks to the removal of a £500 debt from his shoulders, and with it, the need to slouch about *incognito*. For it has turned out that the Captain, like most hardened criminals, is a man of his word.

'Yer done yer duty too well, boyo,' blubbered the Captain while Whitty pretended to study his collection of model ships, thereby avoiding the disconcerting sight of the old man in tears. 'It be to my regret that there be no villain alive to deal with. Our man deserved another fate than to drown while asleep in a nice warm bath.'

'The quality are different from you and I, sir. They do not answer for their actions in the normal way.' Behind the bookcase, Whitty could hear the usual squeaking and rustling of rats. 'May I hope that this does not detract from our original agreement?'

'No, boyo, yer be in the clear and free of debt – though welcome to return to the sport if so-minded.'

'Should I appear so-minded, I beg you to throw me into the cage with the rest of the stock, and leave me there.'

On that note Whitty left the Captain to his rats and his regrets, with his head held high for the first time in several years.

It was with a similarly erect posture that he made his entrance into Plant's, in the turn-out of a gentleman – coat of robin's-egg blue, trousers the colour of faint sunlight – *sans* the taint of outrageous rumour and distasteful quips about backgammon. His meeting with Mrs Plant at her table behind the glass partition proved more than cordial, with a welcome aspect of amusement in her sharp green eyes, and a note passed beneath the table that said, *One o'clock in the morning, side door.*

Upon entering the rear snug, however, he noted the conspicuous absence of Mr Fraser and was met with troubling news from Mr Cobb, who disengaged his forehead from the table long enough to inform him that the correspondent for *Dodd's* had suffered an infirmity and remained bedridden, thanks to a mysterious malady – arising, by all reports, from a daring but ill-advised investigation into the sport of ratting. To which Mr Gosse of the *Yokel's Preceptor* produced from his pocketbook a piece of doggerel intended for publication in *Punch*, hinting that Mr Fraser's illness might be of an unmentionable nature:

> *A Hiberian writer of twaddle*
> *Must his figure in bandages swaddle*
> *A rattus addendum*
> *Hath nipped his pudendum*
> *And now he must walk with a waddle.*

'A poor excuse for humour,' Whitty observed. 'In atrocious taste . . .'

Upon entering the bathroom of the Alhambra, he avoids the glances of two epicene gentlemen in towels, lest he come upon a familiar face. Breathing the salubrious vapours, he settles into a marble armchair in a gentle reverie of orientalism – such a comfort after weeks spent in the mysterious occident, by the end of which the town of Oxford, and the university by that name, had become as foreign to him as the temples of Angkor Wat . . .

'Excuse me, Mr Whitty, sir, but I wonder if we might have a quiet word – uninterrupted by your manly acquaintances?'

The American.

The feeling of languor evaporates, while his neck retracts turtle-like into his shoulders and his back arches in the way of a startled cat. Nonetheless, Whitty's eyes remain closed, in the hope that the American will take the hint and disappear for ever.

'Julius Comfort, at your service once again,' continues the gentleman, without a qualm. 'Would you care for a cheroot?'

'No cheroot, thank you,' Whitty replies, smiling tightly at the tall southern gentleman.

Taking Whitty's rebuff as an invitation to settle in, the American undertakes a genial ramble. 'Speaking as a visitor to your fair land, sir, I have often noted that the Englishman has been unfairly marked as a cold creature. In truth, beneath the phlegmatic veneer lies a passionate, excitable spirit, with an outlook akin to the fellows of Arabia.'

'How interesting,' Whitty replies. 'May I remind you, sir, that since we first met, I have encountered my dead brother, and stood accused of murder. I have been driven mad in Millbank. I was set upon and shot at by man-bashers, and suffered an injury to my ankle which continues to give me trouble. God forbid that I might have met my Maker without hearing your opinion of the English national character.'

'Oh, that is a good one, sir. A good crack, as you might say. But we have more important business to discuss. In awaiting your return, I have become such a frequent visitor to this establishment, I feel as if my skin is turning to sponge.'

With a wink, Mr Comfort retrieves a damp envelope, paper, pen and ink from a spot on the floor beside his chair. 'In my official capacity with the Pinkerton Group, I stand engaged by the same family who underwrote the pursuit of Bill Williams – also known as Dr Gilbert Myers, Professor Zollner, Herr Schrenk-Notting, and so forth. My employers wish to reward you, sir, for your part in bringing to justice a dangerous fraud, who had eluded agents of law enforcement on two continents.'

'The deuce! You still think I actually hanged the man, don't you? – or rather, *lynched* him, is the way I think you people express it.'

'You are a man of action, sir, the breed of man who is taming the West as we speak.'

'I am nothing of the kind, sir. I am an English gentleman. I will have you understand that a gentleman does not go about lynching people or taming the West.'

The American effects a wry smile. 'May I suggest, sir, that it is a foolish man who makes a fetish of his own innocence. Especially when he is about to receive a good deal of money.'

A pause, while the latter sentence sinks in. 'How much?'

'A gold certificate in the amount of $5,000.'

'Is that a good deal of money? I have no grasp of exchange-rates.'

'By my calculation, sir, that would come to approximately 225 troy ounces, or £1,000 sterling. Unless, of course you wish to pound the gold into jewellery and wear it on your person.' He smiles, pleased by his play on the word *pound*, rises to his feet, gives Whitty's hand a damp shake, and is gone.

Envelope in hand, Whitty lies on his back and gazes upward at the skylight directly above him. He can feel a weak beam of sunlight, trickling through the transom, dripping warmly upon his cheeks and forehead. Closing his eyes, he can feel his naked body lift from its marble chair and soar upward, through the panes of glass and up the light-well, to smile upon the face of London.

Epilogue

At the age of eighteen, Emma Lambert married Eric Alger Mindon, a graduate of Christ Church and a champion cricketer for Hampshire, where they settled at Cuffnells, the Mindon family estate. She gave birth to three sons, two of whom died in the Great War. Emma Pleasance Mindon died in 1933, at the age of eighty-six.

Lydia Maude Lambert did not marry. She died in 1876, of peritonitis, aged twenty-five.

Birdie Lambert, née Root, returned to her home in Upper Clodding where she assumed responsibility for the family business upon the illness of her father. She died in 1877 of a fever at the age of forty-four.

Lieutenant-Colonel Robin and Corporal Weeks established a firm, Robin & Weeks, on Duke of York Street, London, dealing in provisions and equipment for foreign travel, at which the partners enjoyed moderate success.

Alasdair Fraser recovered fully and resumed his position with *Dodd's*. Soon thereafter, his exposé concerning 'Corruption in the Fourth Estate' ended a number of careers, including that of Mr Cream of *The Falcon*.

The Reverend William Leffington Boltbyn never took another photograph.